"THE BLOODY TRUTH"

NAILBITER

VOLUME SIX

Story by
JOSHUA WILLIAMSON

Art by
MIKE HENDERSON

Colors by
ADAM GUZOWSKI

Letters & Book Design by
JOHN J. HILL

Edited by
ROB LEVIN

NAILBITER Created by
JOSHUA WILLIAMSON &
MIKE HENDERSON

NAILBITER
VOL. 6: THE BLOODY TRUTH.

First printing. May 2017. Copyright © 2017 Joshua Williamson and Mike Henderson. All rights reserved. Published by Image Comics, Inc. Office of publication: 2701 NW Vaughn St., Suite 780, Portland, OR 97210. Originally published in single magazine form as NAILBITER #26-30, by Image Comics. "Nailbiter," its logos, and the likenesses of all characters herein are trademarks of Joshua Williamson and Mike Henderson, unless otherwise noted. "Image" and the Image Comics logos are registered trademarks of Image Comics, Inc. No part of this publication may be reproduced or transmitted, in any form or by any means (except for short excerpts for journalistic or review purposes), without the express written permission of Joshua Williamson, Mike Henderson or Image Comics, Inc. All names, characters, events, and locales in this publication are entirely fictional. Any resemblance to actual persons (living or dead), events, or places, without satiric intent, is coincidental. Printed in the USA. For information regarding the CPSIA on this printed material call: 203-595-3636 and provide reference #RICH–733896.

For international rights, contact: foreignlicensing@imagecomics.com.

ISBN: 978-1-5343-0155-9

ISSUE TWENTY-SIX

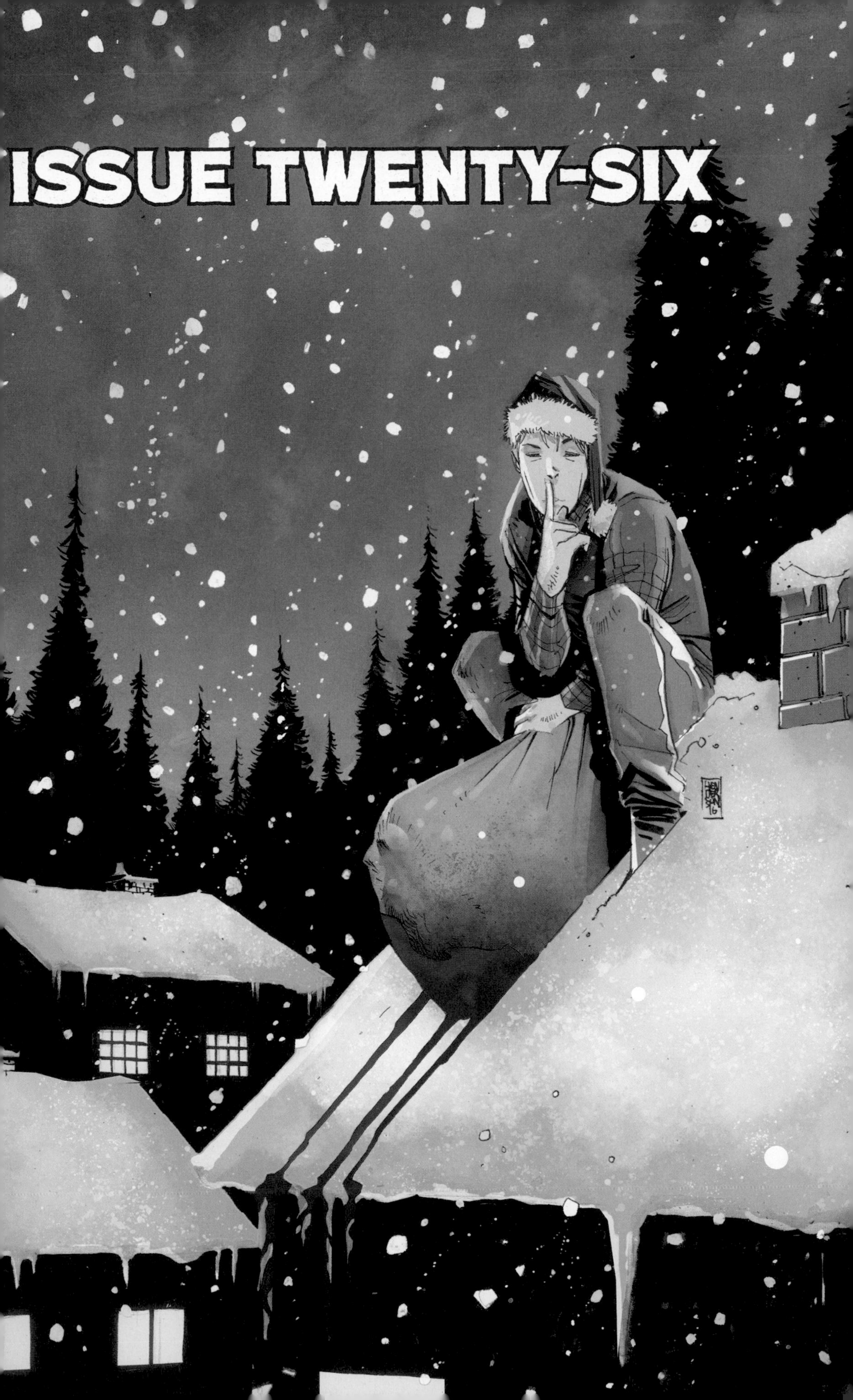

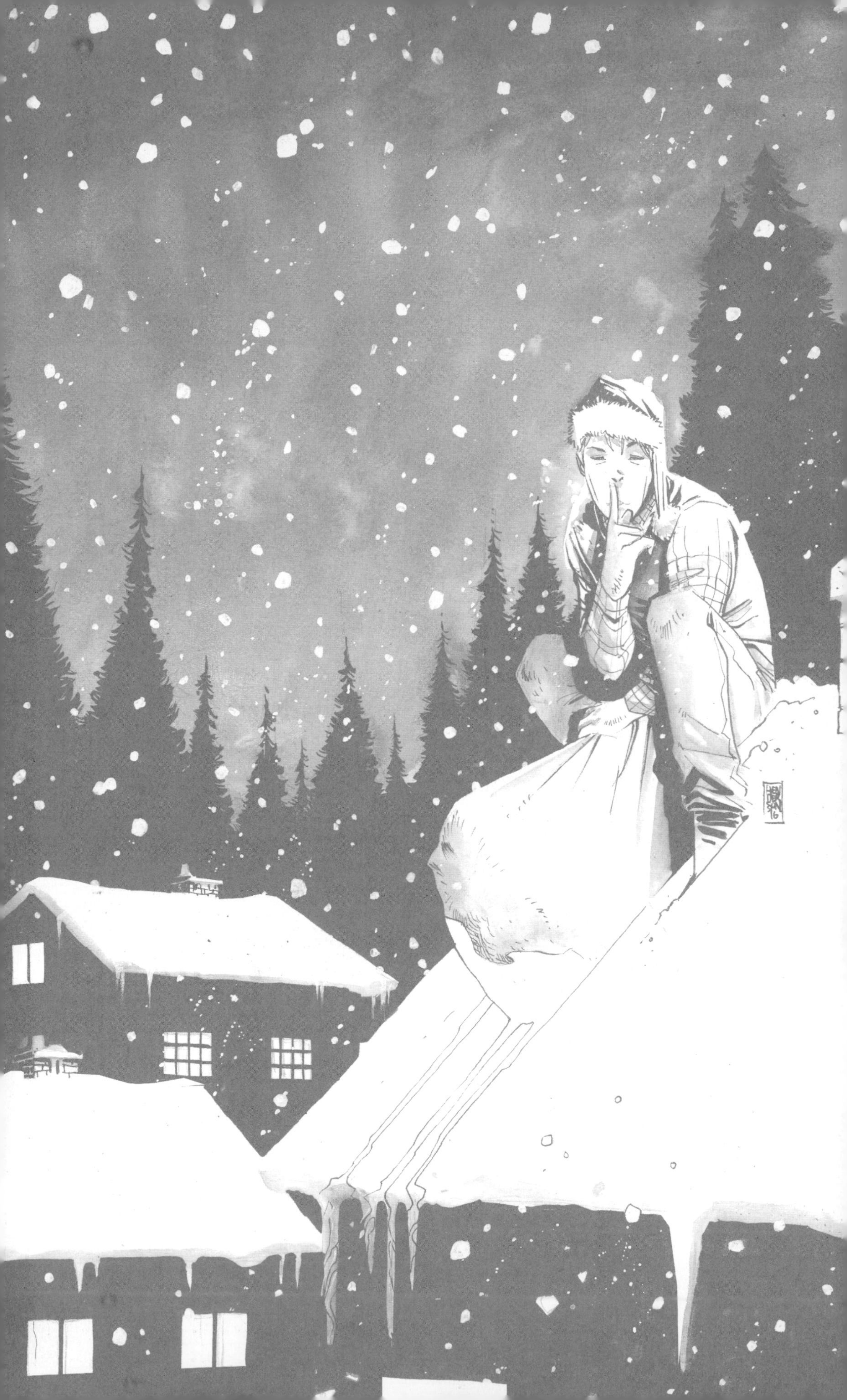

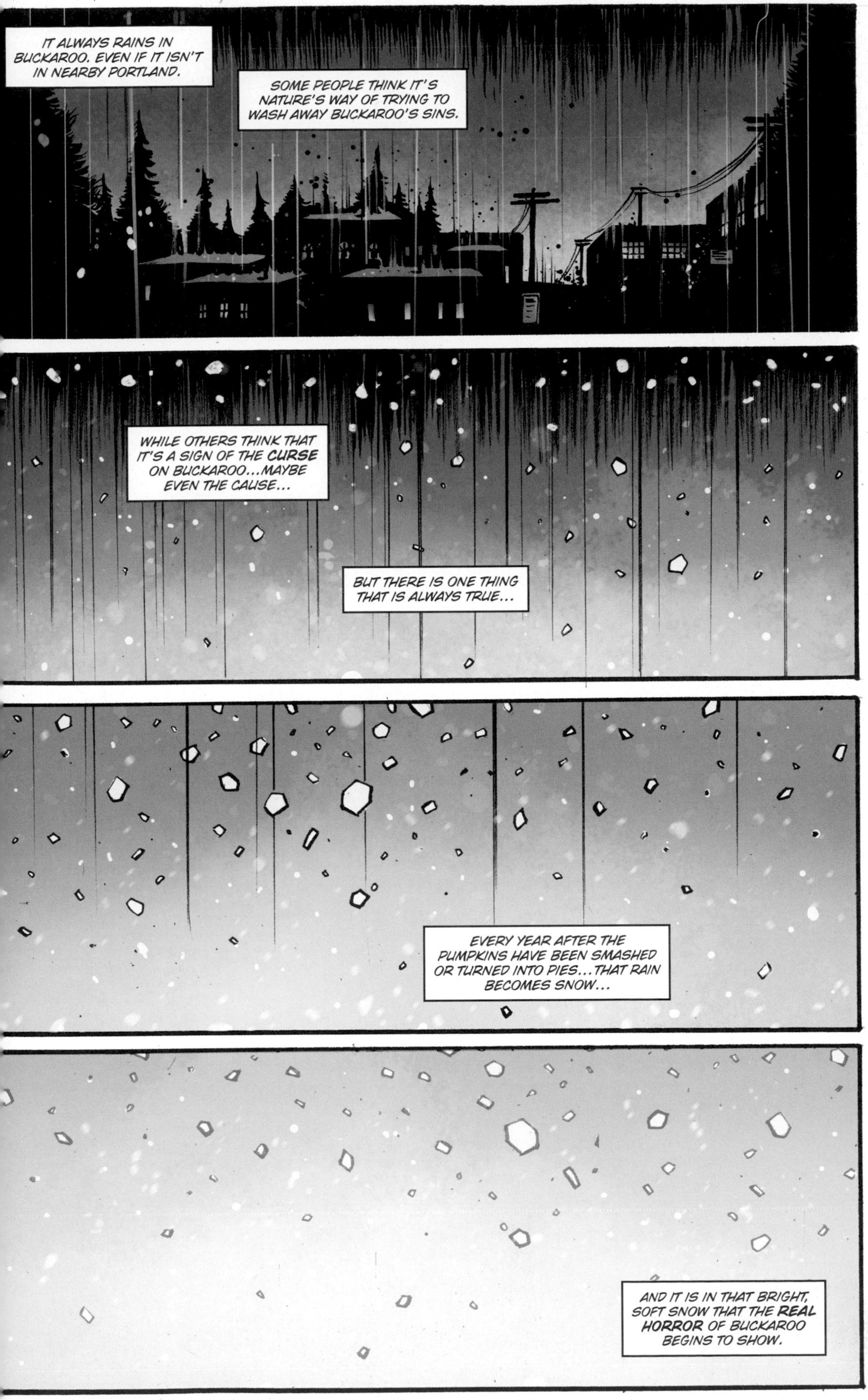
IT ALWAYS RAINS IN BUCKAROO. EVEN IF IT ISN'T IN NEARBY PORTLAND.
SOME PEOPLE THINK IT'S NATURE'S WAY OF TRYING TO WASH AWAY BUCKAROO'S SINS.
WHILE OTHERS THINK THAT IT'S A SIGN OF THE **CURSE** ON BUCKAROO...MAYBE EVEN THE CAUSE...
BUT THERE IS ONE THING THAT IS ALWAYS TRUE...
EVERY YEAR AFTER THE PUMPKINS HAVE BEEN SMASHED OR TURNED INTO PIES...THAT RAIN BECOMES SNOW...
AND IT IS IN THAT BRIGHT, SOFT SNOW THAT THE **REAL HORROR** OF BUCKAROO BEGINS TO SHOW.

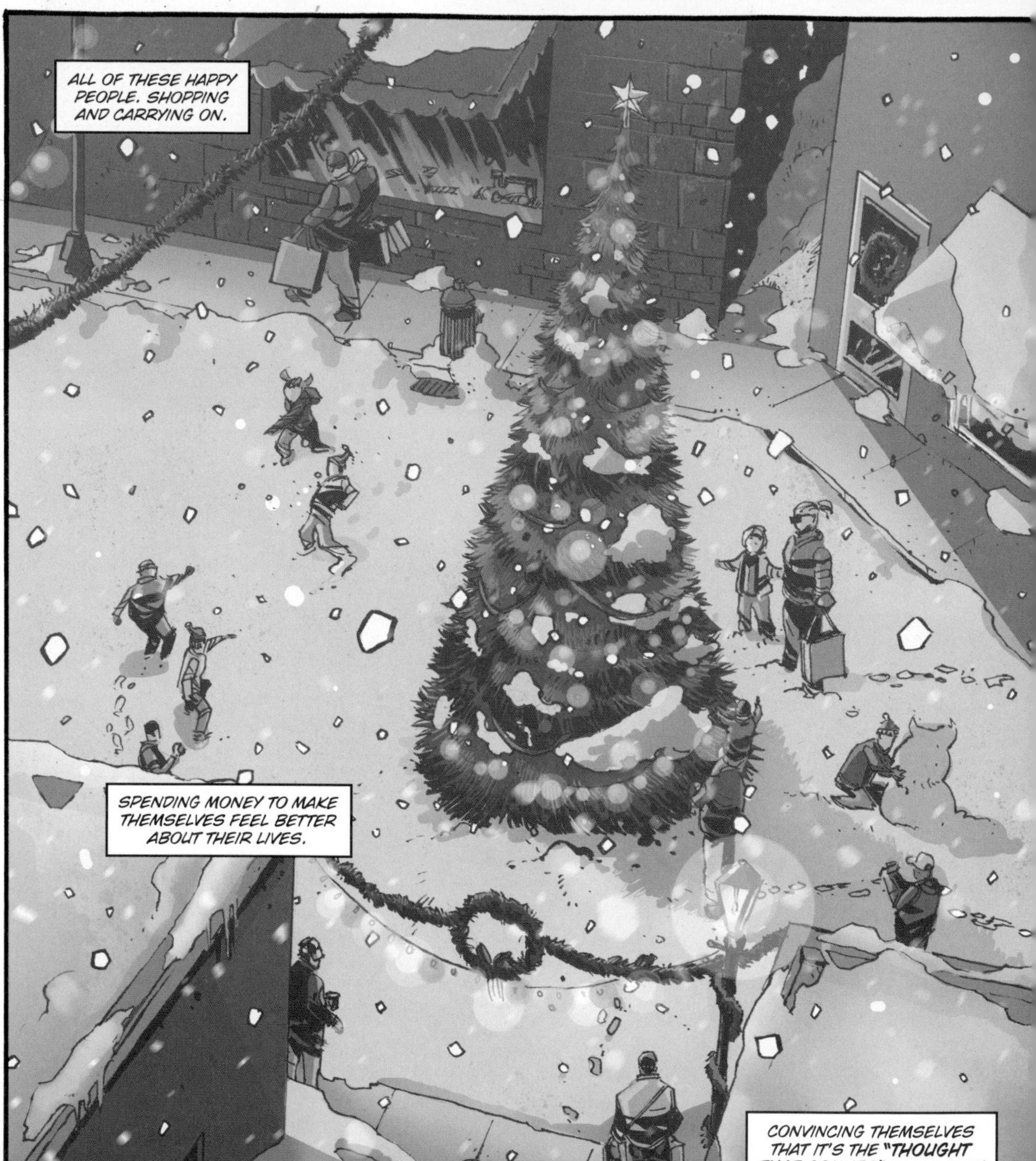
ALL OF THESE HAPPY PEOPLE. SHOPPING AND CARRYING ON.
SPENDING MONEY TO MAKE THEMSELVES FEEL BETTER ABOUT THEIR LIVES.
CONVINCING THEMSELVES THAT IT'S THE "THOUGHT THAT COUNTS" WHILE ONLY THINKING OF THEMSELVES.

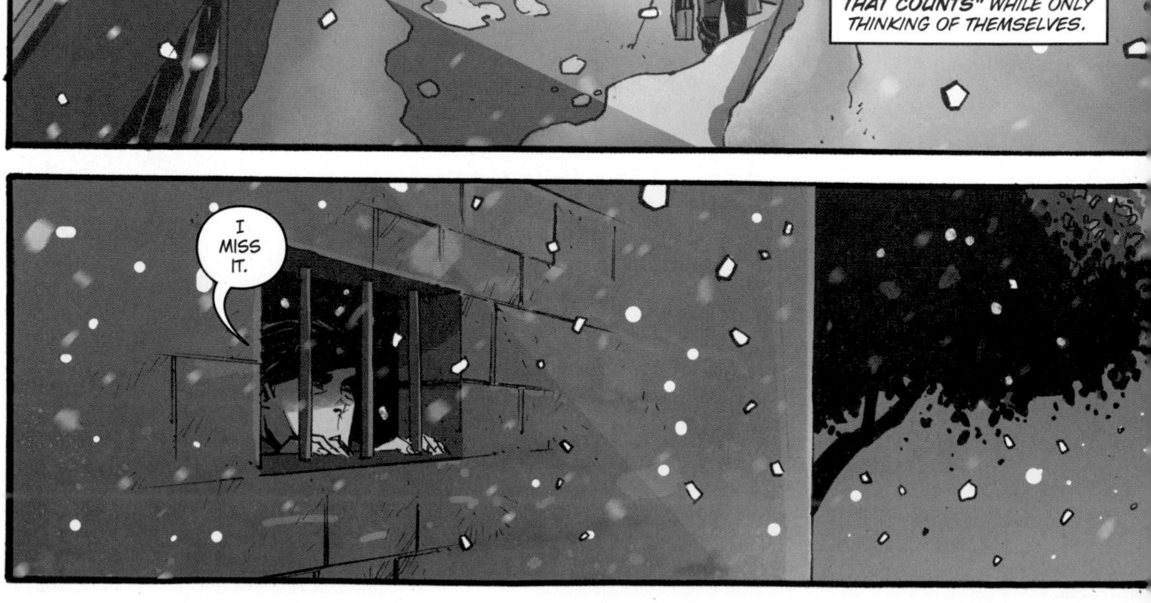
I MISS IT.

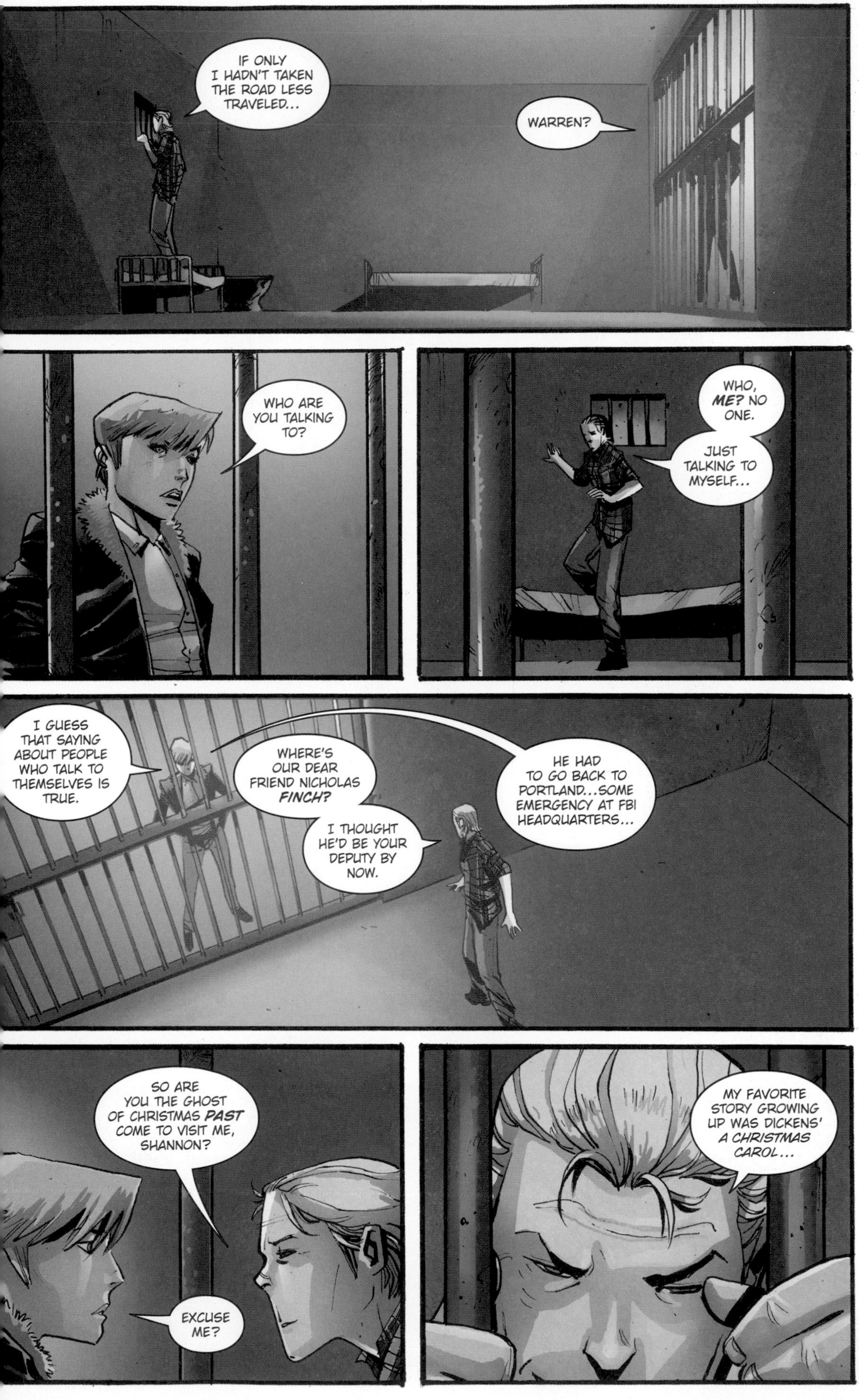
IF ONLY I HADN'T TAKEN THE ROAD LESS TRAVELED...
WARREN?
WHO ARE YOU TALKING TO?
WHO, ME? NO ONE.
JUST TALKING TO MYSELF...
I GUESS THAT SAYING ABOUT PEOPLE WHO TALK TO THEMSELVES IS TRUE.
WHERE'S OUR DEAR FRIEND NICHOLAS FINCH?
I THOUGHT HE'D BE YOUR DEPUTY BY NOW.
HE HAD TO GO BACK TO PORTLAND...SOME EMERGENCY AT FBI HEADQUARTERS...
SO ARE YOU THE GHOST OF CHRISTMAS PAST COME TO VISIT ME, SHANNON?
EXCUSE ME?
MY FAVORITE STORY GROWING UP WAS DICKENS' A CHRISTMAS CAROL...

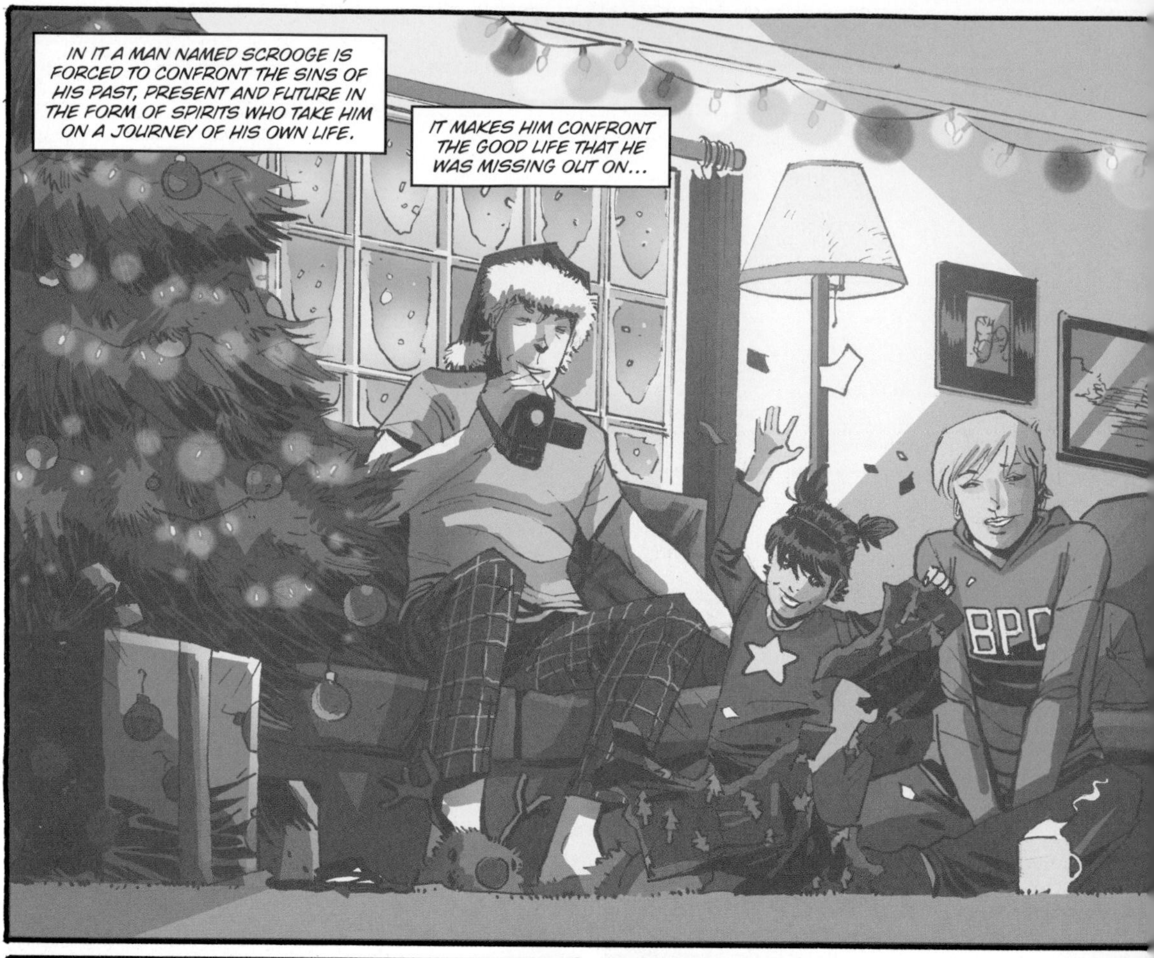
IN IT A MAN NAMED SCROOGE IS FORCED TO CONFRONT THE SINS OF HIS PAST, PRESENT AND FUTURE IN THE FORM OF SPIRITS WHO TAKE HIM ON A JOURNEY OF HIS OWN LIFE.
IT MAKES HIM CONFRONT THE GOOD LIFE THAT HE WAS MISSING OUT ON...
BPC

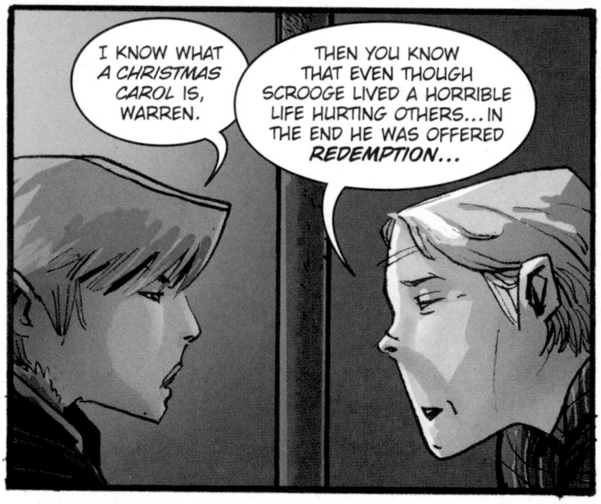
I KNOW WHAT A *CHRISTMAS CAROL* IS, WARREN.
THEN YOU KNOW THAT EVEN THOUGH SCROOGE LIVED A HORRIBLE LIFE HURTING OTHERS... IN THE END HE WAS OFFERED ***REDEMPTION...***

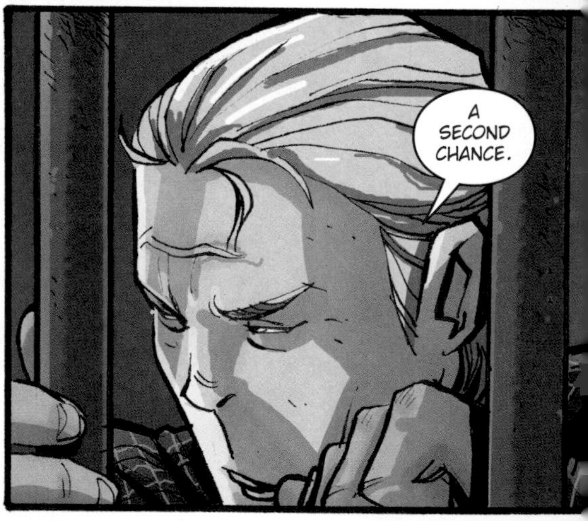
A SECOND CHANCE.

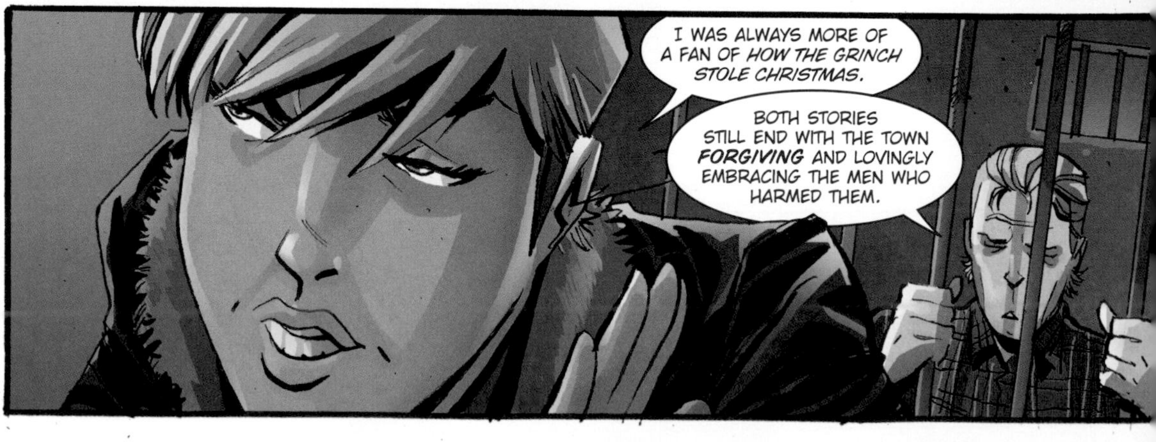
I WAS ALWAYS MORE OF A FAN OF *HOW THE GRINCH STOLE CHRISTMAS*.
BOTH STORIES STILL END WITH THE TOWN ***FORGIVING*** AND LOVINGLY EMBRACING THE MEN WHO HARMED THEM.

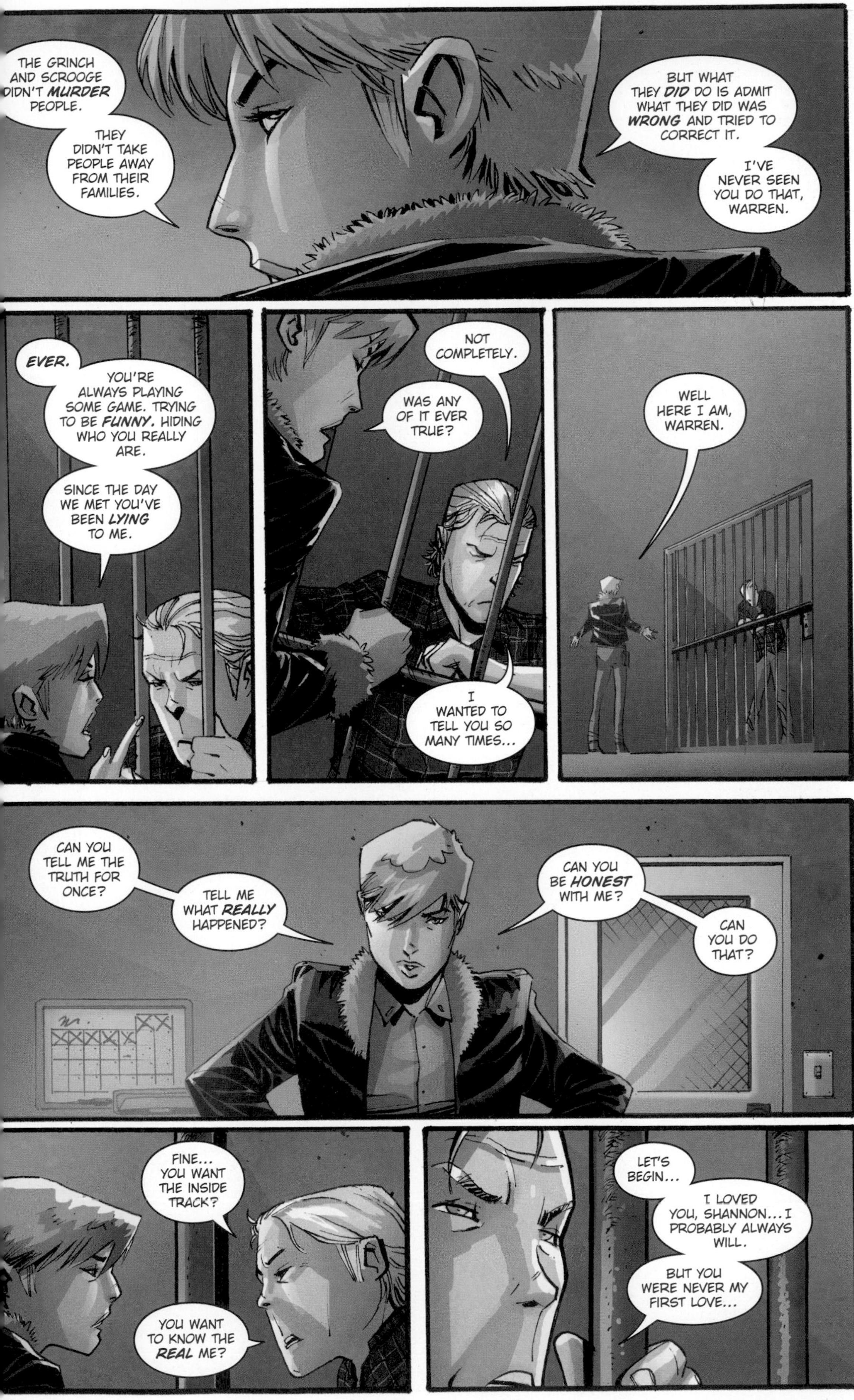

THE GRINCH AND SCROOGE DIDN'T MURDER PEOPLE.
THEY DIDN'T TAKE PEOPLE AWAY FROM THEIR FAMILIES.
BUT WHAT THEY DID DO IS ADMIT WHAT THEY DID WAS WRONG AND TRIED TO CORRECT IT.
I'VE NEVER SEEN YOU DO THAT, WARREN.
EVER.
YOU'RE ALWAYS PLAYING SOME GAME. TRYING TO BE FUNNY. HIDING WHO YOU REALLY ARE.
SINCE THE DAY WE MET YOU'VE BEEN LYING TO ME.
WAS ANY OF IT EVER TRUE?
NOT COMPLETELY.
I WANTED TO TELL YOU SO MANY TIMES...
WELL HERE I AM, WARREN.
CAN YOU TELL ME THE TRUTH FOR ONCE?
TELL ME WHAT REALLY HAPPENED?
CAN YOU BE HONEST WITH ME?
CAN YOU DO THAT?
FINE... YOU WANT THE INSIDE TRACK?
YOU WANT TO KNOW THE REAL ME?
LET'S BEGIN...
I LOVED YOU, SHANNON... I PROBABLY ALWAYS WILL.
BUT YOU WERE NEVER MY FIRST LOVE...

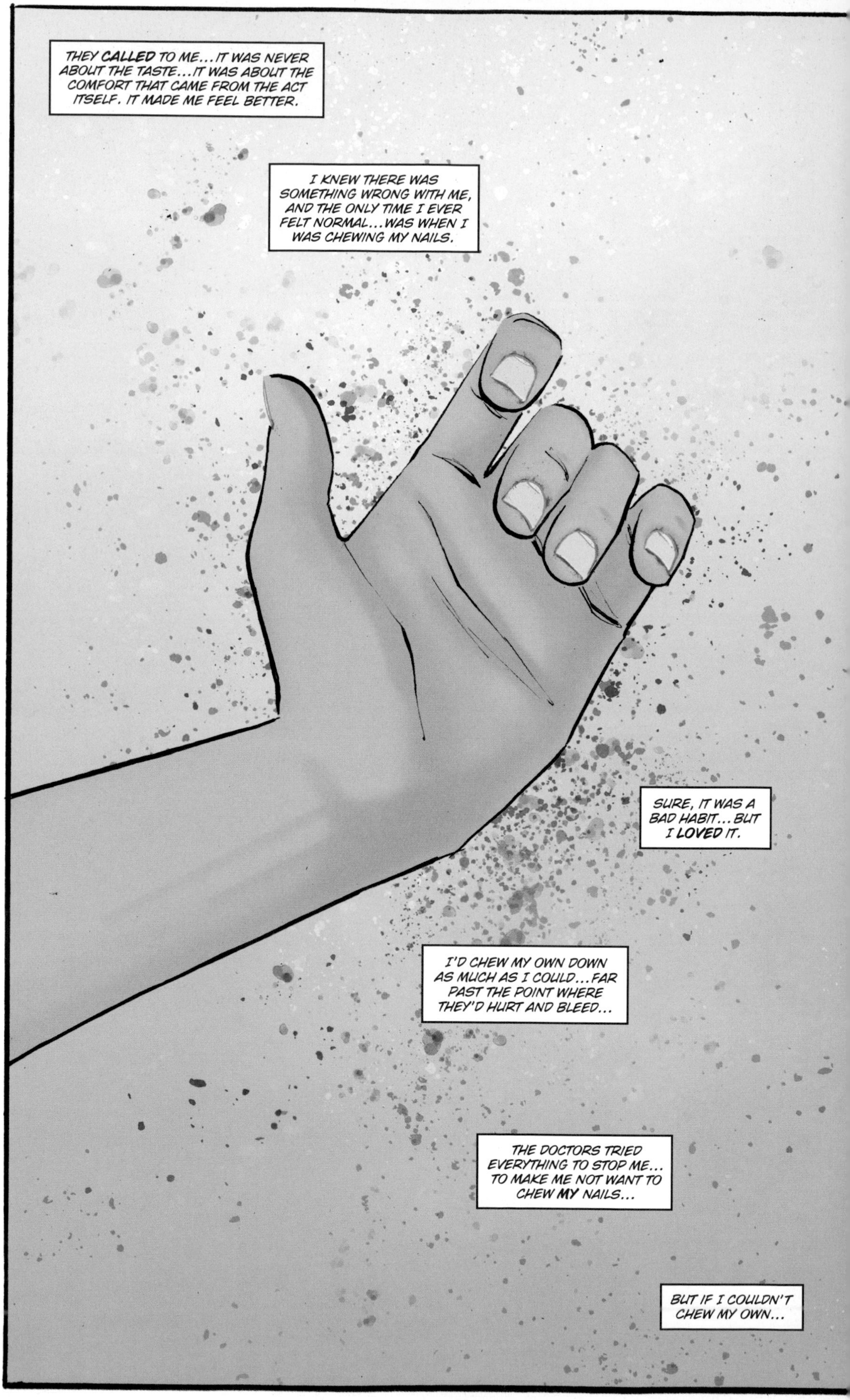
THEY CALLED TO ME... IT WAS NEVER ABOUT THE TASTE... IT WAS ABOUT THE COMFORT THAT CAME FROM THE ACT ITSELF. IT MADE ME FEEL BETTER.
I KNEW THERE WAS SOMETHING WRONG WITH ME, AND THE ONLY TIME I EVER FELT NORMAL... WAS WHEN I WAS CHEWING MY NAILS.
SURE, IT WAS A BAD HABIT... BUT I LOVED IT.
I'D CHEW MY OWN DOWN AS MUCH AS I COULD... FAR PAST THE POINT WHERE THEY'D HURT AND BLEED...
THE DOCTORS TRIED EVERYTHING TO STOP ME... TO MAKE ME NOT WANT TO CHEW MY NAILS...
BUT IF I COULDN'T CHEW MY OWN...

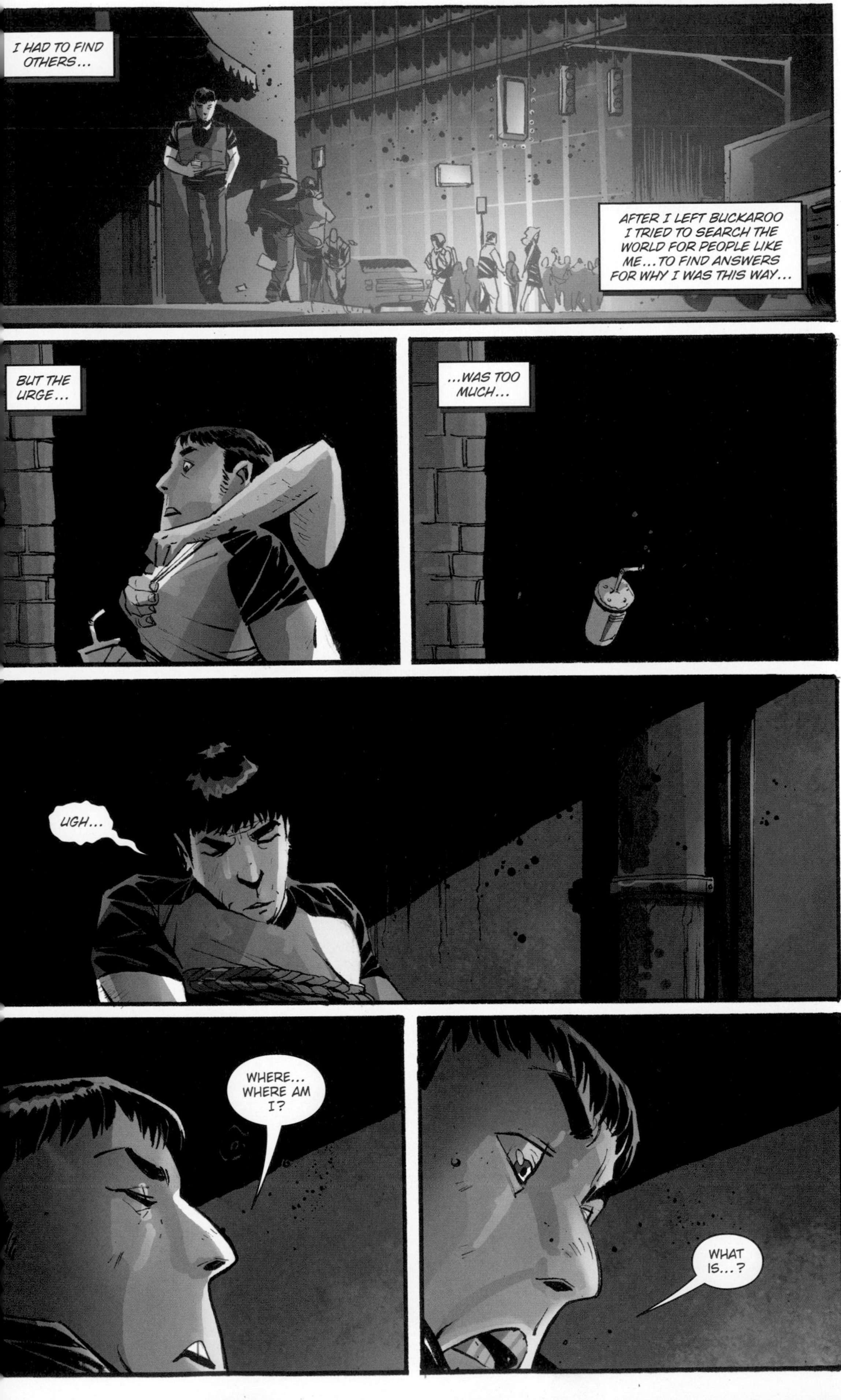
I HAD TO FIND OTHERS...
AFTER I LEFT BUCKAROO I TRIED TO SEARCH THE WORLD FOR PEOPLE LIKE ME...TO FIND ANSWERS FOR WHY I WAS THIS WAY...
BUT THE URGE...
...WAS TOO MUCH...
UGH...
WHERE... WHERE AM I?
WHAT IS...?

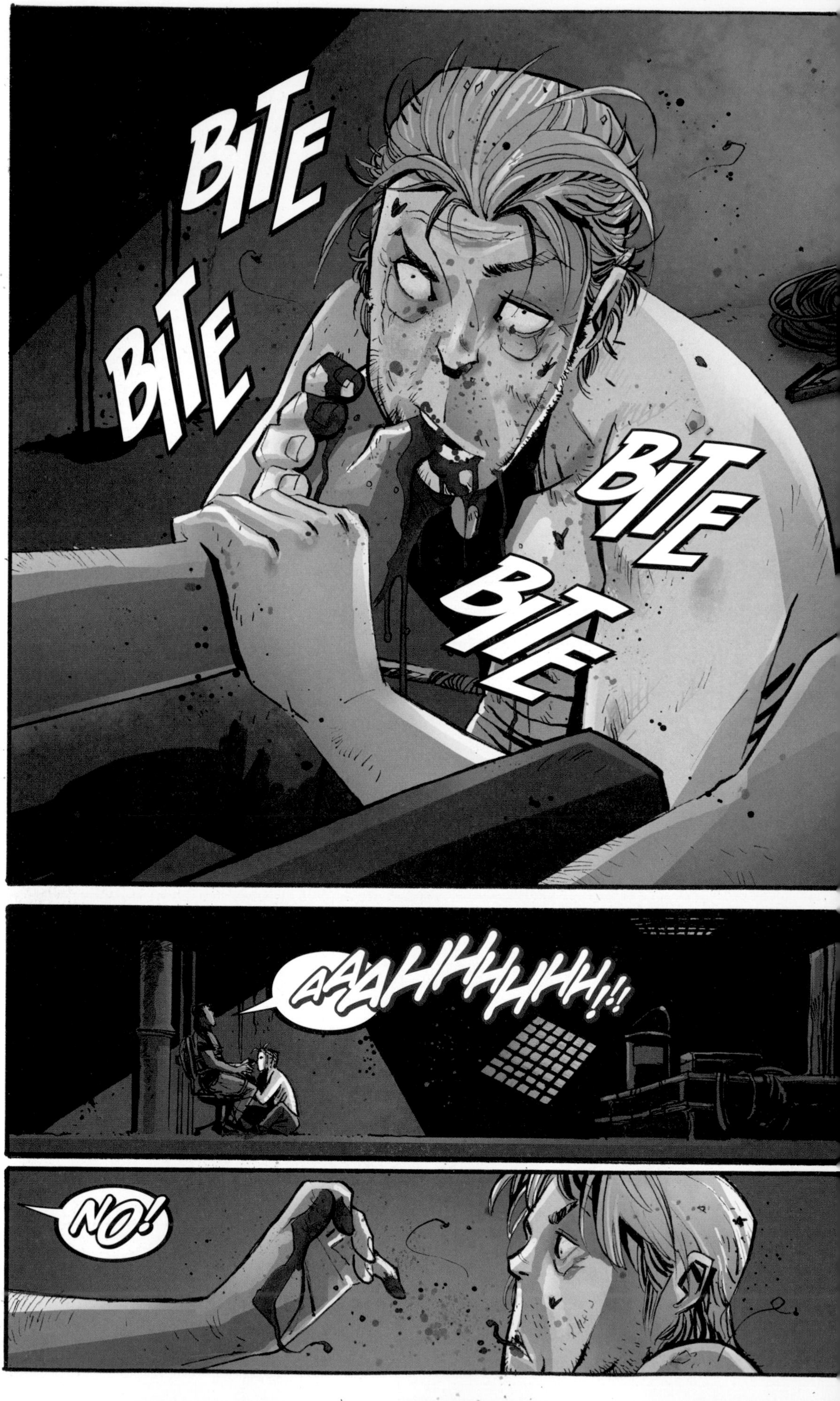
BITE
BITE
BITE
BITE
AAAHHHHHH!!
NO!

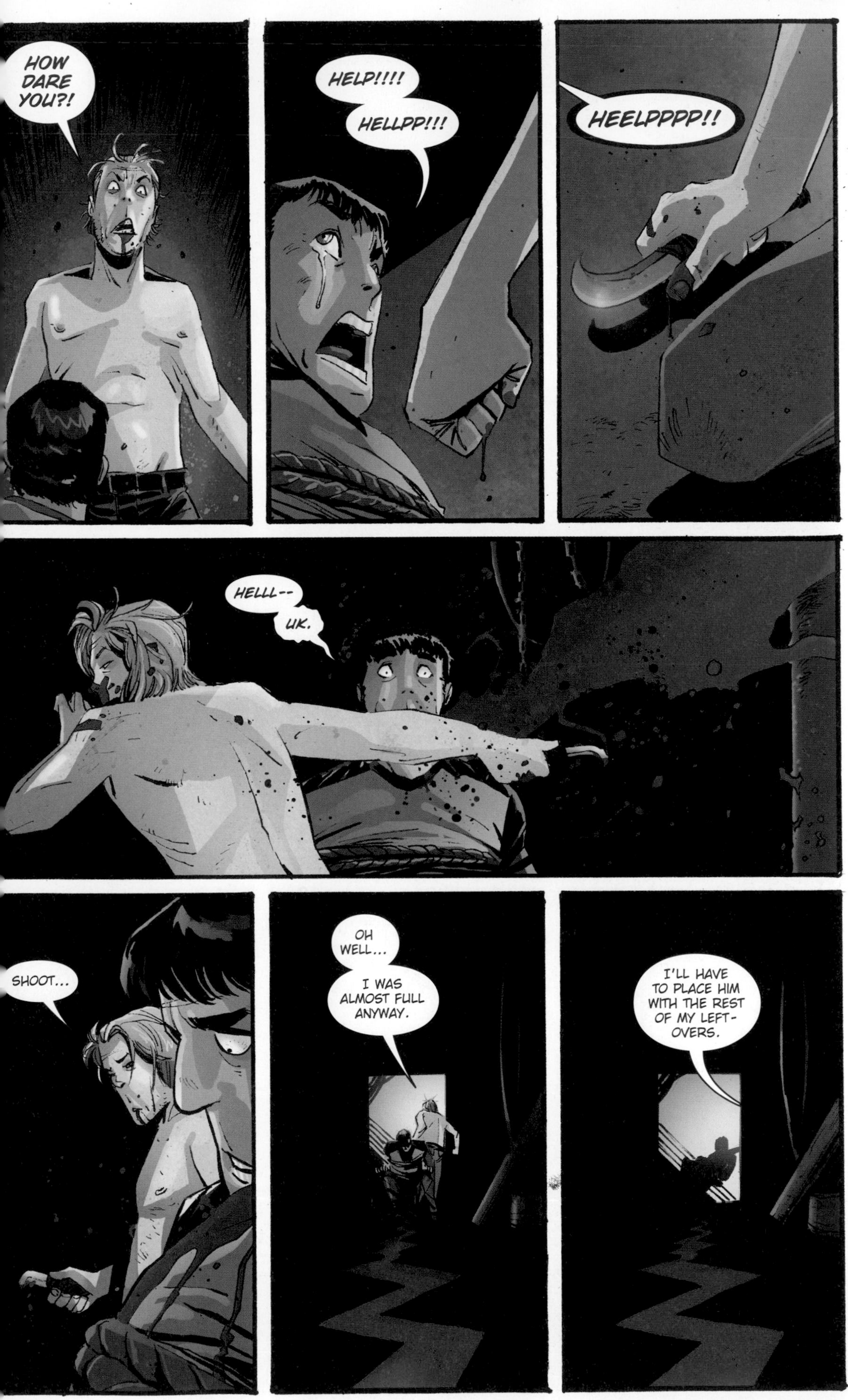
HOW DARE YOU?!
HELP!!!!
HELLPP!!!
HEELPPPP!!
HELLL--
UK.
SHOOT...
OH WELL...
I WAS ALMOST FULL ANYWAY.
I'LL HAVE TO PLACE HIM WITH THE REST OF MY LEFT-OVERS.

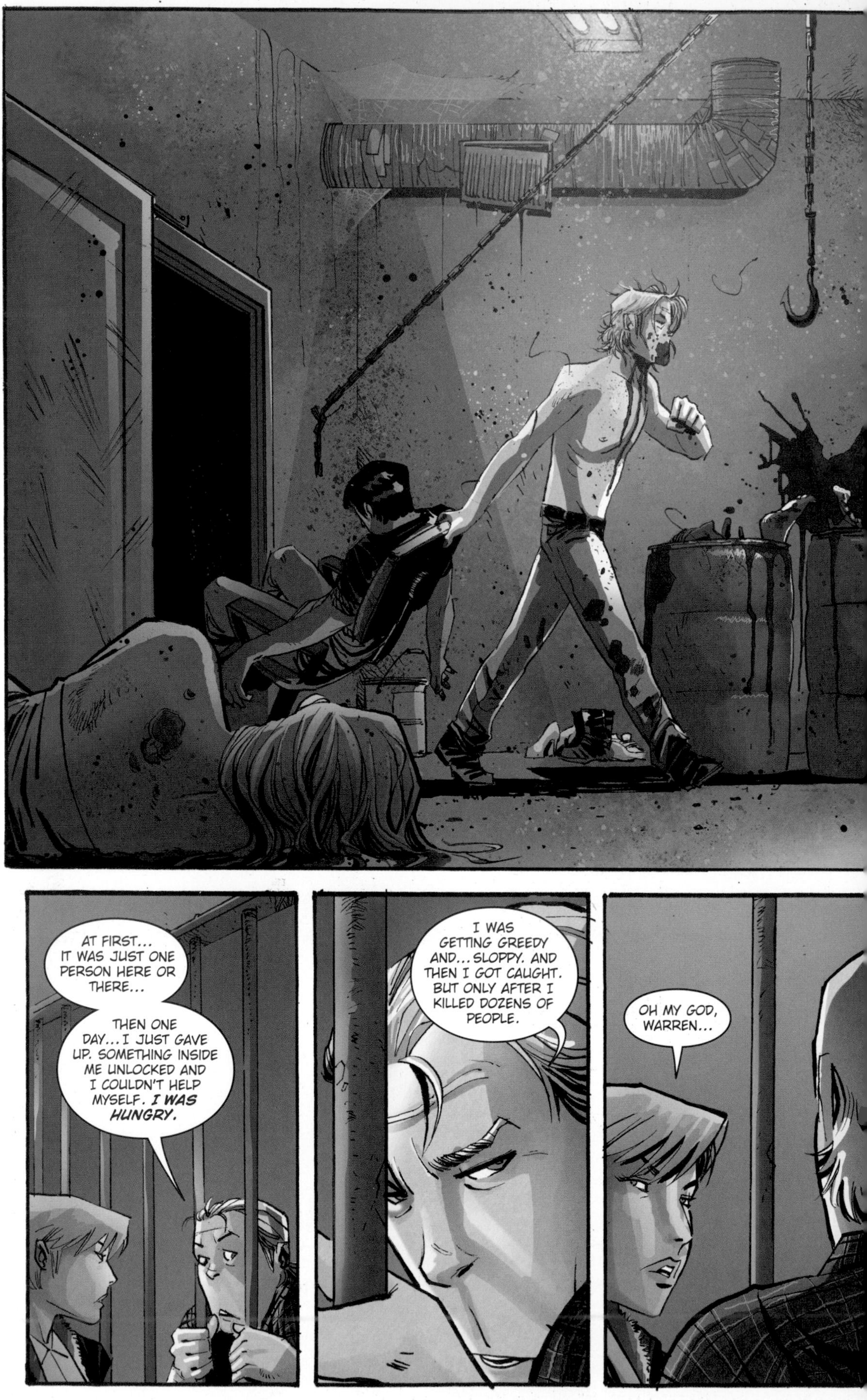
AT FIRST... IT WAS JUST ONE PERSON HERE OR THERE...
THEN ONE DAY... I JUST GAVE UP. SOMETHING INSIDE ME UNLOCKED AND I COULDN'T HELP MYSELF. *I WAS HUNGRY.*
I WAS GETTING GREEDY AND... SLOPPY. AND THEN I GOT CAUGHT. BUT ONLY AFTER I KILLED DOZENS OF PEOPLE.
OH MY GOD, WARREN...

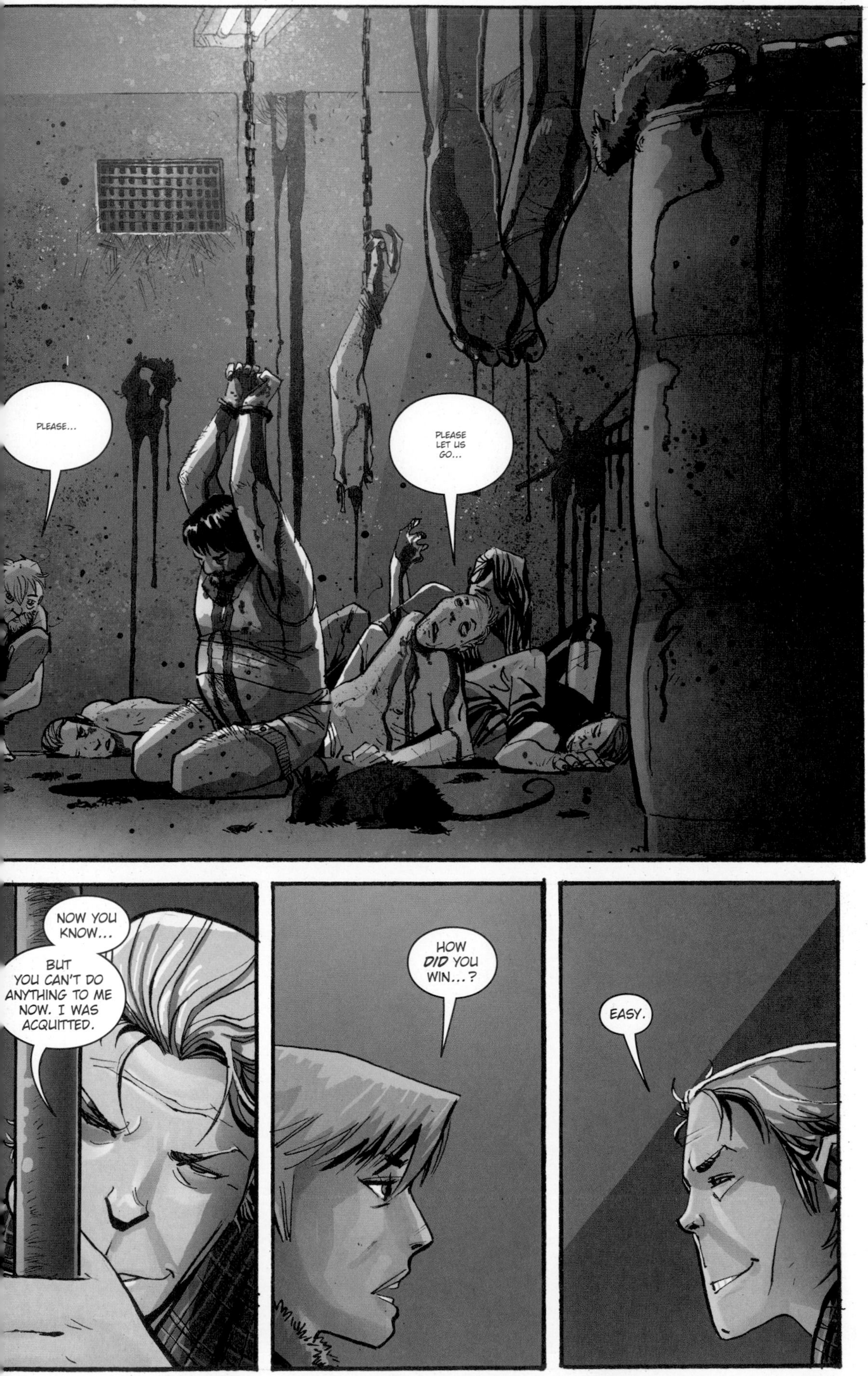
PLEASE...
PLEASE LET US GO...
NOW YOU KNOW...
BUT YOU CAN'T DO ANYTHING TO ME NOW. I WAS ACQUITTED.
HOW *DID* YOU WIN...?
EASY.

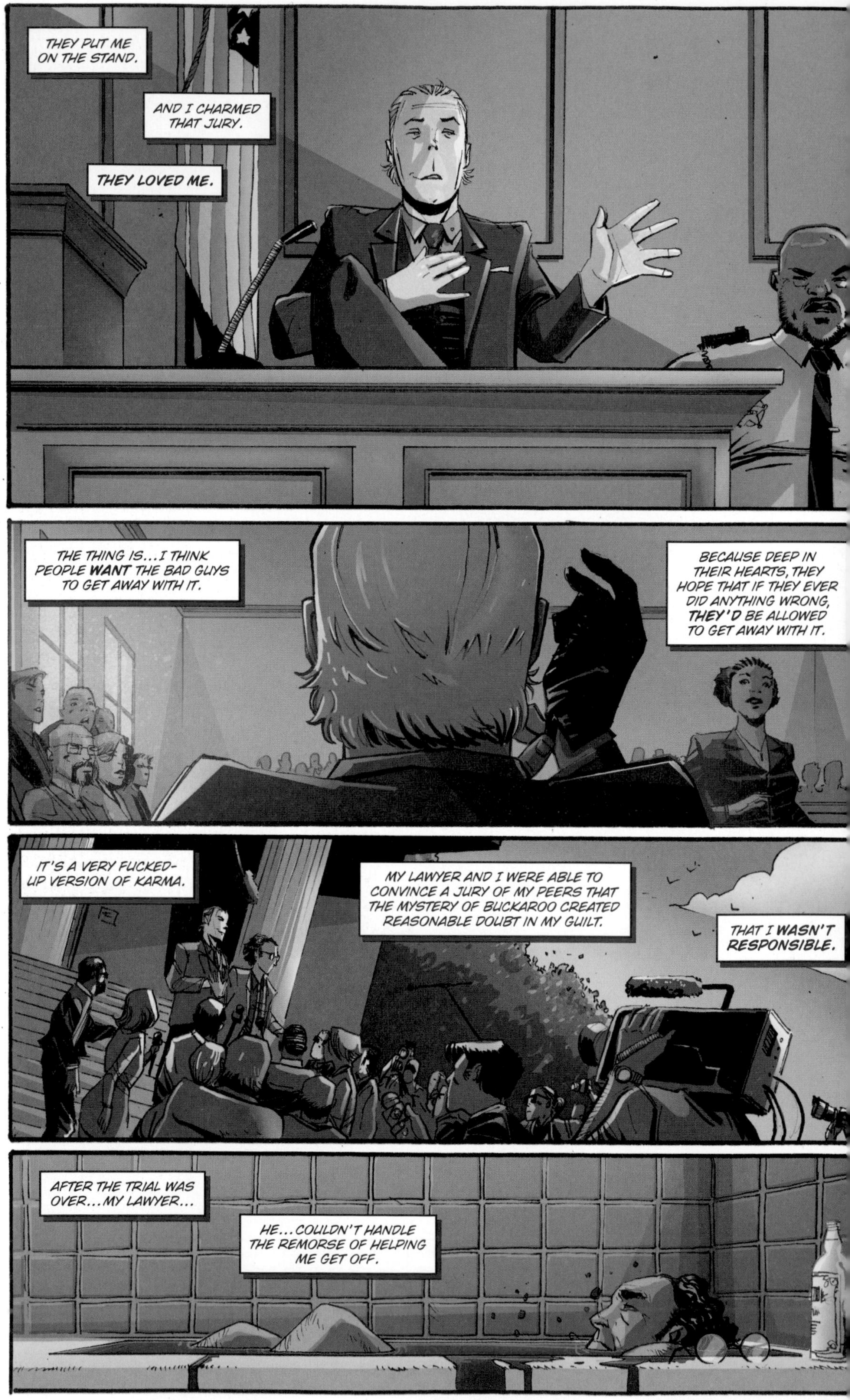
THEY PUT ME ON THE STAND.
AND I CHARMED THAT JURY.
THEY LOVED ME.
THE THING IS...I THINK PEOPLE WANT THE BAD GUYS TO GET AWAY WITH IT.
BECAUSE DEEP IN THEIR HEARTS, THEY HOPE THAT IF THEY EVER DID ANYTHING WRONG, THEY'D BE ALLOWED TO GET AWAY WITH IT.
IT'S A VERY FUCKED-UP VERSION OF KARMA.
MY LAWYER AND I WERE ABLE TO CONVINCE A JURY OF MY PEERS THAT THE MYSTERY OF BUCKAROO CREATED REASONABLE DOUBT IN MY GUILT.
THAT I WASN'T RESPONSIBLE.
AFTER THE TRIAL WAS OVER...MY LAWYER...
HE...COULDN'T HANDLE THE REMORSE OF HELPING ME GET OFF.

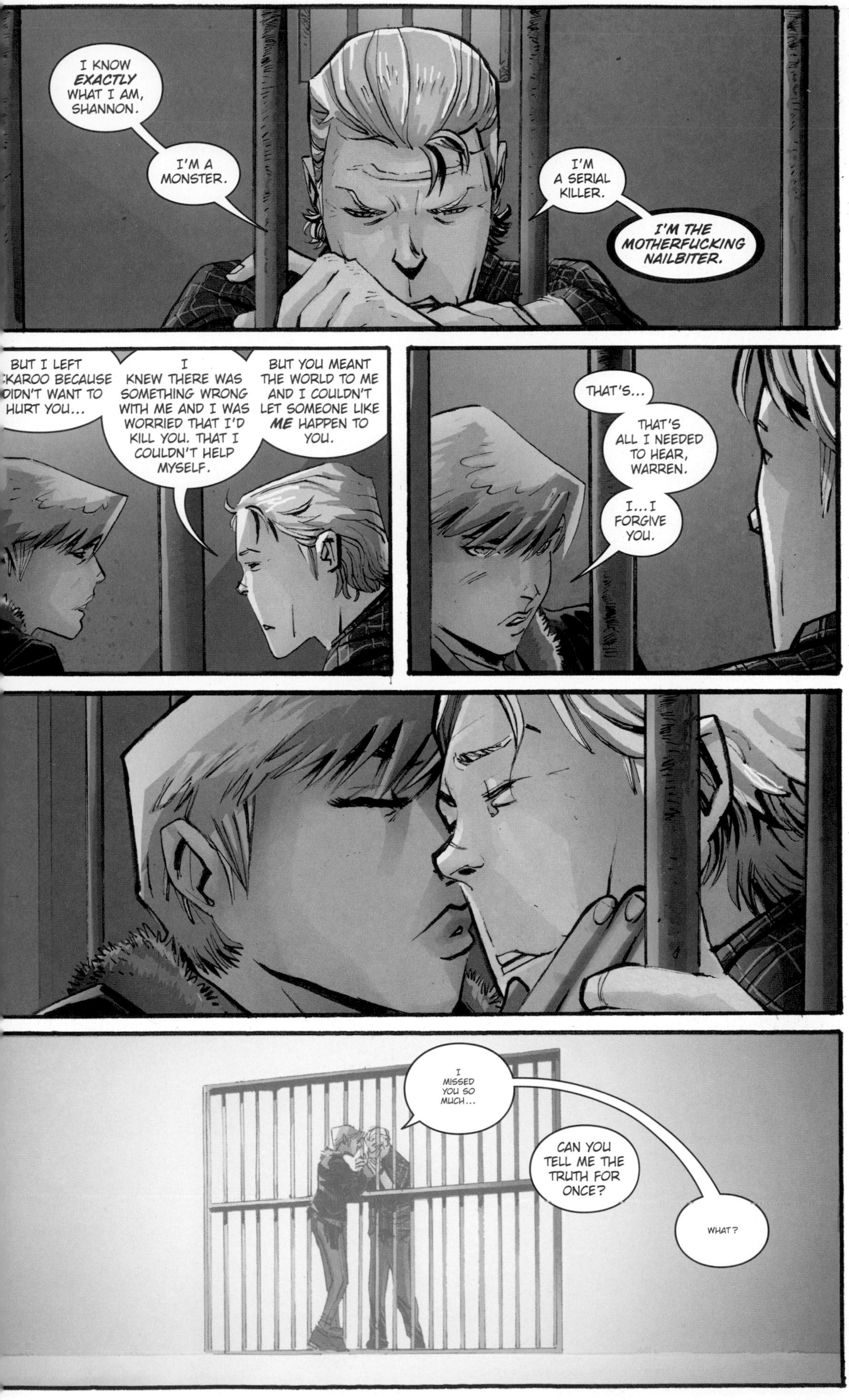
I KNOW *EXACTLY* WHAT I AM, SHANNON.
I'M A MONSTER.
I'M A SERIAL KILLER.
I'M THE MOTHERFUCKING NAILBITER.
BUT I LEFT CKAROO BECAUSE DIDN'T WANT TO HURT YOU...
I KNEW THERE WAS SOMETHING WRONG WITH ME AND I WAS WORRIED THAT I'D KILL YOU. THAT I COULDN'T HELP MYSELF.
BUT YOU MEANT THE WORLD TO ME AND I COULDN'T LET SOMEONE LIKE *ME* HAPPEN TO YOU.
THAT'S...
THAT'S ALL I NEEDED TO HEAR, WARREN.
I... I FORGIVE YOU.
I MISSED YOU SO MUCH...
CAN YOU TELL ME THE TRUTH FOR ONCE?
WHAT?

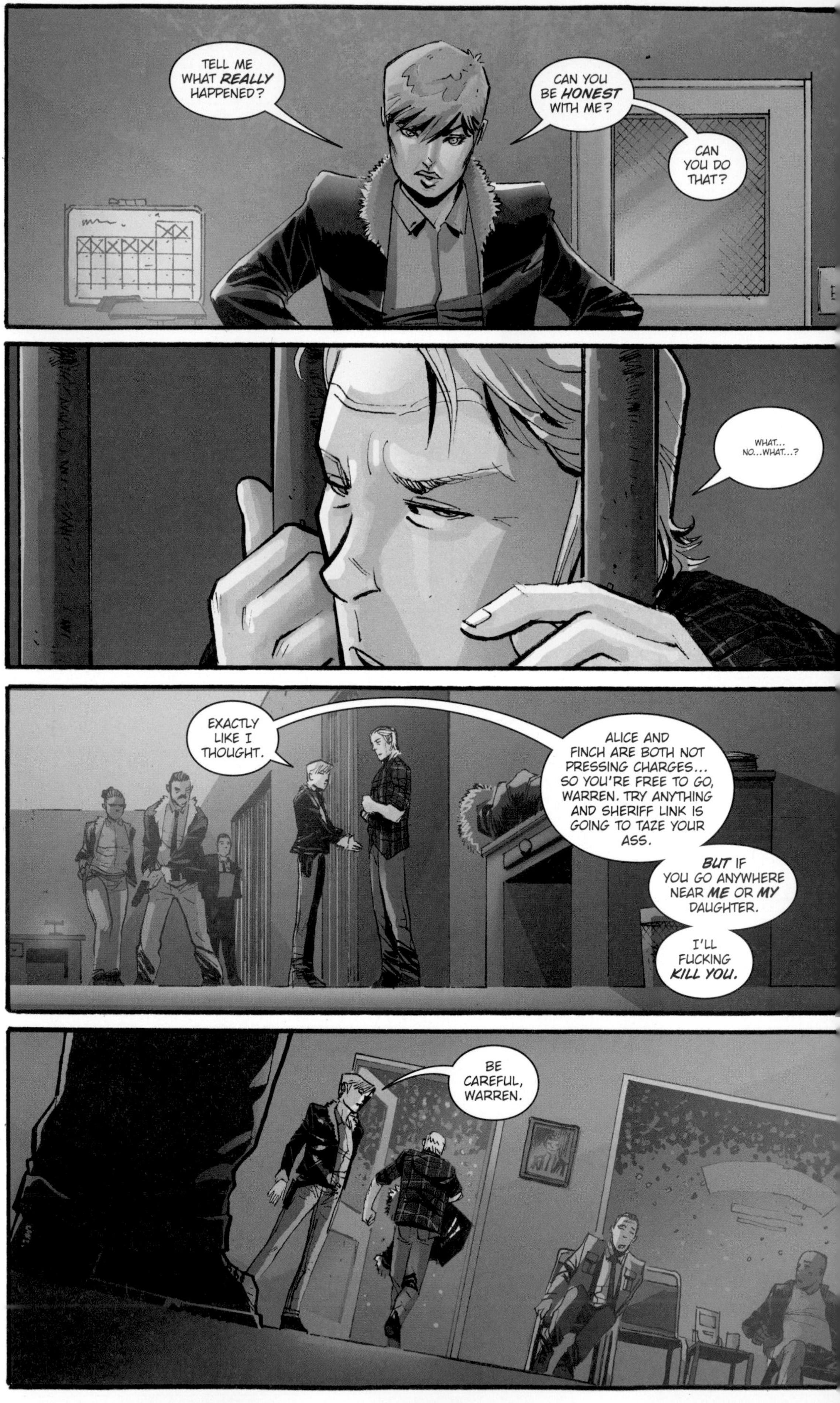
TELL ME WHAT REALLY HAPPENED?
CAN YOU BE HONEST WITH ME?
CAN YOU DO THAT?
WHAT... NO...WHAT...?
EXACTLY LIKE I THOUGHT.
ALICE AND FINCH ARE BOTH NOT PRESSING CHARGES... SO YOU'RE FREE TO GO, WARREN. TRY ANYTHING AND SHERIFF LINK IS GOING TO TAZE YOUR ASS.
BUT IF YOU GO ANYWHERE NEAR ME OR MY DAUGHTER.
I'LL FUCKING KILL YOU.
BE CAREFUL, WARREN.

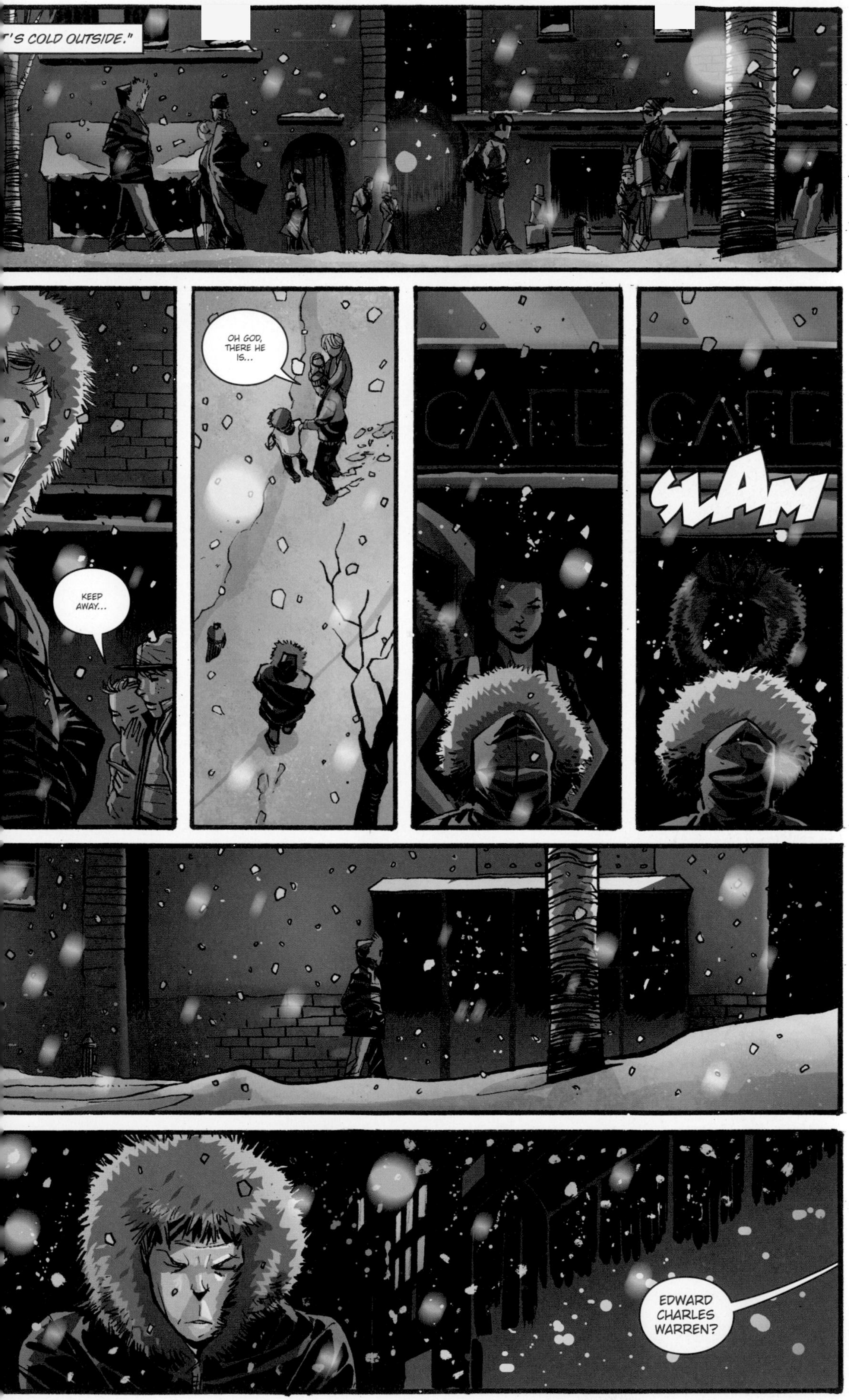
T'S COLD OUTSIDE."
KEEP AWAY...
OH GOD, THERE HE IS...
SLAM
EDWARD CHARLES WARREN?

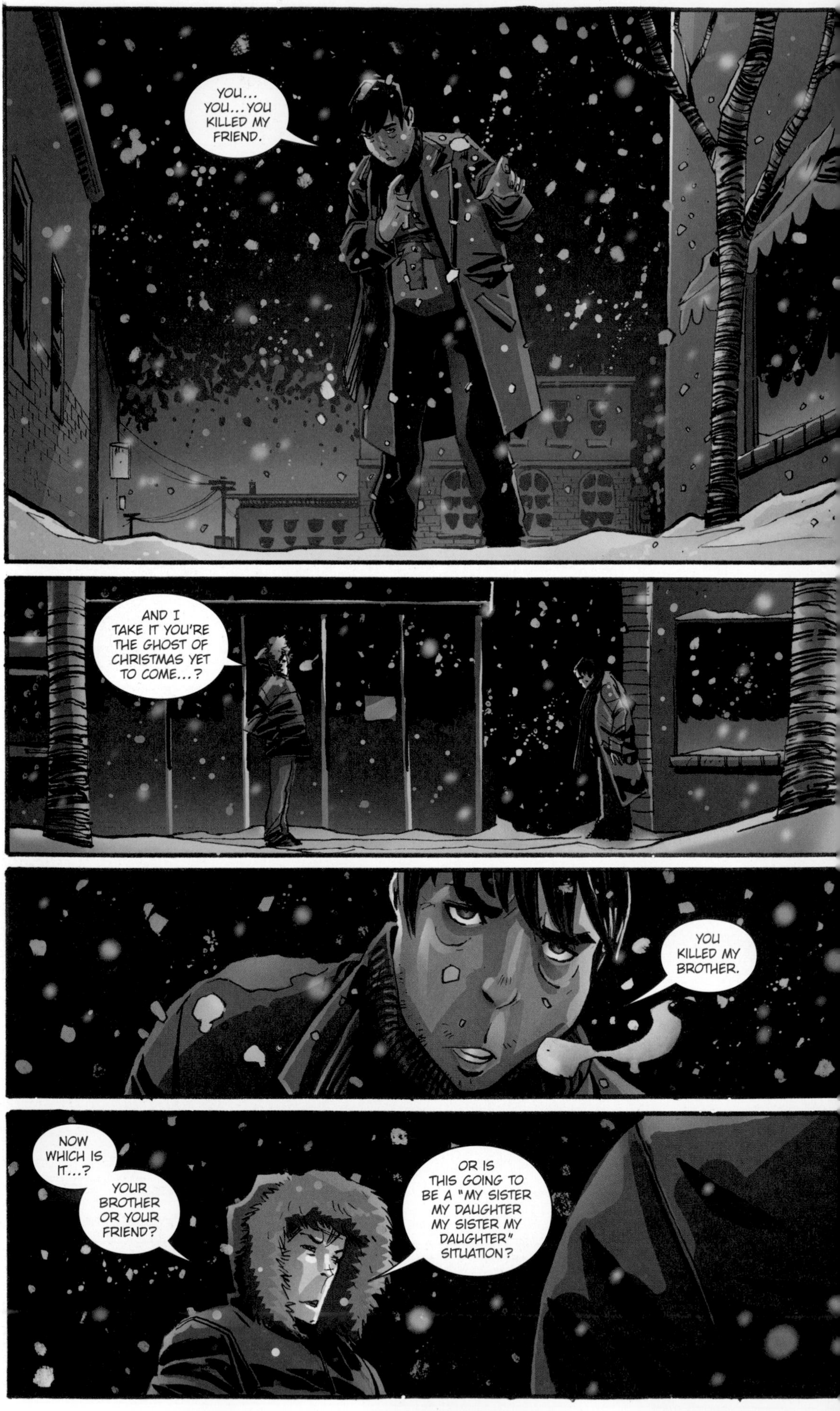
YOU... YOU...YOU KILLED MY FRIEND.
AND I TAKE IT YOU'RE THE GHOST OF CHRISTMAS YET TO COME...?
YOU KILLED MY BROTHER.
NOW WHICH IS IT...?
YOUR BROTHER OR YOUR FRIEND?
OR IS THIS GOING TO BE A "MY SISTER MY DAUGHTER MY SISTER MY DAUGHTER" SITUATION?

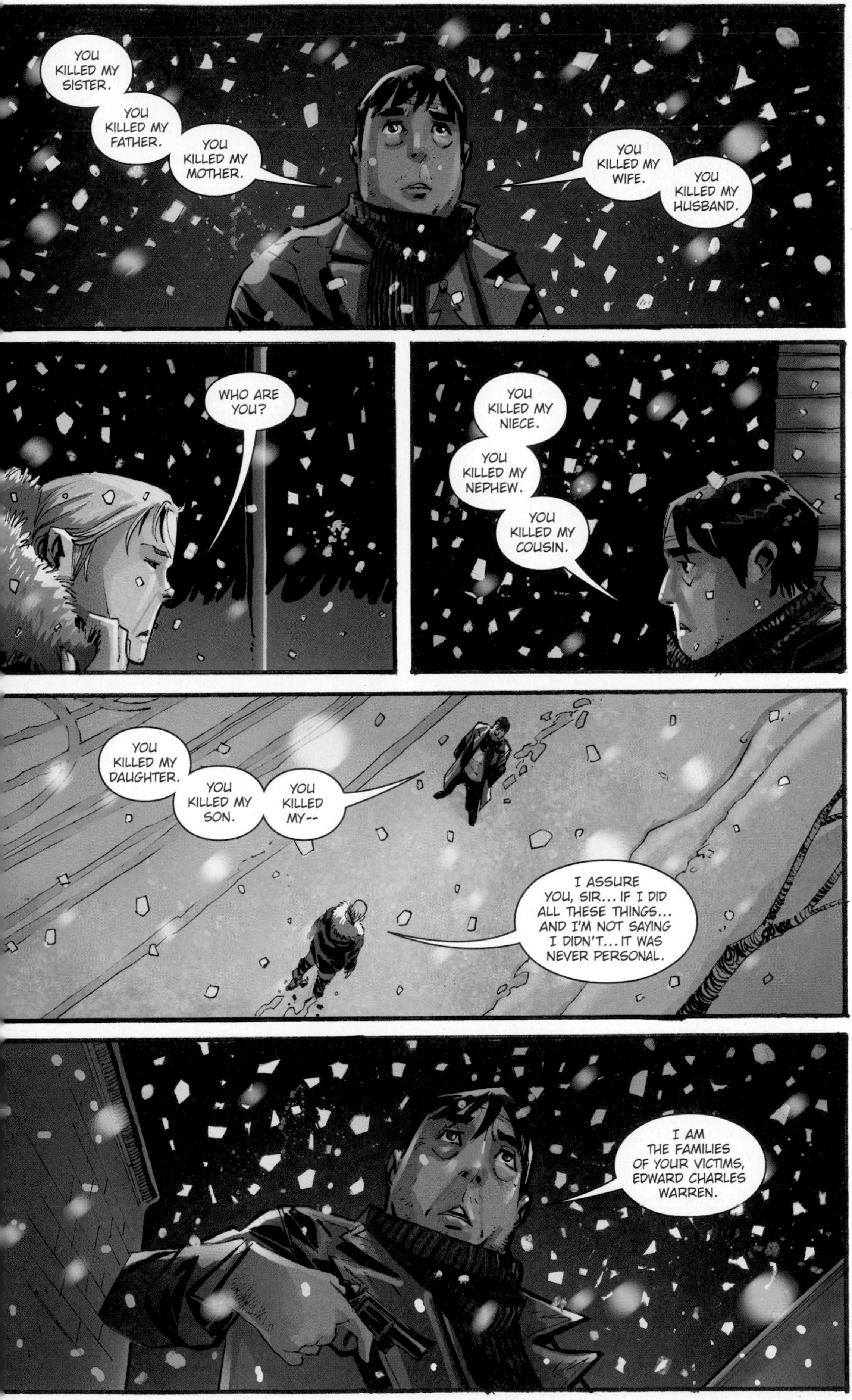
YOU KILLED MY SISTER.
YOU KILLED MY FATHER.
YOU KILLED MY MOTHER.
YOU KILLED MY WIFE.
YOU KILLED MY HUSBAND.
WHO ARE YOU?
YOU KILLED MY NIECE.
YOU KILLED MY NEPHEW.
YOU KILLED MY COUSIN.
YOU KILLED MY DAUGHTER.
YOU KILLED MY SON.
YOU KILLED MY--
I ASSURE YOU, SIR... IF I DID ALL THESE THINGS... AND I'M NOT SAYING I DIDN'T... IT WAS NEVER PERSONAL.
I AM THE FAMILIES OF YOUR VICTIMS, EDWARD CHARLES WARREN.

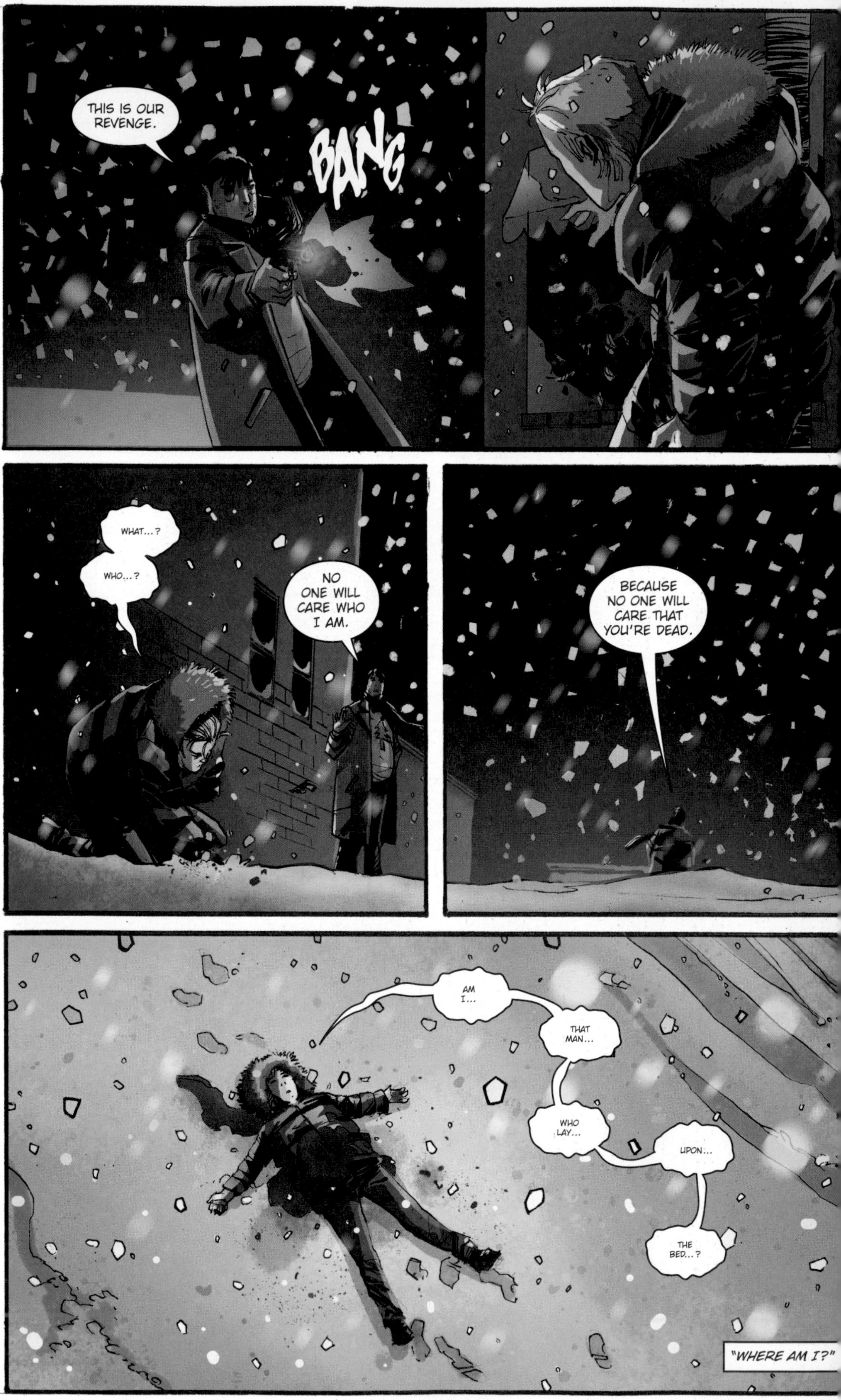
THIS IS OUR REVENGE.
BANG
WHAT...?
WHO...?
NO ONE WILL CARE WHO I AM.
BECAUSE NO ONE WILL CARE THAT YOU'RE DEAD.
AM I...
THAT MAN...
WHO LAY...
UPON...
THE BED...?
"WHERE AM I?"

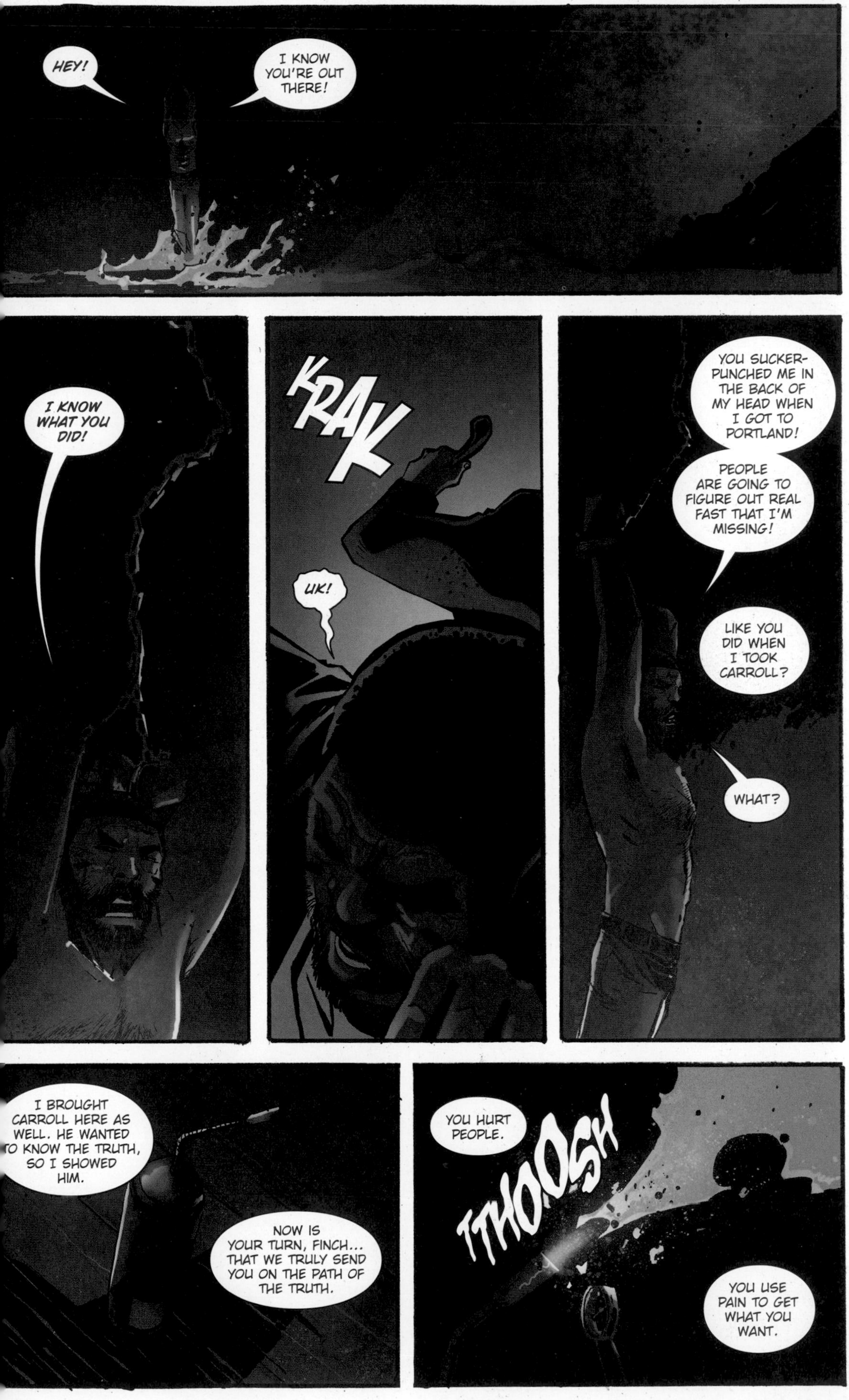
HEY!
I KNOW YOU'RE OUT THERE!
I KNOW WHAT YOU DID!
KRAK
UK!
YOU SUCKER-PUNCHED ME IN THE BACK OF MY HEAD WHEN I GOT TO PORTLAND!
PEOPLE ARE GOING TO FIGURE OUT REAL FAST THAT I'M MISSING!
LIKE YOU DID WHEN I TOOK CARROLL?
WHAT?
I BROUGHT CARROLL HERE AS WELL. HE WANTED TO KNOW THE TRUTH, SO I SHOWED HIM.
NOW IS YOUR TURN, FINCH... THAT WE TRULY SEND YOU ON THE PATH OF THE TRUTH.
YOU HURT PEOPLE.
THOOSH
YOU USE PAIN TO GET WHAT YOU WANT.

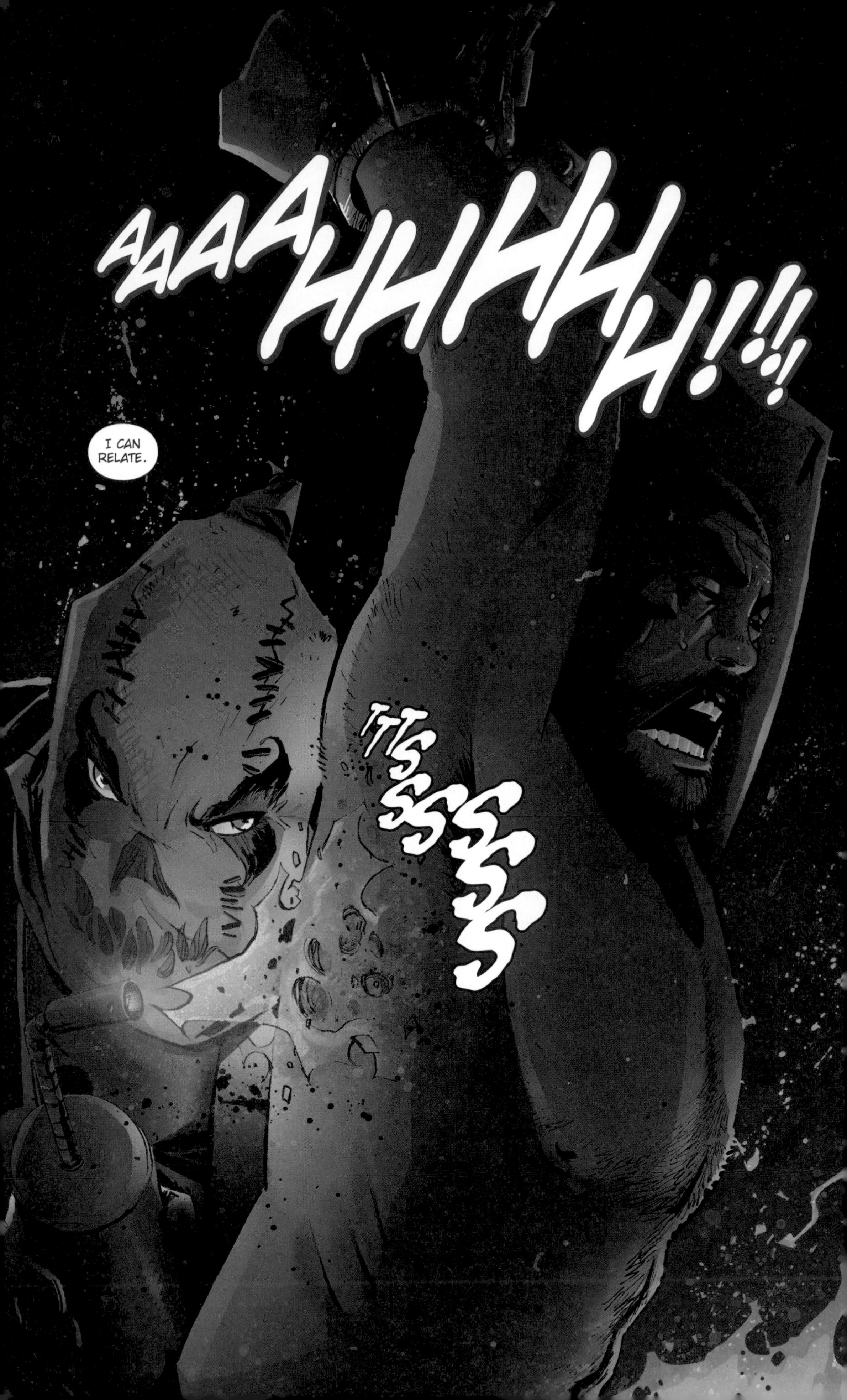
AAAAHHHHH!!!
I CAN RELATE.
TTSSSSSS

ISSUE TWENTY-SEVEN

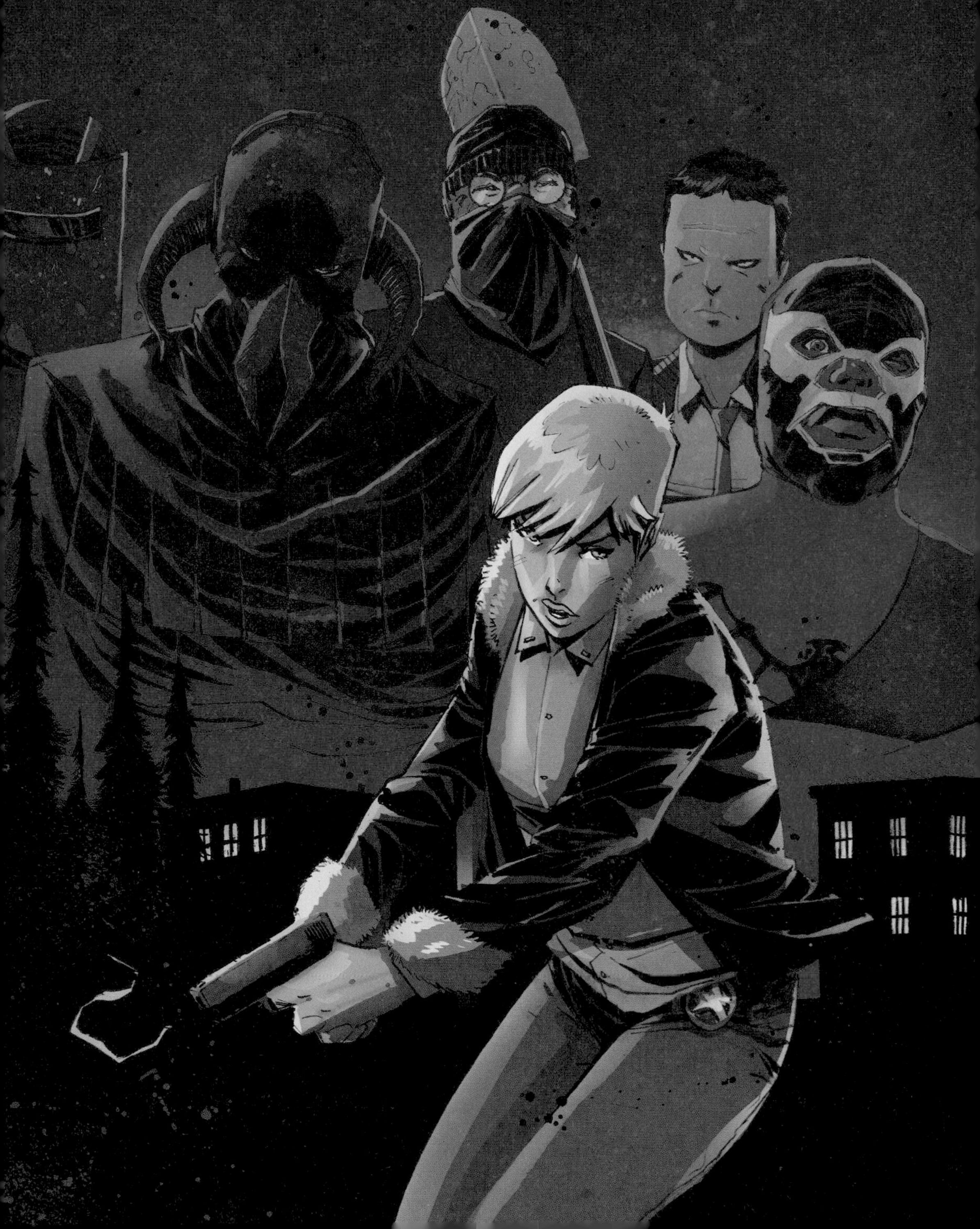

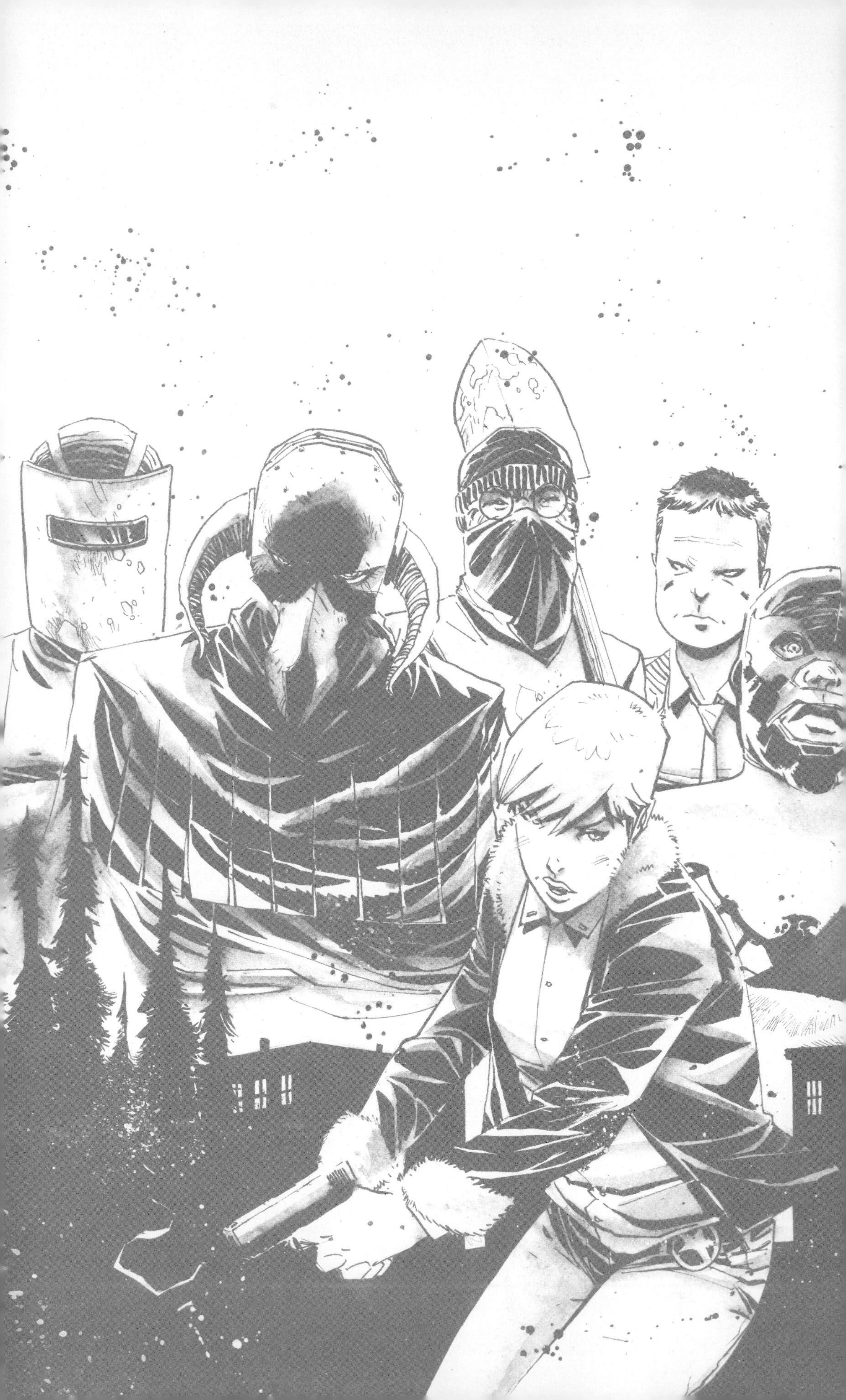

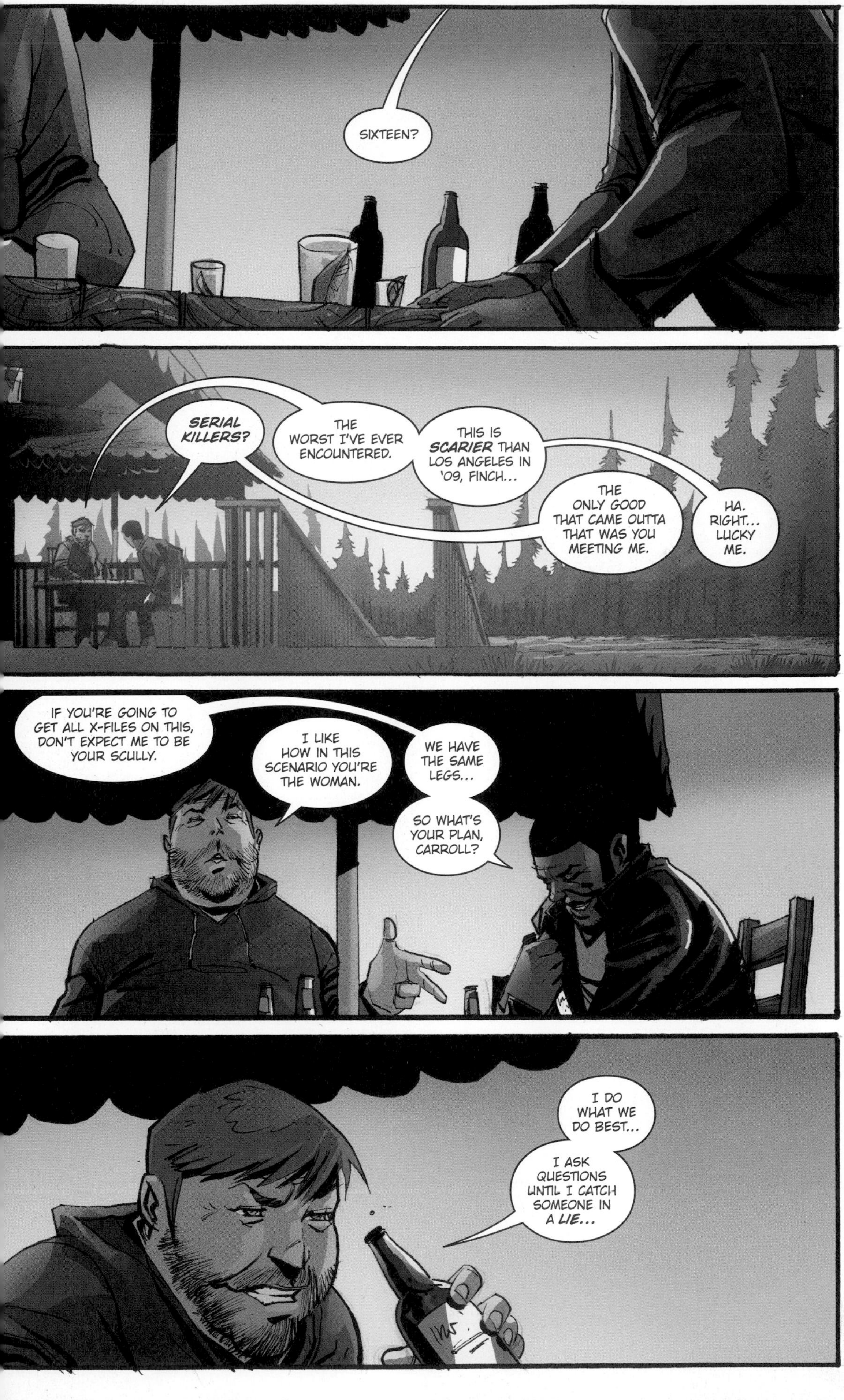
SIXTEEN?
SERIAL KILLERS?
THE WORST I'VE EVER ENCOUNTERED.
THIS IS SCARIER THAN LOS ANGELES IN '09, FINCH...
THE ONLY GOOD THAT CAME OUTTA THAT WAS YOU MEETING ME.
HA. RIGHT... LUCKY ME.
IF YOU'RE GOING TO GET ALL X-FILES ON THIS, DON'T EXPECT ME TO BE YOUR SCULLY.
I LIKE HOW IN THIS SCENARIO YOU'RE THE WOMAN.
WE HAVE THE SAME LEGS...
SO WHAT'S YOUR PLAN, CARROLL?
I DO WHAT WE DO BEST...
I ASK QUESTIONS UNTIL I CATCH SOMEONE IN A LIE...

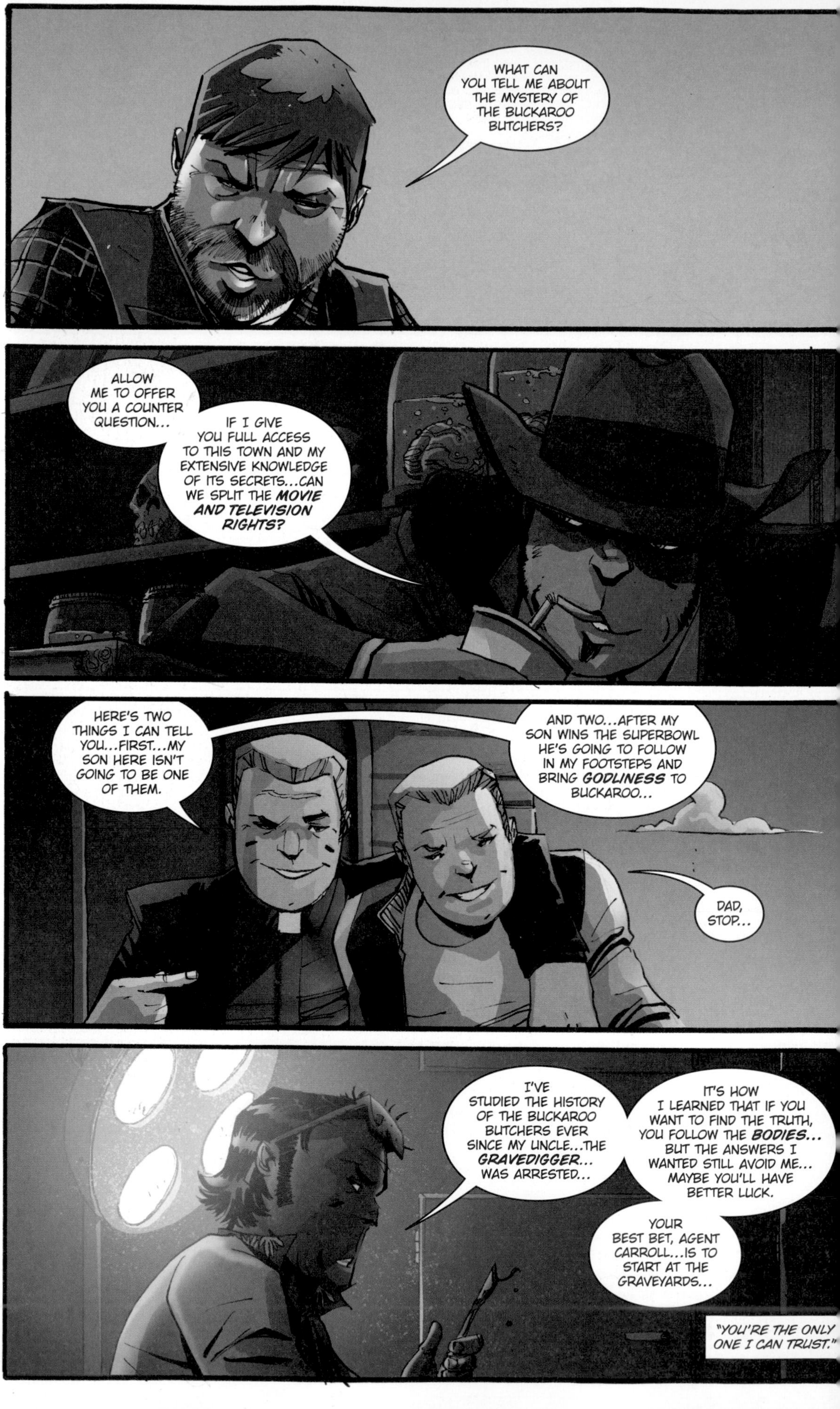
WHAT CAN YOU TELL ME ABOUT THE MYSTERY OF THE BUCKAROO BUTCHERS?
ALLOW ME TO OFFER YOU A COUNTER QUESTION...
IF I GIVE YOU FULL ACCESS TO THIS TOWN AND MY EXTENSIVE KNOWLEDGE OF ITS SECRETS...CAN WE SPLIT THE MOVIE AND TELEVISION RIGHTS?
HERE'S TWO THINGS I CAN TELL YOU...FIRST...MY SON HERE ISN'T GOING TO BE ONE OF THEM.
AND TWO...AFTER MY SON WINS THE SUPERBOWL HE'S GOING TO FOLLOW IN MY FOOTSTEPS AND BRING GODLINESS TO BUCKAROO...
DAD, STOP...
I'VE STUDIED THE HISTORY OF THE BUCKAROO BUTCHERS EVER SINCE MY UNCLE...THE GRAVEDIGGER... WAS ARRESTED...
IT'S HOW I LEARNED THAT IF YOU WANT TO FIND THE TRUTH, YOU FOLLOW THE BODIES... BUT THE ANSWERS I WANTED STILL AVOID ME... MAYBE YOU'LL HAVE BETTER LUCK.
YOUR BEST BET, AGENT CARROLL...IS TO START AT THE GRAVEYARDS...
"YOU'RE THE ONLY ONE I CAN TRUST."

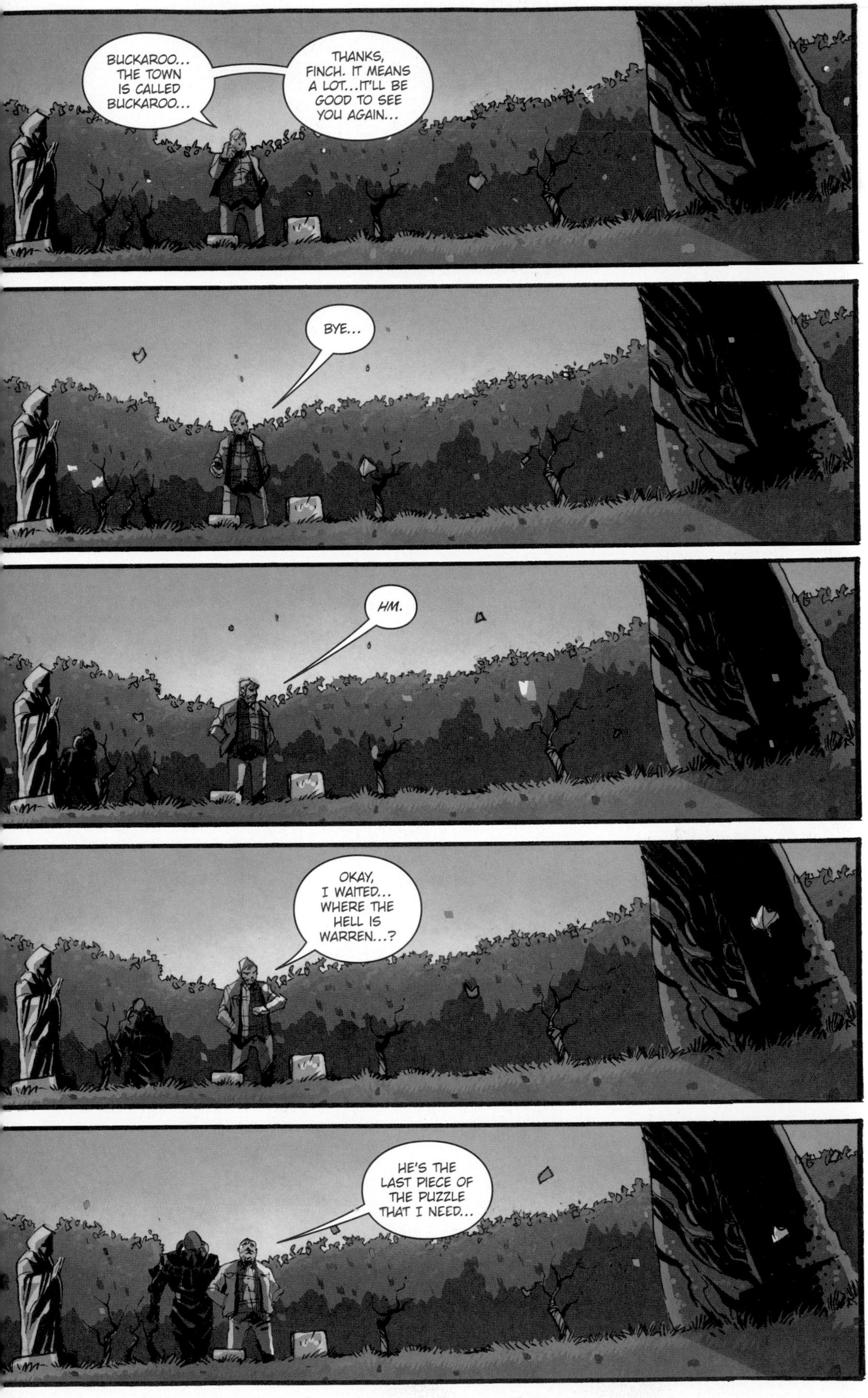
BUCKAROO... THE TOWN IS CALLED BUCKAROO...
THANKS, FINCH. IT MEANS A LOT...IT'LL BE GOOD TO SEE YOU AGAIN...
BYE...
HM.
OKAY, I WAITED... WHERE THE HELL IS WARREN...?
HE'S THE LAST PIECE OF THE PUZZLE THAT I NEED...

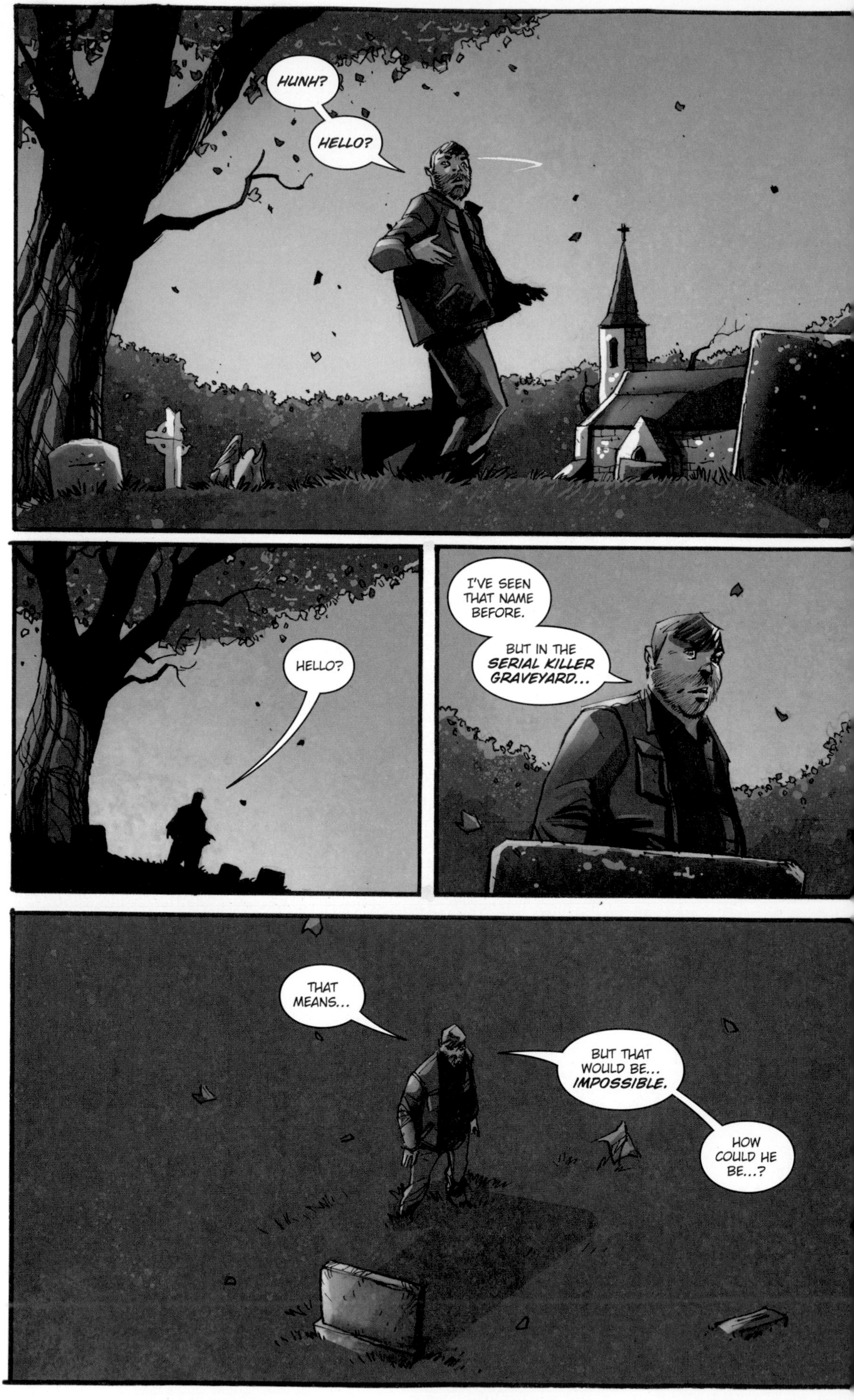
HUNH?
HELLO?
HELLO?
I'VE SEEN THAT NAME BEFORE.
BUT IN THE SERIAL KILLER GRAVEYARD...
THAT MEANS...
BUT THAT WOULD BE... IMPOSSIBLE.
HOW COULD HE BE...?

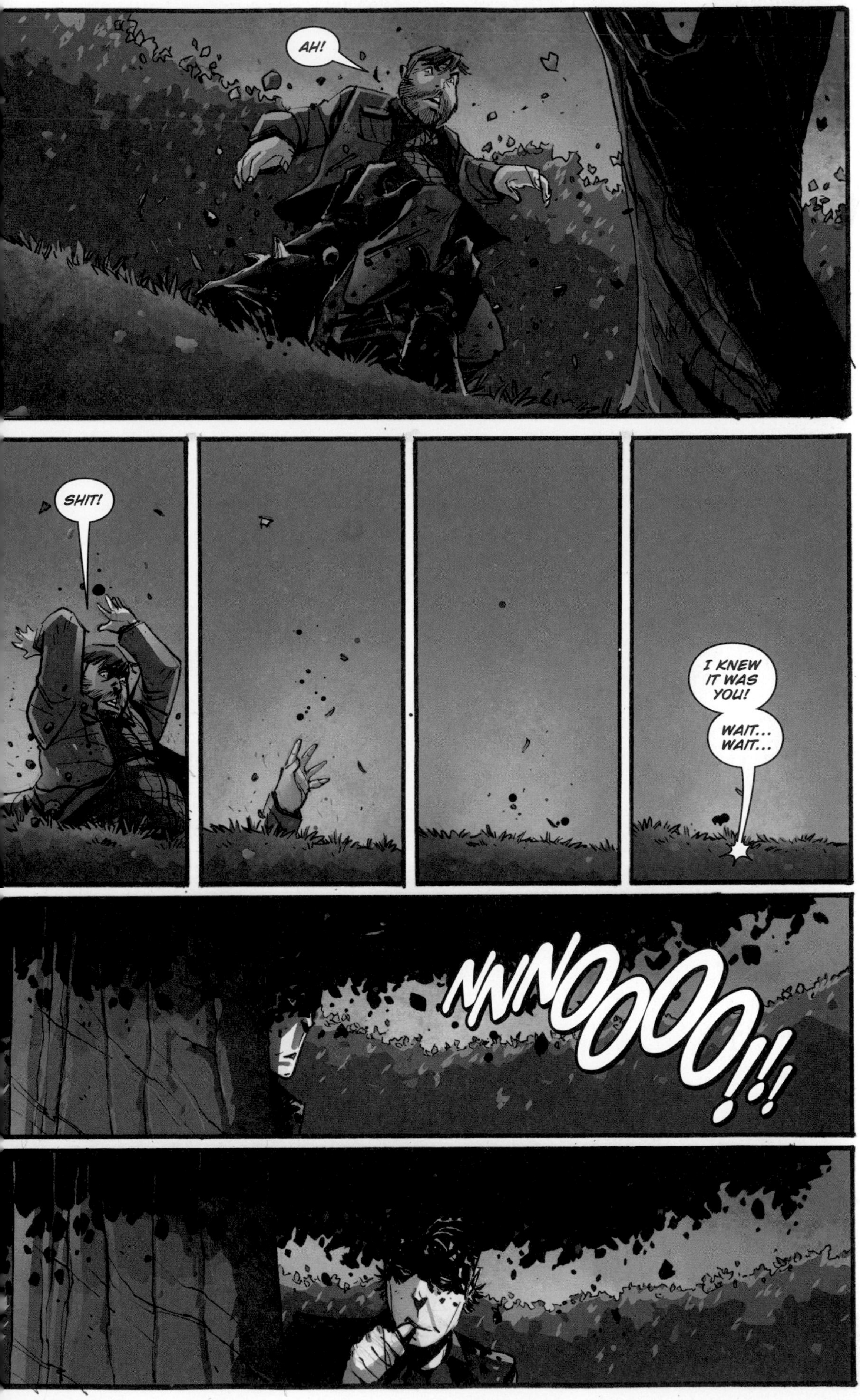
AH!
SHIT!
I KNEW IT WAS YOU!
WAIT... WAIT...
NNNOOOOO!!!

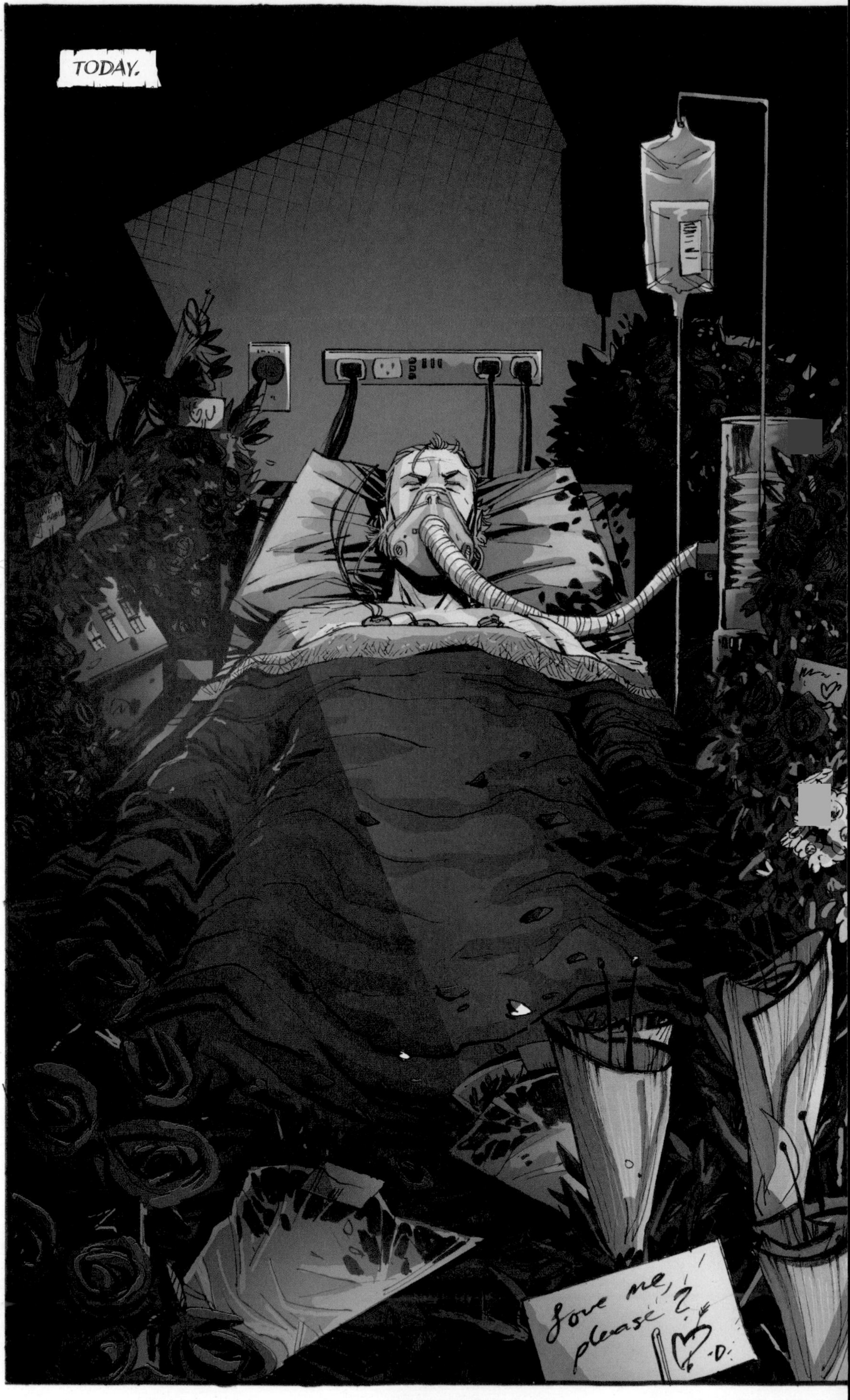

TODAY.
Love me, please? -D.

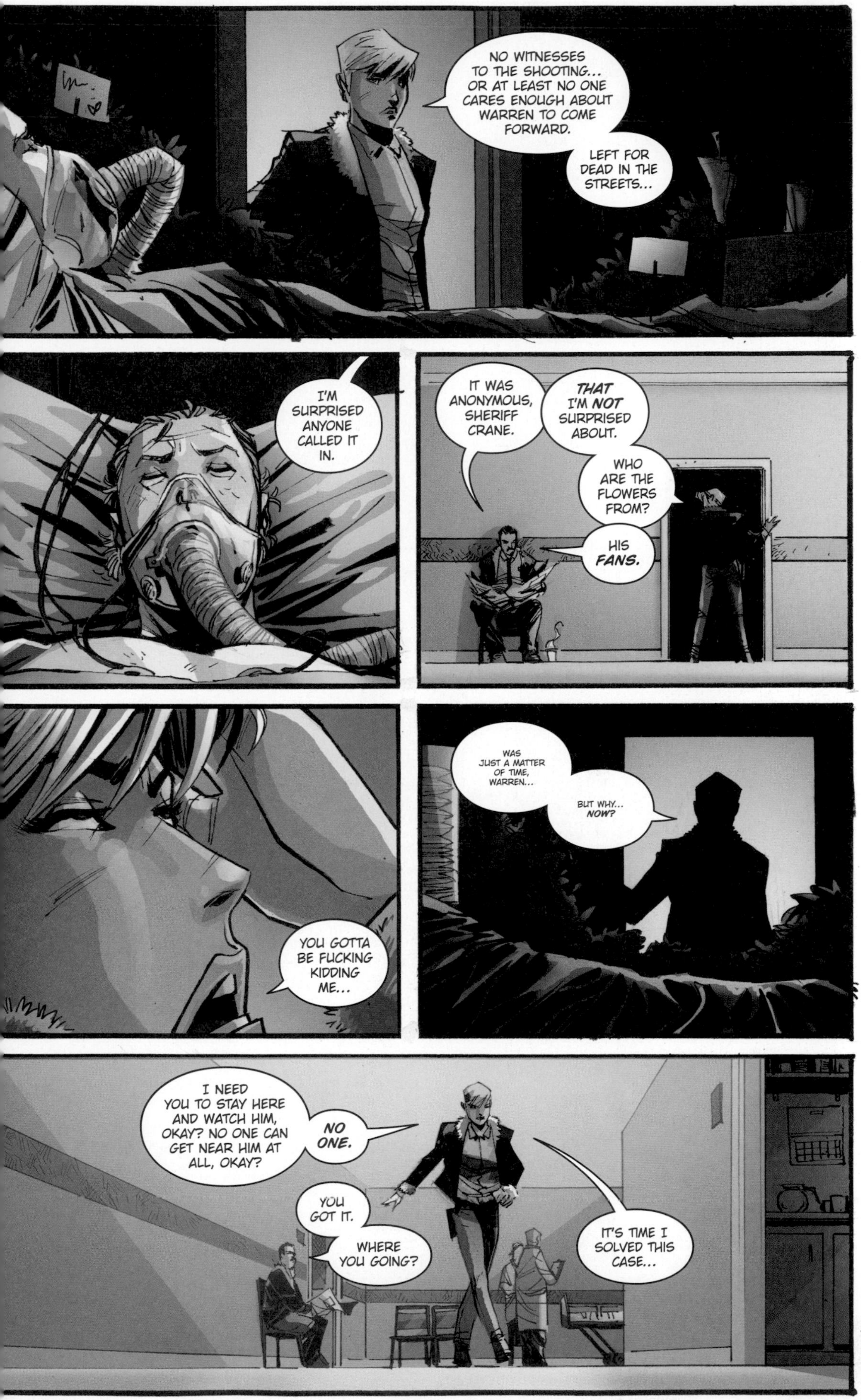
NO WITNESSES TO THE SHOOTING... OR AT LEAST NO ONE CARES ENOUGH ABOUT WARREN TO COME FORWARD.
LEFT FOR DEAD IN THE STREETS...
I'M SURPRISED ANYONE CALLED IT IN.
IT WAS ANONYMOUS, SHERIFF CRANE.
THAT I'M NOT SURPRISED ABOUT.
WHO ARE THE FLOWERS FROM?
HIS FANS.
YOU GOTTA BE FUCKING KIDDING ME...
WAS JUST A MATTER OF TIME, WARREN...
BUT WHY... NOW?
I NEED YOU TO STAY HERE AND WATCH HIM, OKAY? NO ONE CAN GET NEAR HIM AT ALL, OKAY?
NO ONE.
YOU GOT IT.
WHERE YOU GOING?
IT'S TIME I SOLVED THIS CASE...

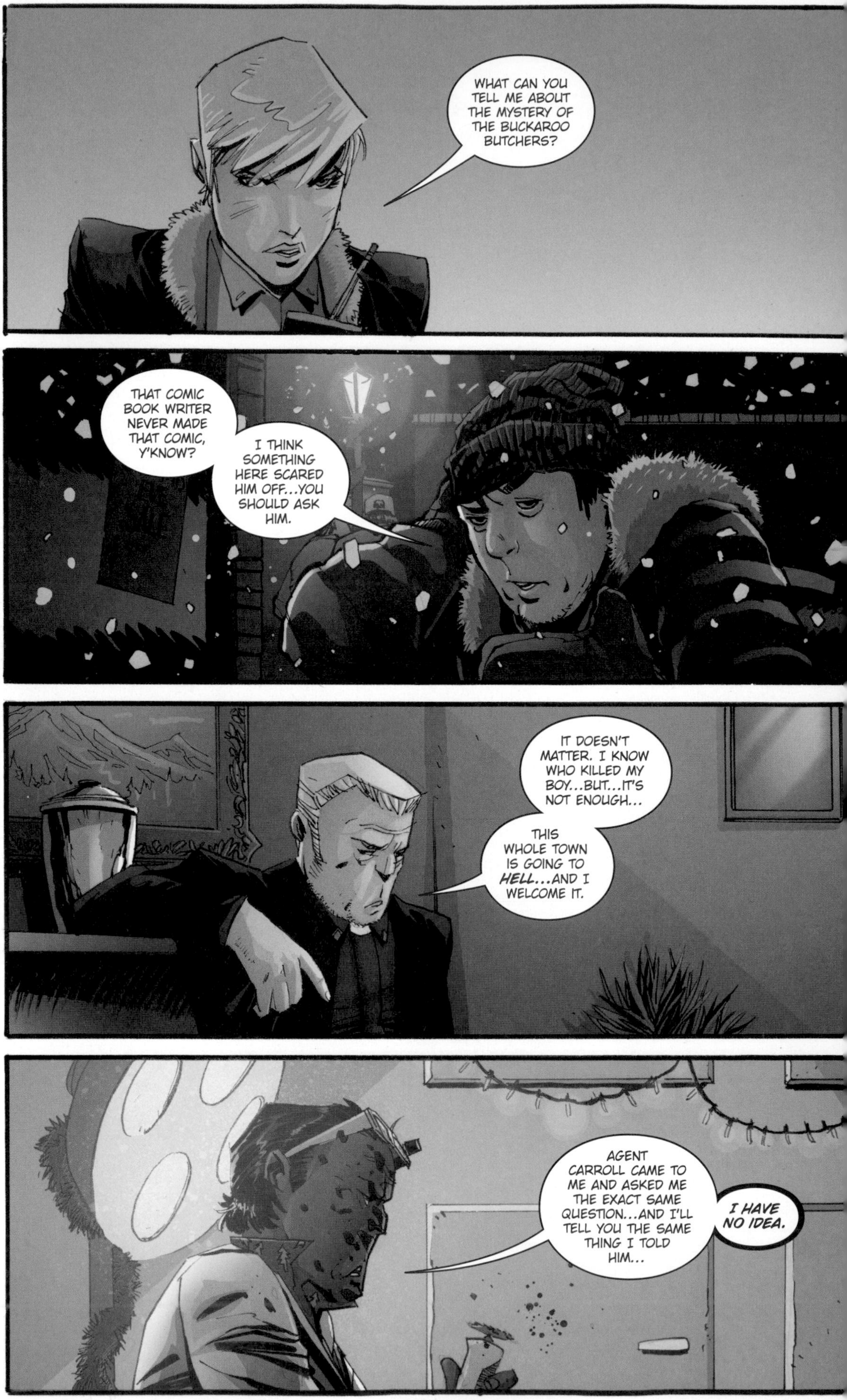
WHAT CAN YOU TELL ME ABOUT THE MYSTERY OF THE BUCKAROO BUTCHERS?
THAT COMIC BOOK WRITER NEVER MADE THAT COMIC, Y'KNOW?
I THINK SOMETHING HERE SCARED HIM OFF...YOU SHOULD ASK HIM.
IT DOESN'T MATTER. I KNOW WHO KILLED MY BOY...BUT...IT'S NOT ENOUGH...
THIS WHOLE TOWN IS GOING TO *HELL*...AND I WELCOME IT.
AGENT CARROLL CAME TO ME AND ASKED ME THE EXACT SAME QUESTION...AND I'LL TELL YOU THE SAME THING I TOLD HIM...
I HAVE NO IDEA.

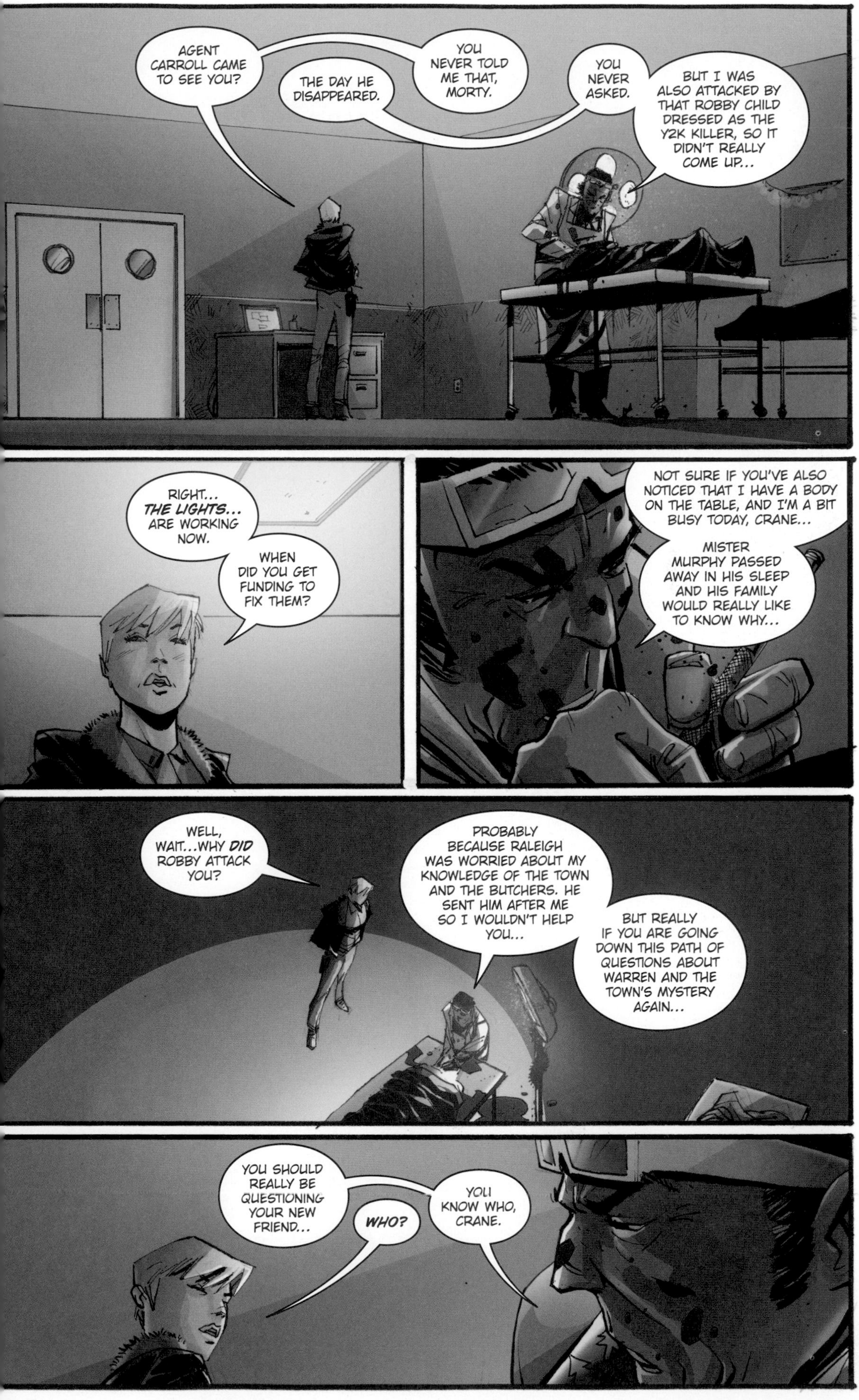
AGENT CARROLL CAME TO SEE YOU?
THE DAY HE DISAPPEARED.
YOU NEVER TOLD ME THAT, MORTY.
YOU NEVER ASKED.
BUT I WAS ALSO ATTACKED BY THAT ROBBY CHILD DRESSED AS THE Y2K KILLER, SO IT DIDN'T REALLY COME UP...
RIGHT... THE LIGHTS... ARE WORKING NOW.
WHEN DID YOU GET FUNDING TO FIX THEM?
NOT SURE IF YOU'VE ALSO NOTICED THAT I HAVE A BODY ON THE TABLE, AND I'M A BIT BUSY TODAY, CRANE...
MISTER MURPHY PASSED AWAY IN HIS SLEEP AND HIS FAMILY WOULD REALLY LIKE TO KNOW WHY...
WELL, WAIT...WHY DID ROBBY ATTACK YOU?
PROBABLY BECAUSE RALEIGH WAS WORRIED ABOUT MY KNOWLEDGE OF THE TOWN AND THE BUTCHERS. HE SENT HIM AFTER ME SO I WOULDN'T HELP YOU...
BUT REALLY IF YOU ARE GOING DOWN THIS PATH OF QUESTIONS ABOUT WARREN AND THE TOWN'S MYSTERY AGAIN...
YOU SHOULD REALLY BE QUESTIONING YOUR NEW FRIEND...
WHO?
YOU KNOW WHO, CRANE.

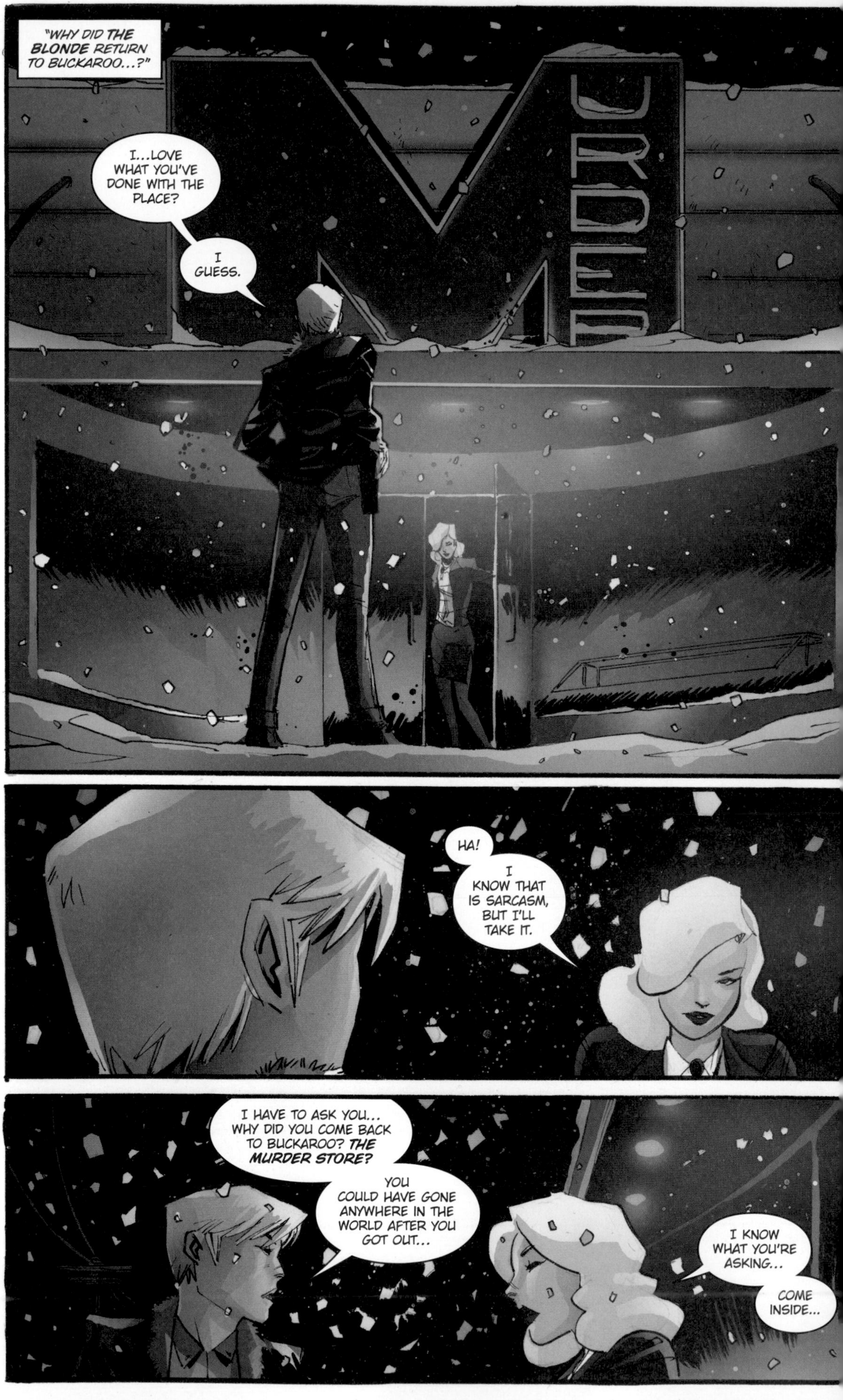
"WHY DID THE BLONDE RETURN TO BUCKAROO...?"
URDER
I...LOVE WHAT YOU'VE DONE WITH THE PLACE?
I GUESS.
HA!
I KNOW THAT IS SARCASM, BUT I'LL TAKE IT.
I HAVE TO ASK YOU... WHY DID YOU COME BACK TO BUCKAROO? THE MURDER STORE?
YOU COULD HAVE GONE ANYWHERE IN THE WORLD AFTER YOU GOT OUT...
I KNOW WHAT YOU'RE ASKING...
COME INSIDE...

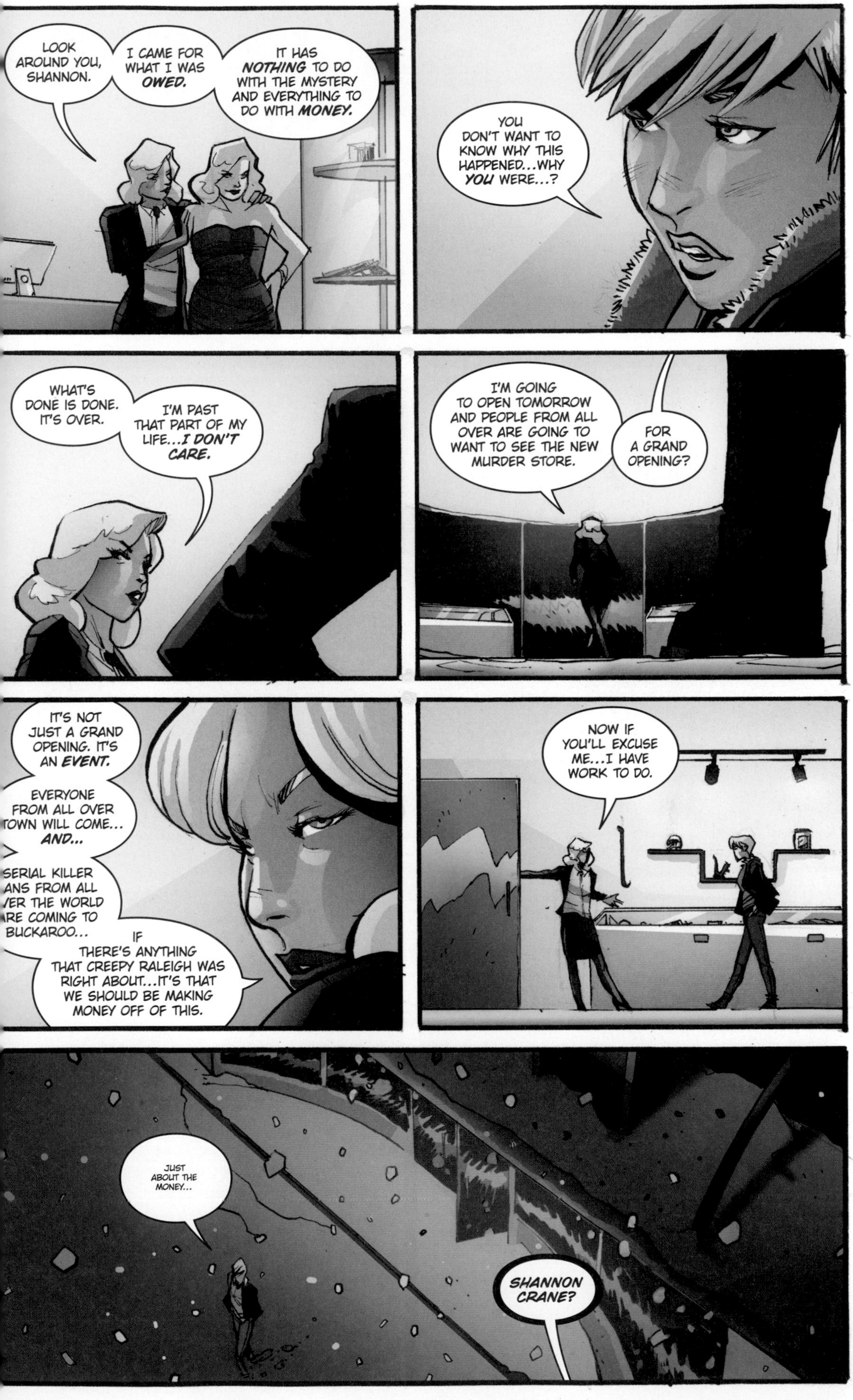
LOOK AROUND YOU, SHANNON.
I CAME FOR WHAT I WAS **OWED.**
IT HAS **NOTHING** TO DO WITH THE MYSTERY AND EVERYTHING TO DO WITH **MONEY.**
YOU DON'T WANT TO KNOW WHY THIS HAPPENED...WHY **YOU** WERE...?
WHAT'S DONE IS DONE. IT'S OVER.
I'M PAST THAT PART OF MY LIFE...**I DON'T CARE.**
I'M GOING TO OPEN TOMORROW AND PEOPLE FROM ALL OVER ARE GOING TO WANT TO SEE THE NEW MURDER STORE.
FOR A GRAND OPENING?
IT'S NOT JUST A GRAND OPENING. IT'S AN **EVENT.**
EVERYONE FROM ALL OVER TOWN WILL COME... **AND...**
SERIAL KILLER ANS FROM ALL VER THE WORLD RE COMING TO BUCKAROO...
IF THERE'S ANYTHING THAT CREEPY RALEIGH WAS RIGHT ABOUT...IT'S THAT WE SHOULD BE MAKING MONEY OFF OF THIS.
NOW IF YOU'LL EXCUSE ME...I HAVE WORK TO DO.
JUST ABOUT THE MONEY...
SHANNON CRANE?

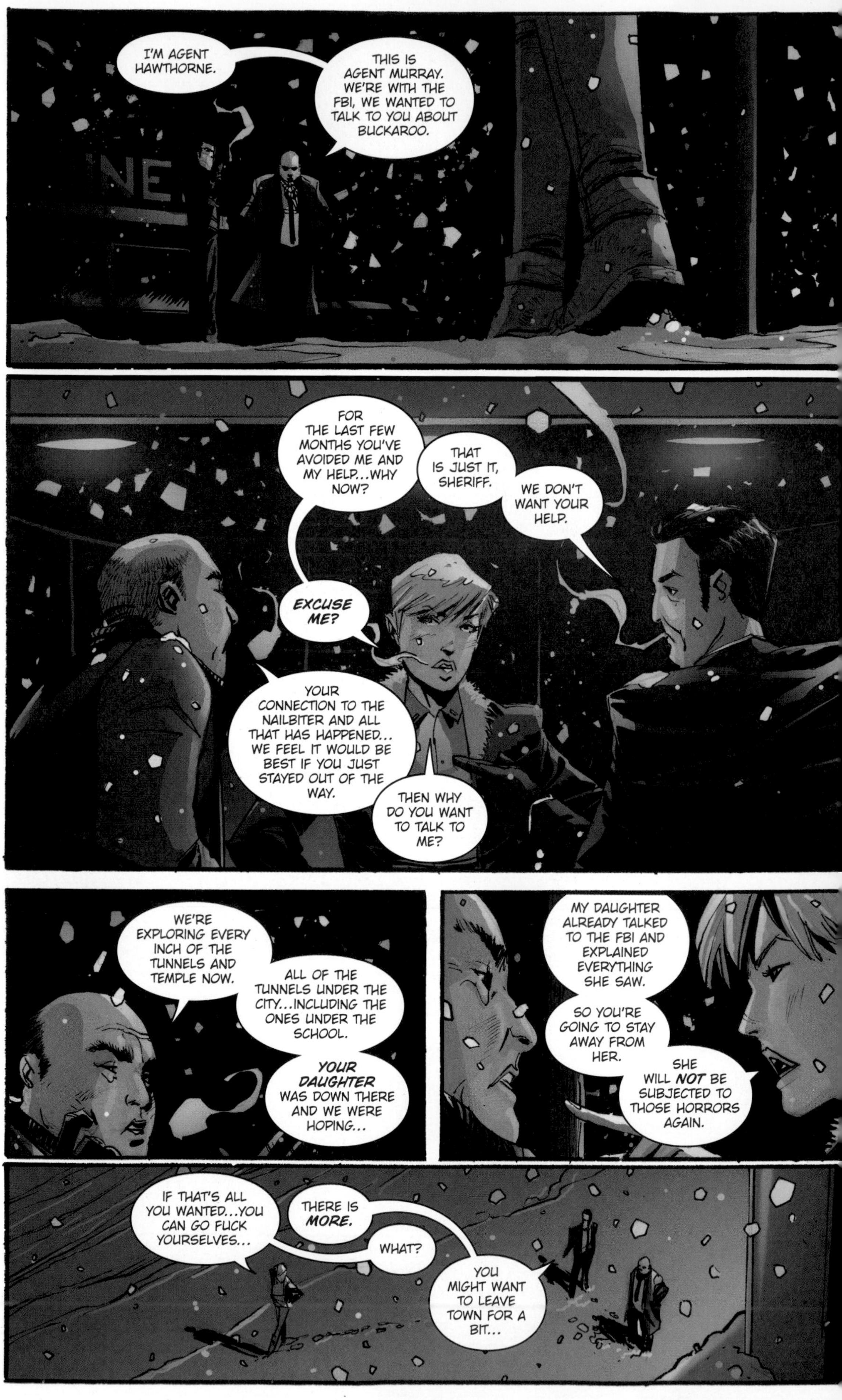
I'M AGENT HAWTHORNE.
THIS IS AGENT MURRAY. WE'RE WITH THE FBI, WE WANTED TO TALK TO YOU ABOUT BUCKAROO.
FOR THE LAST FEW MONTHS YOU'VE AVOIDED ME AND MY HELP...WHY NOW?
THAT IS JUST IT, SHERIFF.
WE DON'T WANT YOUR HELP.
EXCUSE ME?
YOUR CONNECTION TO THE NAILBITER AND ALL THAT HAS HAPPENED... WE FEEL IT WOULD BE BEST IF YOU JUST STAYED OUT OF THE WAY.
THEN WHY DO YOU WANT TO TALK TO ME?
WE'RE EXPLORING EVERY INCH OF THE TUNNELS AND TEMPLE NOW.
ALL OF THE TUNNELS UNDER THE CITY...INCLUDING THE ONES UNDER THE SCHOOL.
YOUR DAUGHTER WAS DOWN THERE AND WE WERE HOPING...
MY DAUGHTER ALREADY TALKED TO THE FBI AND EXPLAINED EVERYTHING SHE SAW.
SO YOU'RE GOING TO STAY AWAY FROM HER.
SHE WILL NOT BE SUBJECTED TO THOSE HORRORS AGAIN.
IF THAT'S ALL YOU WANTED...YOU CAN GO FUCK YOURSELVES...
THERE IS MORE.
WHAT?
YOU MIGHT WANT TO LEAVE TOWN FOR A BIT...

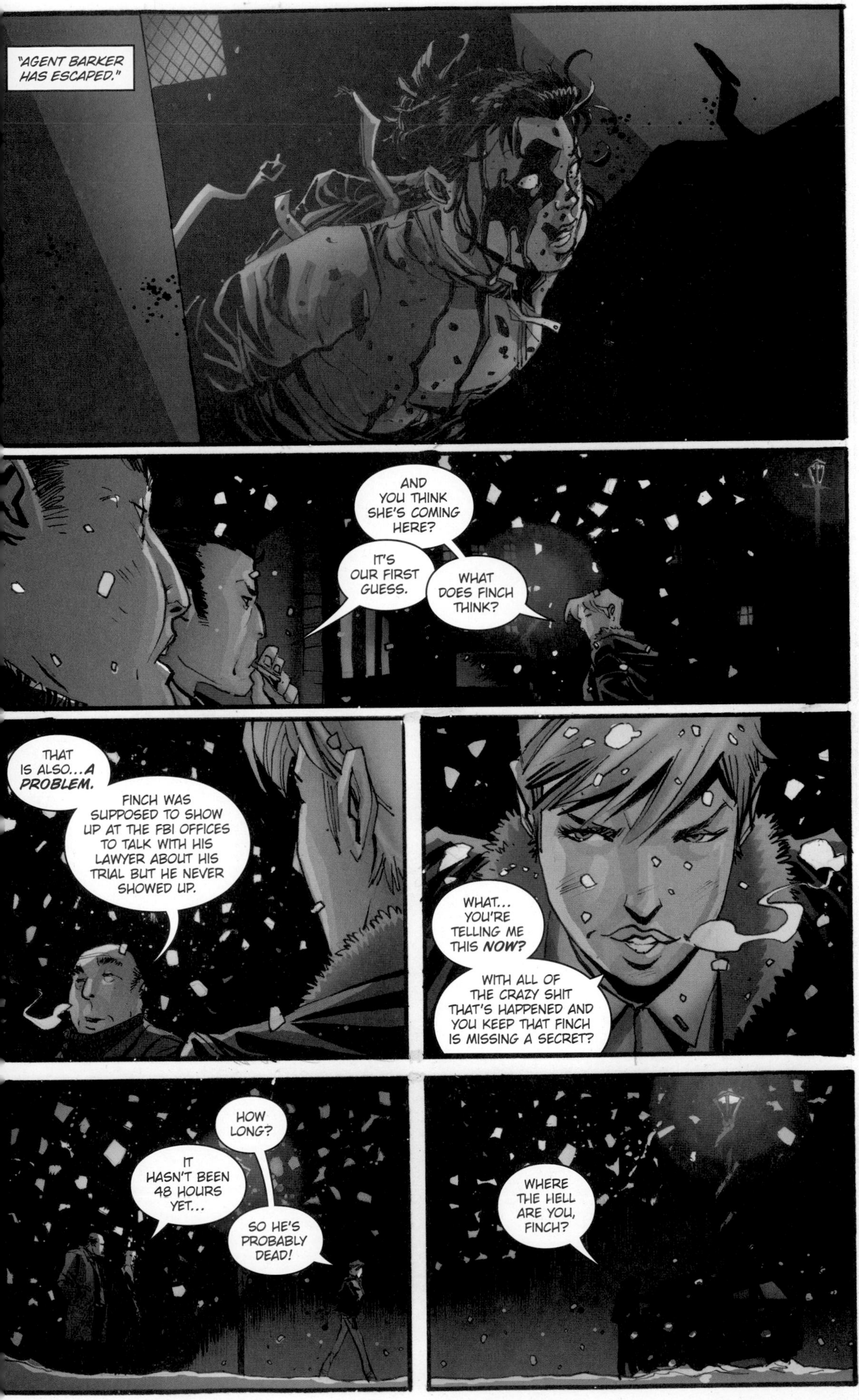
"AGENT BARKER HAS ESCAPED."
AND YOU THINK SHE'S COMING HERE?
IT'S OUR FIRST GUESS.
WHAT DOES FINCH THINK?
THAT IS ALSO... A PROBLEM.
FINCH WAS SUPPOSED TO SHOW UP AT THE FBI OFFICES TO TALK WITH HIS LAWYER ABOUT HIS TRIAL BUT HE NEVER SHOWED UP.
WHAT... YOU'RE TELLING ME THIS NOW?
WITH ALL OF THE CRAZY SHIT THAT'S HAPPENED AND YOU KEEP THAT FINCH IS MISSING A SECRET?
HOW LONG?
IT HASN'T BEEN 48 HOURS YET...
SO HE'S PROBABLY DEAD!
WHERE THE HELL ARE YOU, FINCH?

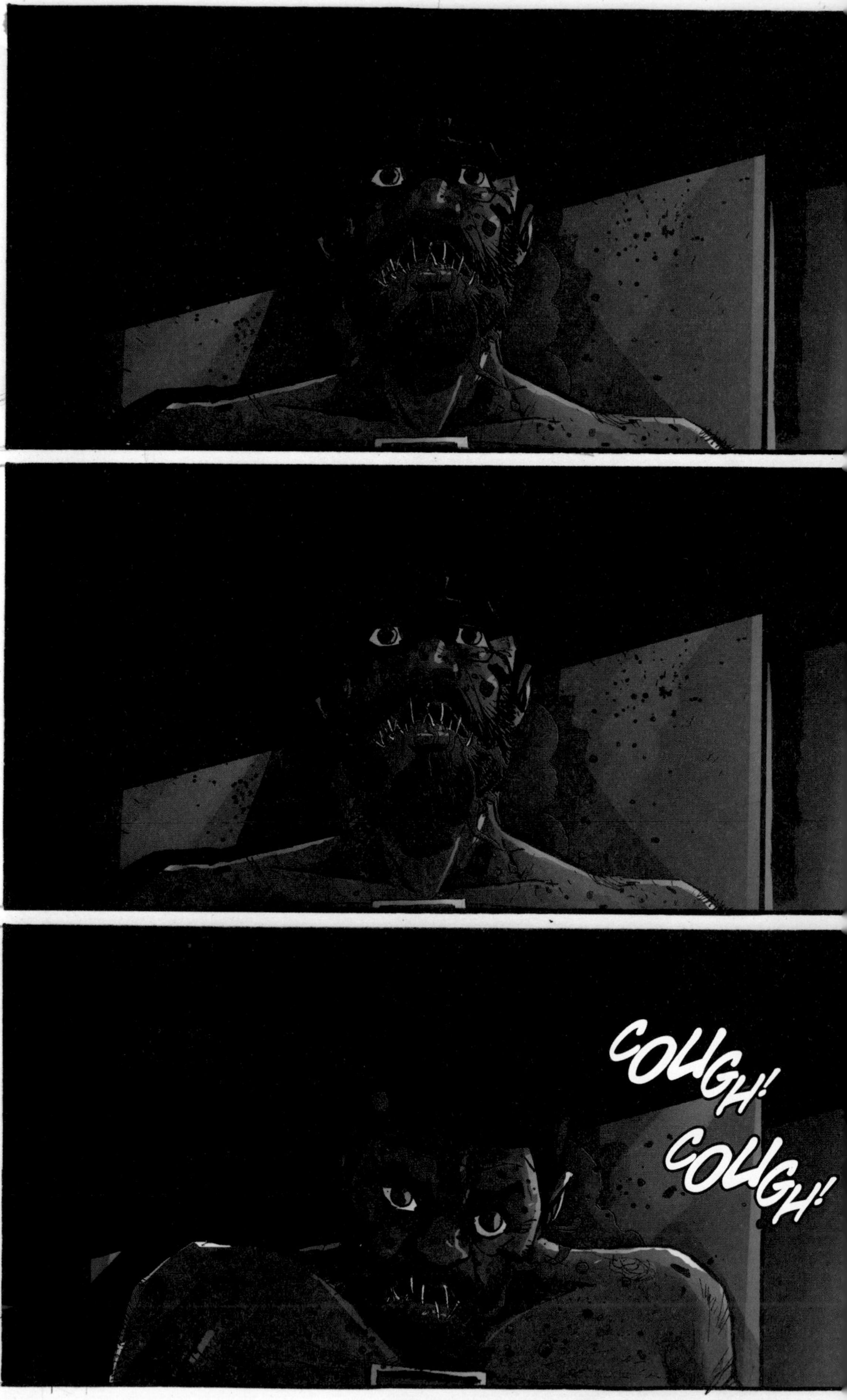
COUGH!
COUGH!

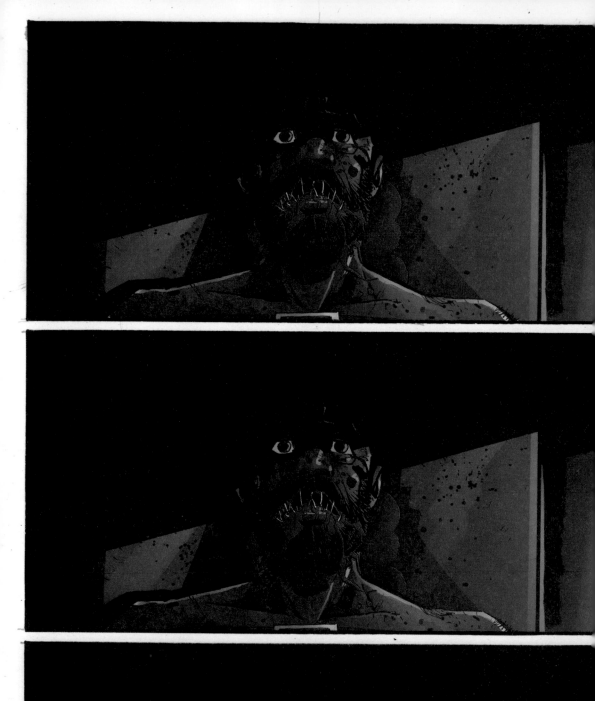

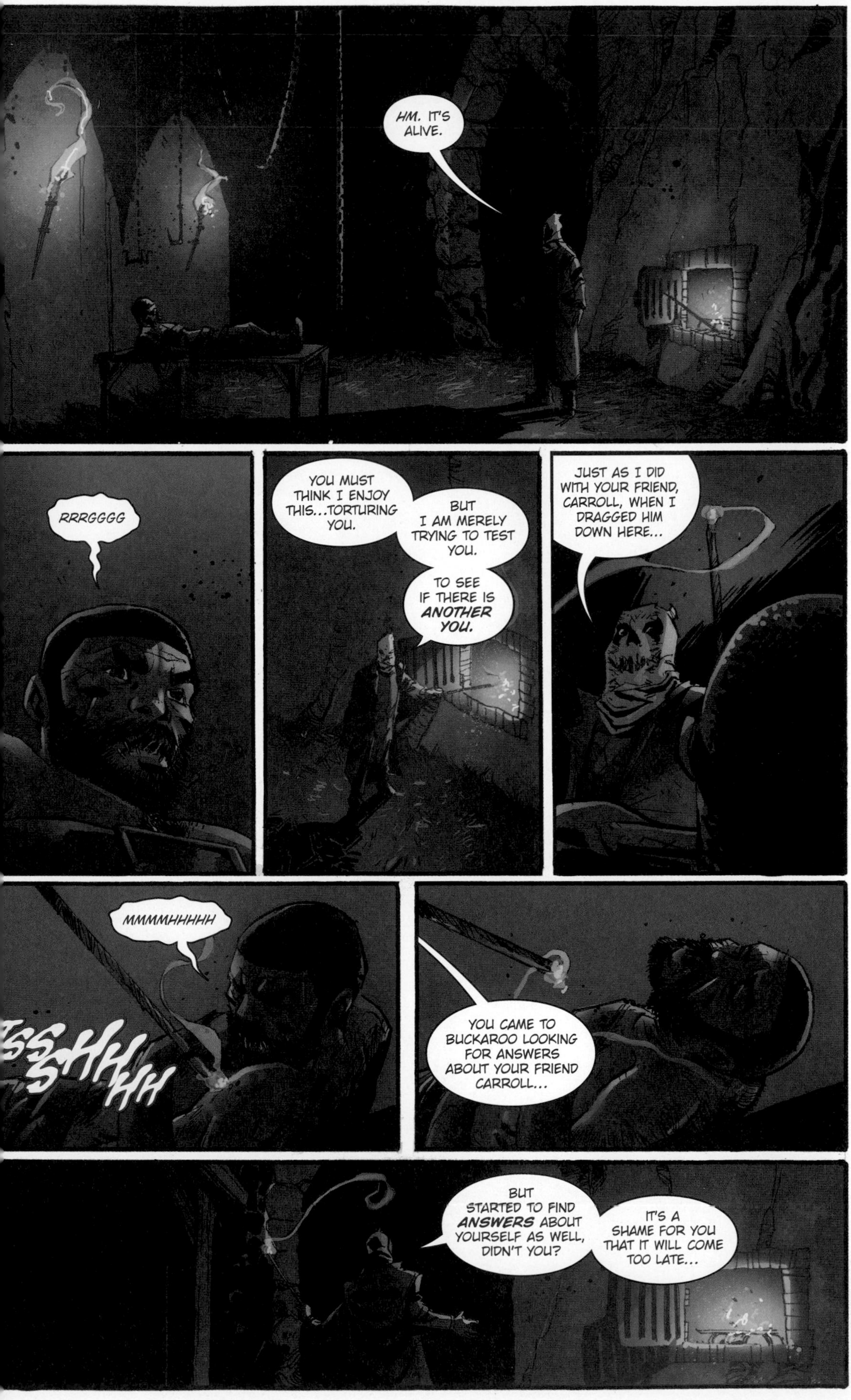
HM. IT'S ALIVE.
RRRGGGG
YOU MUST THINK I ENJOY THIS...TORTURING YOU.
BUT I AM MERELY TRYING TO TEST YOU.
TO SEE IF THERE IS ANOTHER YOU.
JUST AS I DID WITH YOUR FRIEND, CARROLL, WHEN I DRAGGED HIM DOWN HERE...
MMMMHHHHH
SSSHHHHH
YOU CAME TO BUCKAROO LOOKING FOR ANSWERS ABOUT YOUR FRIEND CARROLL...
BUT STARTED TO FIND ANSWERS ABOUT YOURSELF AS WELL, DIDN'T YOU?
IT'S A SHAME FOR YOU THAT IT WILL COME TOO LATE...

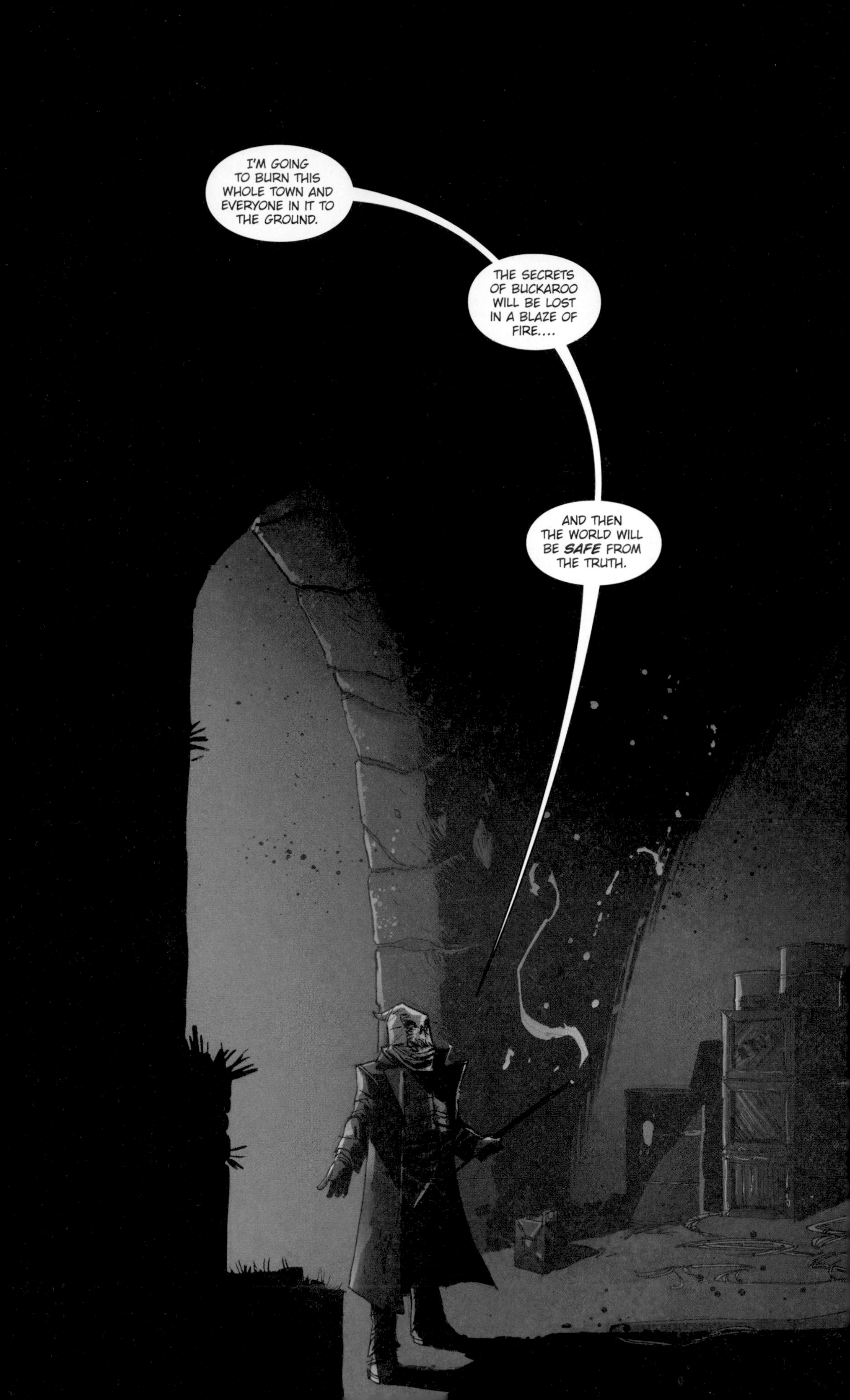
I'M GOING TO BURN THIS WHOLE TOWN AND EVERYONE IN IT TO THE GROUND.
THE SECRETS OF BUCKAROO WILL BE LOST IN A BLAZE OF FIRE....
AND THEN THE WORLD WILL BE **SAFE** FROM THE TRUTH.

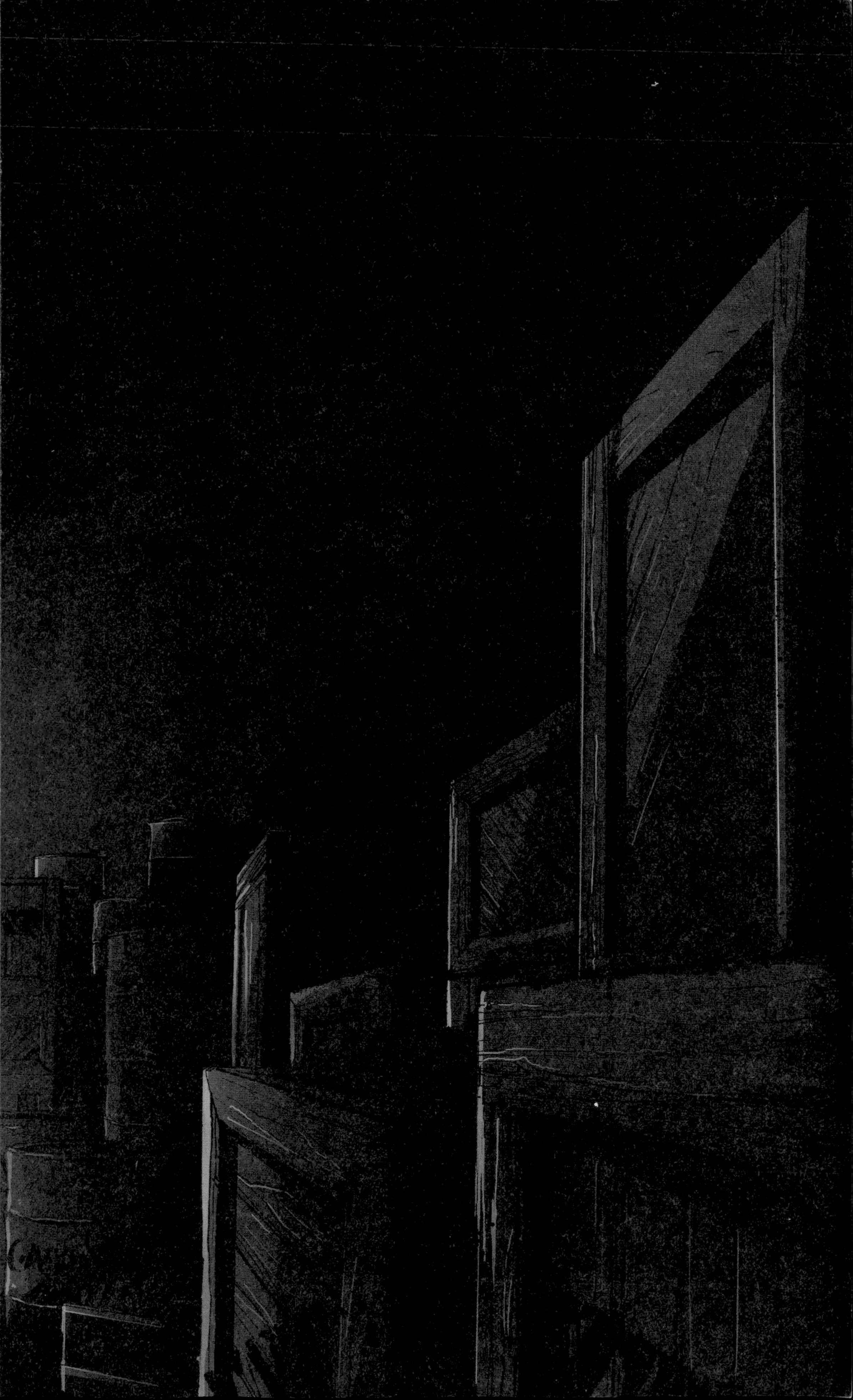

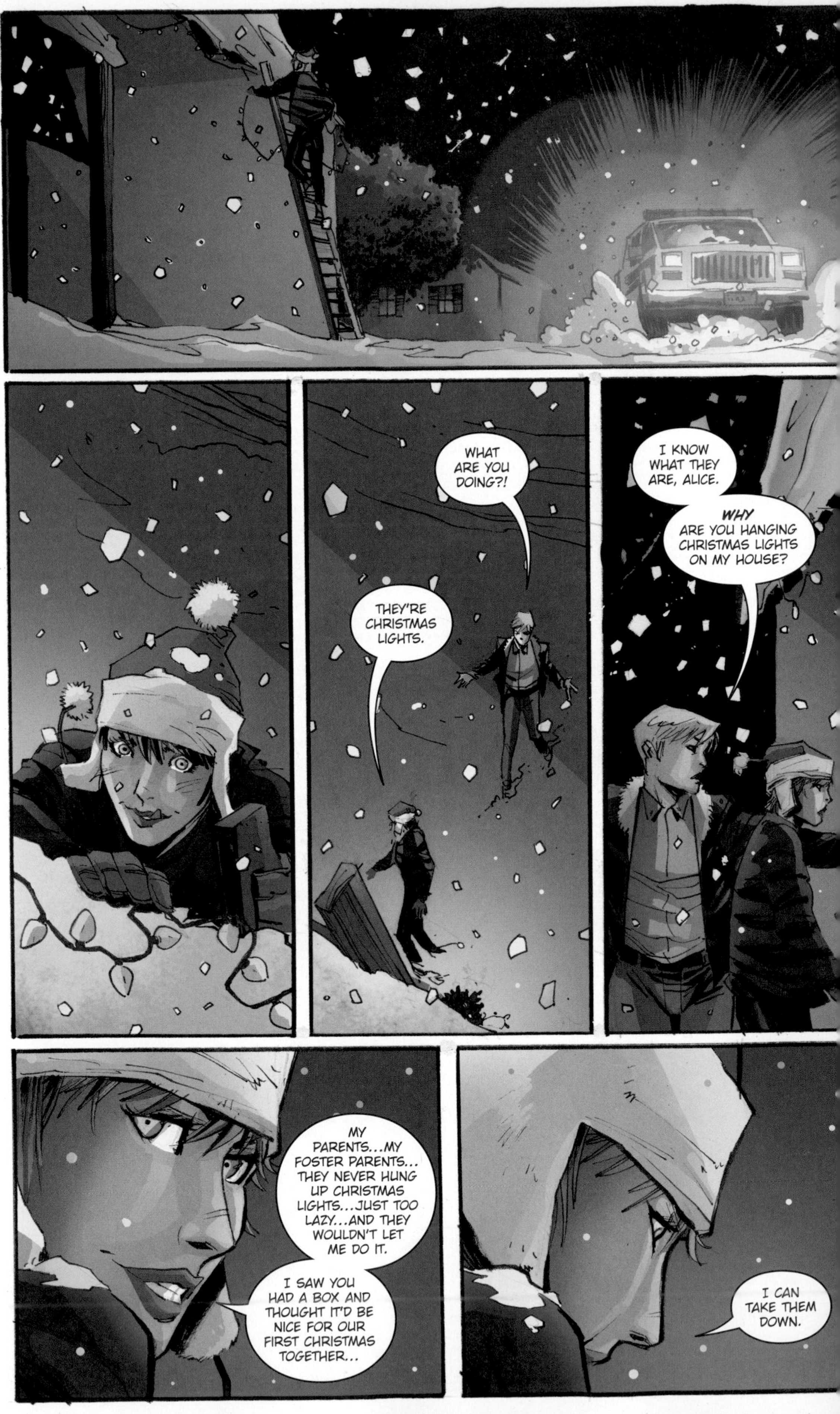
WHAT ARE YOU DOING?!
THEY'RE CHRISTMAS LIGHTS.
I KNOW WHAT THEY ARE, ALICE.
WHY ARE YOU HANGING CHRISTMAS LIGHTS ON MY HOUSE?
MY PARENTS...MY FOSTER PARENTS... THEY NEVER HUNG UP CHRISTMAS LIGHTS...JUST TOO LAZY...AND THEY WOULDN'T LET ME DO IT.
I SAW YOU HAD A BOX AND THOUGHT IT'D BE NICE FOR OUR FIRST CHRISTMAS TOGETHER...
I CAN TAKE THEM DOWN.

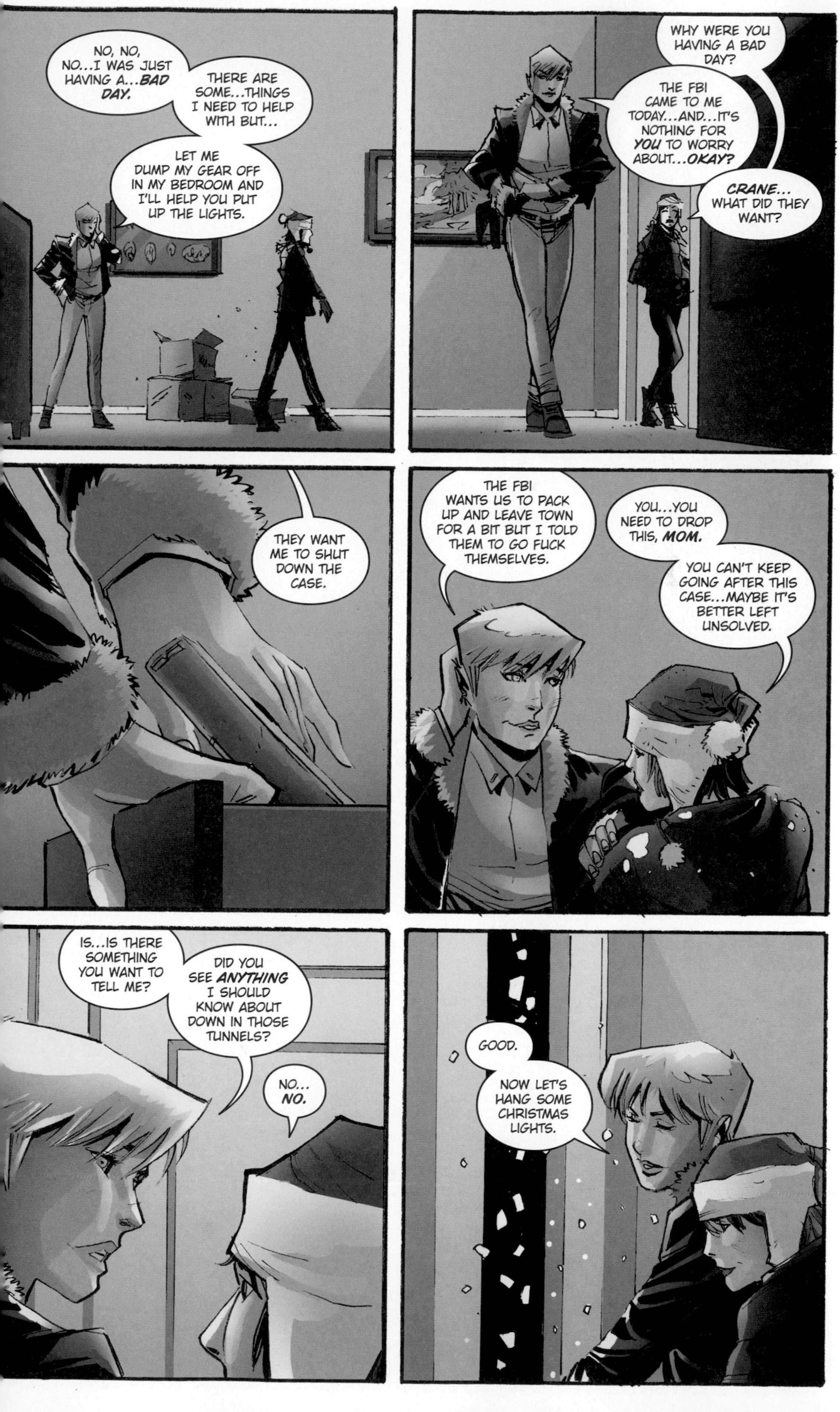
NO, NO, NO...I WAS JUST HAVING A...BAD DAY.
THERE ARE SOME...THINGS I NEED TO HELP WITH BUT...
LET ME DUMP MY GEAR OFF IN MY BEDROOM AND I'LL HELP YOU PUT UP THE LIGHTS.
WHY WERE YOU HAVING A BAD DAY?
THE FBI CAME TO ME TODAY...AND...IT'S NOTHING FOR YOU TO WORRY ABOUT...OKAY?
CRANE... WHAT DID THEY WANT?
THEY WANT ME TO SHUT DOWN THE CASE.
THE FBI WANTS US TO PACK UP AND LEAVE TOWN FOR A BIT BUT I TOLD THEM TO GO FUCK THEMSELVES.
YOU...YOU NEED TO DROP THIS, MOM.
YOU CAN'T KEEP GOING AFTER THIS CASE...MAYBE IT'S BETTER LEFT UNSOLVED.
IS...IS THERE SOMETHING YOU WANT TO TELL ME?
DID YOU SEE ANYTHING I SHOULD KNOW ABOUT DOWN IN THOSE TUNNELS?
NO... NO.
GOOD.
NOW LET'S HANG SOME CHRISTMAS LIGHTS.

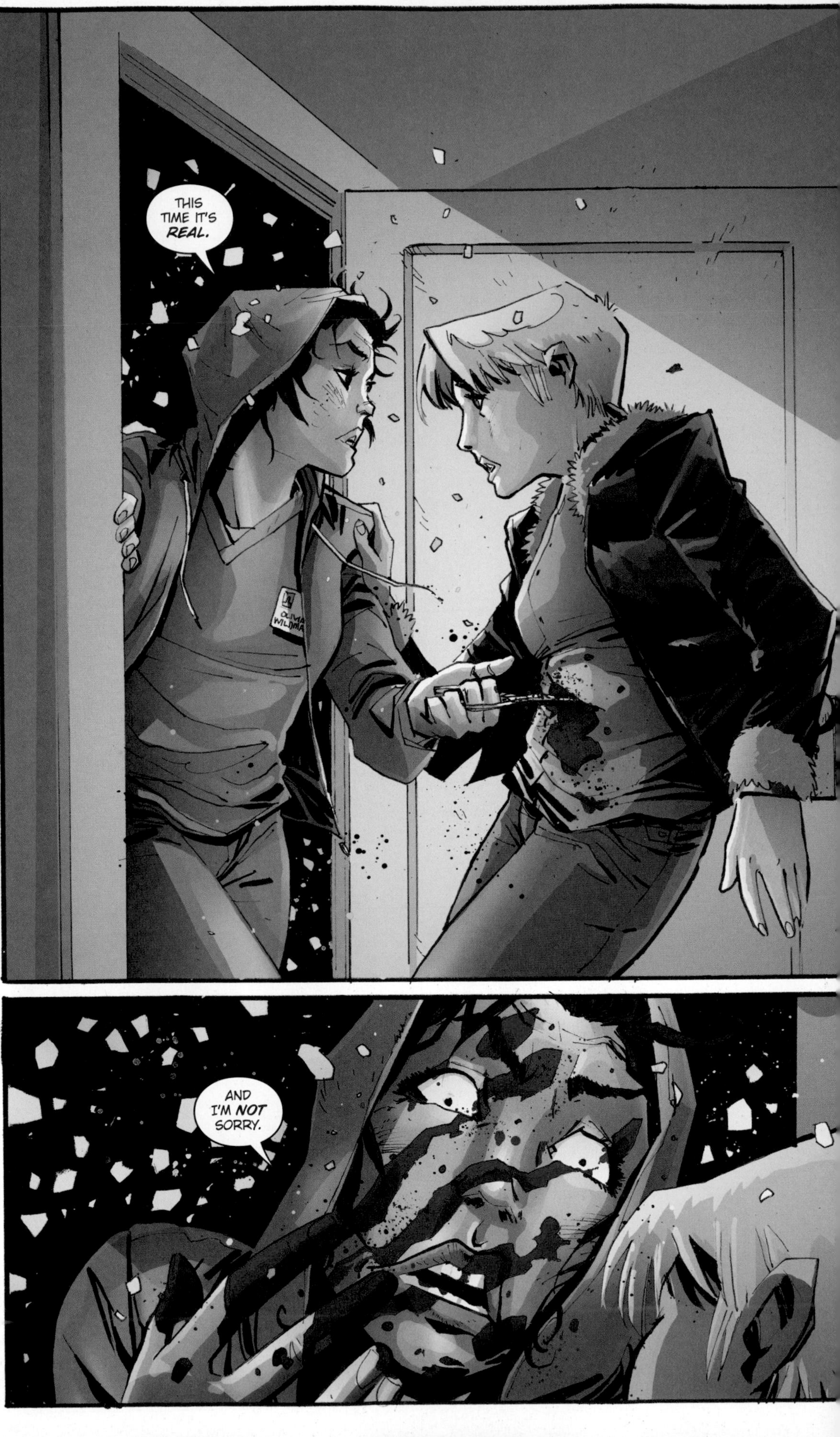
THIS TIME IT'S REAL.
AND I'M NOT SORRY.

ISSUE TWENTY-EIGHT

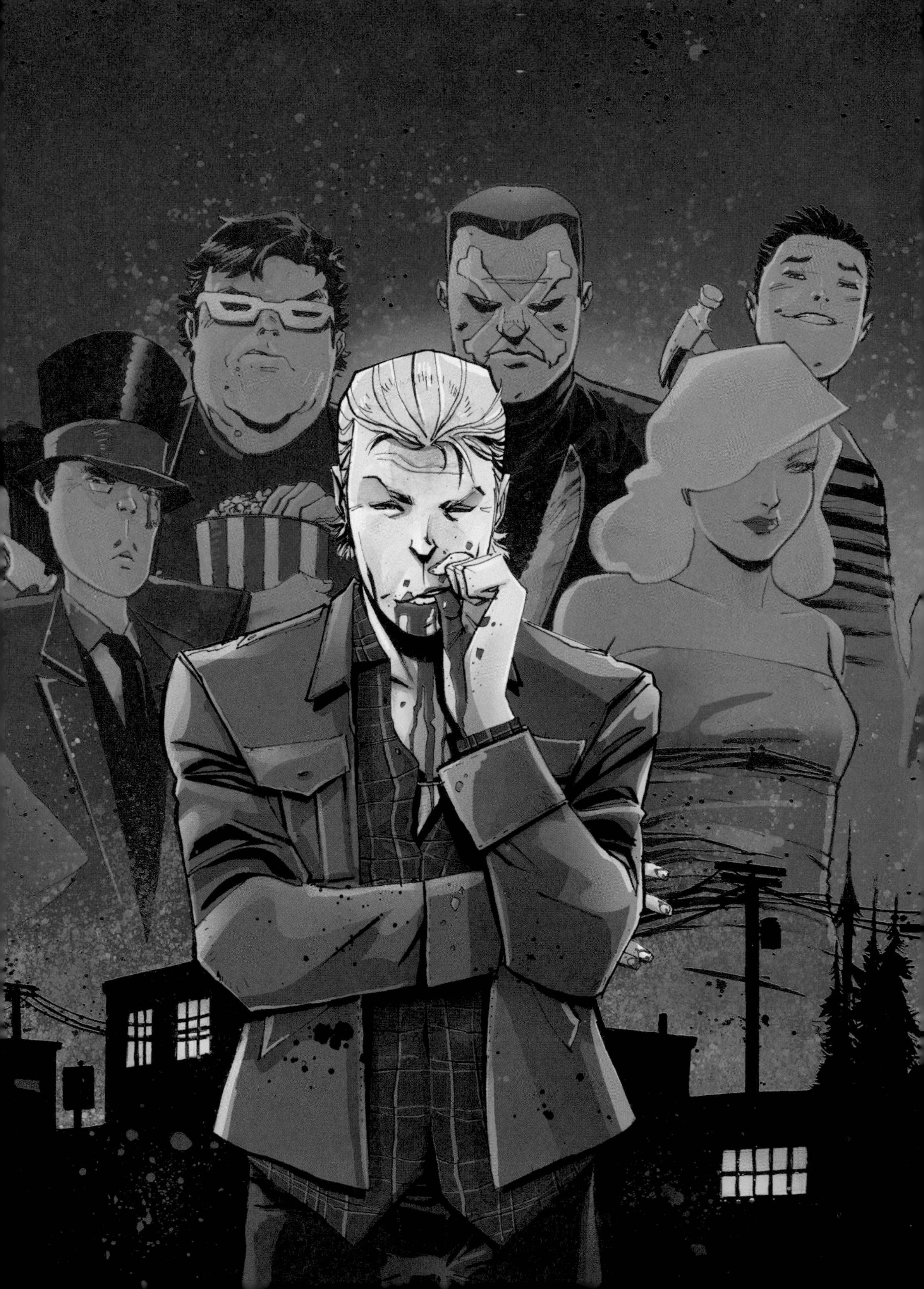

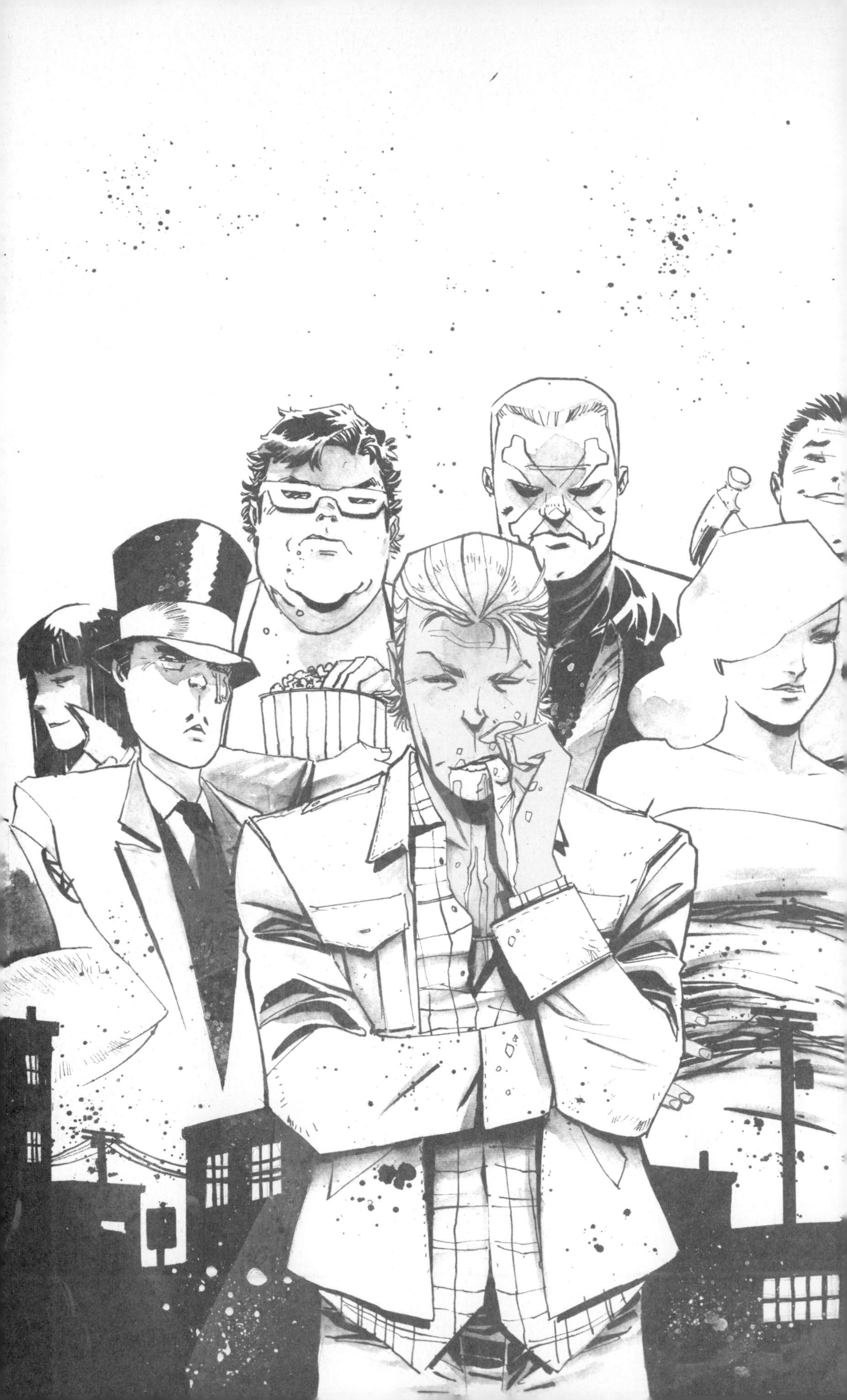

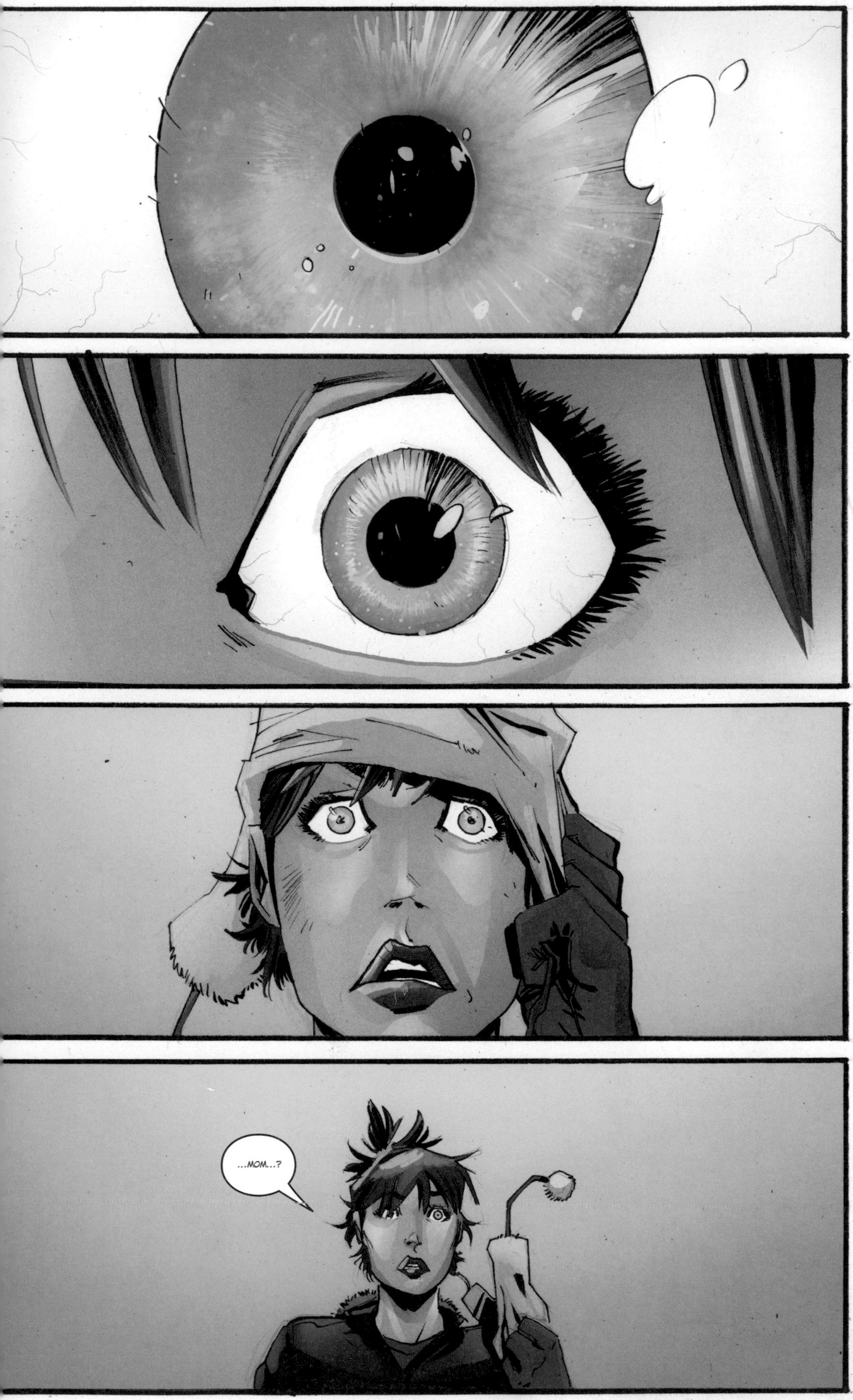
...MOM...?

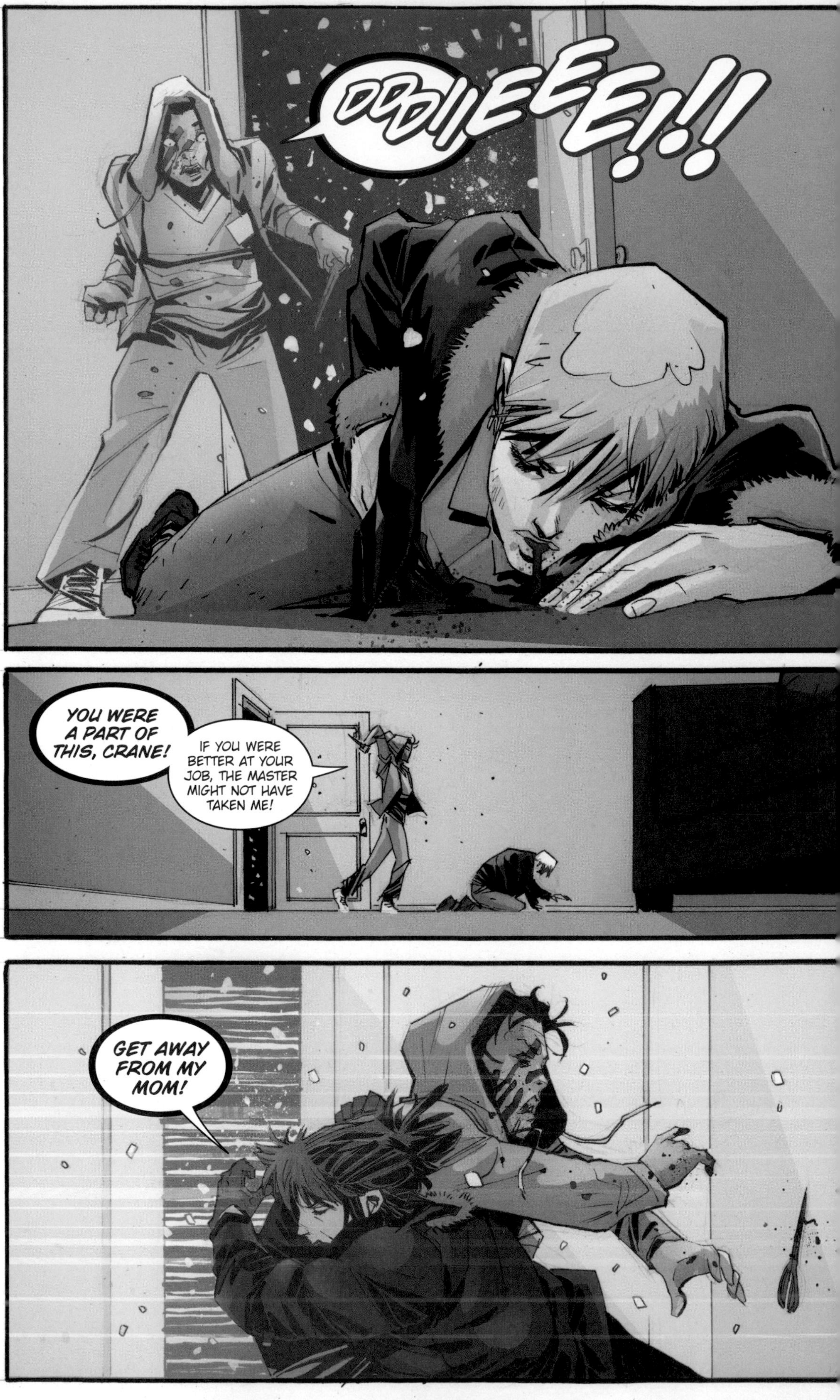
DDDIIEEEE!!!
YOU WERE A PART OF THIS, CRANE!
IF YOU WERE BETTER AT YOUR JOB, THE MASTER MIGHT NOT HAVE TAKEN ME!
GET AWAY FROM MY MOM!

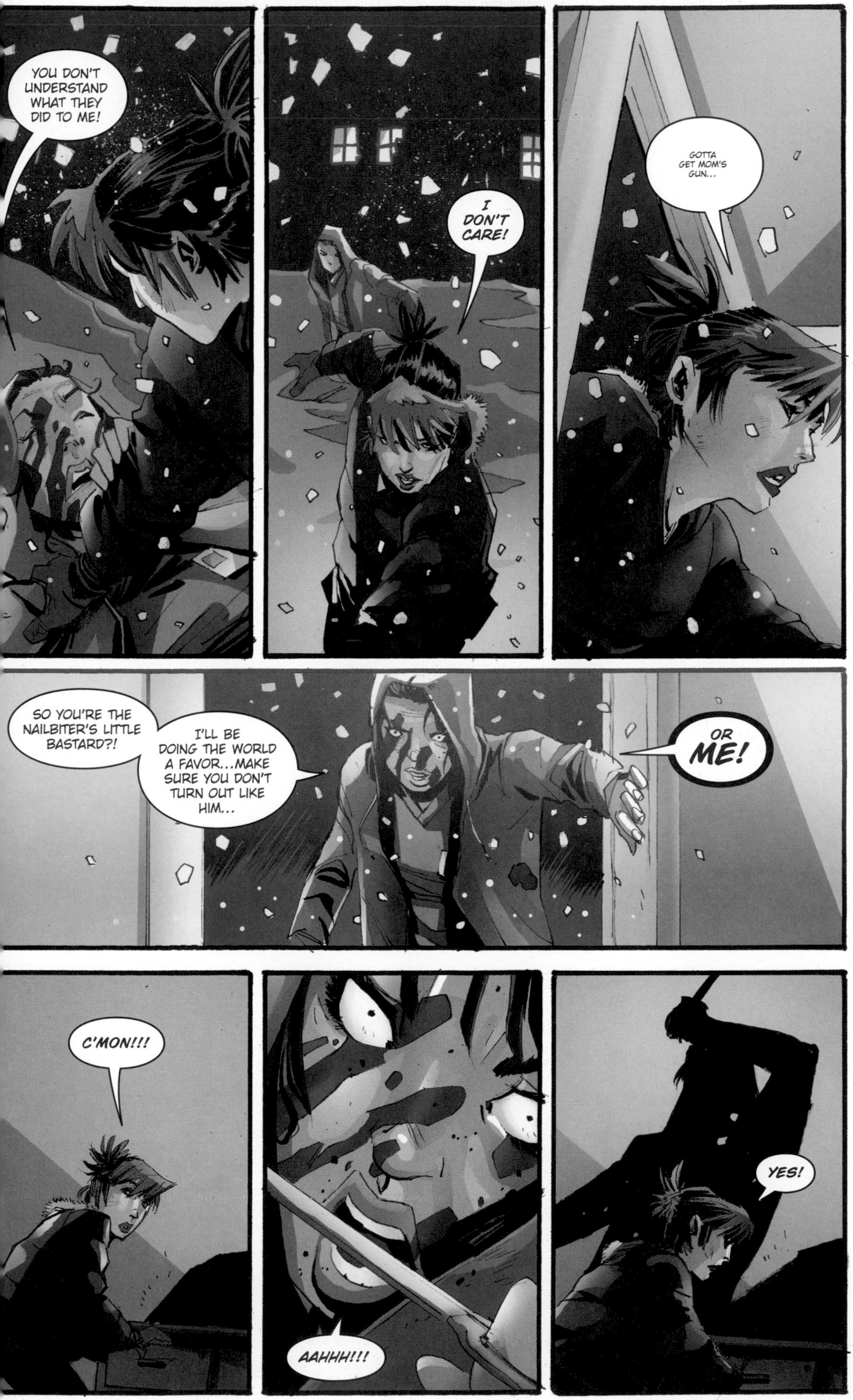
YOU DON'T UNDERSTAND WHAT THEY DID TO ME!
I DON'T CARE!
GOTTA GET MOM'S GUN...
SO YOU'RE THE NAILBITER'S LITTLE BASTARD?!
I'LL BE DOING THE WORLD A FAVOR...MAKE SURE YOU DON'T TURN OUT LIKE HIM...
OR ME!
C'MON!!!
AAHHH!!!
YES!

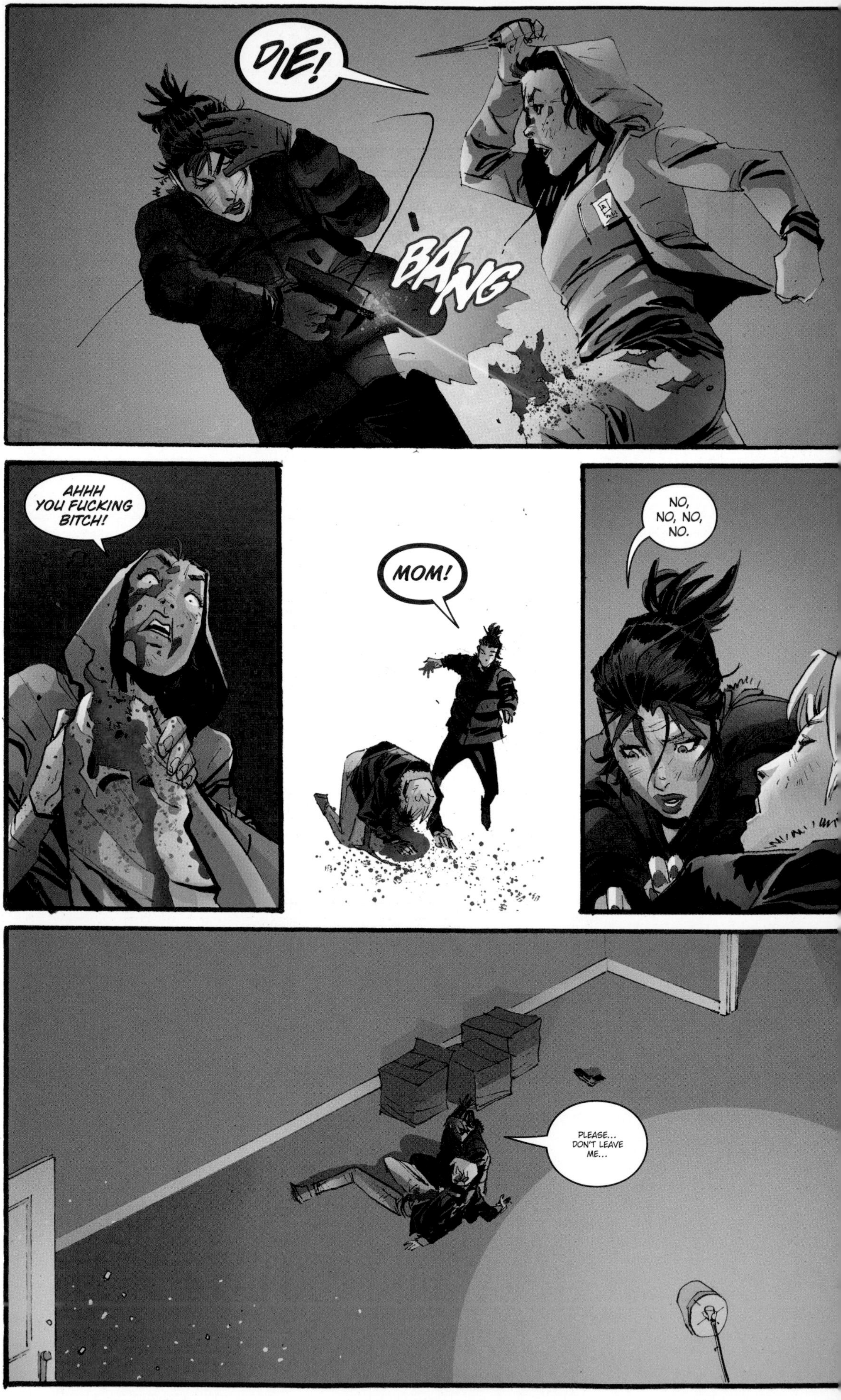
DIE!
BANG
AHHH YOU FUCKING BITCH!
MOM!
NO, NO, NO, NO.
PLEASE... DON'T LEAVE ME...

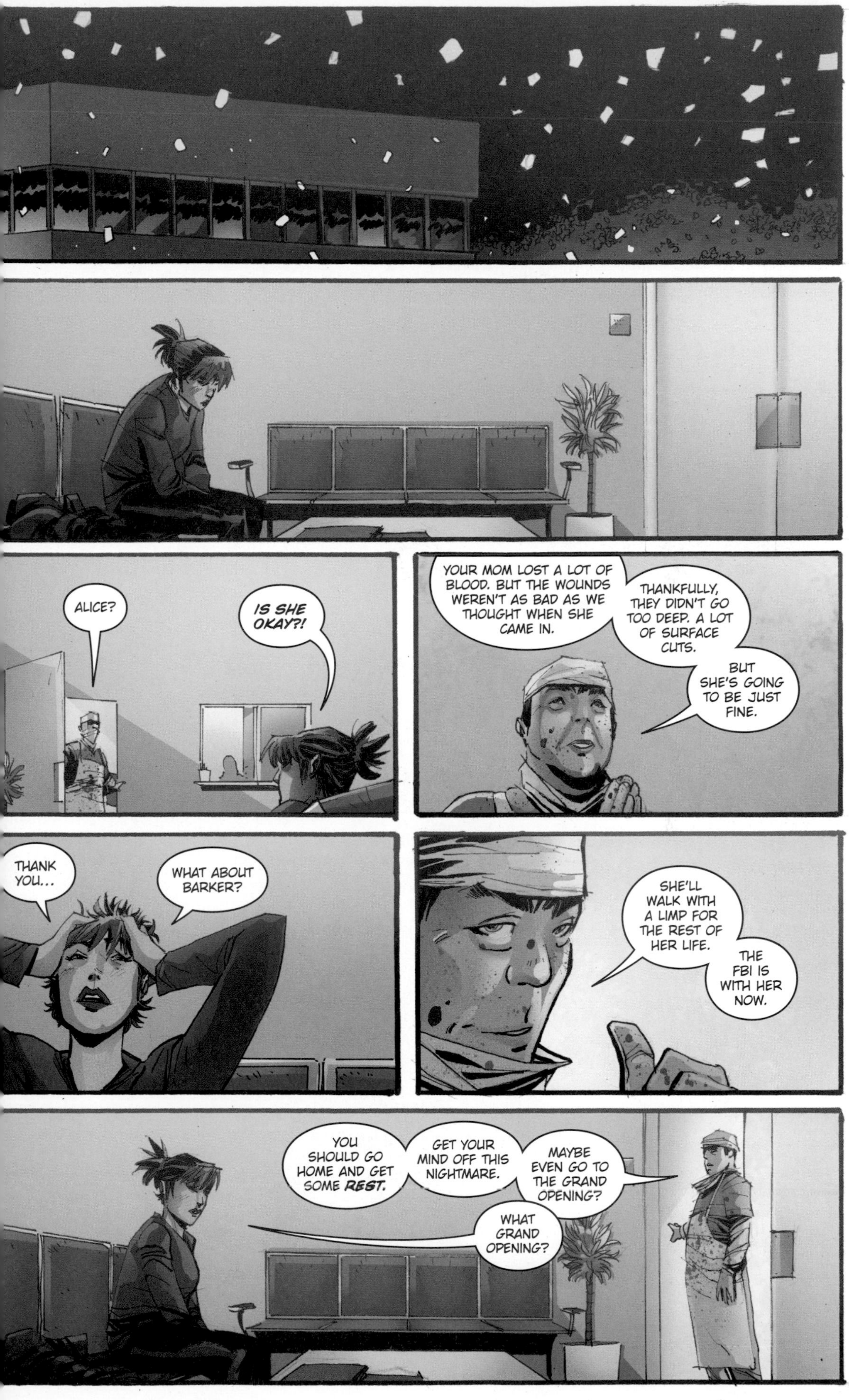
ALICE?
IS SHE OKAY?!
YOUR MOM LOST A LOT OF BLOOD. BUT THE WOUNDS WEREN'T AS BAD AS WE THOUGHT WHEN SHE CAME IN.
THANKFULLY, THEY DIDN'T GO TOO DEEP. A LOT OF SURFACE CUTS.
BUT SHE'S GOING TO BE JUST FINE.
THANK YOU...
WHAT ABOUT BARKER?
SHE'LL WALK WITH A LIMP FOR THE REST OF HER LIFE.
THE FBI IS WITH HER NOW.
YOU SHOULD GO HOME AND GET SOME REST.
GET YOUR MIND OFF THIS NIGHTMARE.
MAYBE EVEN GO TO THE GRAND OPENING?
WHAT GRAND OPENING?

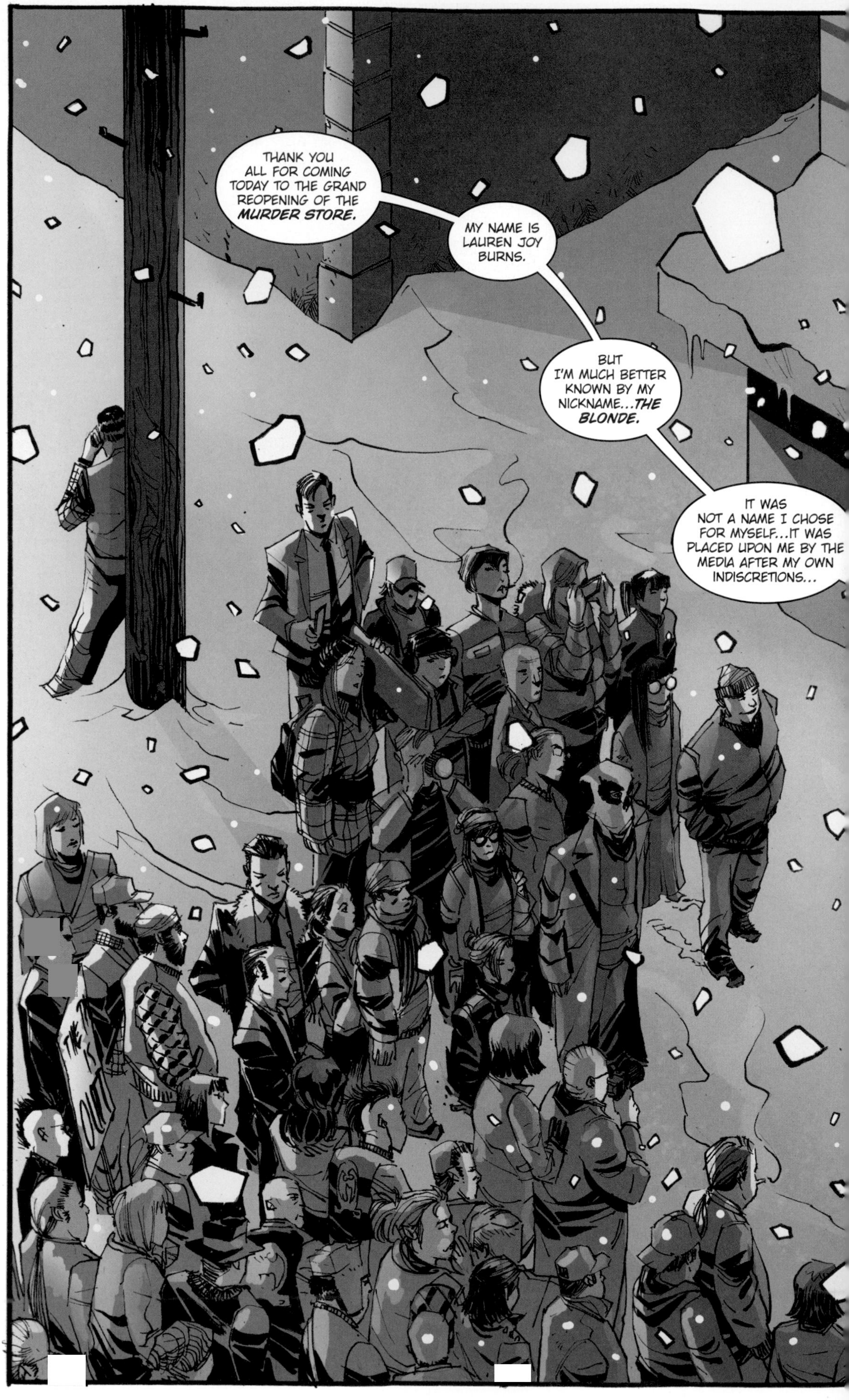
THANK YOU ALL FOR COMING TODAY TO THE GRAND REOPENING OF THE MURDER STORE.
MY NAME IS LAUREN JOY BURNS.
BUT I'M MUCH BETTER KNOWN BY MY NICKNAME...THE BLONDE.
IT WAS NOT A NAME I CHOSE FOR MYSELF...IT WAS PLACED UPON ME BY THE MEDIA AFTER MY OWN INDISCRETIONS...

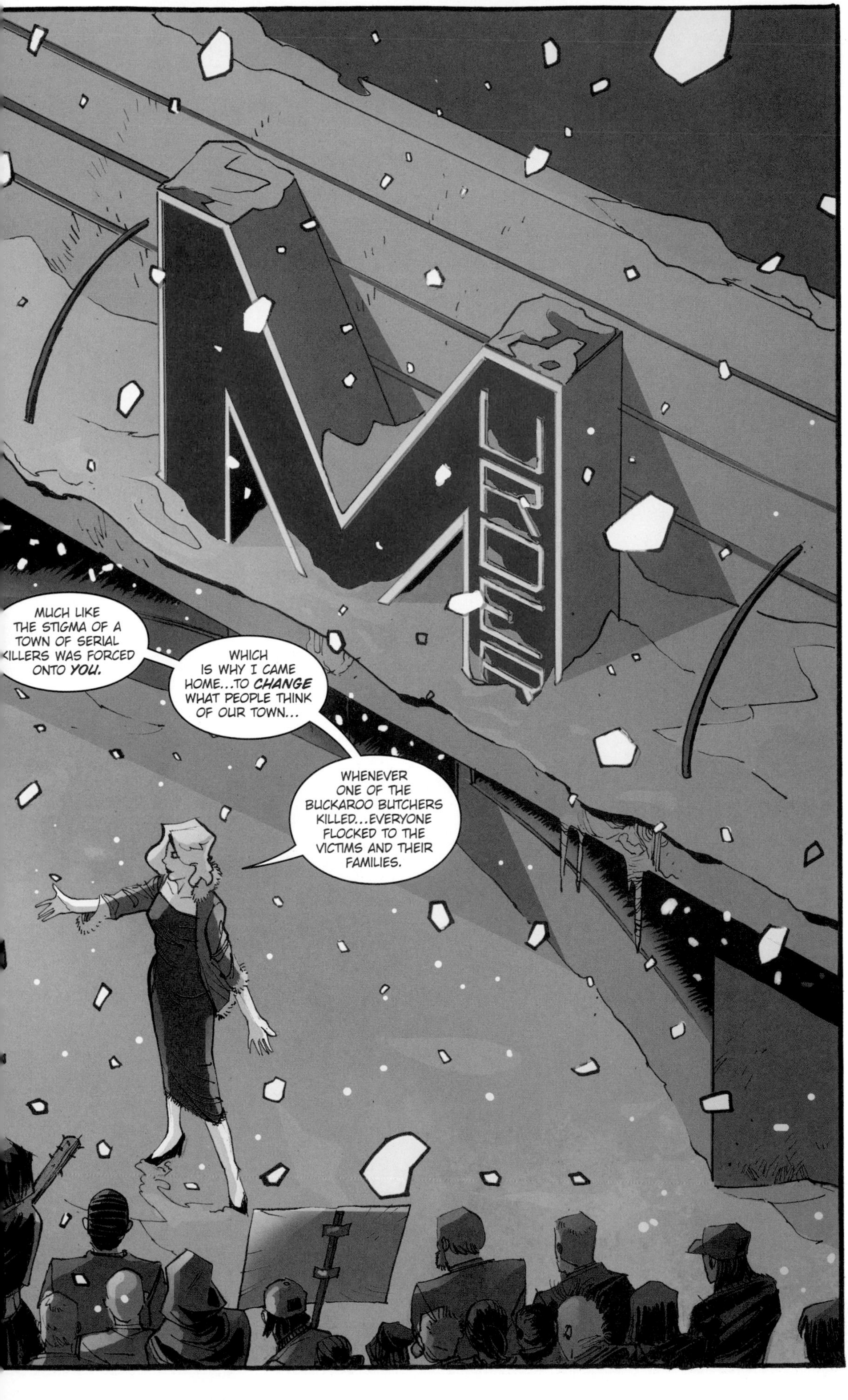
MUCH LIKE THE STIGMA OF A TOWN OF SERIAL KILLERS WAS FORCED ONTO *YOU.*
WHICH IS WHY I CAME HOME...TO *CHANGE* WHAT PEOPLE THINK OF OUR TOWN...
WHENEVER ONE OF THE BUCKAROO BUTCHERS KILLED...EVERYONE FLOCKED TO THE VICTIMS AND THEIR FAMILIES.

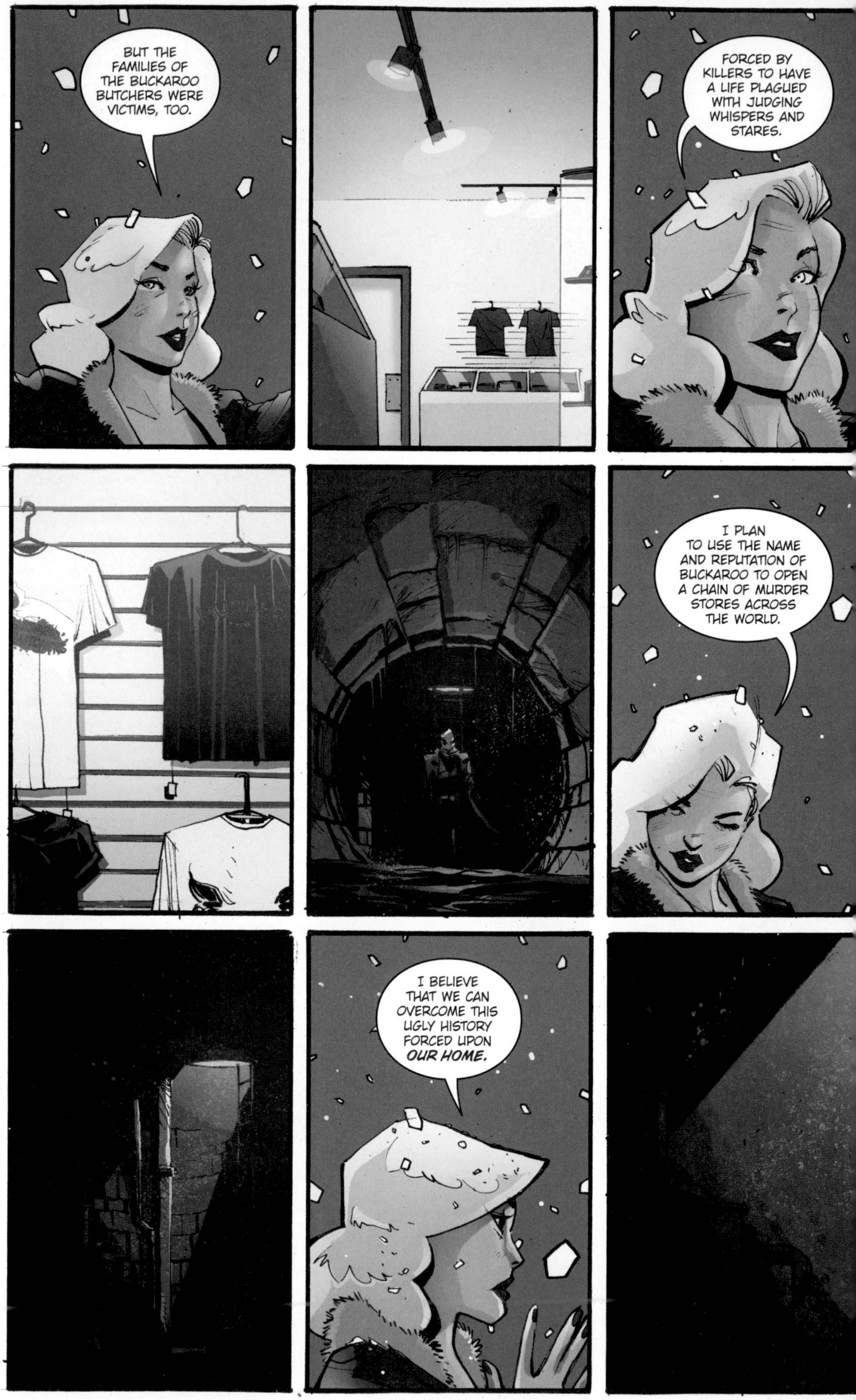
BUT THE FAMILIES OF THE BUCKAROO BUTCHERS WERE VICTIMS, TOO.
FORCED BY KILLERS TO HAVE A LIFE PLAGUED WITH JUDGING WHISPERS AND STARES.
I PLAN TO USE THE NAME AND REPUTATION OF BUCKAROO TO OPEN A CHAIN OF MURDER STORES ACROSS THE WORLD.
I BELIEVE THAT WE CAN OVERCOME THIS UGLY HISTORY FORCED UPON OUR HOME.

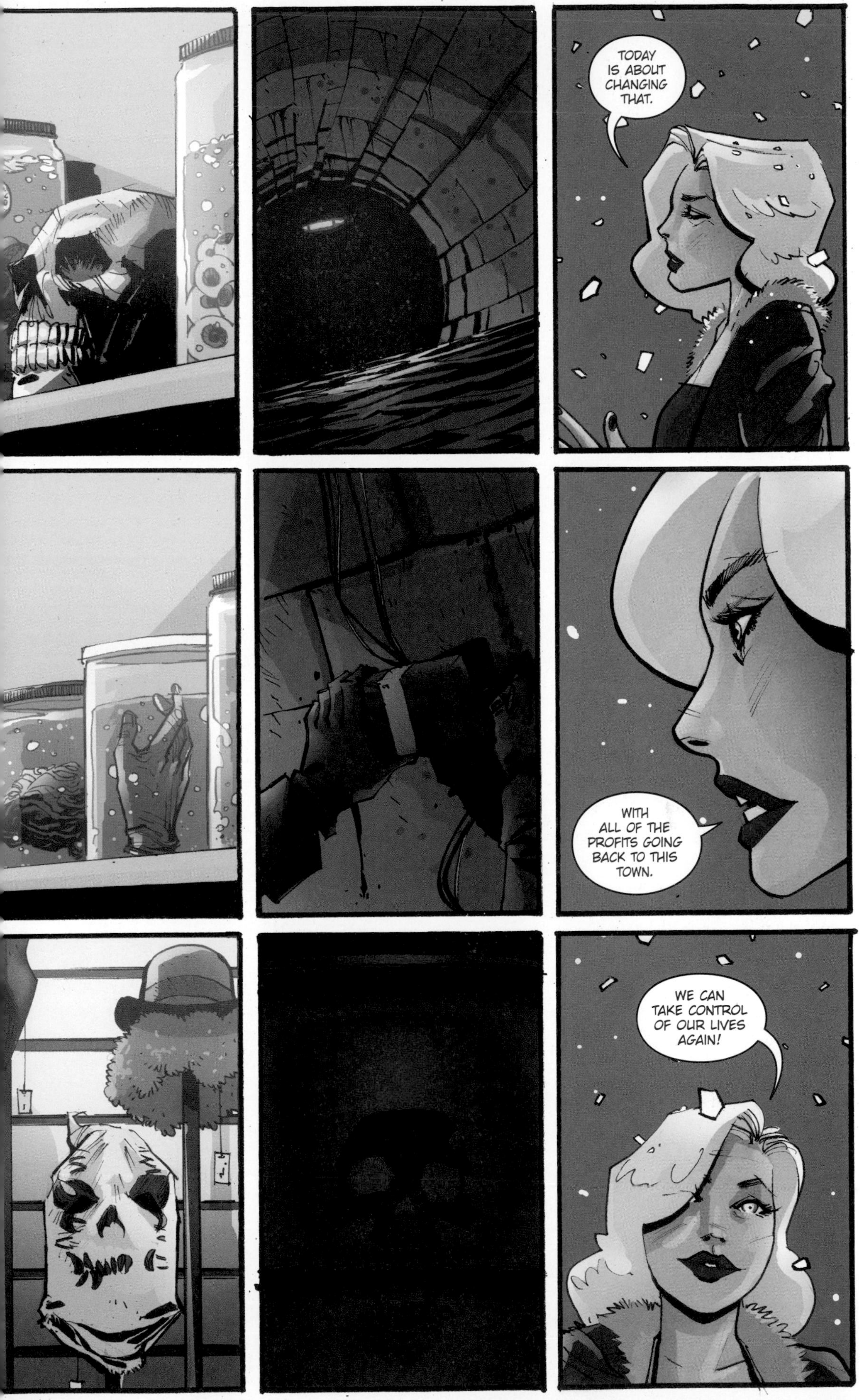
TODAY IS ABOUT CHANGING THAT.
WITH ALL OF THE PROFITS GOING BACK TO THIS TOWN.
WE CAN TAKE CONTROL OF OUR LIVES AGAIN!

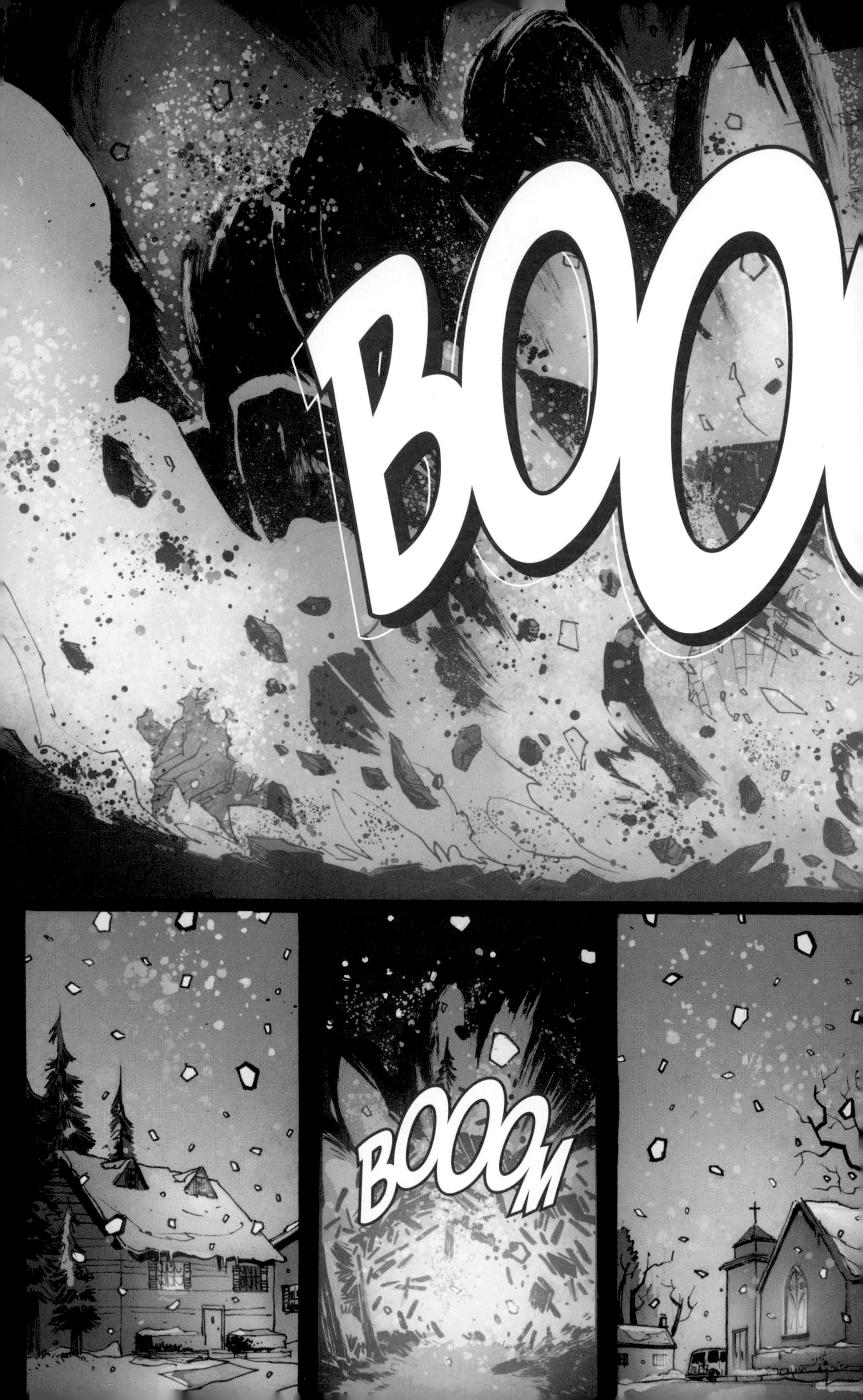
BOO
BOOOM

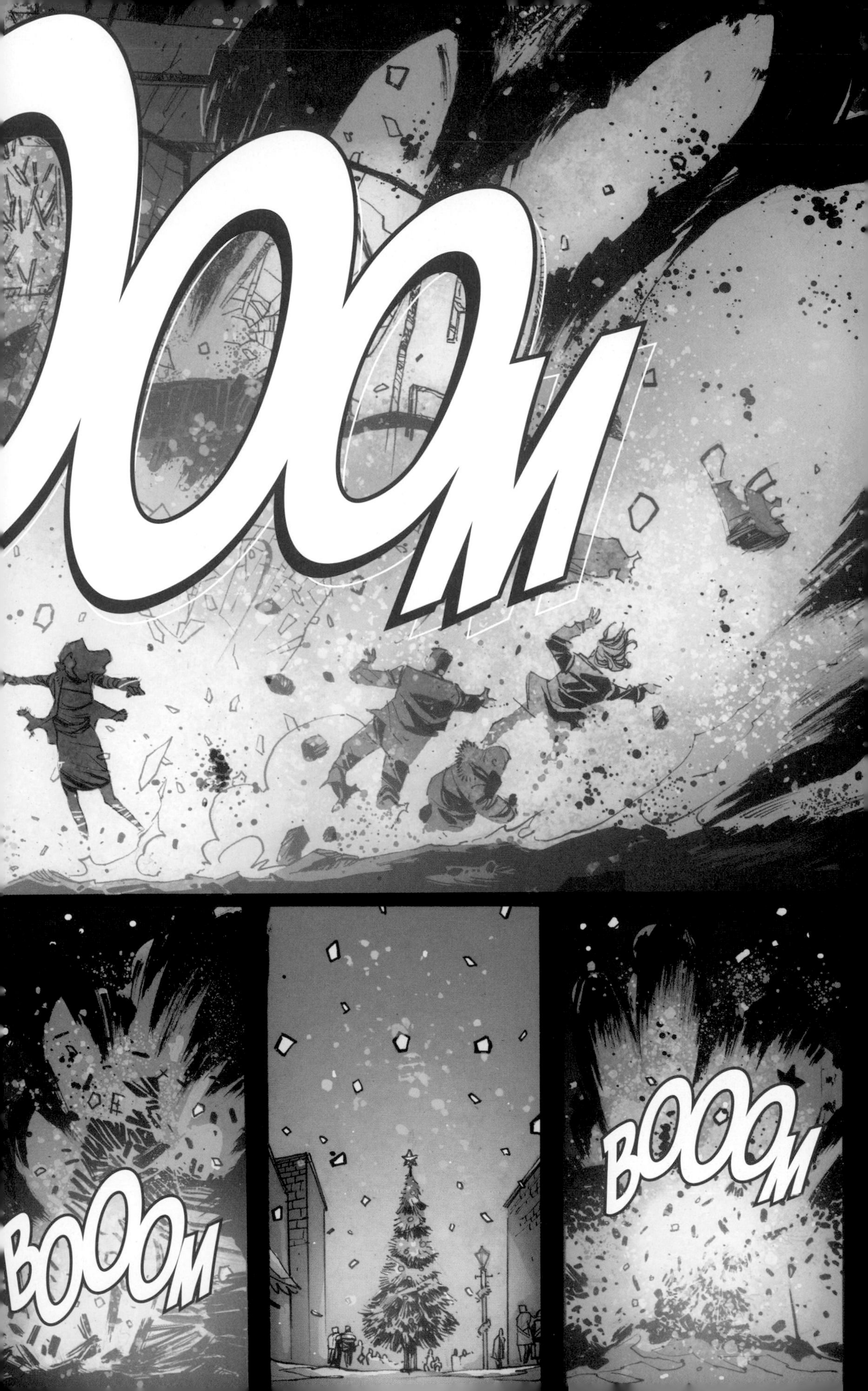
BOOOM
BOOOM

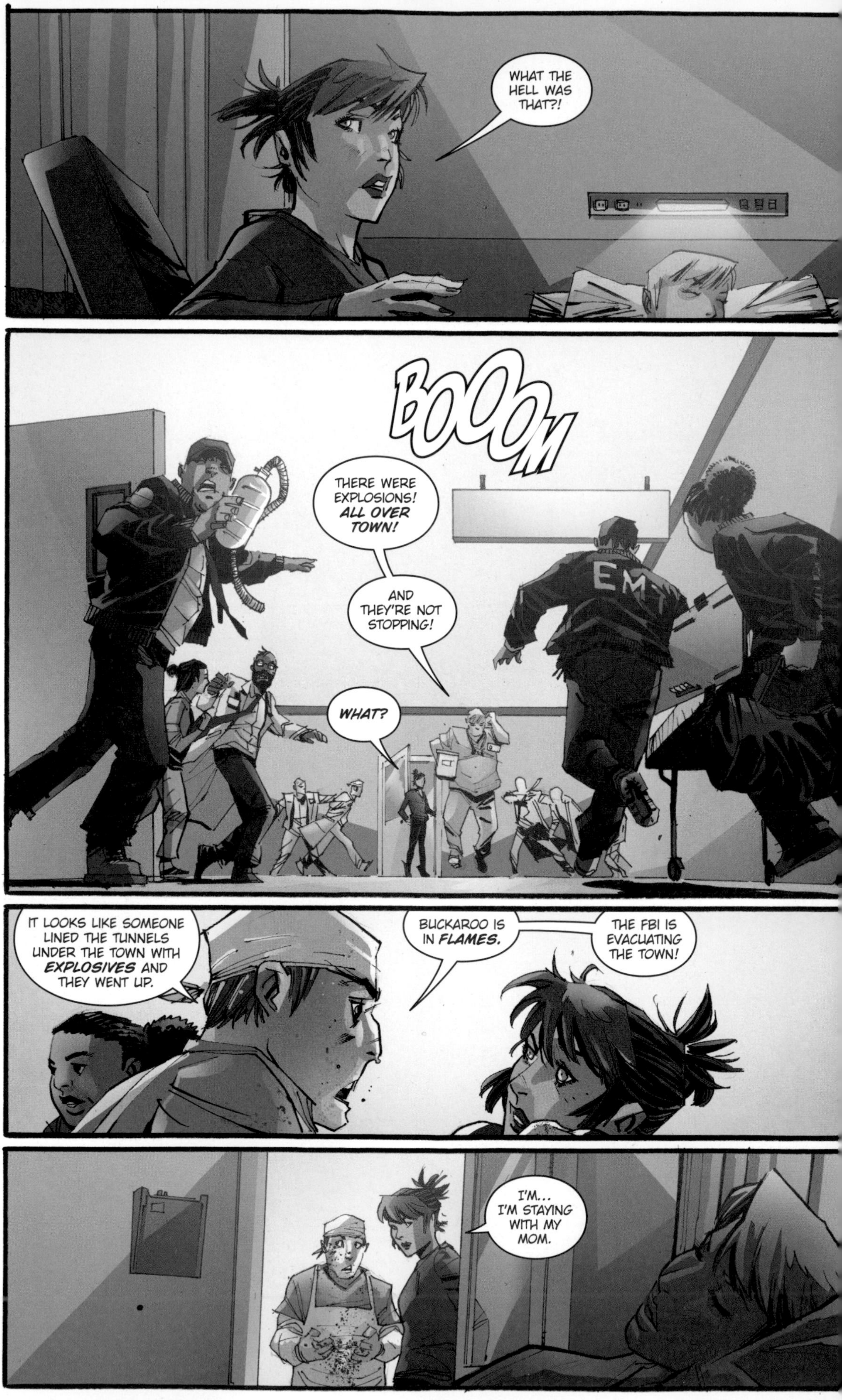
WHAT THE HELL WAS THAT?!
BOOOOM
THERE WERE EXPLOSIONS! ALL OVER TOWN!
AND THEY'RE NOT STOPPING!
WHAT?
IT LOOKS LIKE SOMEONE LINED THE TUNNELS UNDER THE TOWN WITH EXPLOSIVES AND THEY WENT UP.
BUCKAROO IS IN FLAMES.
THE FBI IS EVACUATING THE TOWN!
I'M... I'M STAYING WITH MY MOM.

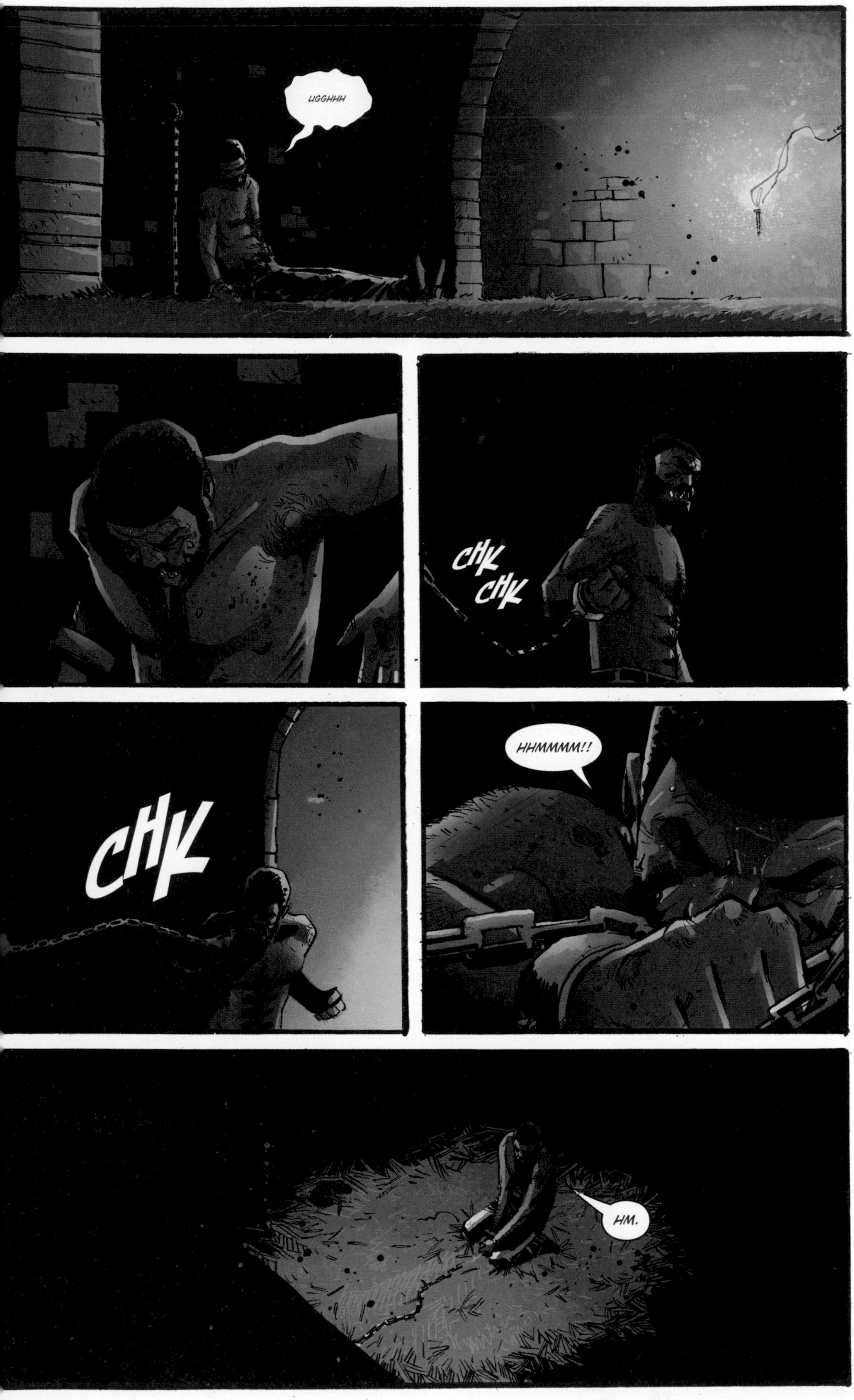
UGGHHH
CHK
CHK
CHK
HHMMMM!!
HM.

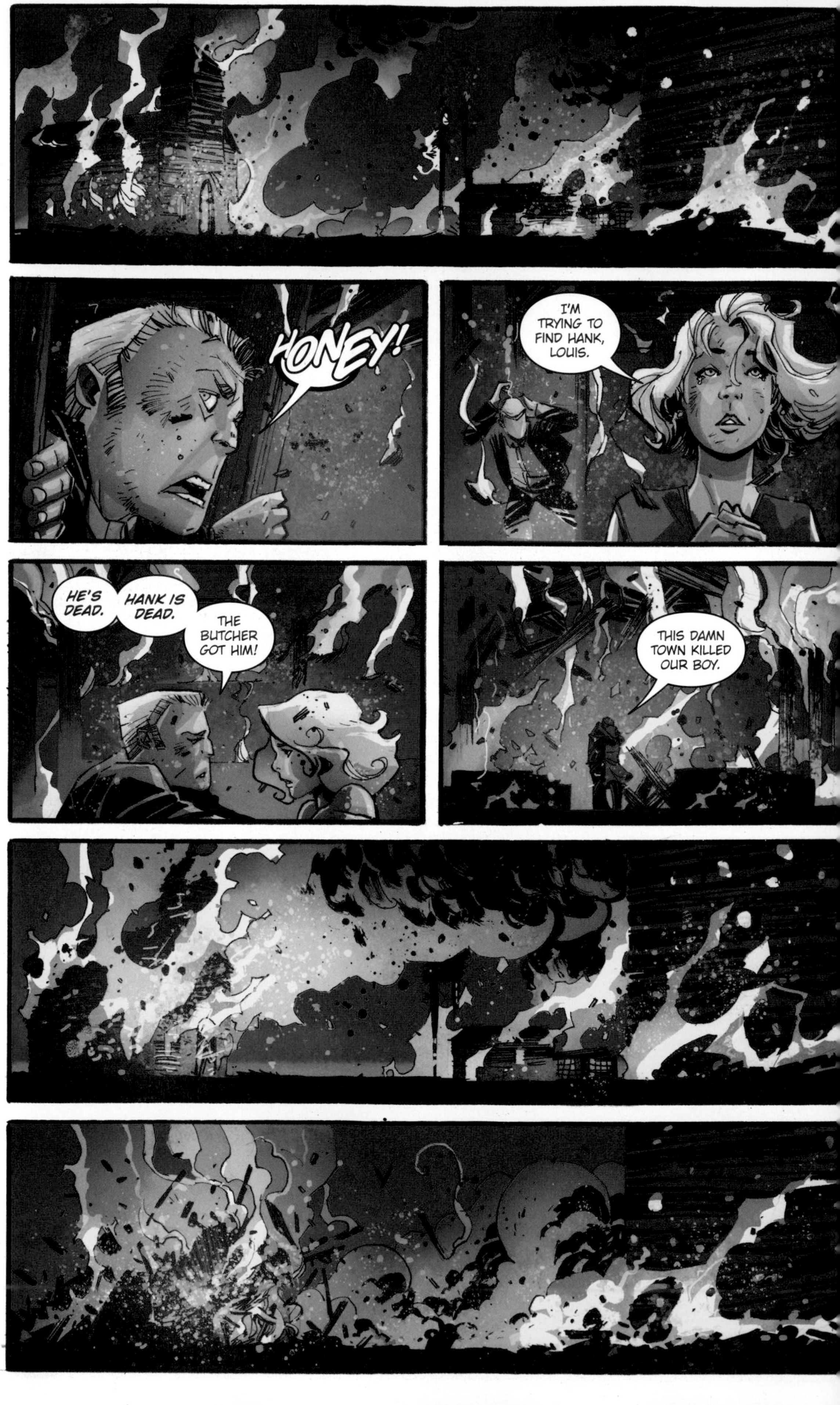
HONEY!
I'M TRYING TO FIND HANK, LOUIS.
HE'S DEAD.
HANK IS DEAD.
THE BUTCHER GOT HIM!
THIS DAMN TOWN KILLED OUR BOY.

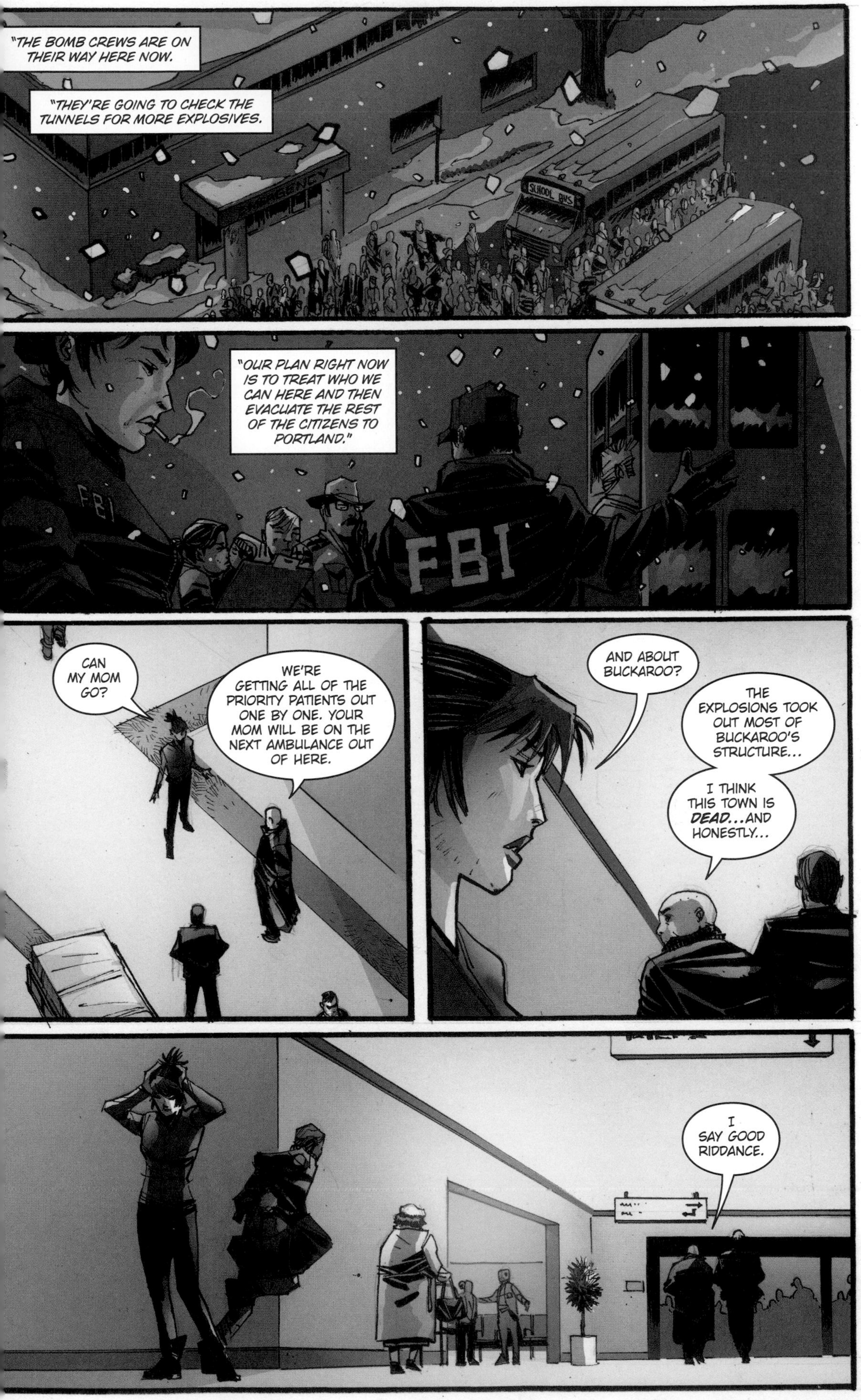
"THE BOMB CREWS ARE ON THEIR WAY HERE NOW.
"THEY'RE GOING TO CHECK THE TUNNELS FOR MORE EXPLOSIVES.
EMERGENCY
SCHOOL BUS
"OUR PLAN RIGHT NOW IS TO TREAT WHO WE CAN HERE AND THEN EVACUATE THE REST OF THE CITIZENS TO PORTLAND."
FBI
FBI
CAN MY MOM GO?
WE'RE GETTING ALL OF THE PRIORITY PATIENTS OUT ONE BY ONE. YOUR MOM WILL BE ON THE NEXT AMBULANCE OUT OF HERE.
AND ABOUT BUCKAROO?
THE EXPLOSIONS TOOK OUT MOST OF BUCKAROO'S STRUCTURE...
I THINK THIS TOWN IS DEAD...AND HONESTLY...
I SAY GOOD RIDDANCE.

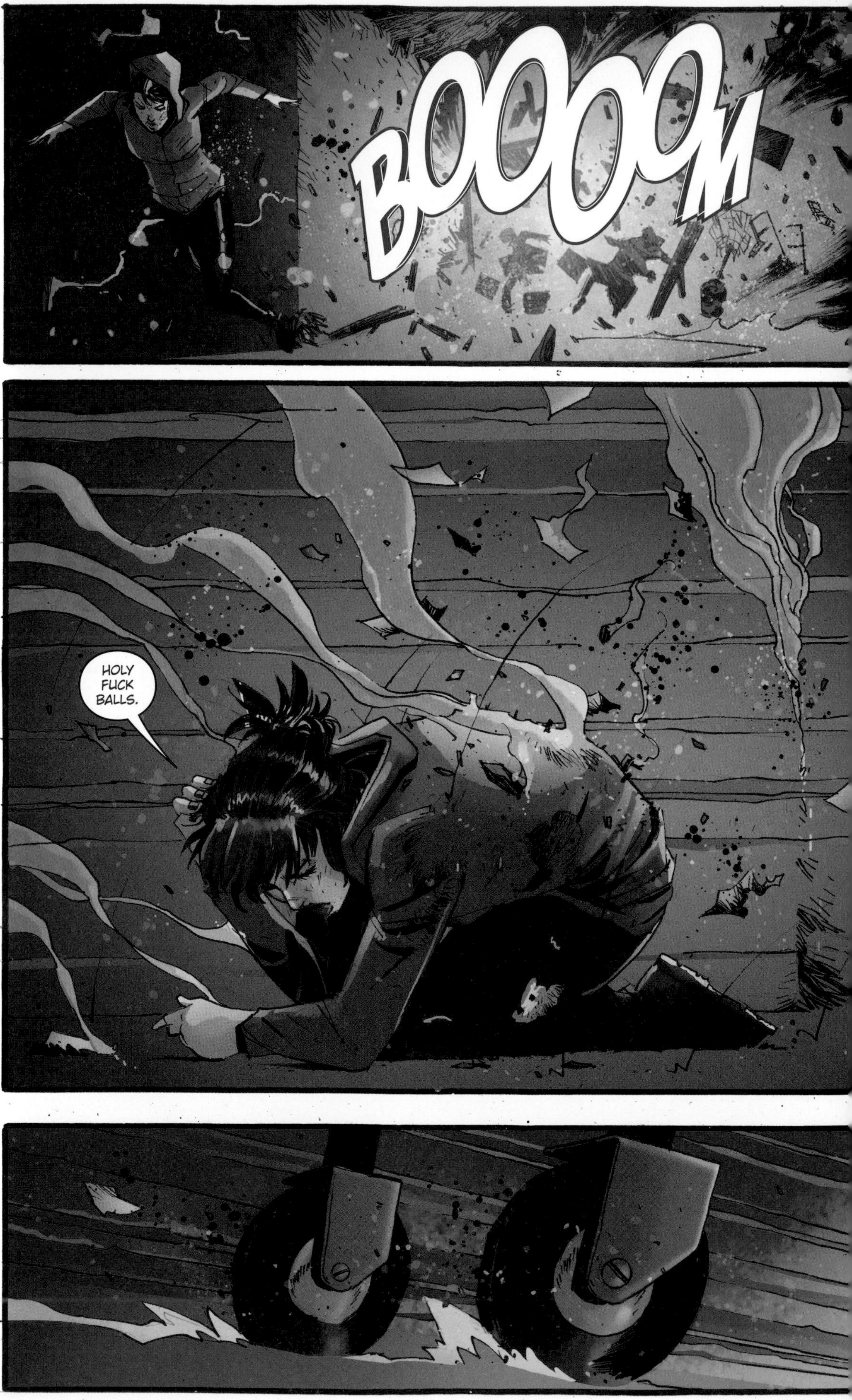
BOOOOM
HOLY FUCK BALLS.

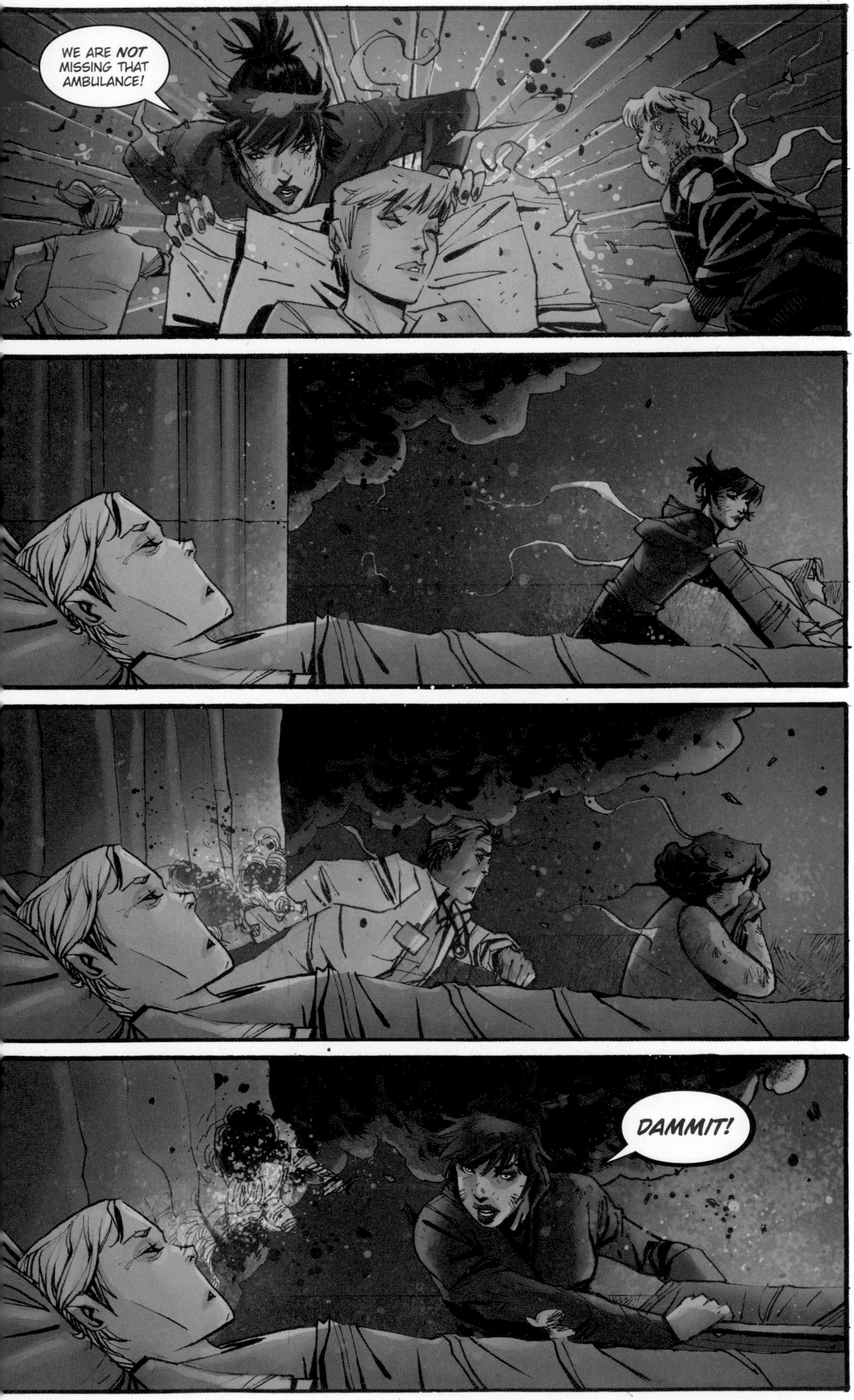
WE ARE NOT MISSING THAT AMBULANCE!
DAMMIT!

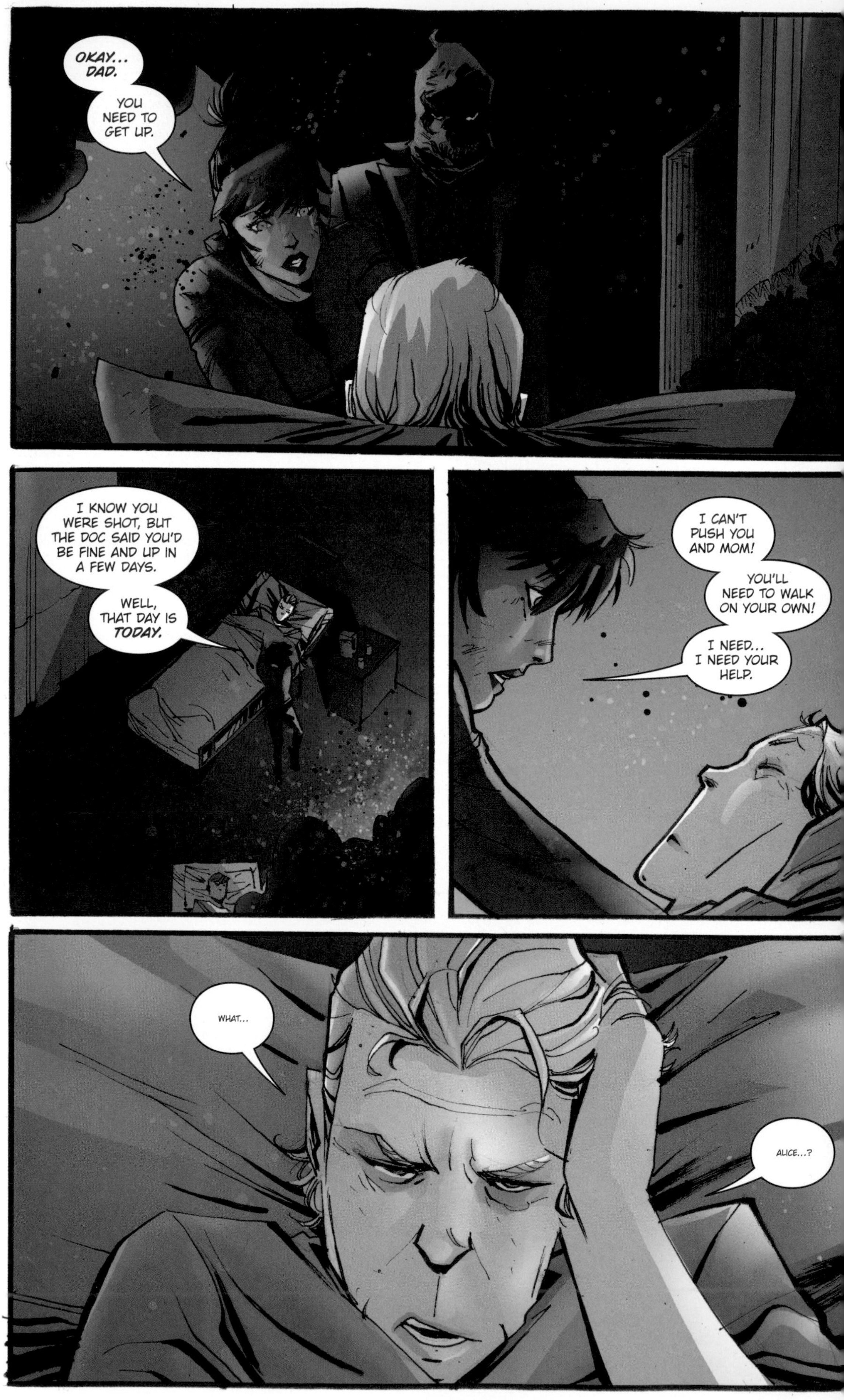
OKAY... DAD.
YOU NEED TO GET UP.
I KNOW YOU WERE SHOT, BUT THE DOC SAID YOU'D BE FINE AND UP IN A FEW DAYS.
WELL, THAT DAY IS TODAY.
I CAN'T PUSH YOU AND MOM!
YOU'LL NEED TO WALK ON YOUR OWN!
I NEED... I NEED YOUR HELP.
WHAT...
ALICE...?

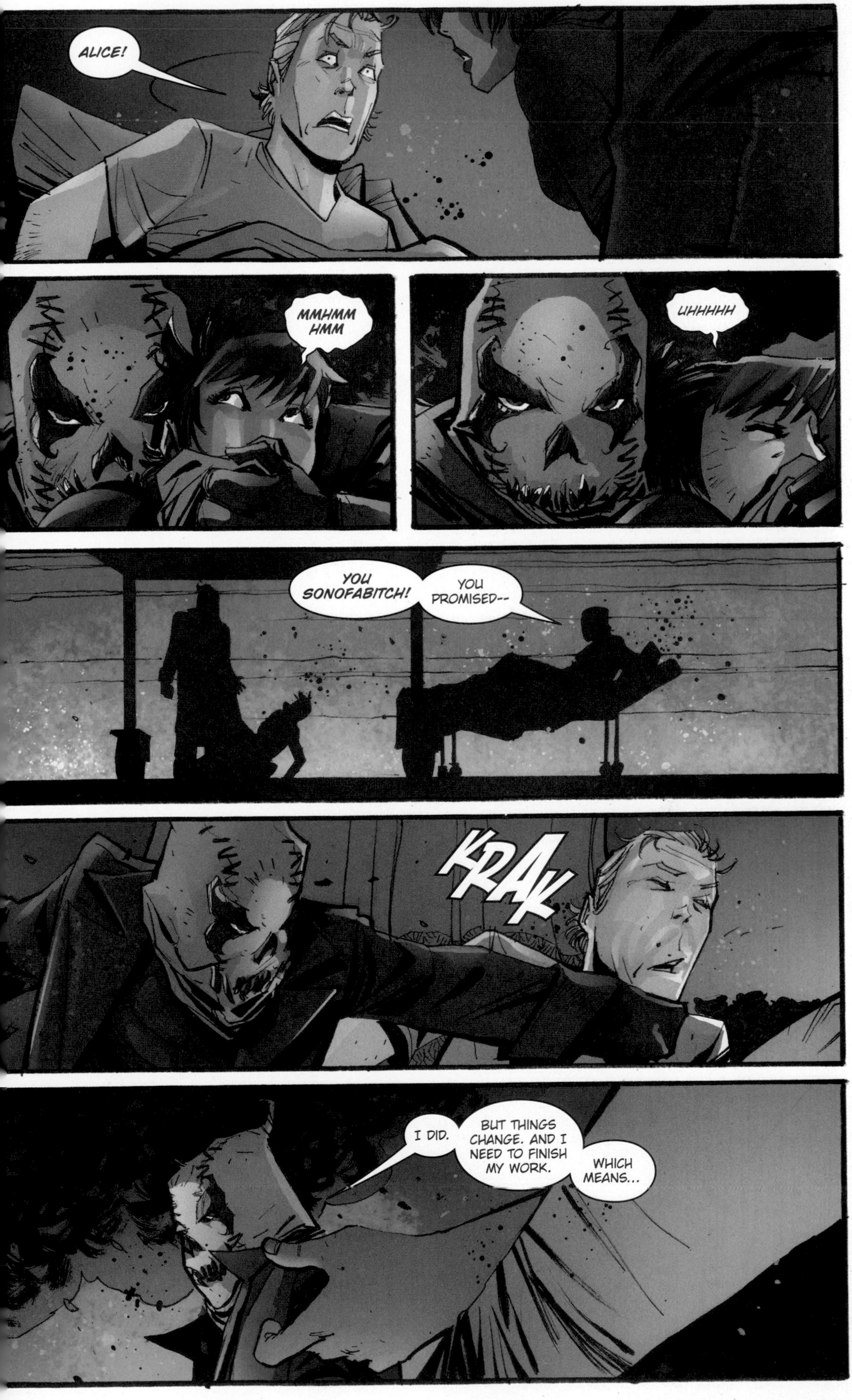
ALICE!
MMHMM HMM
UHHHHH
YOU SONOFABITCH!
YOU PROMISED--
KRAK
I DID.
BUT THINGS CHANGE. AND I NEED TO FINISH MY WORK.
WHICH MEANS...

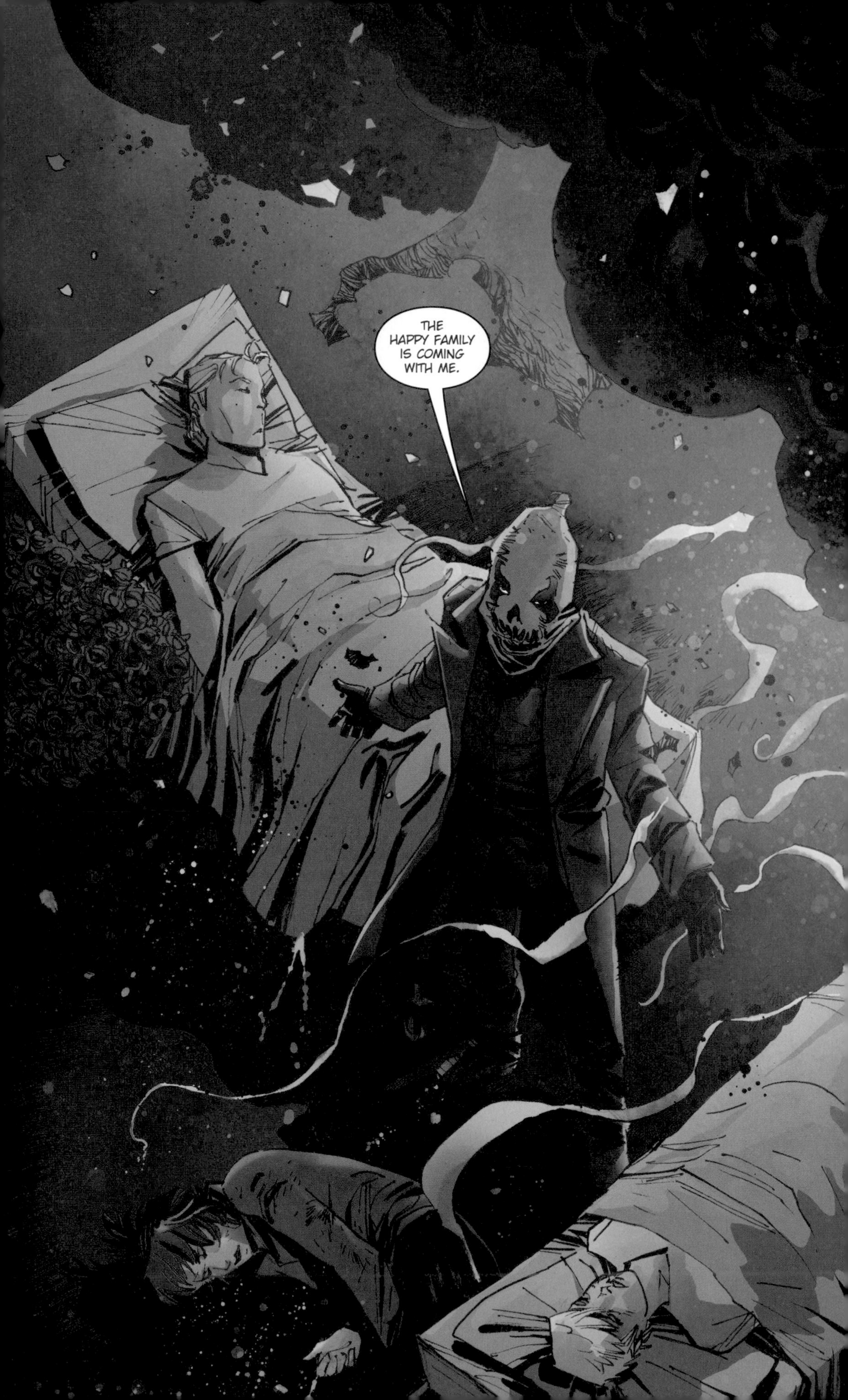
THE HAPPY FAMILY IS COMING WITH ME.

ISSUE TWENTY-NINE

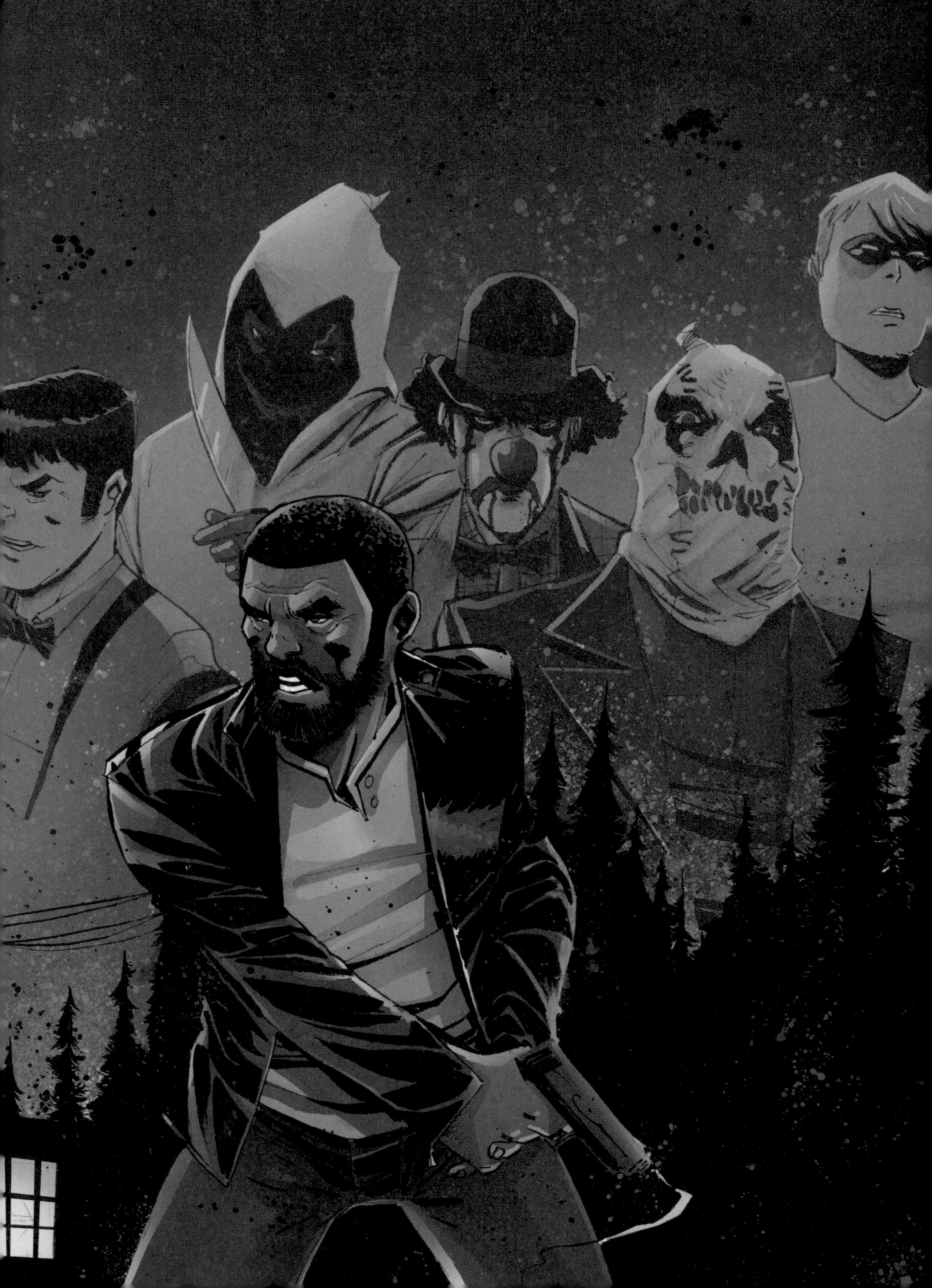

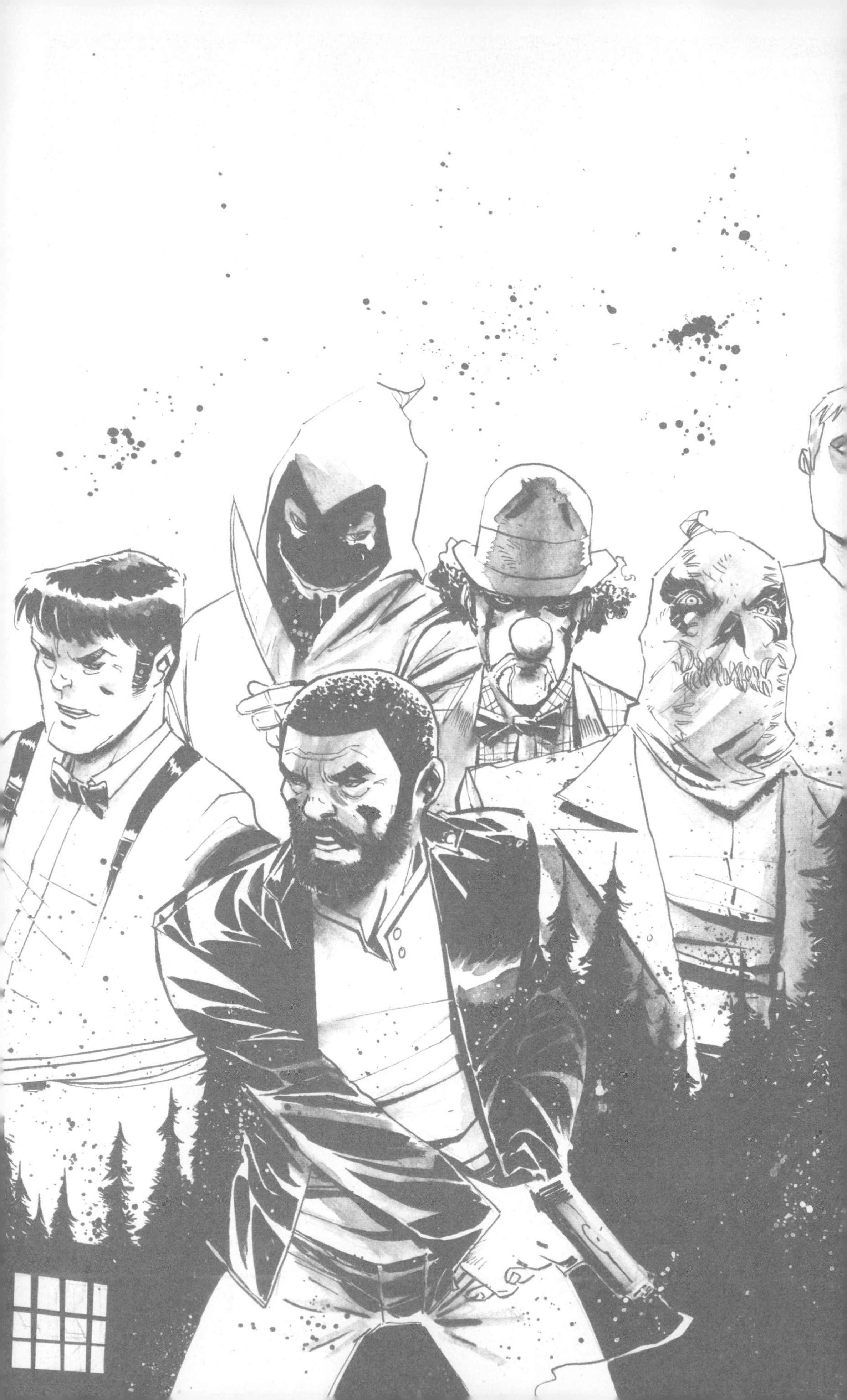

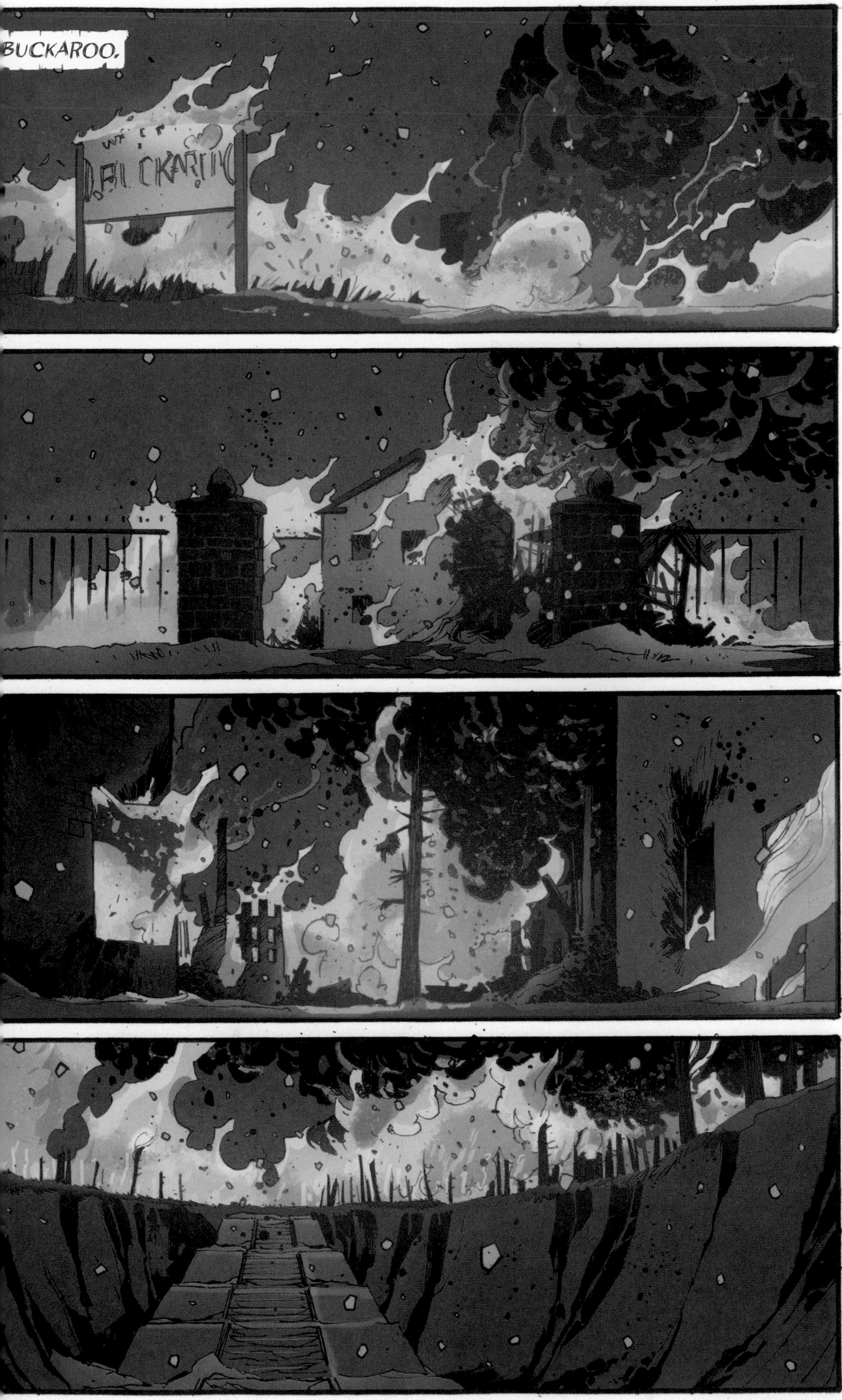
BUCKAROO.

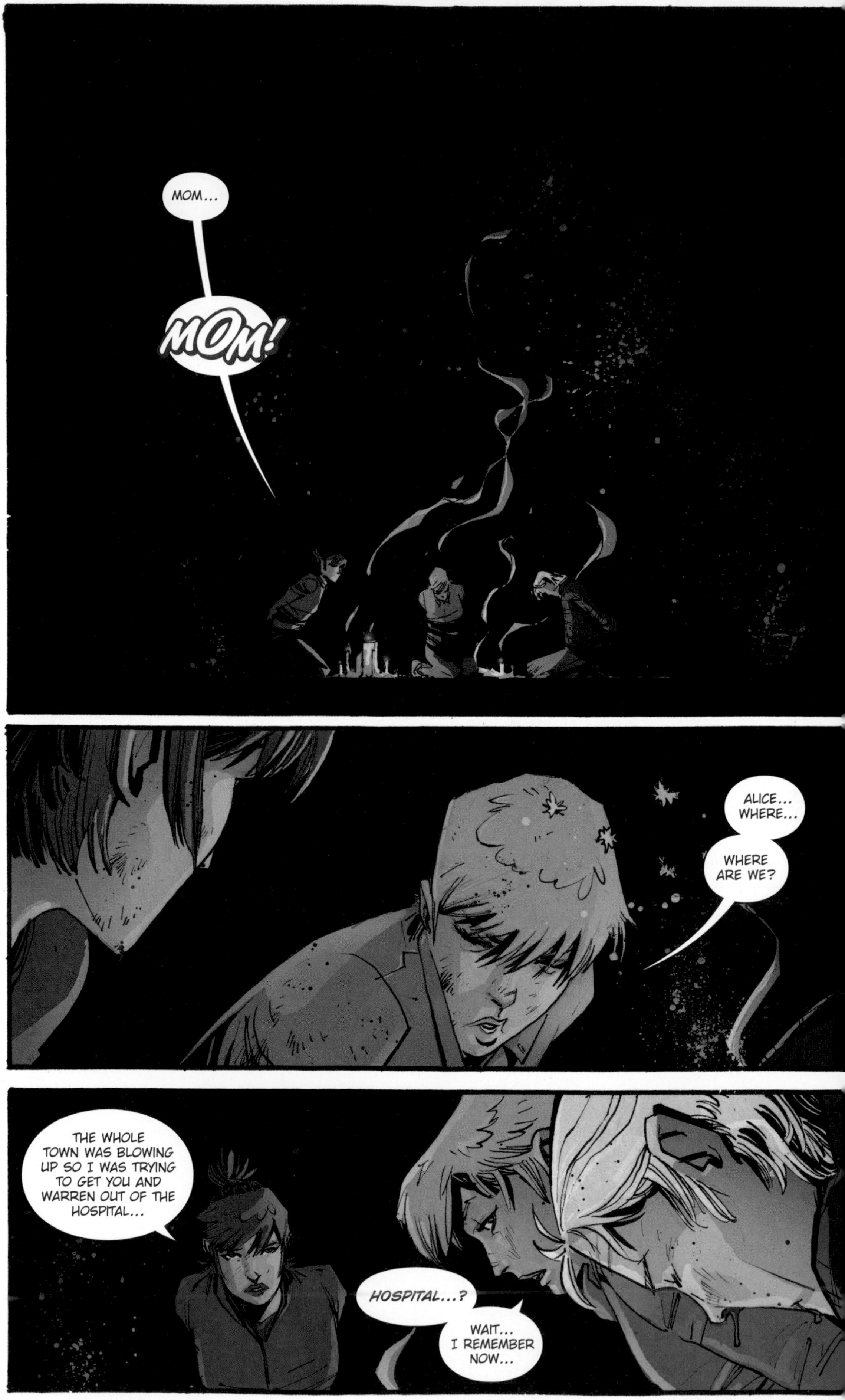

MOM...
MOM!
ALICE... WHERE...
WHERE ARE WE?
THE WHOLE TOWN WAS BLOWING UP SO I WAS TRYING TO GET YOU AND WARREN OUT OF THE HOSPITAL...
HOSPITAL...?
WAIT... I REMEMBER NOW...

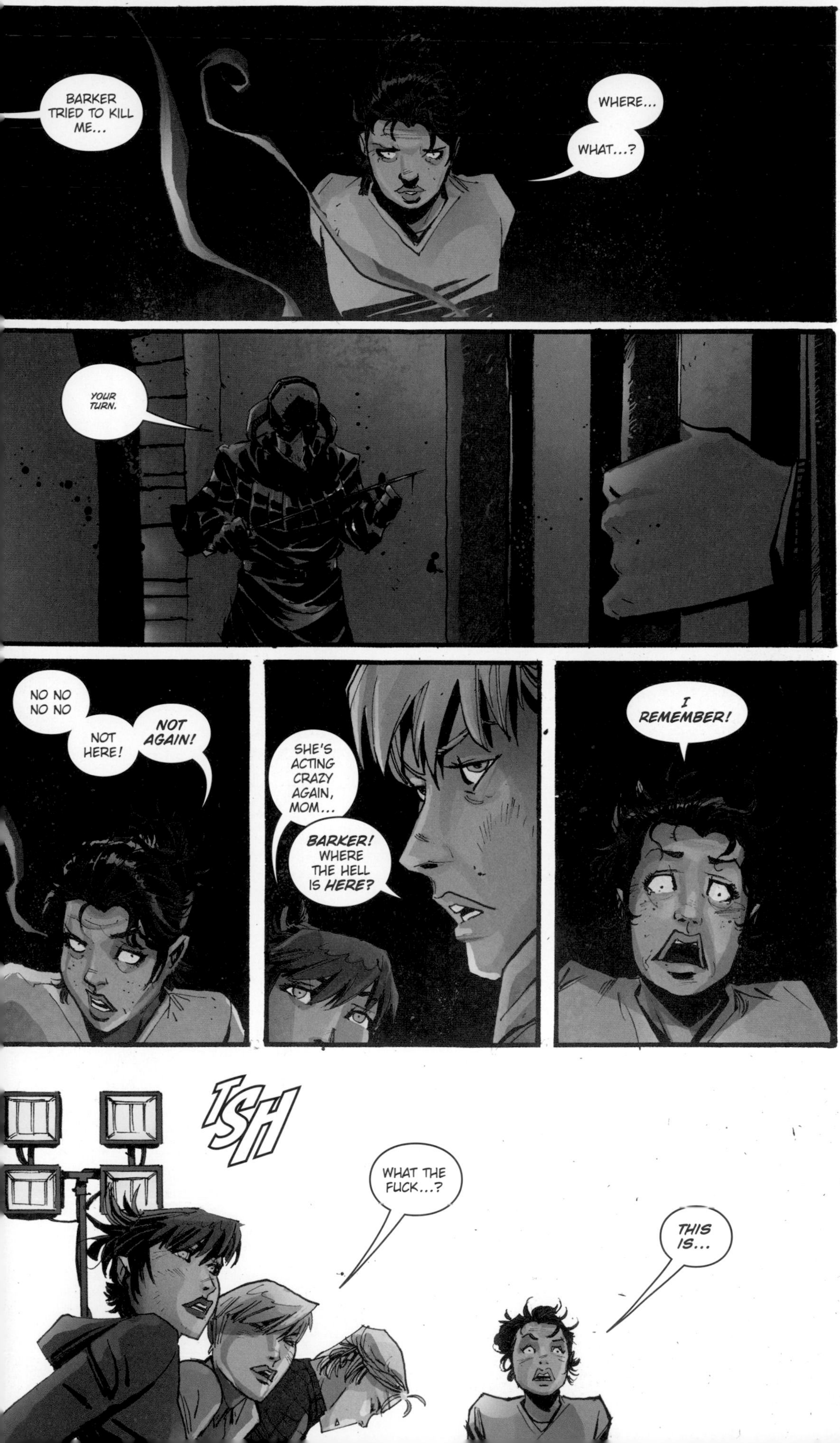
BARKER TRIED TO KILL ME...
WHERE...
WHAT...?
YOUR TURN.
NO NO NO NO
NOT HERE!
NOT AGAIN!
SHE'S ACTING CRAZY AGAIN, MOM...
BARKER! WHERE THE HELL IS HERE?
I REMEMBER!
TSH
WHAT THE FUCK...?
THIS IS...

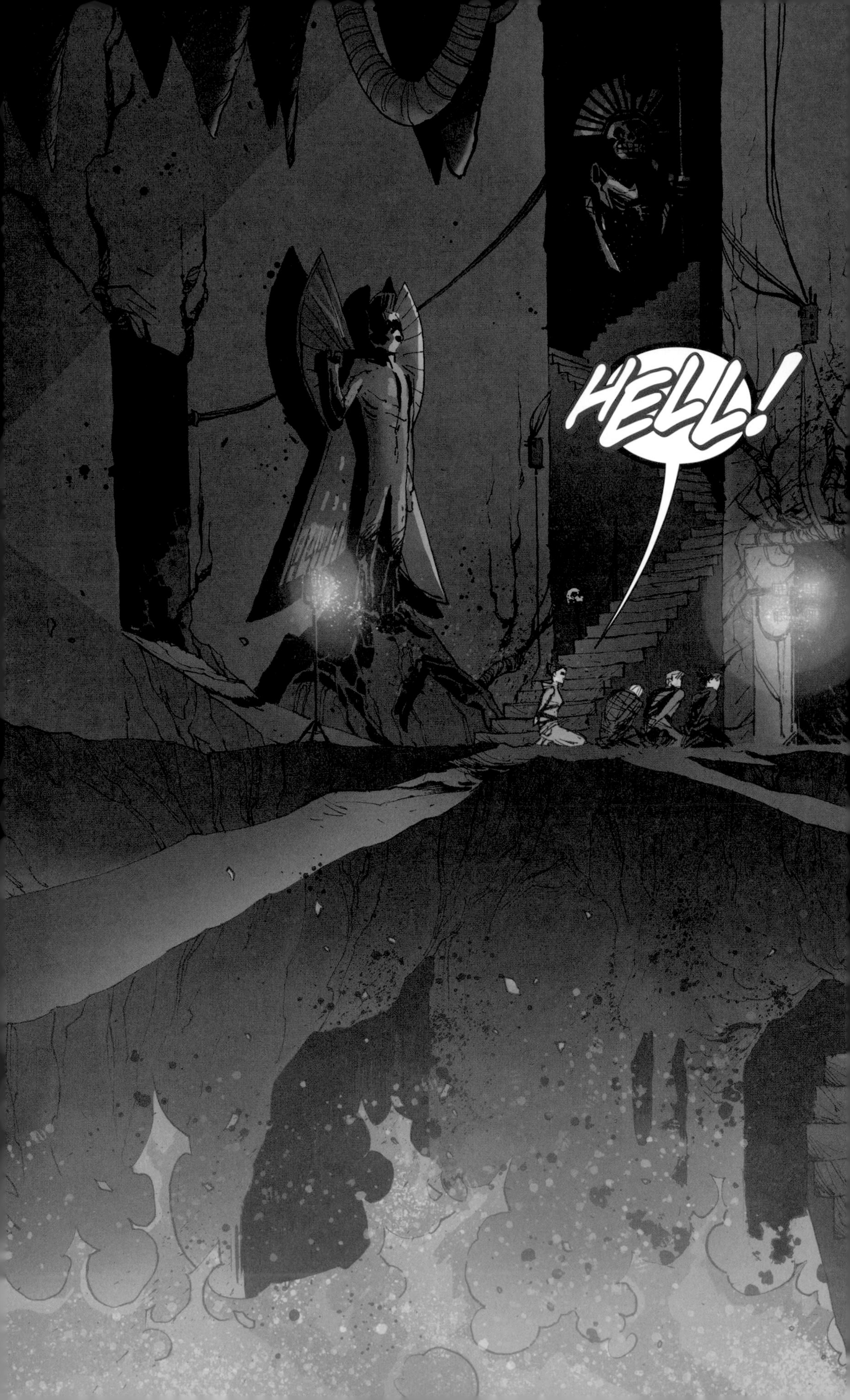
HELL!

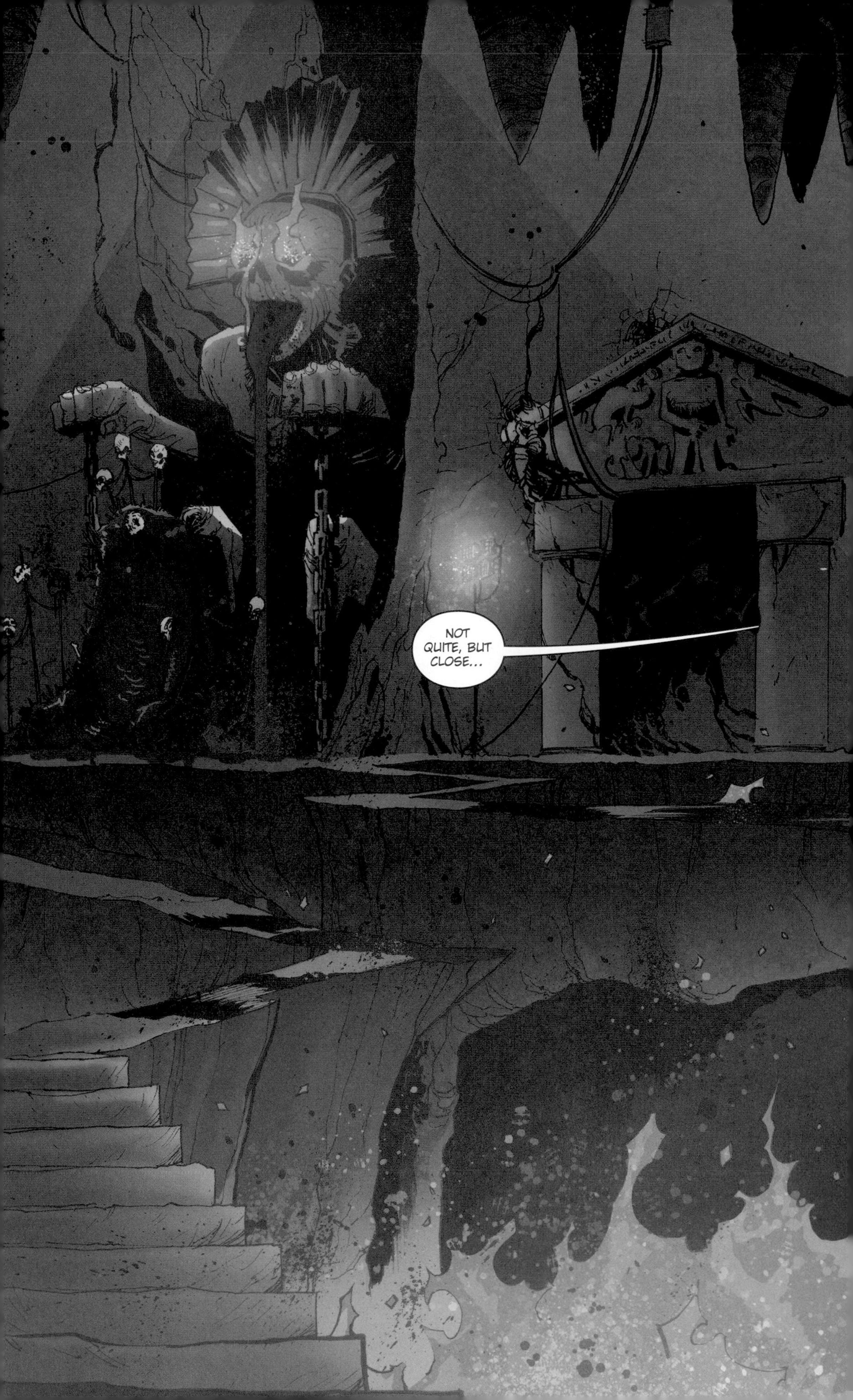
NOT QUITE, BUT CLOSE...

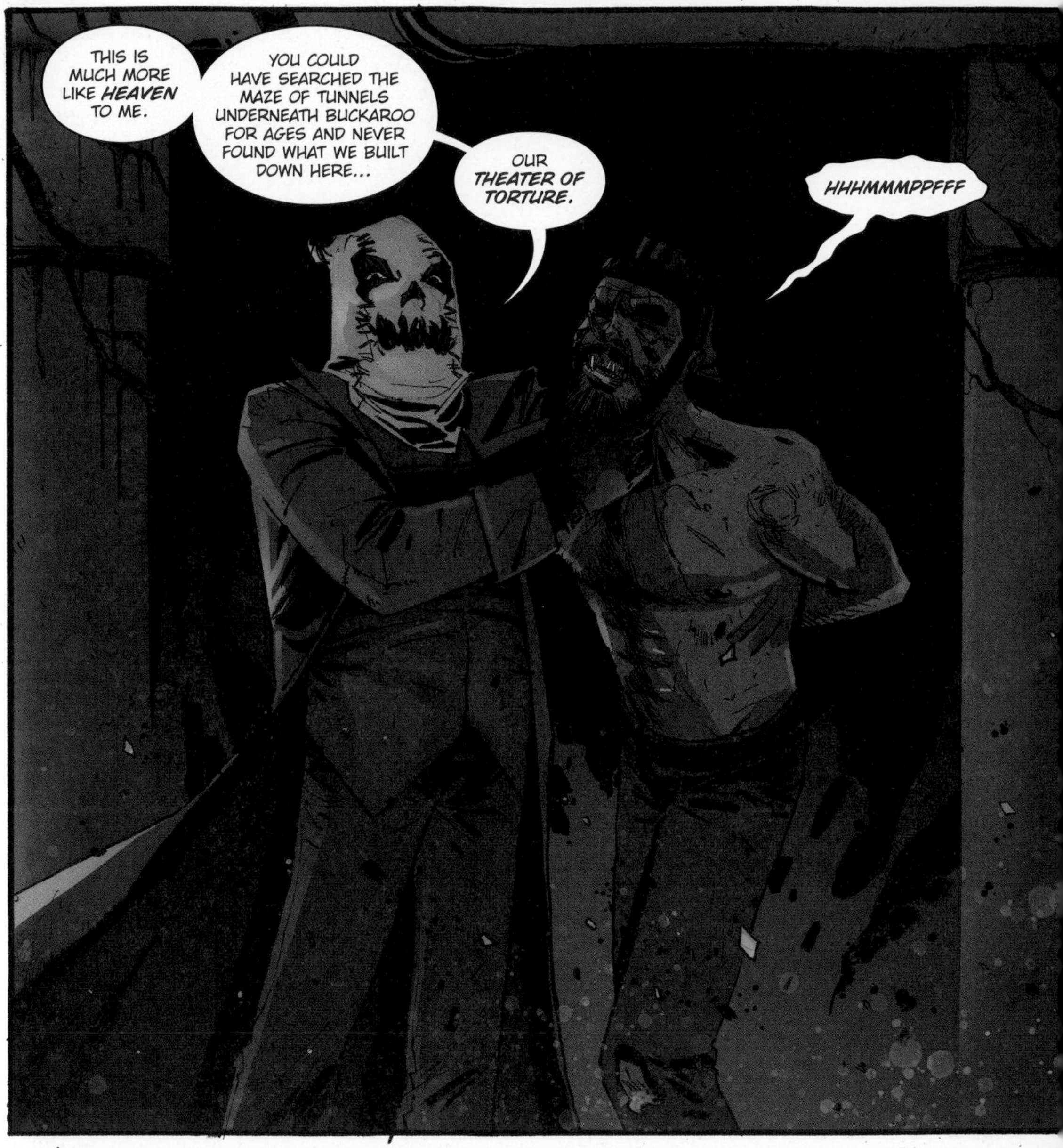
THIS IS MUCH MORE LIKE *HEAVEN* TO ME.
YOU COULD HAVE SEARCHED THE MAZE OF TUNNELS UNDERNEATH BUCKAROO FOR AGES AND NEVER FOUND WHAT WE BUILT DOWN HERE...
OUR *THEATER OF TORTURE.*
HHHMMMPPFFF

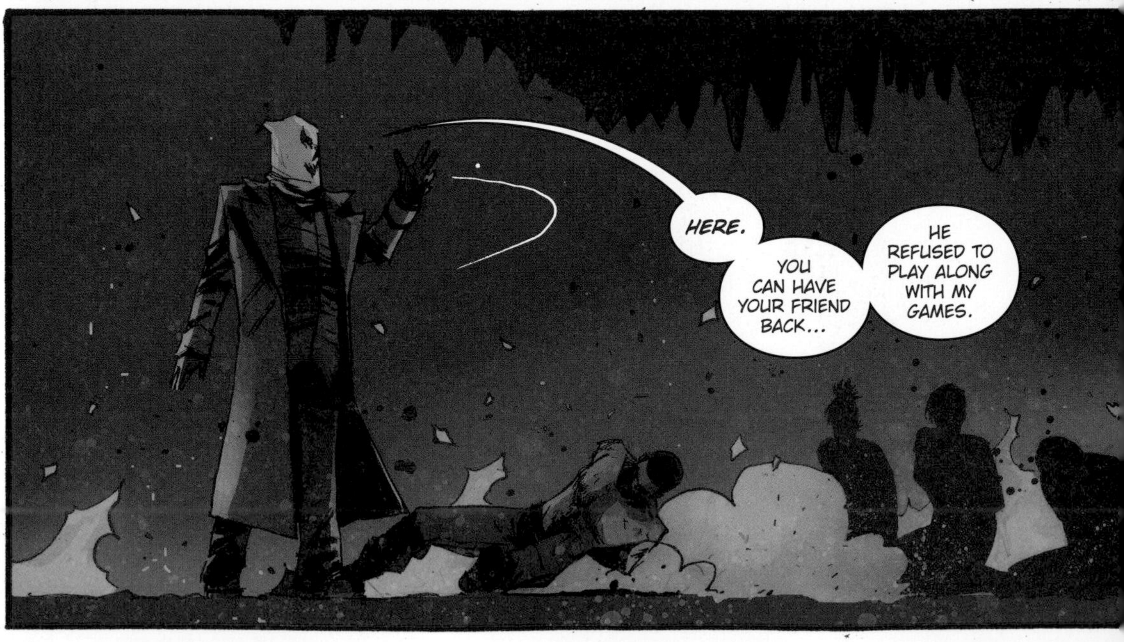
HERE.
YOU CAN HAVE YOUR FRIEND BACK...
HE REFUSED TO PLAY ALONG WITH MY GAMES.

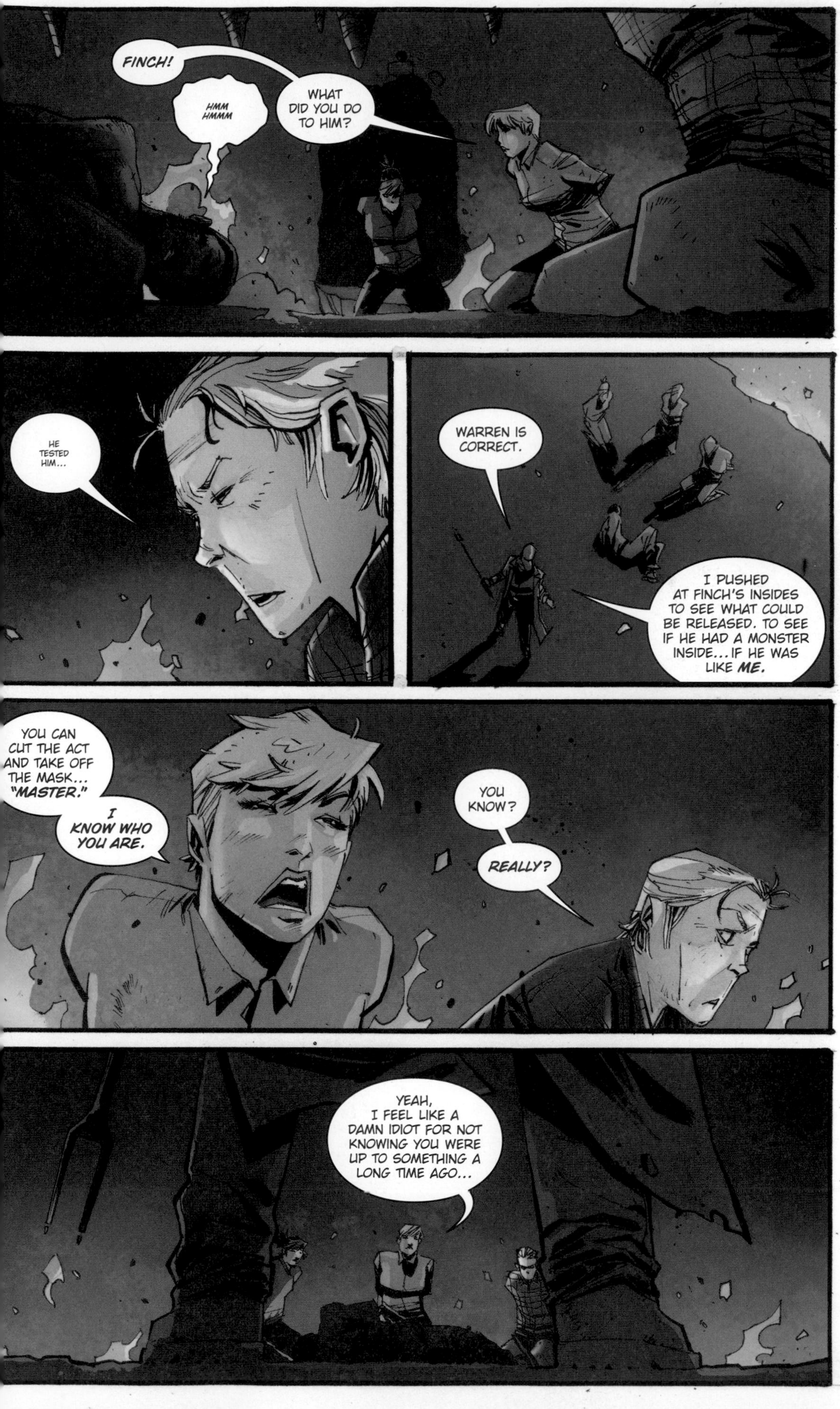
FINCH!
HMM HMMM
WHAT DID YOU DO TO HIM?
HE TESTED HIM...
WARREN IS CORRECT.
I PUSHED AT FINCH'S INSIDES TO SEE WHAT COULD BE RELEASED. TO SEE IF HE HAD A MONSTER INSIDE... IF HE WAS LIKE ME.
YOU CAN CUT THE ACT AND TAKE OFF THE MASK... "MASTER."
I KNOW WHO YOU ARE.
YOU KNOW?
REALLY?
YEAH, I FEEL LIKE A DAMN IDIOT FOR NOT KNOWING YOU WERE UP TO SOMETHING A LONG TIME AGO...

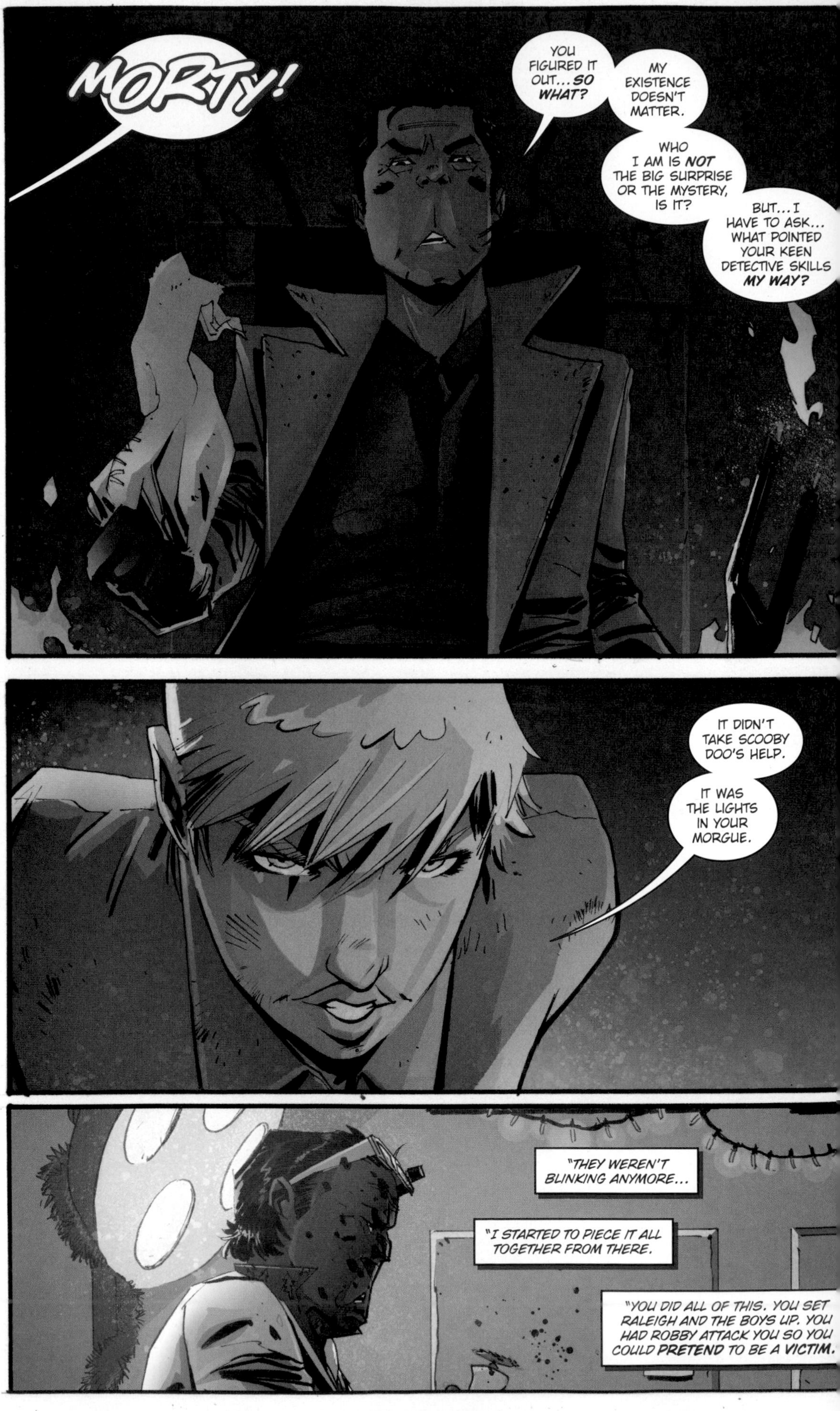
MORTY!
YOU FIGURED IT OUT... SO WHAT?
MY EXISTENCE DOESN'T MATTER.
WHO I AM IS NOT THE BIG SURPRISE OR THE MYSTERY, IS IT?
BUT... I HAVE TO ASK... WHAT POINTED YOUR KEEN DETECTIVE SKILLS MY WAY?
IT DIDN'T TAKE SCOOBY DOO'S HELP.
IT WAS THE LIGHTS IN YOUR MORGUE.
"THEY WEREN'T BLINKING ANYMORE...
"I STARTED TO PIECE IT ALL TOGETHER FROM THERE.
"YOU DID ALL OF THIS. YOU SET RALEIGH AND THE BOYS UP. YOU HAD ROBBY ATTACK YOU SO YOU COULD PRETEND TO BE A VICTIM.

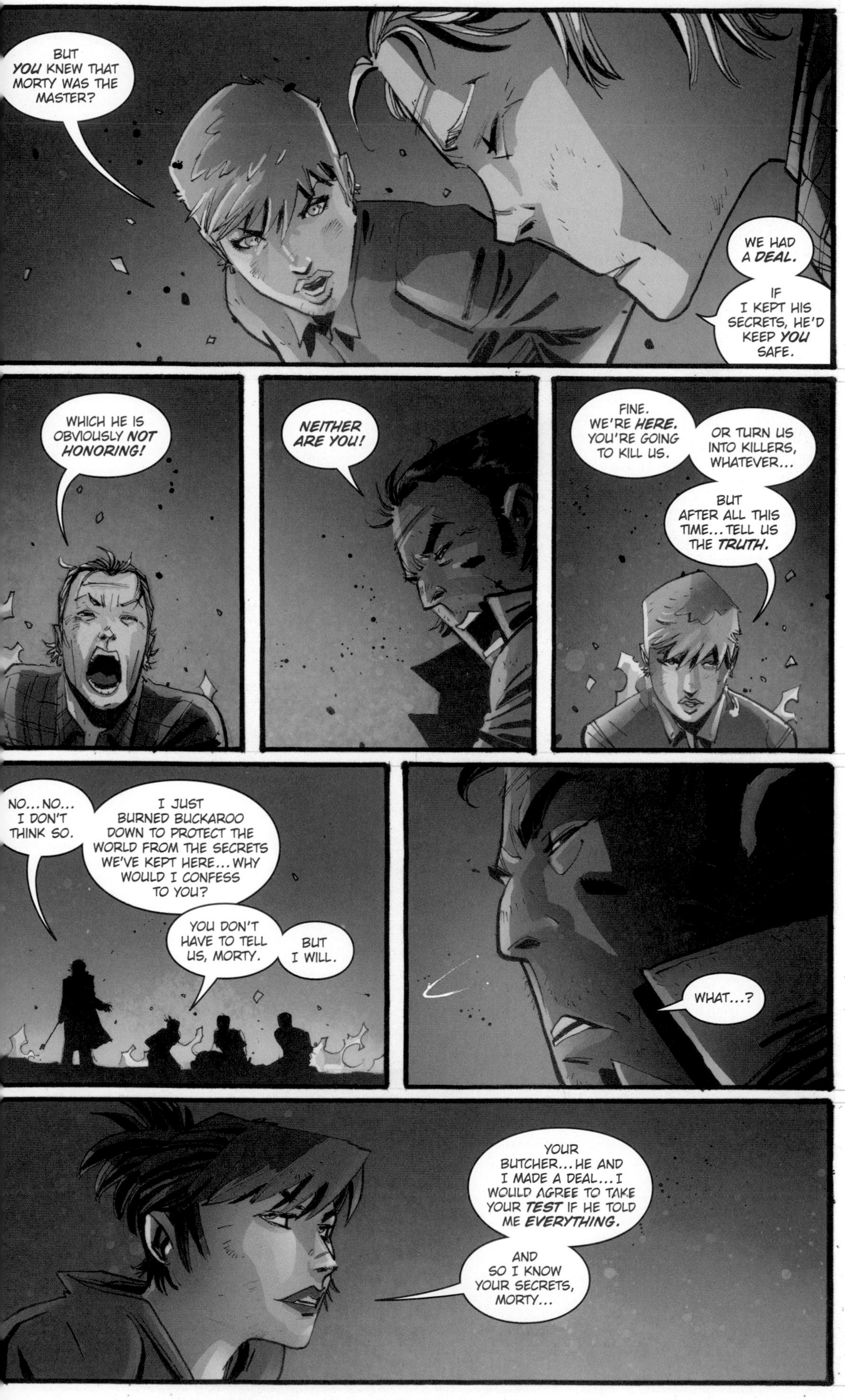
BUT *YOU* KNEW THAT MORTY WAS THE MASTER?
WE HAD A *DEAL.*
IF I KEPT HIS SECRETS, HE'D KEEP *YOU* SAFE.
WHICH HE IS OBVIOUSLY *NOT HONORING!*
NEITHER ARE YOU!
FINE. WE'RE *HERE.* YOU'RE GOING TO KILL US.
OR TURN US INTO KILLERS, WHATEVER...
BUT AFTER ALL THIS TIME... TELL US THE *TRUTH.*
NO... NO... I DON'T THINK SO.
I JUST BURNED BUCKAROO DOWN TO PROTECT THE WORLD FROM THE SECRETS WE'VE KEPT HERE... WHY WOULD I CONFESS TO YOU?
YOU DON'T HAVE TO TELL US, MORTY.
BUT I WILL.
WHAT...?
YOUR BUTCHER... HE AND I MADE A DEAL... I WOULD AGREE TO TAKE YOUR *TEST* IF HE TOLD ME *EVERYTHING.*
AND SO I KNOW YOUR SECRETS, MORTY...

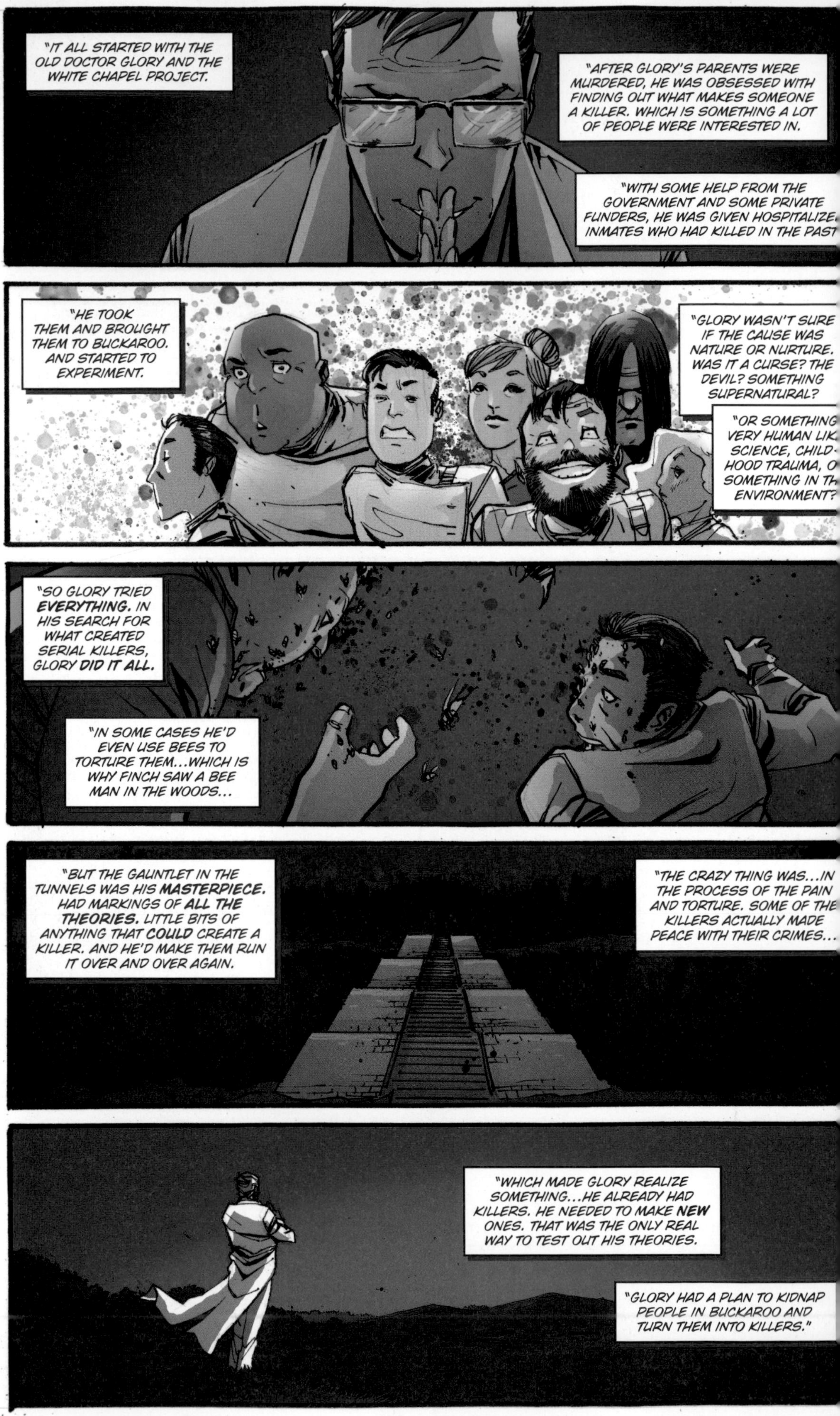
"IT ALL STARTED WITH THE OLD DOCTOR GLORY AND THE WHITE CHAPEL PROJECT.
"AFTER GLORY'S PARENTS WERE MURDERED, HE WAS OBSESSED WITH FINDING OUT WHAT MAKES SOMEONE A KILLER. WHICH IS SOMETHING A LOT OF PEOPLE WERE INTERESTED IN.
"WITH SOME HELP FROM THE GOVERNMENT AND SOME PRIVATE FUNDERS, HE WAS GIVEN HOSPITALIZE INMATES WHO HAD KILLED IN THE PAST
"HE TOOK THEM AND BROUGHT THEM TO BUCKAROO. AND STARTED TO EXPERIMENT.
"GLORY WASN'T SURE IF THE CAUSE WAS NATURE OR NURTURE. WAS IT A CURSE? THE DEVIL? SOMETHING SUPERNATURAL?
"OR SOMETHING VERY HUMAN LIK SCIENCE, CHILD-HOOD TRAUMA, O SOMETHING IN TH ENVIRONMENT?
"SO GLORY TRIED EVERYTHING. IN HIS SEARCH FOR WHAT CREATED SERIAL KILLERS, GLORY DID IT ALL.
"IN SOME CASES HE'D EVEN USE BEES TO TORTURE THEM...WHICH IS WHY FINCH SAW A BEE MAN IN THE WOODS...
"BUT THE GAUNTLET IN THE TUNNELS WAS HIS MASTERPIECE. HAD MARKINGS OF ALL THE THEORIES. LITTLE BITS OF ANYTHING THAT COULD CREATE A KILLER. AND HE'D MAKE THEM RUN IT OVER AND OVER AGAIN.
"THE CRAZY THING WAS...IN THE PROCESS OF THE PAIN AND TORTURE. SOME OF THE KILLERS ACTUALLY MADE PEACE WITH THEIR CRIMES...
"WHICH MADE GLORY REALIZE SOMETHING...HE ALREADY HAD KILLERS. HE NEEDED TO MAKE NEW ONES. THAT WAS THE ONLY REAL WAY TO TEST OUT HIS THEORIES.
"GLORY HAD A PLAN TO KIDNAP PEOPLE IN BUCKAROO AND TURN THEM INTO KILLERS."

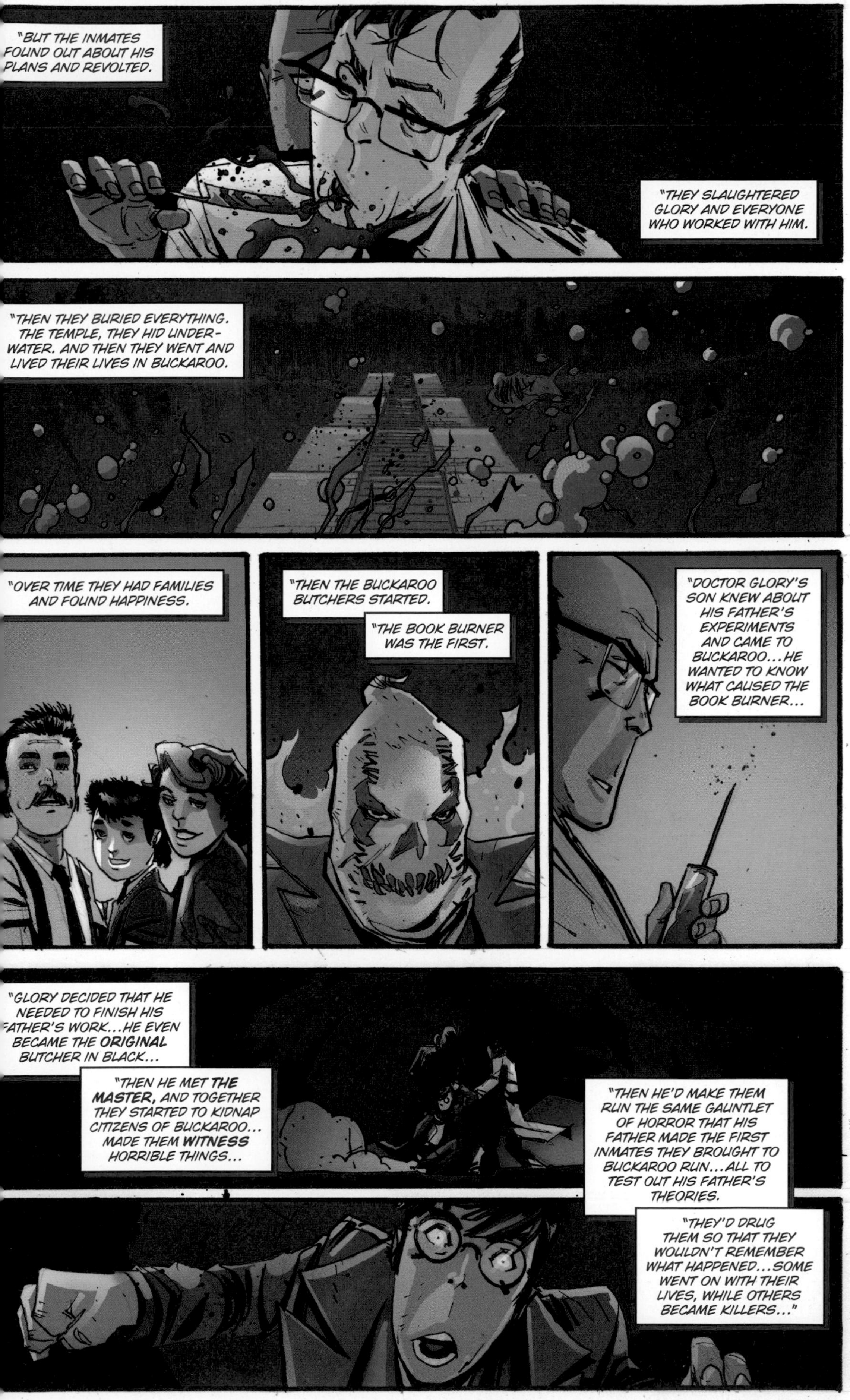
"BUT THE INMATES FOUND OUT ABOUT HIS PLANS AND REVOLTED.
"THEY SLAUGHTERED GLORY AND EVERYONE WHO WORKED WITH HIM.
"THEN THEY BURIED EVERYTHING. THE TEMPLE, THEY HID UNDER-WATER. AND THEN THEY WENT AND LIVED THEIR LIVES IN BUCKAROO.
"OVER TIME THEY HAD FAMILIES AND FOUND HAPPINESS.
"THEN THE BUCKAROO BUTCHERS STARTED.
"THE BOOK BURNER WAS THE FIRST.
"DOCTOR GLORY'S SON KNEW ABOUT HIS FATHER'S EXPERIMENTS AND CAME TO BUCKAROO...HE WANTED TO KNOW WHAT CAUSED THE BOOK BURNER...
"GLORY DECIDED THAT HE NEEDED TO FINISH HIS FATHER'S WORK...HE EVEN BECAME THE ORIGINAL BUTCHER IN BLACK...
"THEN HE MET THE MASTER, AND TOGETHER THEY STARTED TO KIDNAP CITIZENS OF BUCKAROO... MADE THEM WITNESS HORRIBLE THINGS...
"THEN HE'D MAKE THEM RUN THE SAME GAUNTLET OF HORROR THAT HIS FATHER MADE THE FIRST INMATES THEY BROUGHT TO BUCKAROO RUN...ALL TO TEST OUT HIS FATHER'S THEORIES.
"THEY'D DRUG THEM SO THAT THEY WOULDN'T REMEMBER WHAT HAPPENED...SOME WENT ON WITH THEIR LIVES, WHILE OTHERS BECAME KILLERS..."

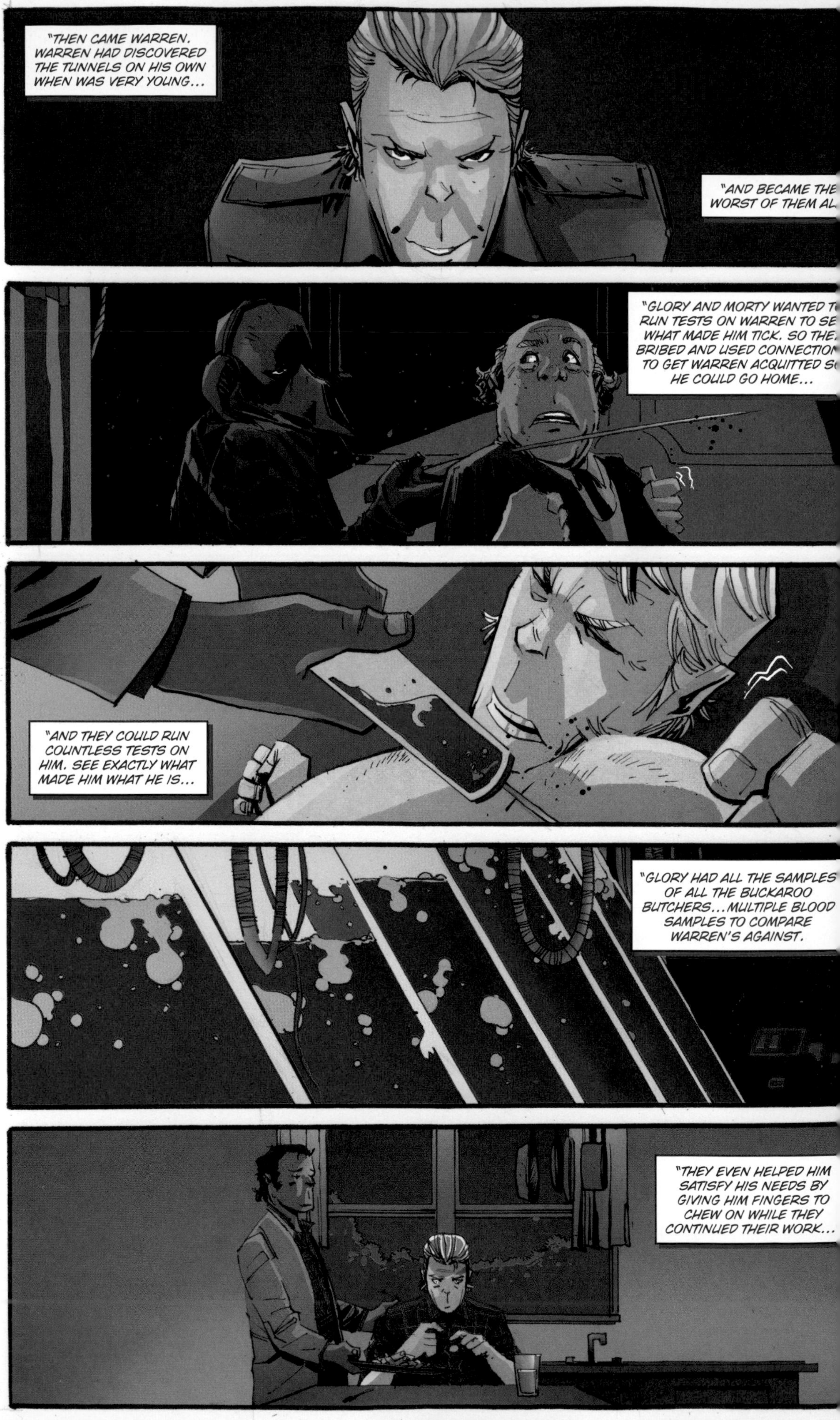
"THEN CAME WARREN. WARREN HAD DISCOVERED THE TUNNELS ON HIS OWN WHEN WAS VERY YOUNG...
"AND BECAME THE WORST OF THEM AL
"GLORY AND MORTY WANTED T RUN TESTS ON WARREN TO SE WHAT MADE HIM TICK. SO THE BRIBED AND USED CONNECTION TO GET WARREN ACQUITTED S HE COULD GO HOME...
"AND THEY COULD RUN COUNTLESS TESTS ON HIM. SEE EXACTLY WHAT MADE HIM WHAT HE IS...
"GLORY HAD ALL THE SAMPLES OF ALL THE BUCKAROO BUTCHERS...MULTIPLE BLOOD SAMPLES TO COMPARE WARREN'S AGAINST.
"THEY EVEN HELPED HIM SATISFY HIS NEEDS BY GIVING HIM FINGERS TO CHEW ON WHILE THEY CONTINUED THEIR WORK...

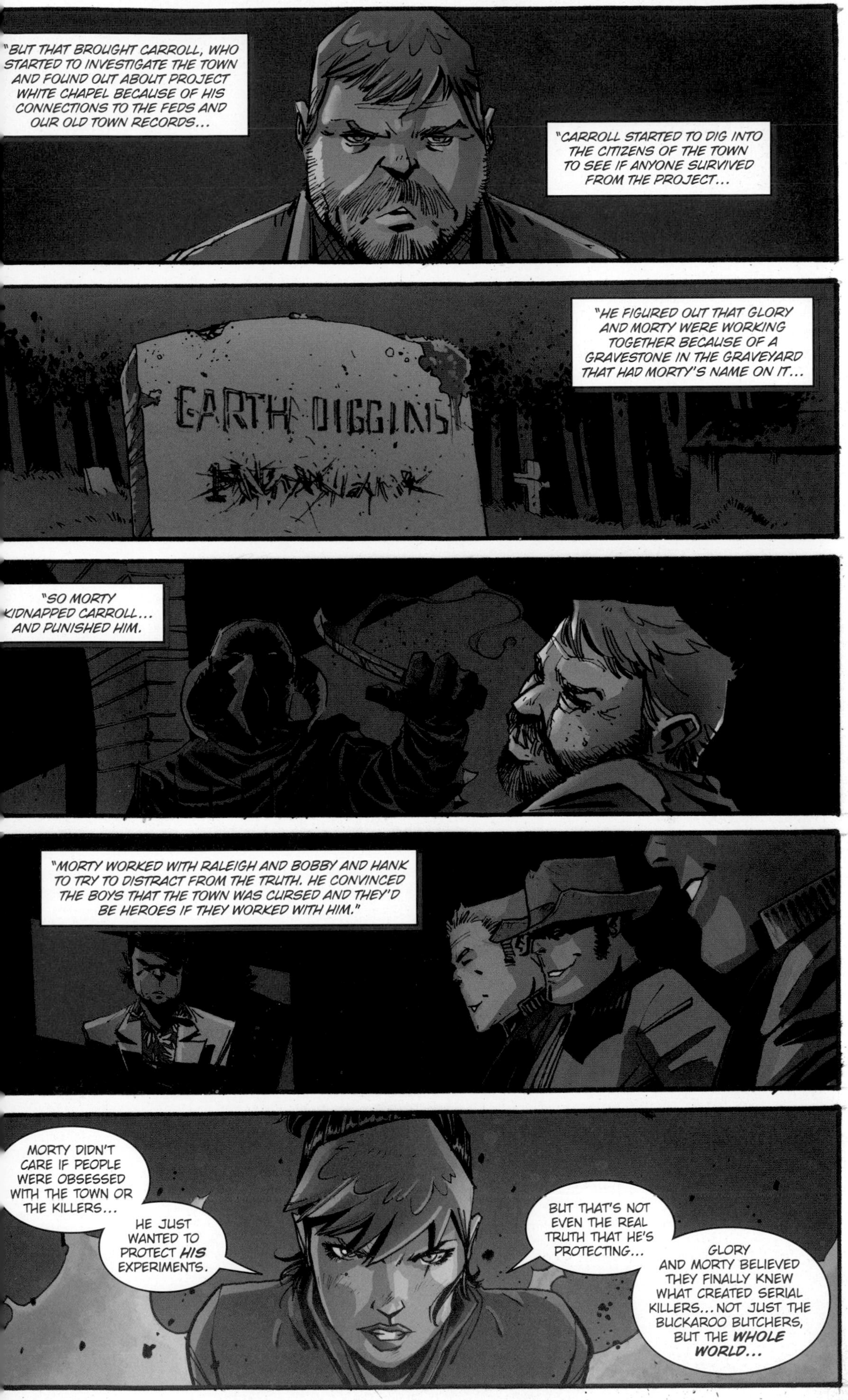
"BUT THAT BROUGHT CARROLL, WHO STARTED TO INVESTIGATE THE TOWN AND FOUND OUT ABOUT PROJECT WHITE CHAPEL BECAUSE OF HIS CONNECTIONS TO THE FEDS AND OUR OLD TOWN RECORDS...
"CARROLL STARTED TO DIG INTO THE CITIZENS OF THE TOWN TO SEE IF ANYONE SURVIVED FROM THE PROJECT...
"HE FIGURED OUT THAT GLORY AND MORTY WERE WORKING TOGETHER BECAUSE OF A GRAVESTONE IN THE GRAVEYARD THAT HAD MORTY'S NAME ON IT...
GARTH DIGGINS
"SO MORTY KIDNAPPED CARROLL... AND PUNISHED HIM.
"MORTY WORKED WITH RALEIGH AND BOBBY AND HANK TO TRY TO DISTRACT FROM THE TRUTH. HE CONVINCED THE BOYS THAT THE TOWN WAS CURSED AND THEY'D BE HEROES IF THEY WORKED WITH HIM."
MORTY DIDN'T CARE IF PEOPLE WERE OBSESSED WITH THE TOWN OR THE KILLERS...
HE JUST WANTED TO PROTECT HIS EXPERIMENTS.
BUT THAT'S NOT EVEN THE REAL TRUTH THAT HE'S PROTECTING...
GLORY AND MORTY BELIEVED THEY FINALLY KNEW WHAT CREATED SERIAL KILLERS...NOT JUST THE BUCKAROO BUTCHERS, BUT THE WHOLE WORLD...

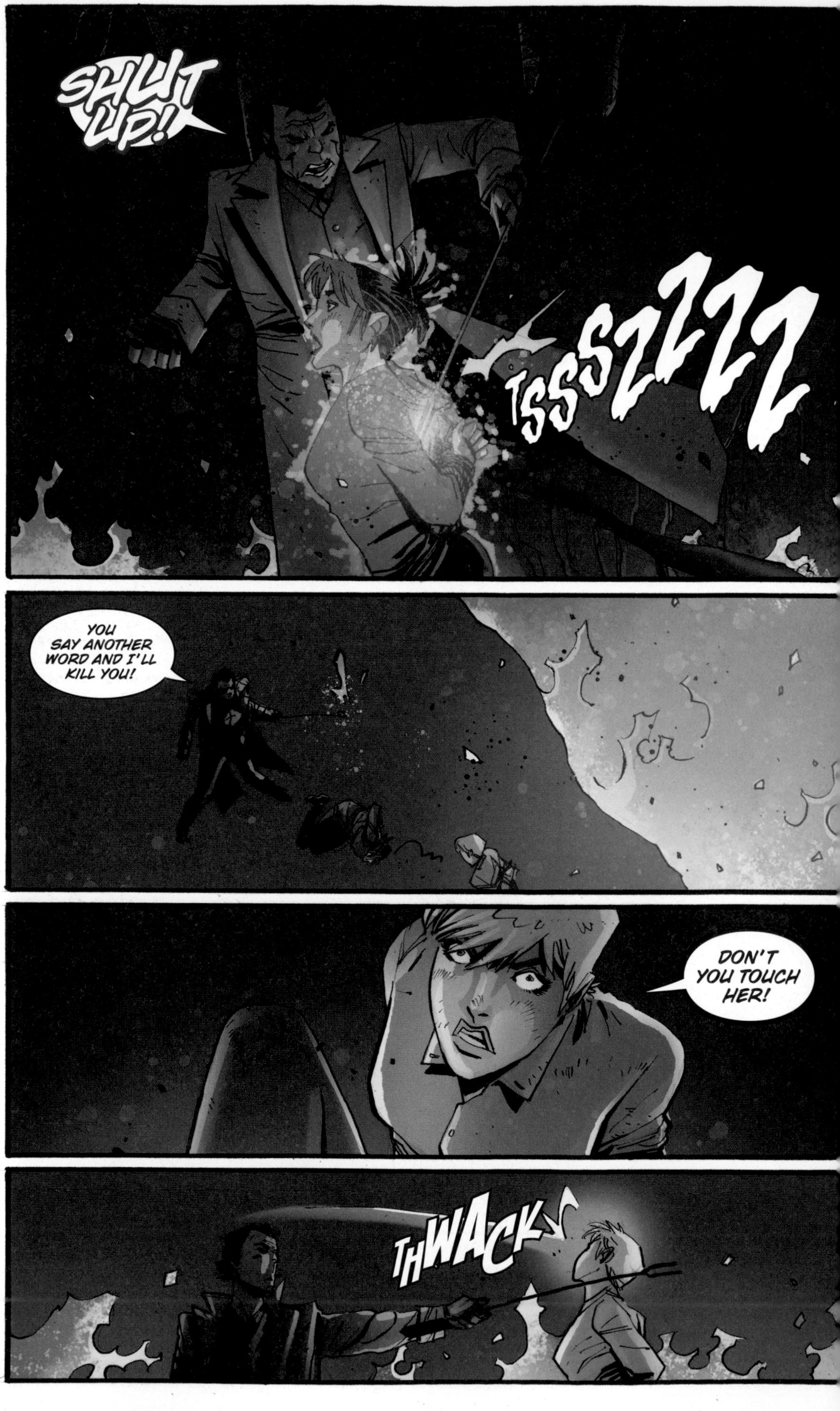
SHUT UP!!
TSSSZZZZ
YOU SAY ANOTHER WORD AND I'LL KILL YOU!
DON'T YOU TOUCH HER!
THWACK

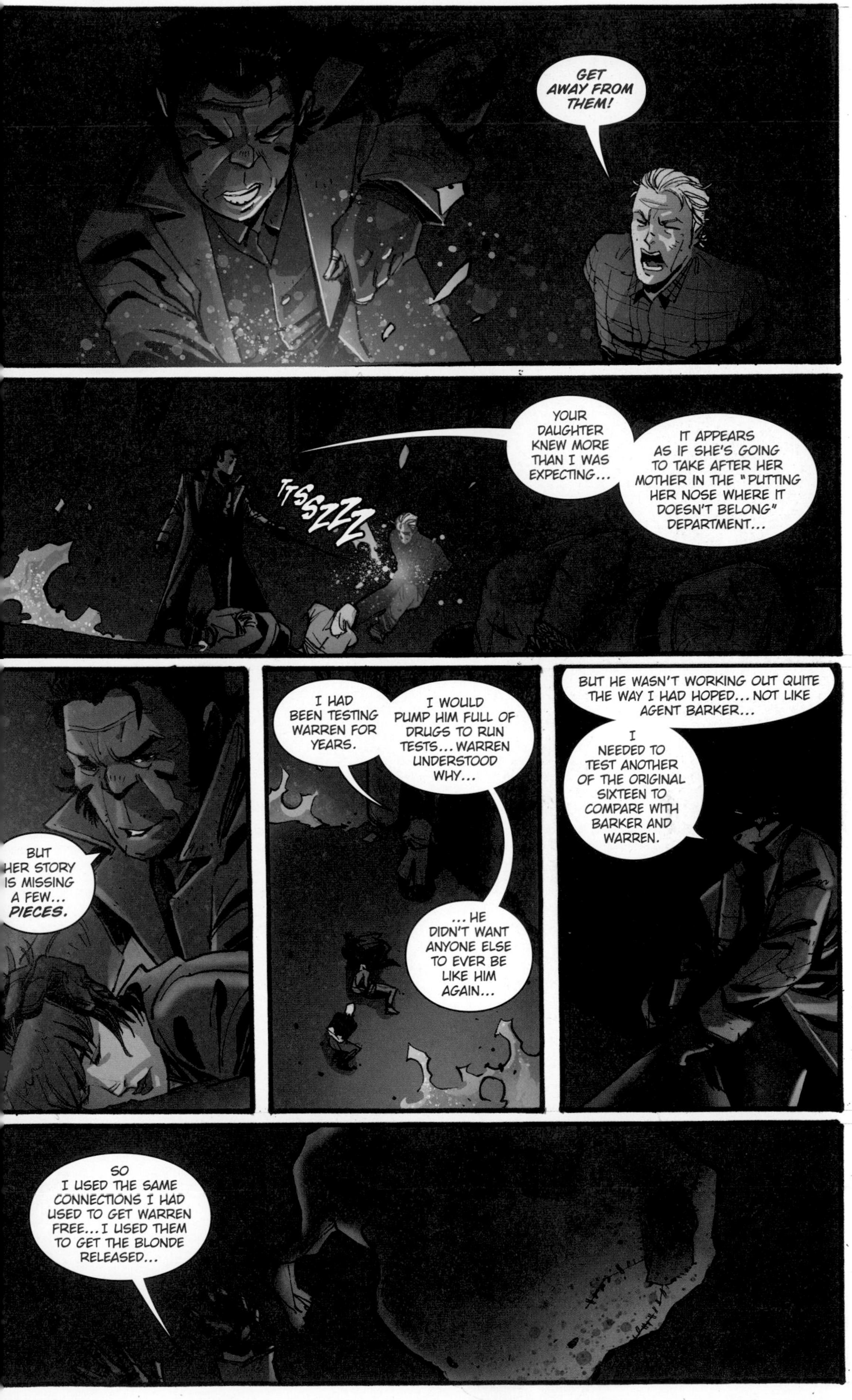
GET AWAY FROM THEM!
YOUR DAUGHTER KNEW MORE THAN I WAS EXPECTING...
IT APPEARS AS IF SHE'S GOING TO TAKE AFTER HER MOTHER IN THE "PUTTING HER NOSE WHERE IT DOESN'T BELONG" DEPARTMENT...
TTSSZZZZ
BUT HER STORY IS MISSING A FEW... PIECES.
I HAD BEEN TESTING WARREN FOR YEARS.
I WOULD PUMP HIM FULL OF DRUGS TO RUN TESTS... WARREN UNDERSTOOD WHY...
...HE DIDN'T WANT ANYONE ELSE TO EVER BE LIKE HIM AGAIN...
BUT HE WASN'T WORKING OUT QUITE THE WAY I HAD HOPED... NOT LIKE AGENT BARKER...
I NEEDED TO TEST ANOTHER OF THE ORIGINAL SIXTEEN TO COMPARE WITH BARKER AND WARREN.
SO I USED THE SAME CONNECTIONS I HAD USED TO GET WARREN FREE... I USED THEM TO GET THE BLONDE RELEASED...

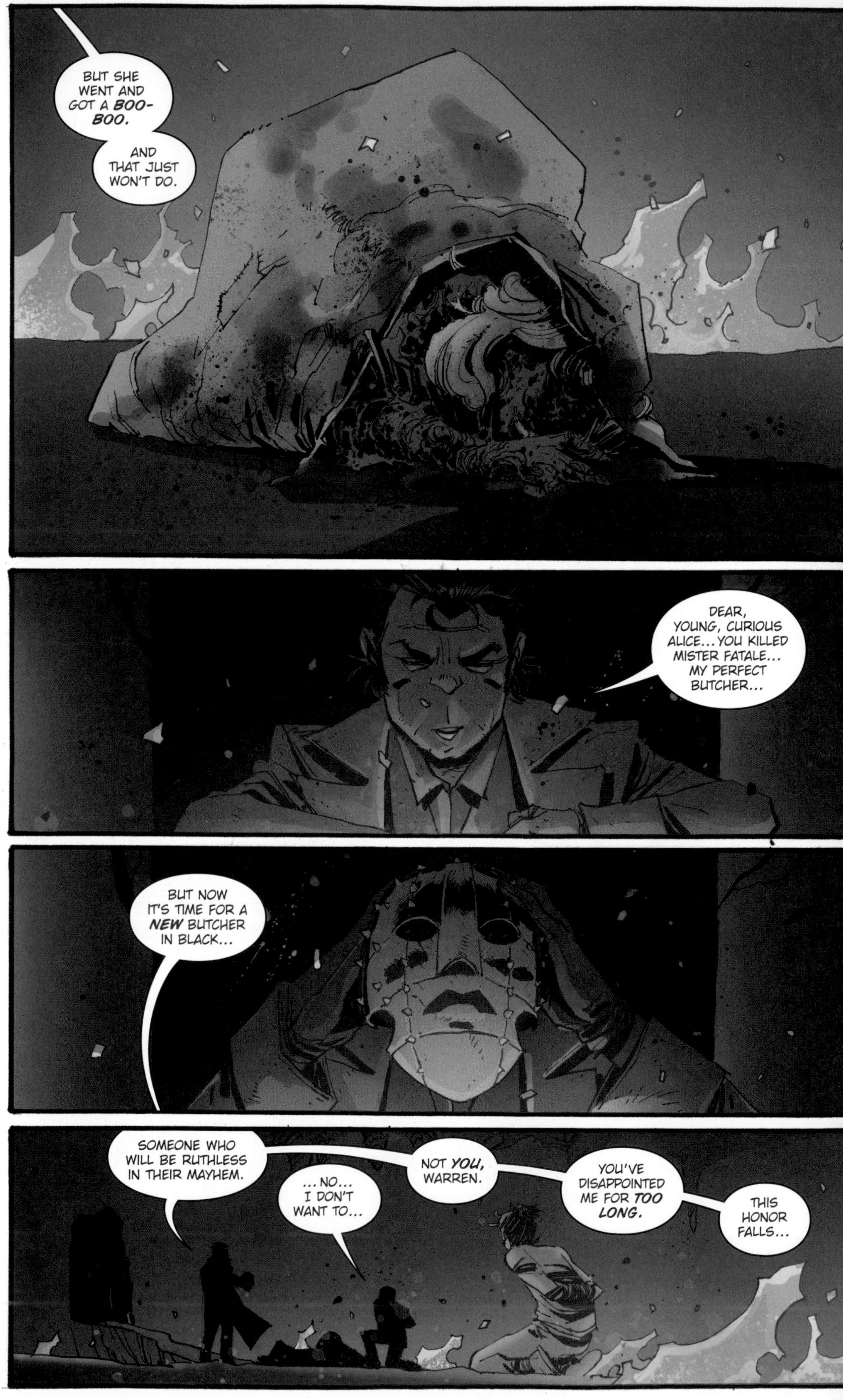

BUT SHE WENT AND GOT A ***BOO-BOO.***
AND THAT JUST WON'T DO.
DEAR, YOUNG, CURIOUS ALICE... YOU KILLED MISTER FATALE... MY PERFECT BUTCHER...
BUT NOW IT'S TIME FOR A ***NEW*** BUTCHER IN BLACK...
SOMEONE WHO WILL BE RUTHLESS IN THEIR MAYHEM.
...NO... I DON'T WANT TO...
NOT ***YOU,*** WARREN.
YOU'VE DISAPPOINTED ME FOR ***TOO LONG.***
THIS HONOR FALLS...

ON AGENT **ABIGAIL BARKER.**

NNNNOOOO!!!!

DON'T CRY, PET.

YOU'VE DONE SUCH A GREAT JOB SO FAR... YOU DID *EXACTLY* WHAT I WANTED YOU TO DO WHEN YOU KILLED AGENT CARROLL...

I DON'T WANT THIS...

I WANT MY OLD LIFE BACK!

NNNOOOOOOOOOOOOOOOOOOOOC

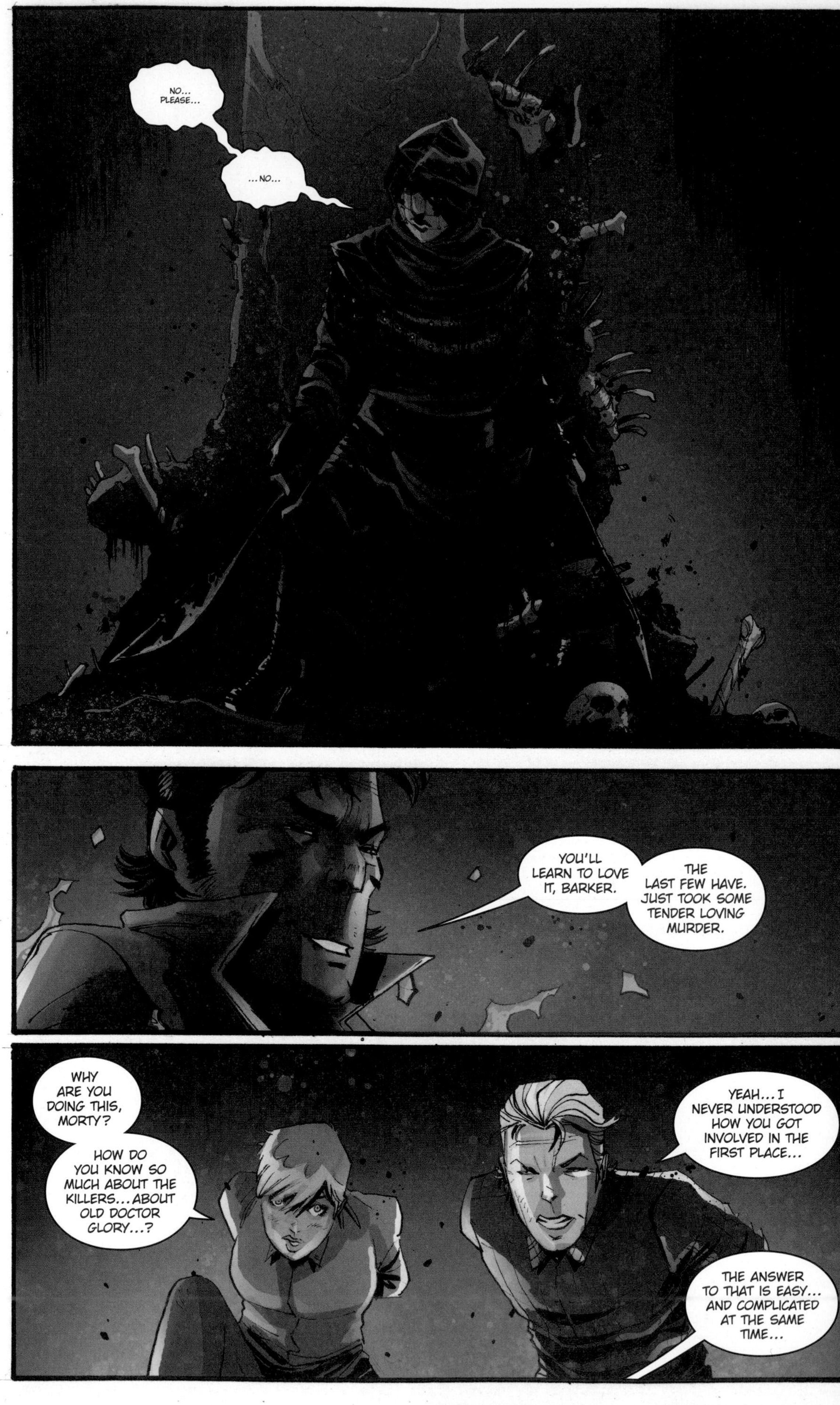
NO... PLEASE...
...NO...
YOU'LL LEARN TO LOVE IT, BARKER.
THE LAST FEW HAVE. JUST TOOK SOME TENDER LOVING MURDER.
WHY ARE YOU DOING THIS, MORTY?
HOW DO YOU KNOW SO MUCH ABOUT THE KILLERS...ABOUT OLD DOCTOR GLORY...?
YEAH... I NEVER UNDERSTOOD HOW YOU GOT INVOLVED IN THE FIRST PLACE...
THE ANSWER TO THAT IS EASY... AND COMPLICATED AT THE SAME TIME...

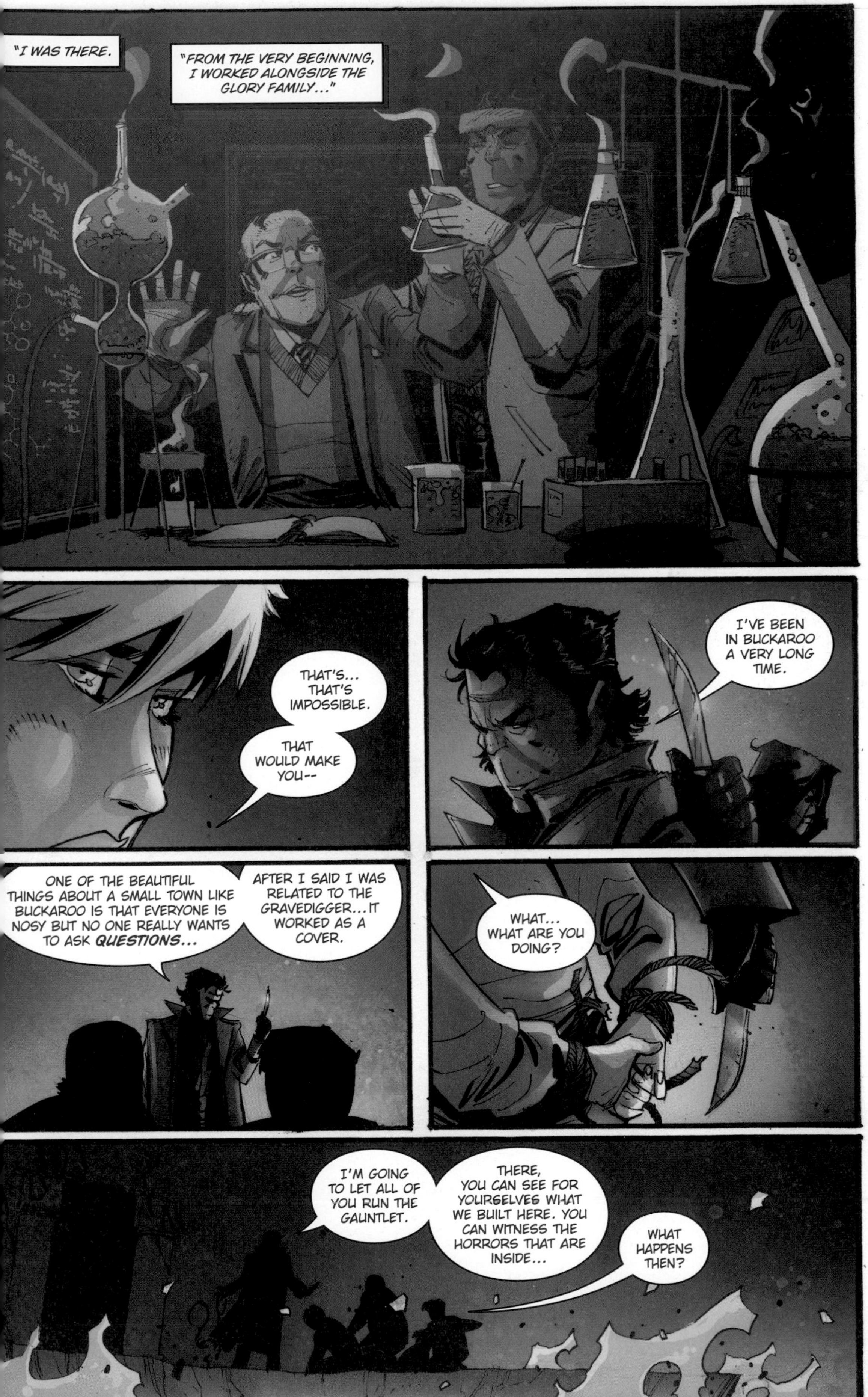
"I WAS THERE.
"FROM THE VERY BEGINNING, I WORKED ALONGSIDE THE GLORY FAMILY..."
THAT'S... THAT'S IMPOSSIBLE.
THAT WOULD MAKE YOU--
I'VE BEEN IN BUCKAROO A VERY LONG TIME.
ONE OF THE BEAUTIFUL THINGS ABOUT A SMALL TOWN LIKE BUCKAROO IS THAT EVERYONE IS NOSY BUT NO ONE REALLY WANTS TO ASK QUESTIONS...
AFTER I SAID I WAS RELATED TO THE GRAVEDIGGER... IT WORKED AS A COVER.
WHAT... WHAT ARE YOU DOING?
I'M GOING TO LET ALL OF YOU RUN THE GAUNTLET.
THERE, YOU CAN SEE FOR YOURSELVES WHAT WE BUILT HERE. YOU CAN WITNESS THE HORRORS THAT ARE INSIDE...
WHAT HAPPENS THEN?

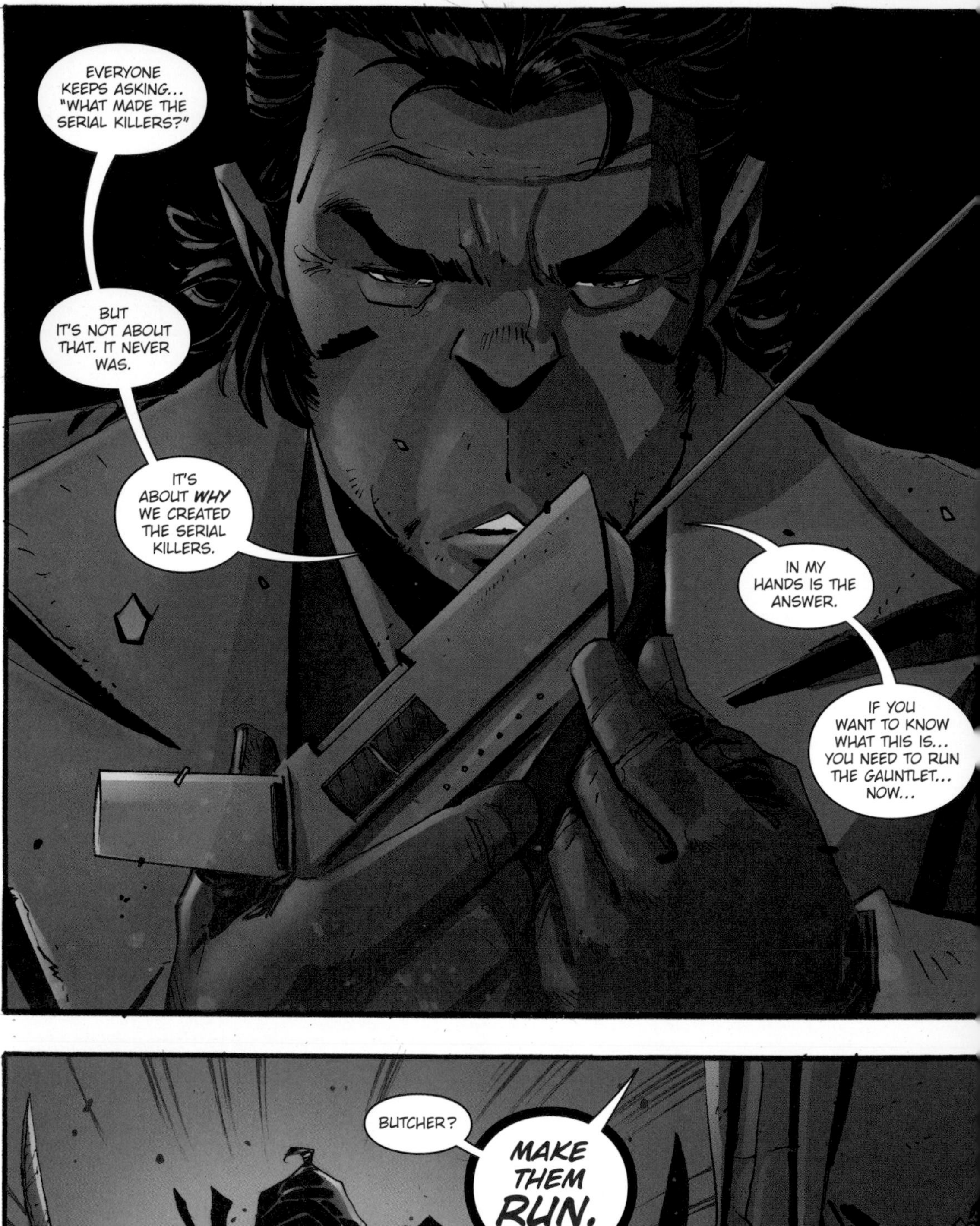
EVERYONE KEEPS ASKING... "WHAT MADE THE SERIAL KILLERS?"
BUT IT'S NOT ABOUT THAT. IT NEVER WAS.
IT'S ABOUT *WHY* WE CREATED THE SERIAL KILLERS.
IN MY HANDS IS THE ANSWER.
IF YOU WANT TO KNOW WHAT THIS IS... YOU NEED TO RUN THE GAUNTLET... NOW...

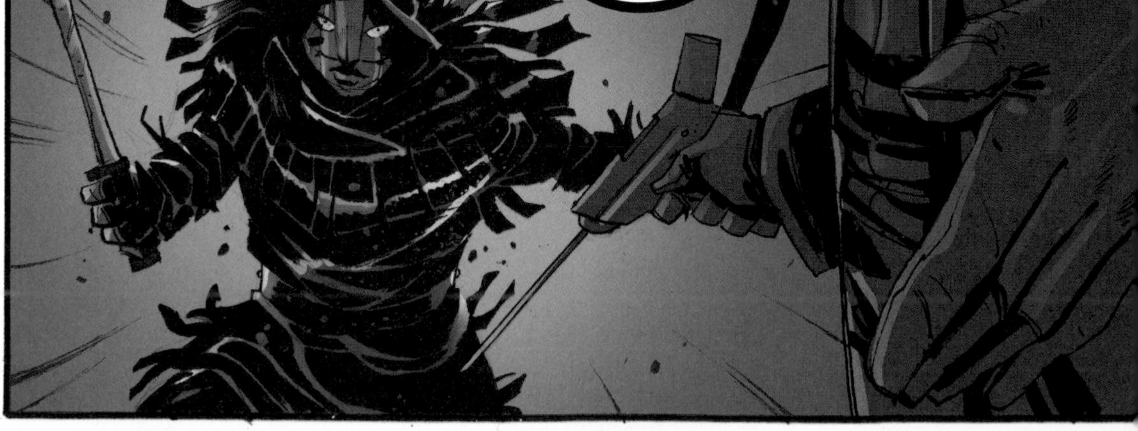
BUTCHER?
MAKE THEM RUN.

ISSUE THIRTY

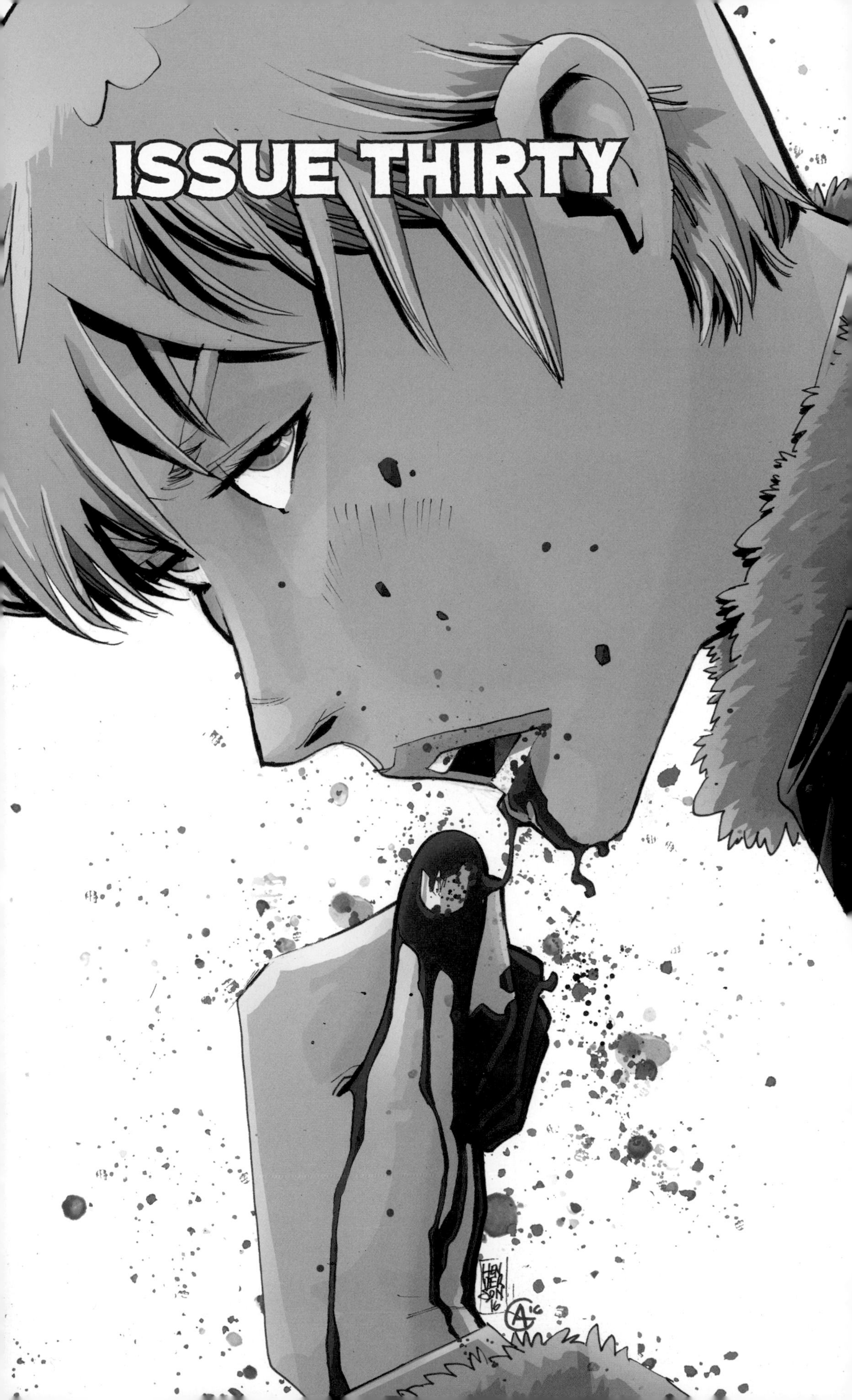

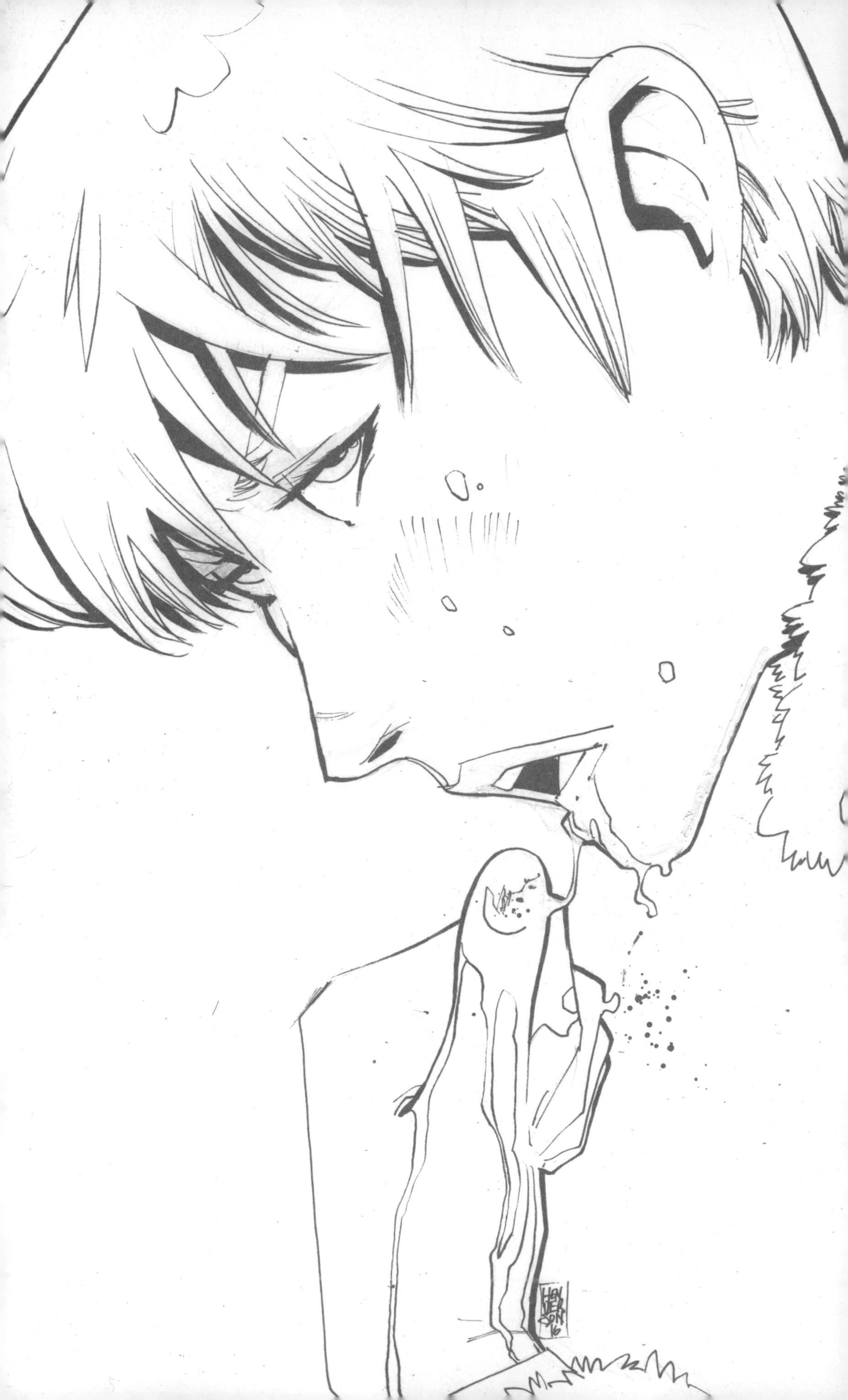

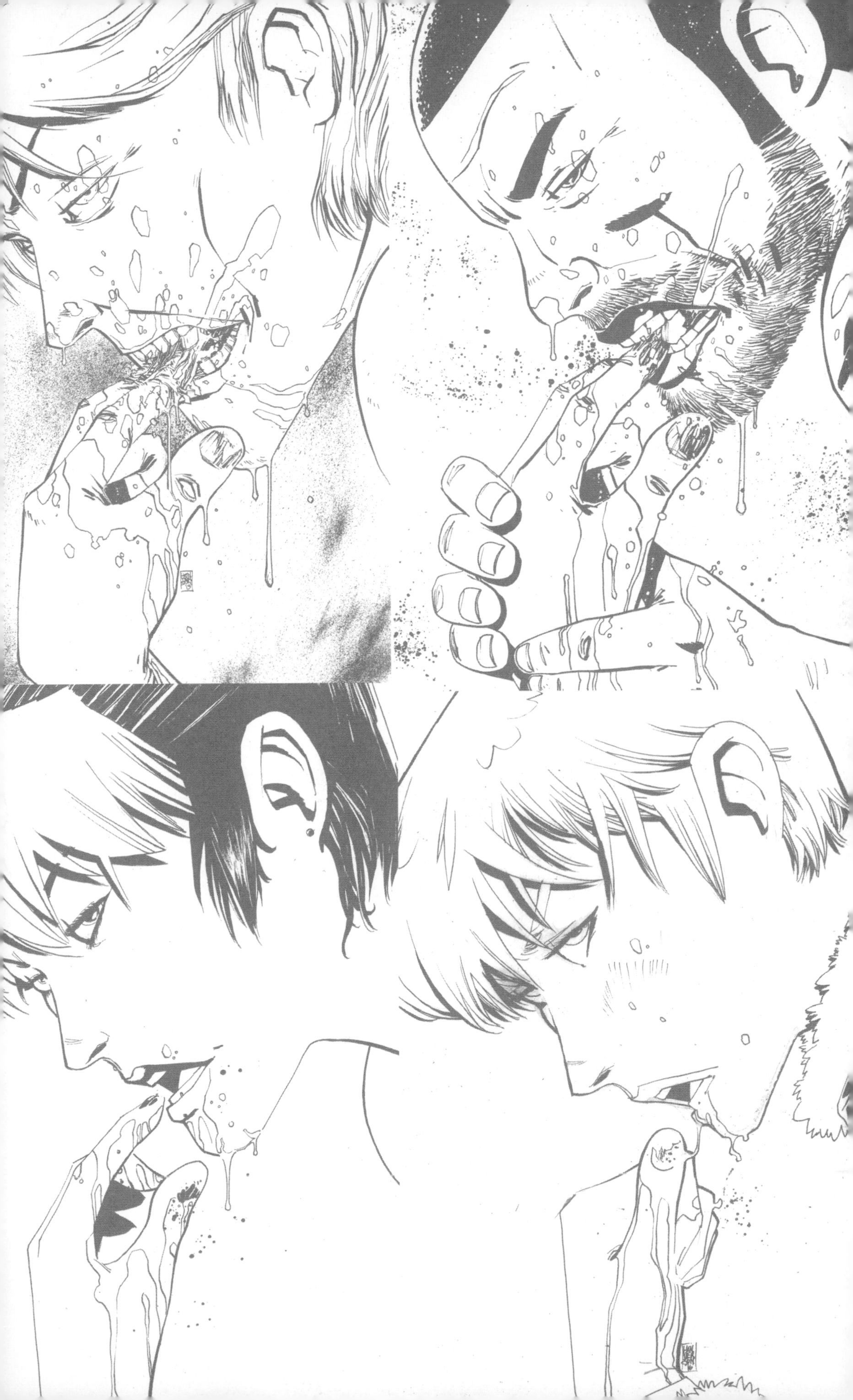

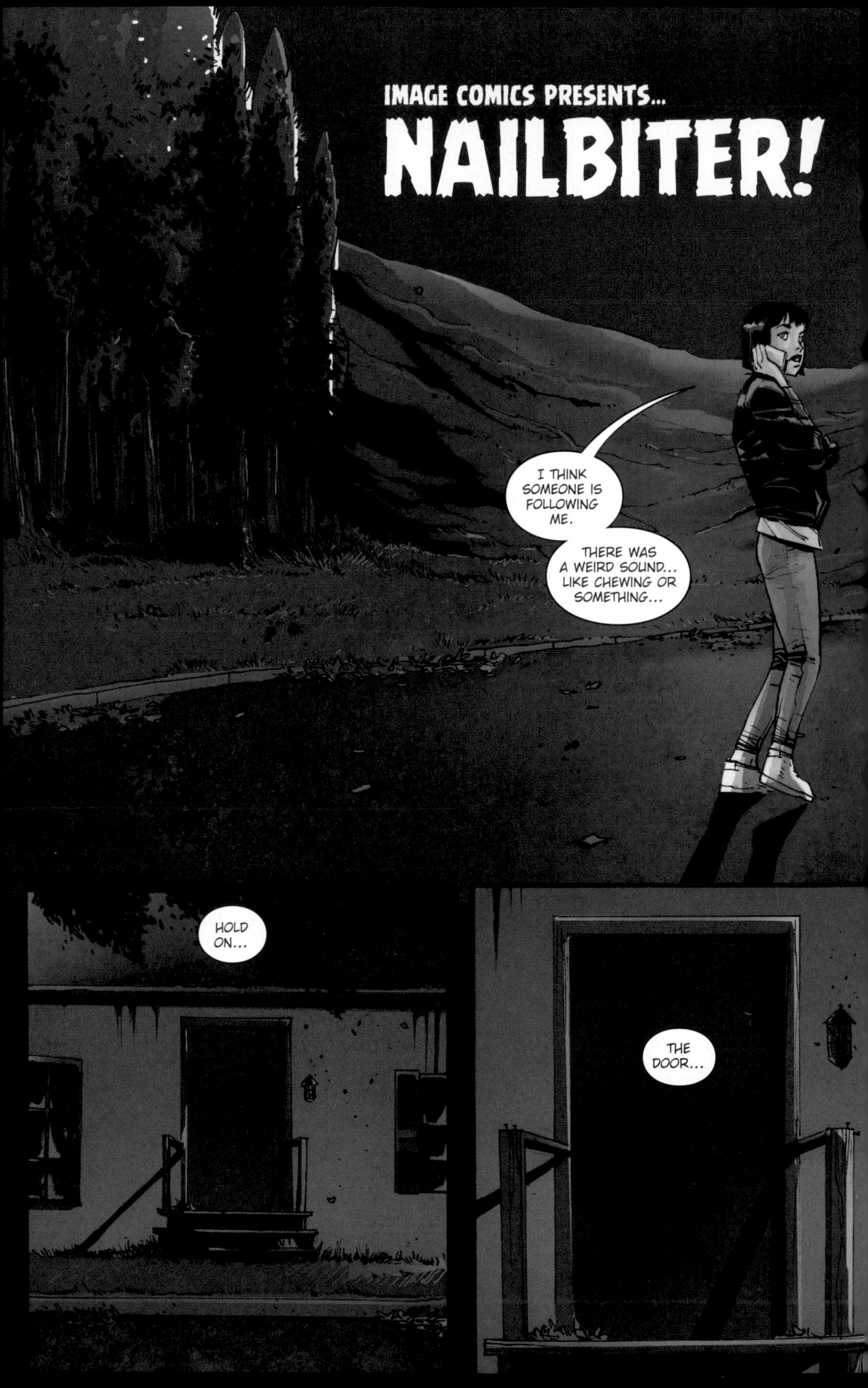
IMAGE COMICS PRESENTS...
NAILBITER!
I THINK SOMEONE IS FOLLOWING ME.
THERE WAS A WEIRD SOUND... LIKE CHEWING OR SOMETHING...
HOLD ON...
THE DOOR...

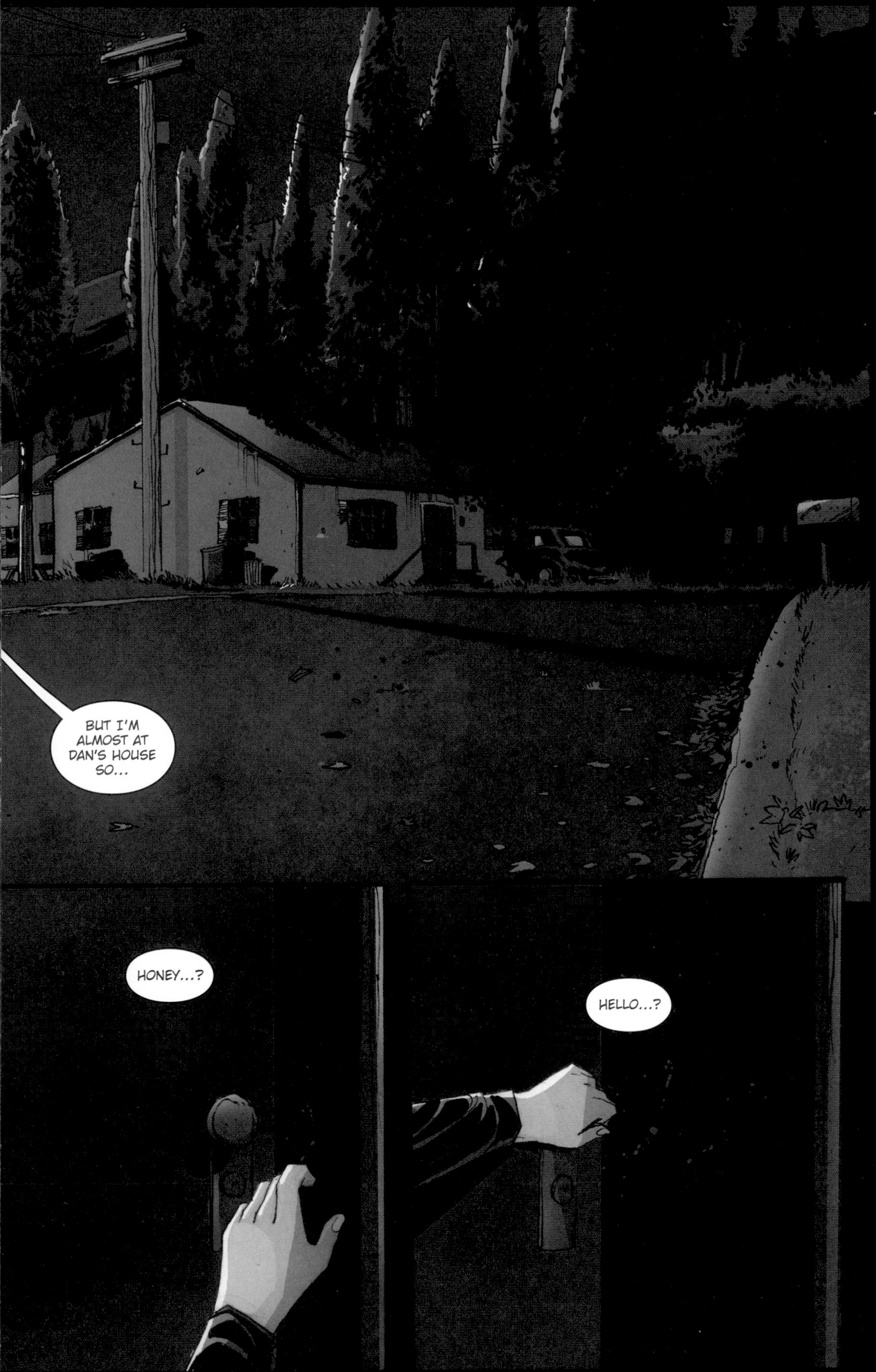
BUT I'M ALMOST AT DAN'S HOUSE SO...
HONEY...?
HELLO...?

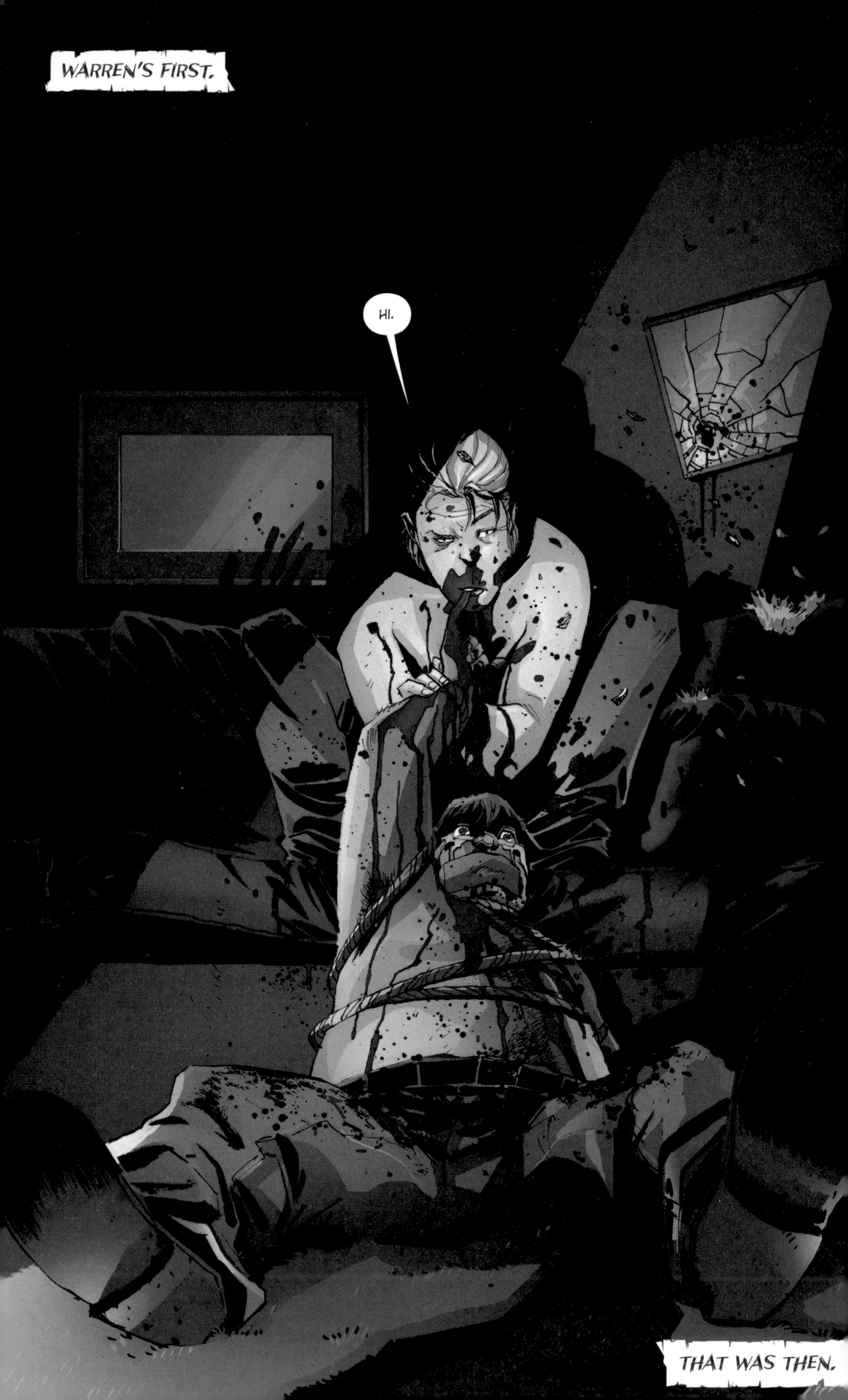
WARREN'S FIRST.
HI.
THAT WAS THEN.

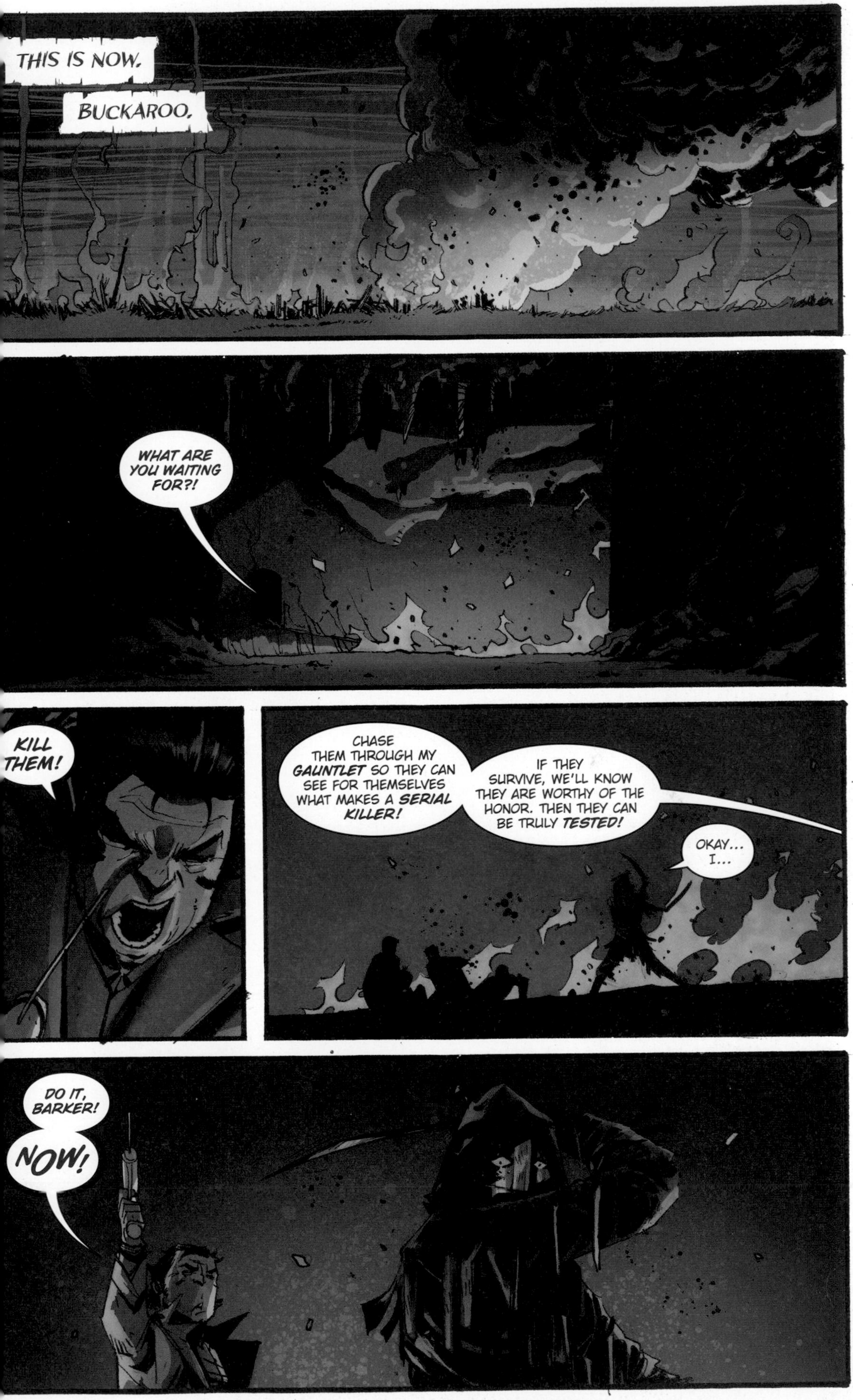
THIS IS NOW.
BUCKAROO.
WHAT ARE YOU WAITING FOR?!
KILL THEM!
CHASE THEM THROUGH MY GAUNTLET SO THEY CAN SEE FOR THEMSELVES WHAT MAKES A SERIAL KILLER!
IF THEY SURVIVE, WE'LL KNOW THEY ARE WORTHY OF THE HONOR. THEN THEY CAN BE TRULY TESTED!
OKAY... I...
DO IT, BARKER!
NOW!

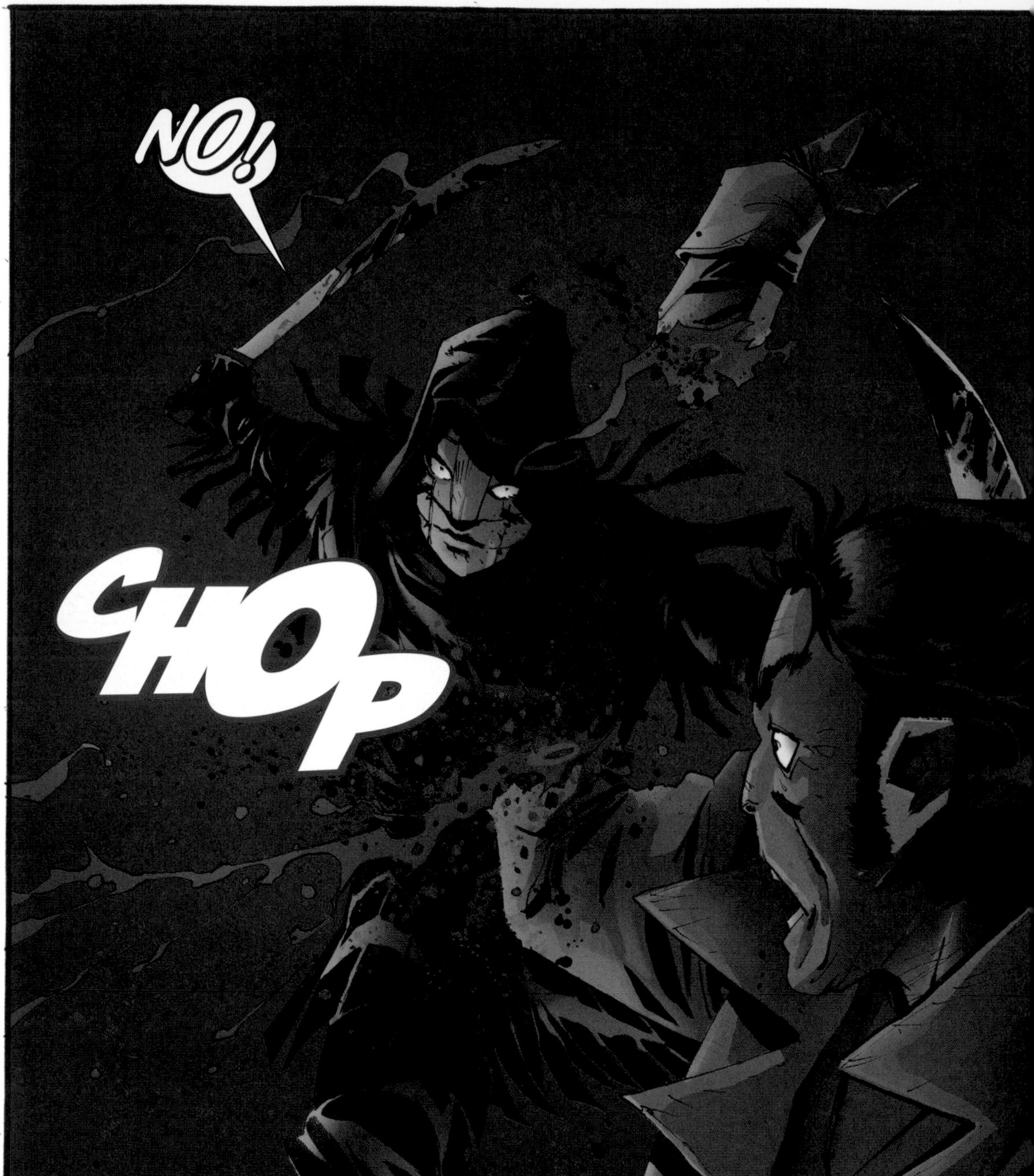
NO!
CHOP

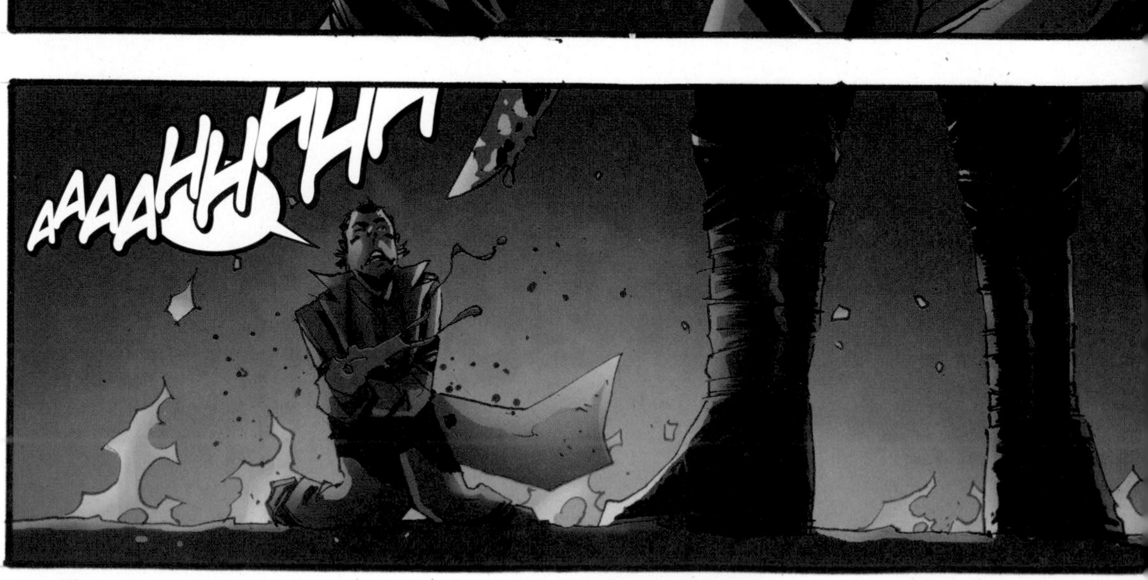
AAAAHHHHH

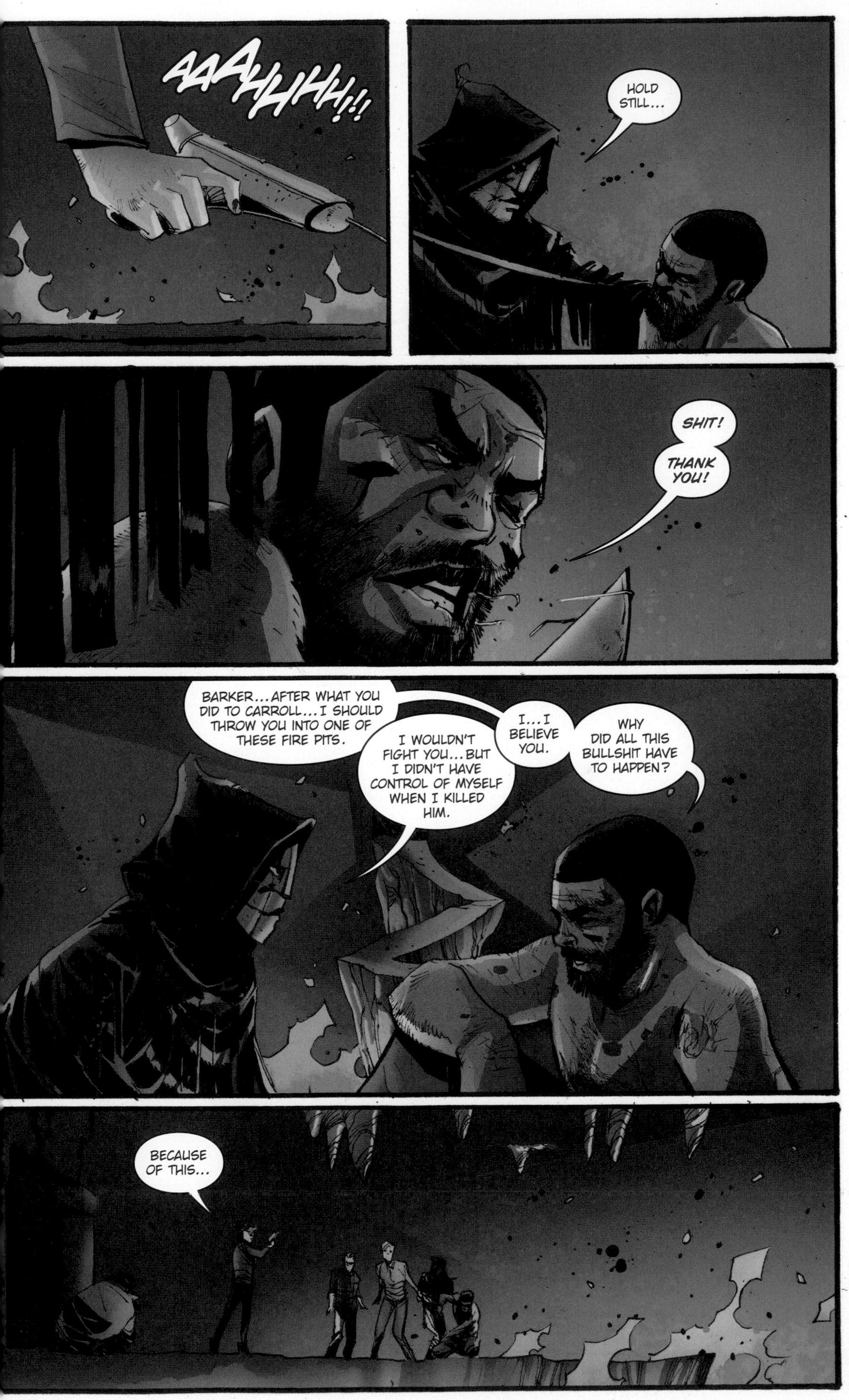
AAAHHHH!!!
HOLD STILL...
SHIT!
THANK YOU!
BARKER... AFTER WHAT YOU DID TO CARROLL... I SHOULD THROW YOU INTO ONE OF THESE FIRE PITS.
I WOULDN'T FIGHT YOU... BUT I DIDN'T HAVE CONTROL OF MYSELF WHEN I KILLED HIM.
I... I BELIEVE YOU.
WHY DID ALL THIS BULLSHIT HAVE TO HAPPEN?
BECAUSE OF THIS...

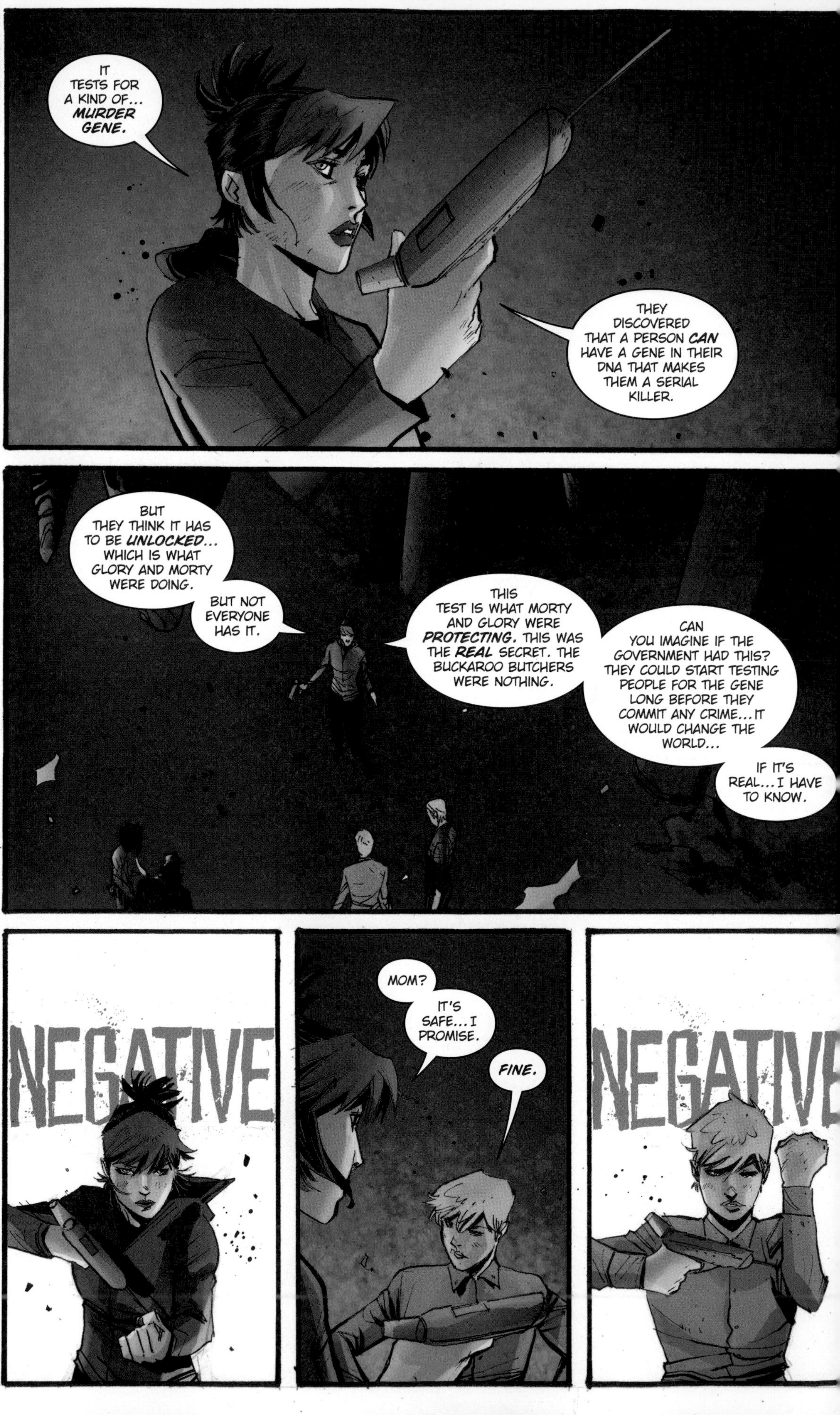
IT TESTS FOR A KIND OF... MURDER GENE.
THEY DISCOVERED THAT A PERSON CAN HAVE A GENE IN THEIR DNA THAT MAKES THEM A SERIAL KILLER.
BUT THEY THINK IT HAS TO BE UNLOCKED... WHICH IS WHAT GLORY AND MORTY WERE DOING.
BUT NOT EVERYONE HAS IT.
THIS TEST IS WHAT MORTY AND GLORY WERE PROTECTING. THIS WAS THE REAL SECRET. THE BUCKAROO BUTCHERS WERE NOTHING.
CAN YOU IMAGINE IF THE GOVERNMENT HAD THIS? THEY COULD START TESTING PEOPLE FOR THE GENE LONG BEFORE THEY COMMIT ANY CRIME... IT WOULD CHANGE THE WORLD...
IF IT'S REAL... I HAVE TO KNOW.
NEGATIVE
MOM?
IT'S SAFE... I PROMISE.
FINE.
NEGATIVE

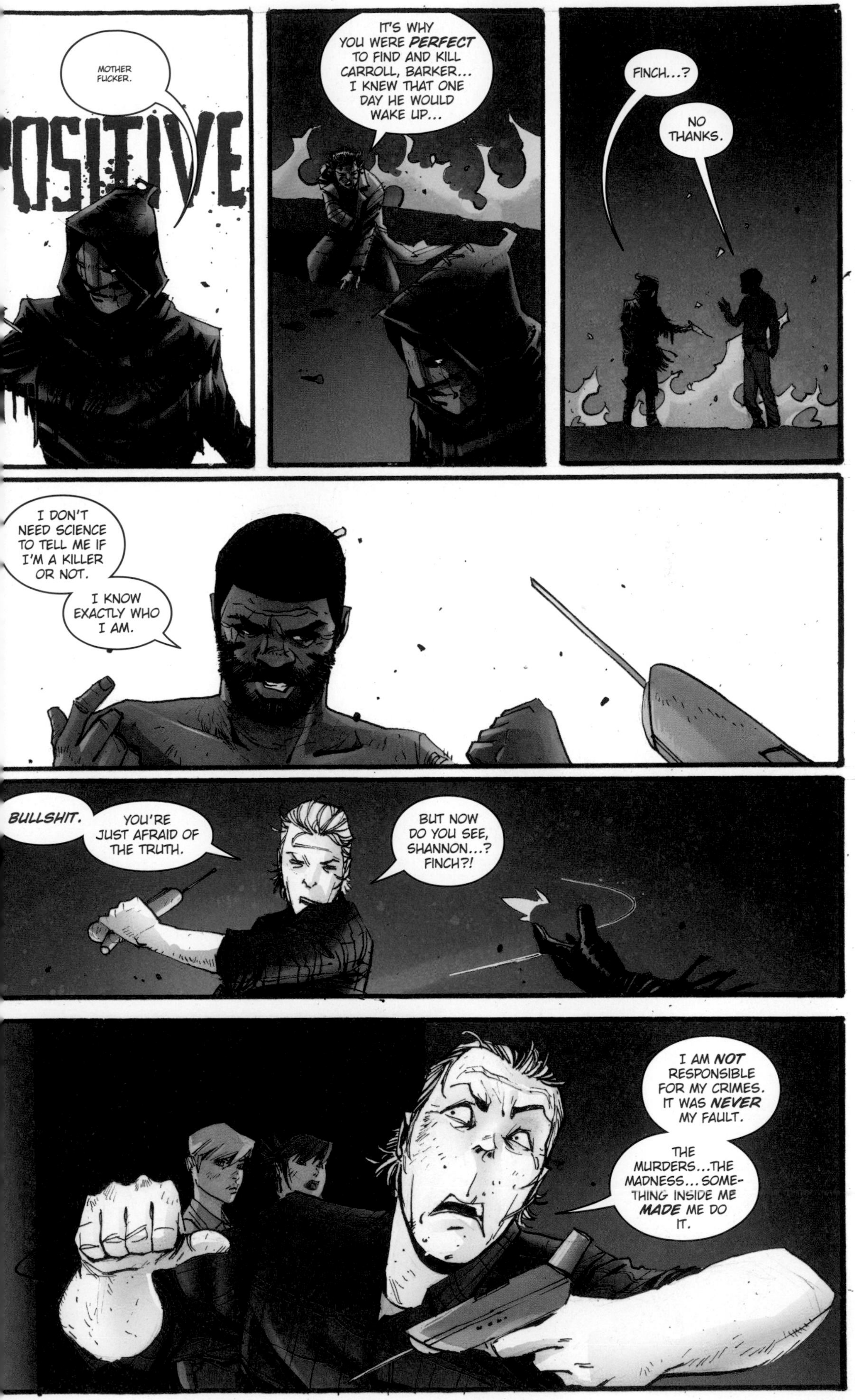

MOTHER FUCKER.
POSITIVE
IT'S WHY YOU WERE PERFECT TO FIND AND KILL CARROLL, BARKER... I KNEW THAT ONE DAY HE WOULD WAKE UP...
FINCH...?
NO THANKS.
I DON'T NEED SCIENCE TO TELL ME IF I'M A KILLER OR NOT.
I KNOW EXACTLY WHO I AM.
BULLSHIT.
YOU'RE JUST AFRAID OF THE TRUTH.
BUT NOW DO YOU SEE, SHANNON...? FINCH?!
I AM NOT RESPONSIBLE FOR MY CRIMES. IT WAS NEVER MY FAULT.
THE MURDERS...THE MADNESS... SOMETHING INSIDE ME MADE ME DO IT.

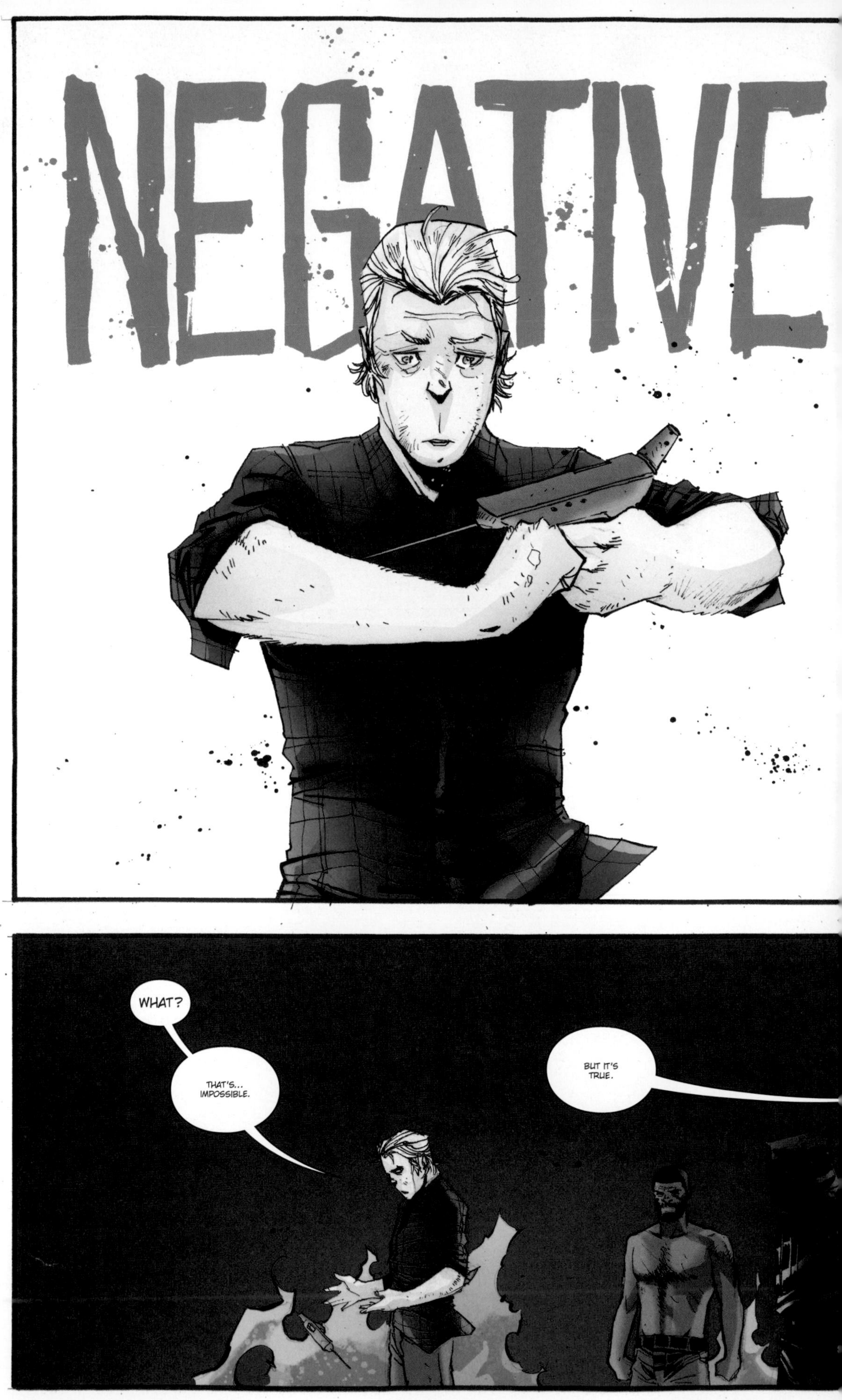
NEGATIVE
WHAT?
THAT'S... IMPOSSIBLE.
BUT IT'S TRUE.

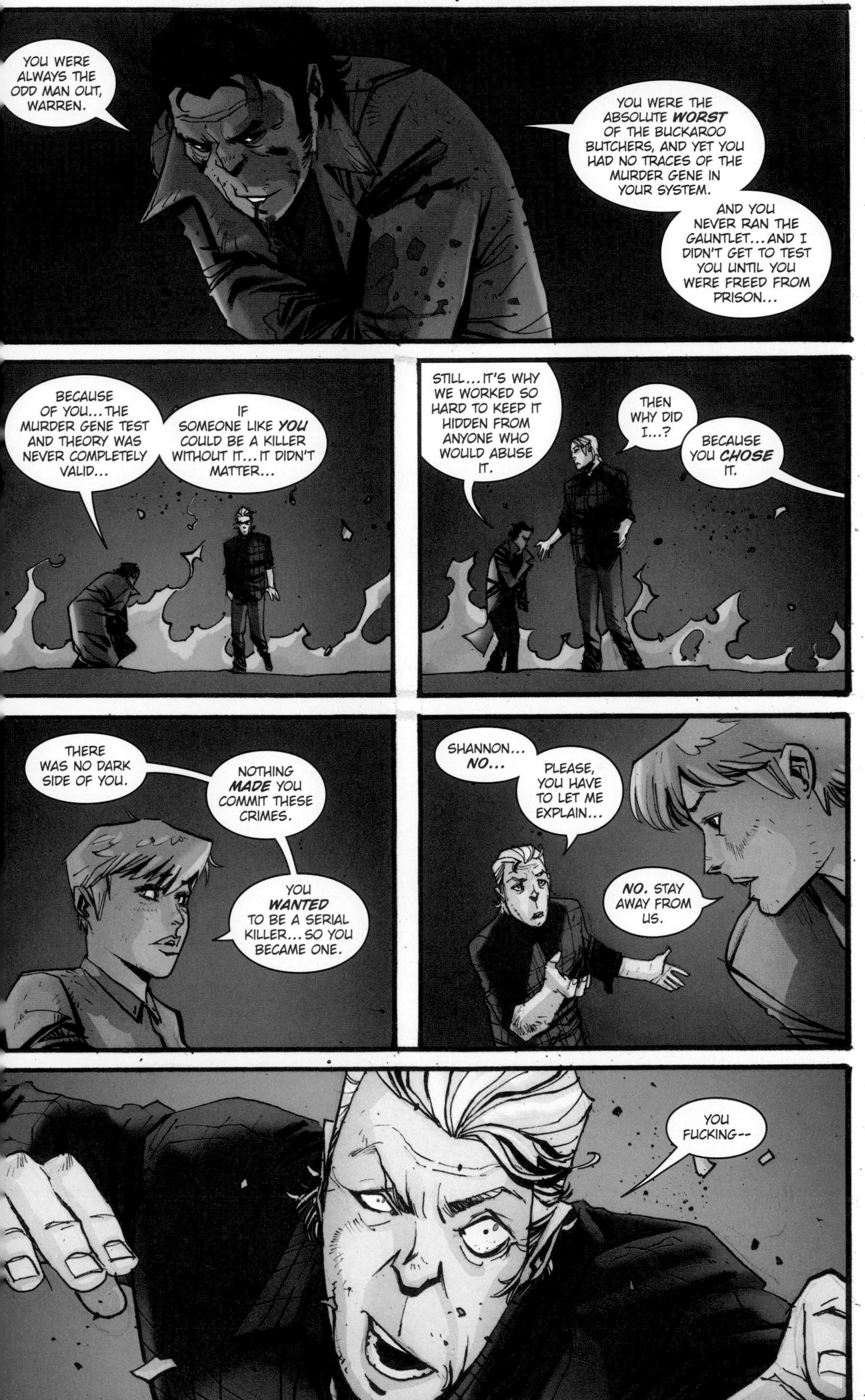

YOU WERE ALWAYS THE ODD MAN OUT, WARREN.
YOU WERE THE ABSOLUTE WORST OF THE BUCKAROO BUTCHERS, AND YET YOU HAD NO TRACES OF THE MURDER GENE IN YOUR SYSTEM.
AND YOU NEVER RAN THE GAUNTLET... AND I DIDN'T GET TO TEST YOU UNTIL YOU WERE FREED FROM PRISON...
BECAUSE OF YOU... THE MURDER GENE TEST AND THEORY WAS NEVER COMPLETELY VALID...
IF SOMEONE LIKE YOU COULD BE A KILLER WITHOUT IT... IT DIDN'T MATTER...
STILL... IT'S WHY WE WORKED SO HARD TO KEEP IT HIDDEN FROM ANYONE WHO WOULD ABUSE IT.
THEN WHY DID I...?
BECAUSE YOU CHOSE IT.
THERE WAS NO DARK SIDE OF YOU.
NOTHING MADE YOU COMMIT THESE CRIMES.
YOU WANTED TO BE A SERIAL KILLER... SO YOU BECAME ONE.
SHANNON... NO...
PLEASE, YOU HAVE TO LET ME EXPLAIN...
NO. STAY AWAY FROM US.
YOU FUCKING--

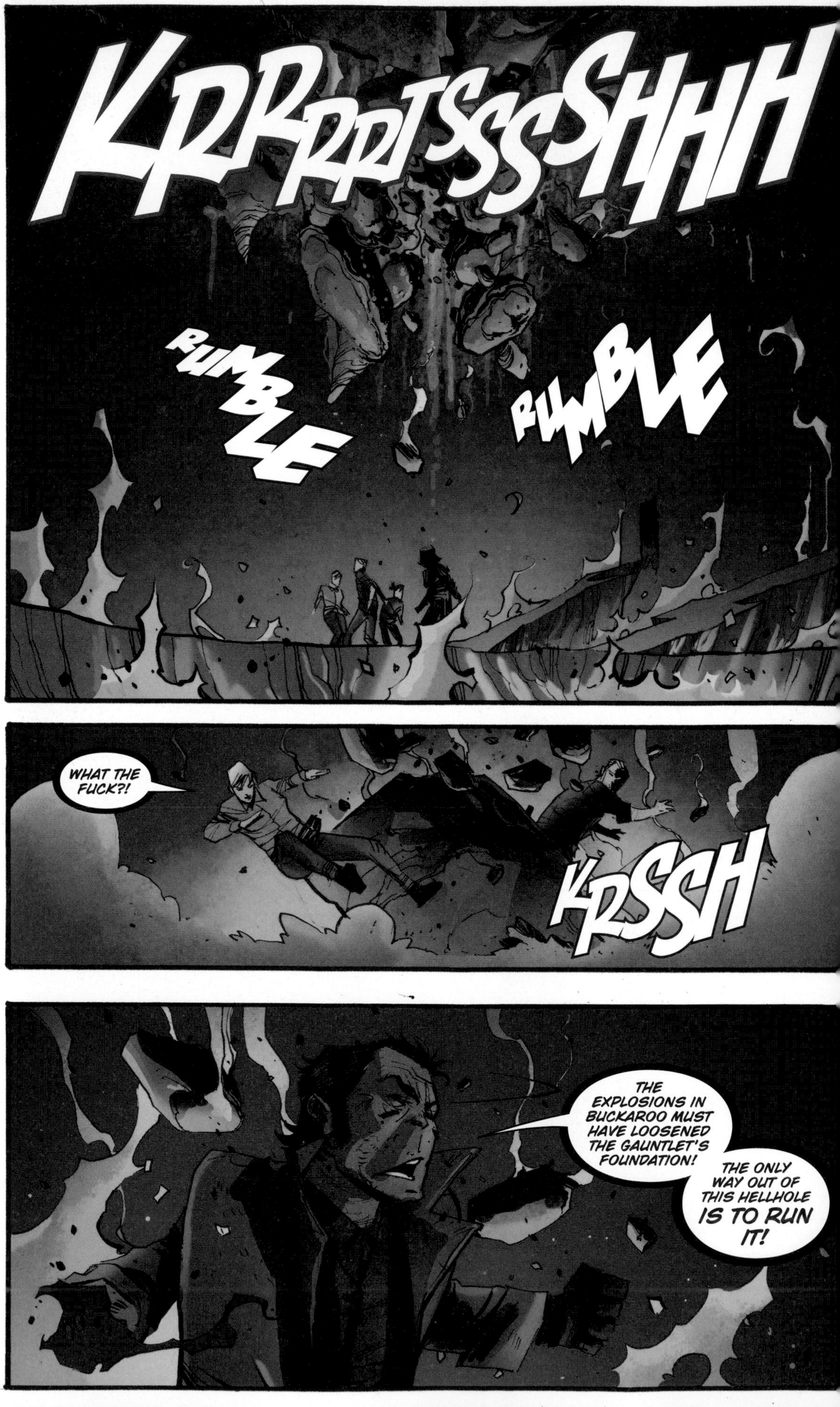
KRRRRISSSSHHH
RUMBLE
RUMBLE
WHAT THE FUCK?!
KRSSH
THE EXPLOSIONS IN BUCKAROO MUST HAVE LOOSENED THE GAUNTLET'S FOUNDATION!
THE ONLY WAY OUT OF THIS HELLHOLE IS TO RUN IT!

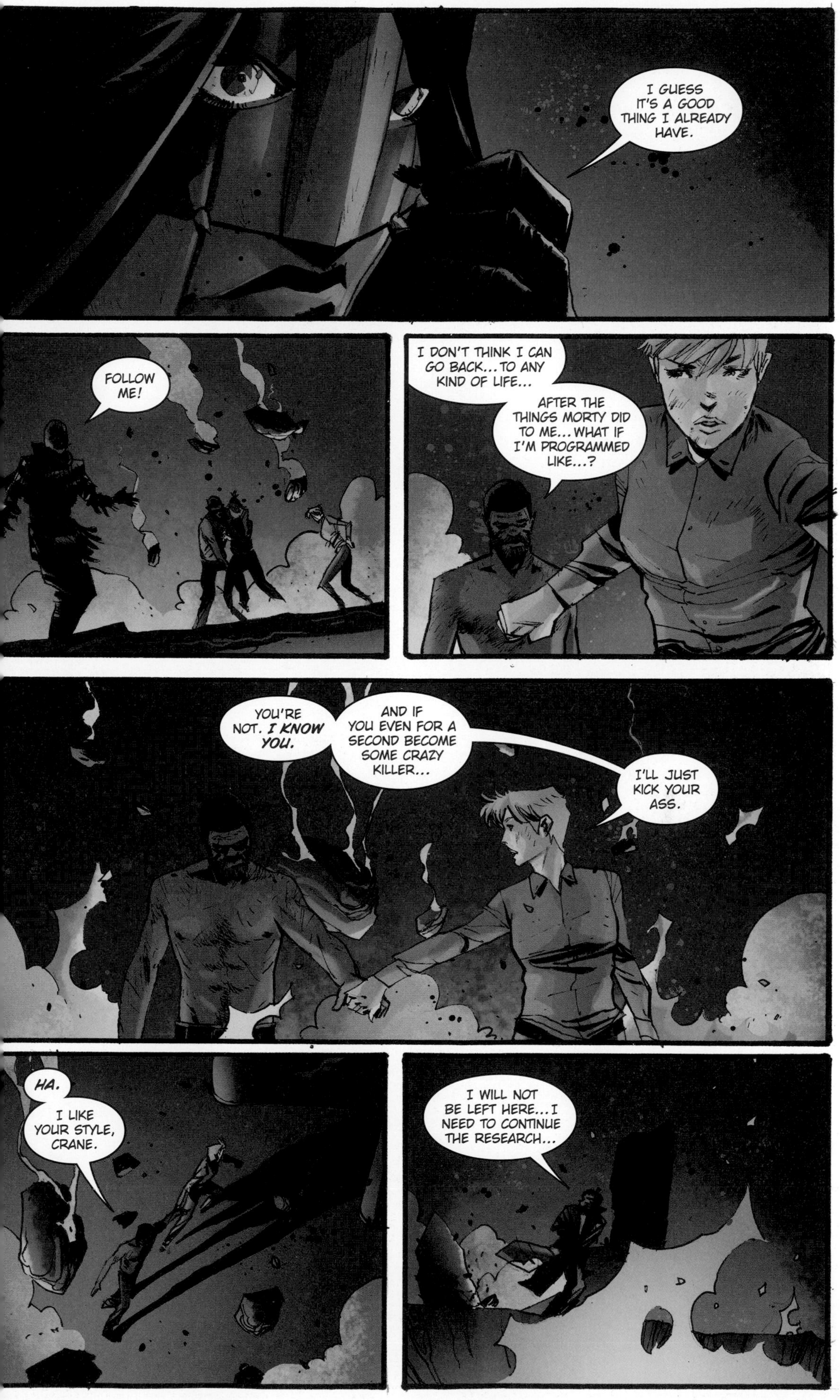
I GUESS IT'S A GOOD THING I ALREADY HAVE.
FOLLOW ME!
I DON'T THINK I CAN GO BACK... TO ANY KIND OF LIFE...
AFTER THE THINGS MORTY DID TO ME... WHAT IF I'M PROGRAMMED LIKE...?
YOU'RE NOT. *I KNOW YOU.*
AND IF YOU EVEN FOR A SECOND BECOME SOME CRAZY KILLER...
I'LL JUST KICK YOUR ASS.
HA.
I LIKE YOUR STYLE, CRANE.
I WILL NOT BE LEFT HERE... I NEED TO CONTINUE THE RESEARCH...

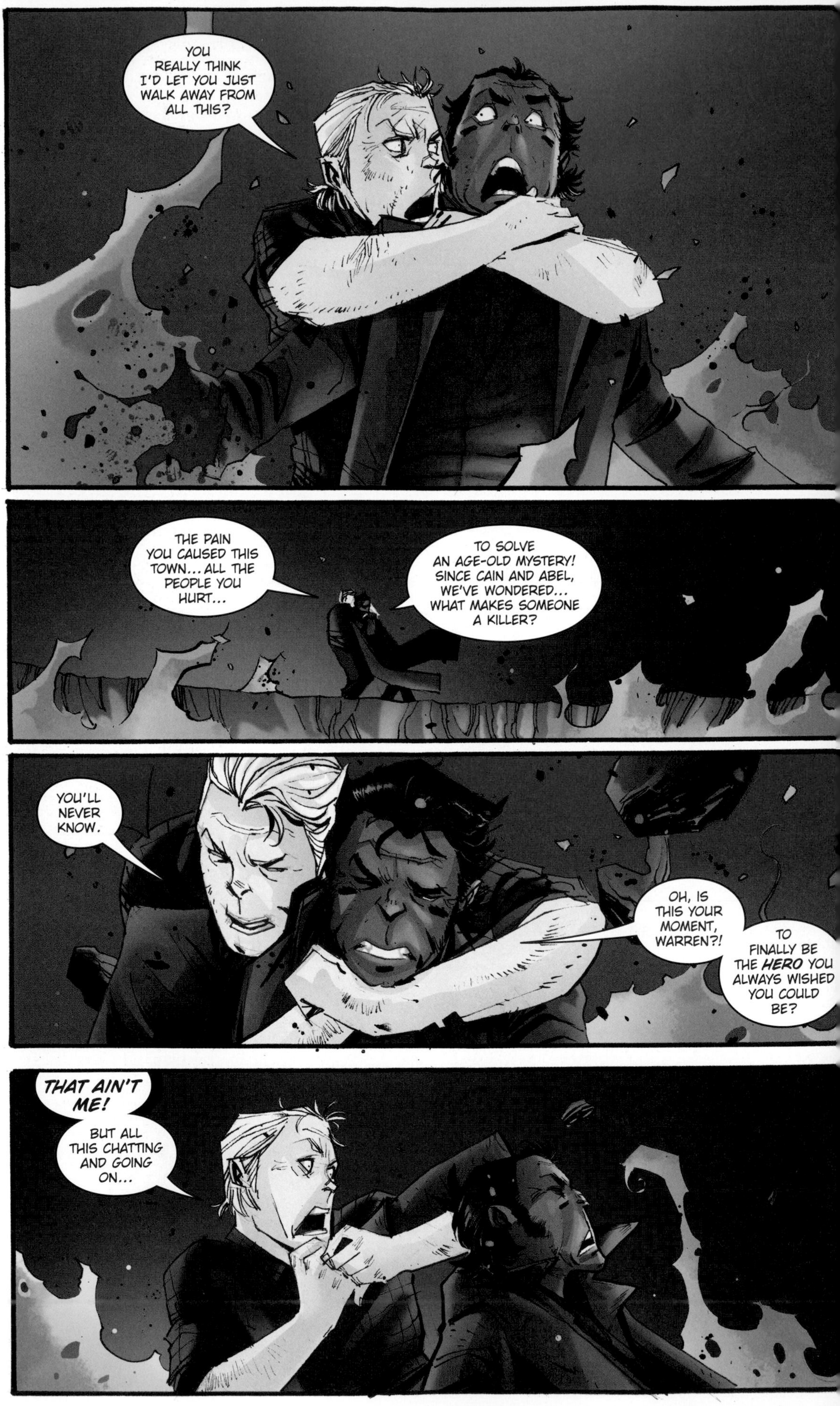
YOU REALLY THINK I'D LET YOU JUST WALK AWAY FROM ALL THIS?
THE PAIN YOU CAUSED THIS TOWN... ALL THE PEOPLE YOU HURT...
TO SOLVE AN AGE-OLD MYSTERY! SINCE CAIN AND ABEL, WE'VE WONDERED... WHAT MAKES SOMEONE A KILLER?
YOU'LL NEVER KNOW.
OH, IS THIS YOUR MOMENT, WARREN?!
TO FINALLY BE THE HERO YOU ALWAYS WISHED YOU COULD BE?
THAT AIN'T ME!
BUT ALL THIS CHATTING AND GOING ON...

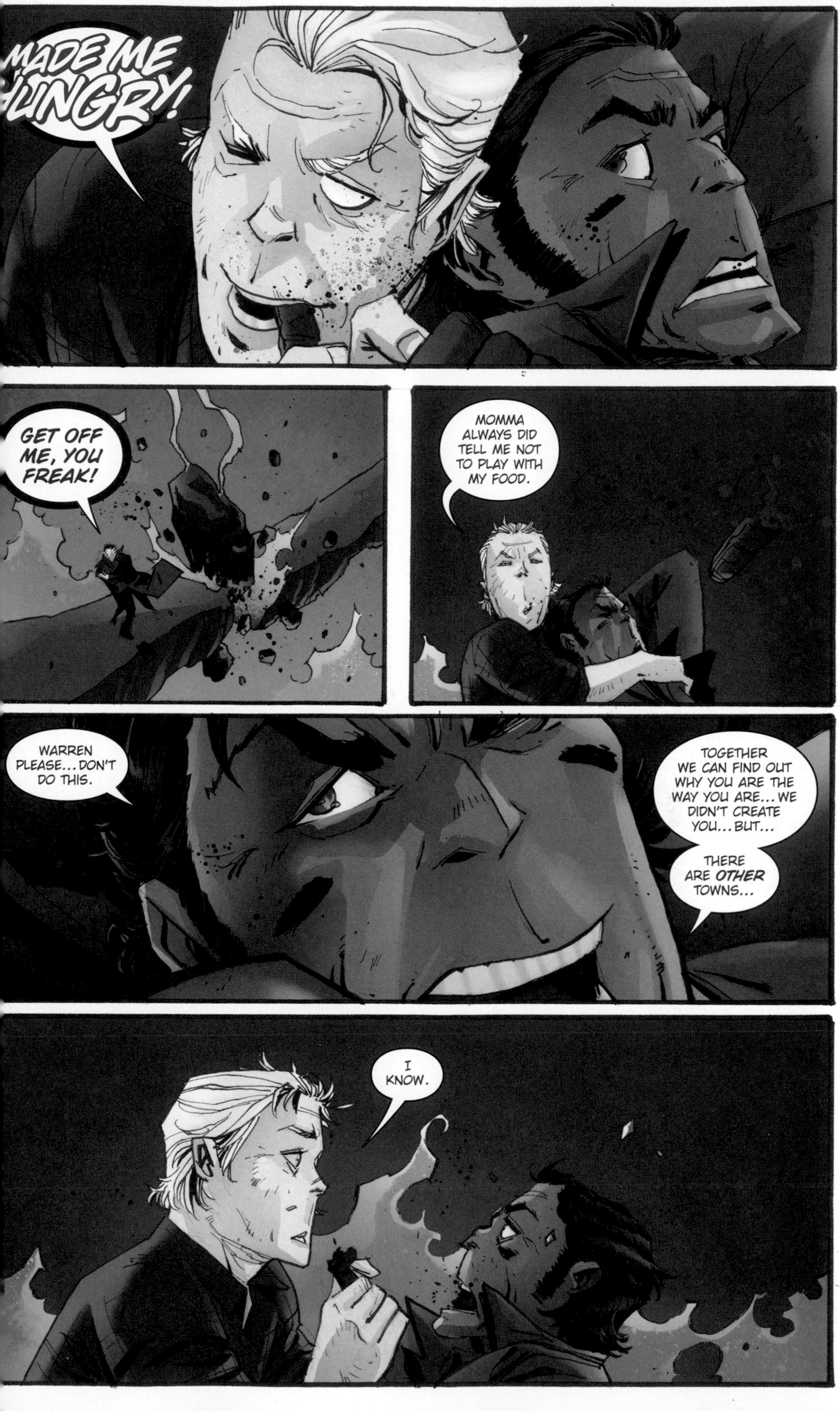
MADE ME HUNGRY!
GET OFF ME, YOU FREAK!
MOMMA ALWAYS DID TELL ME NOT TO PLAY WITH MY FOOD.
WARREN PLEASE... DON'T DO THIS.
TOGETHER WE CAN FIND OUT WHY YOU ARE THE WAY YOU ARE... WE DIDN'T CREATE YOU... BUT...
THERE ARE *OTHER* TOWNS...
I KNOW.

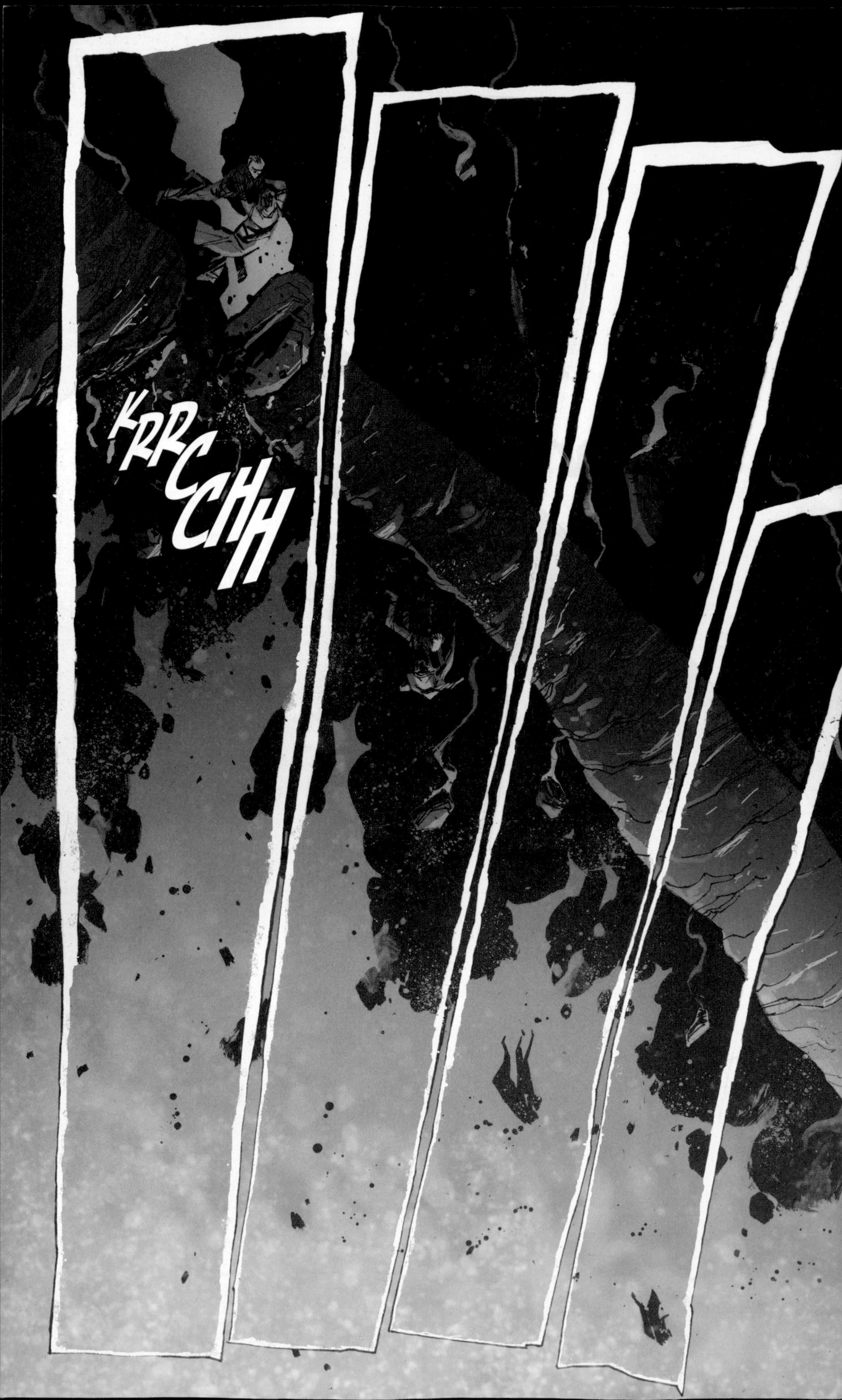
KRRCHH

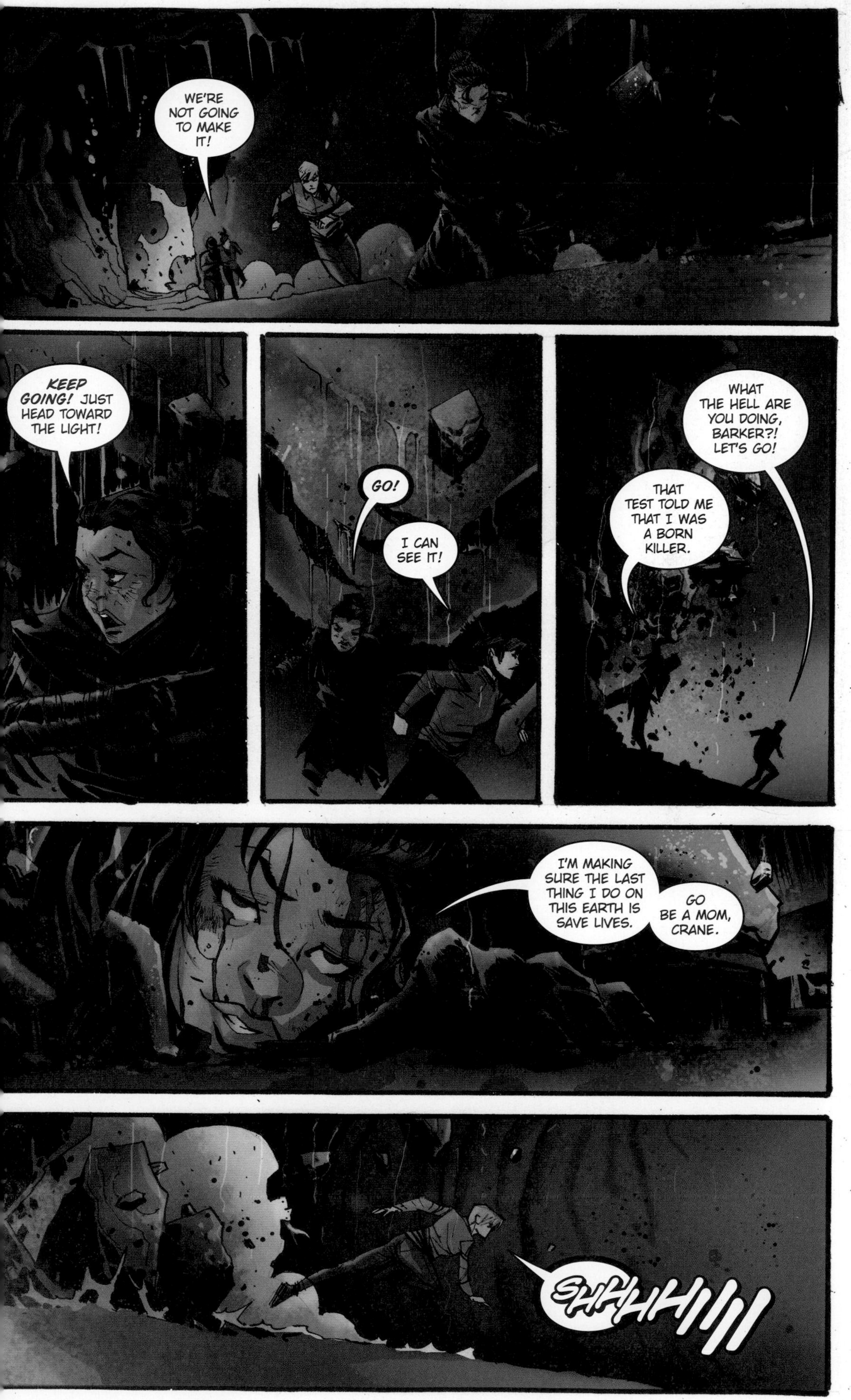
WE'RE NOT GOING TO MAKE IT!
KEEP GOING! JUST HEAD TOWARD THE LIGHT!
GO!
I CAN SEE IT!
WHAT THE HELL ARE YOU DOING, BARKER?! LET'S GO!
THAT TEST TOLD ME THAT I WAS A BORN KILLER.
I'M MAKING SURE THE LAST THING I DO ON THIS EARTH IS SAVE LIVES.
GO BE A MOM, CRANE.
SHHHHH

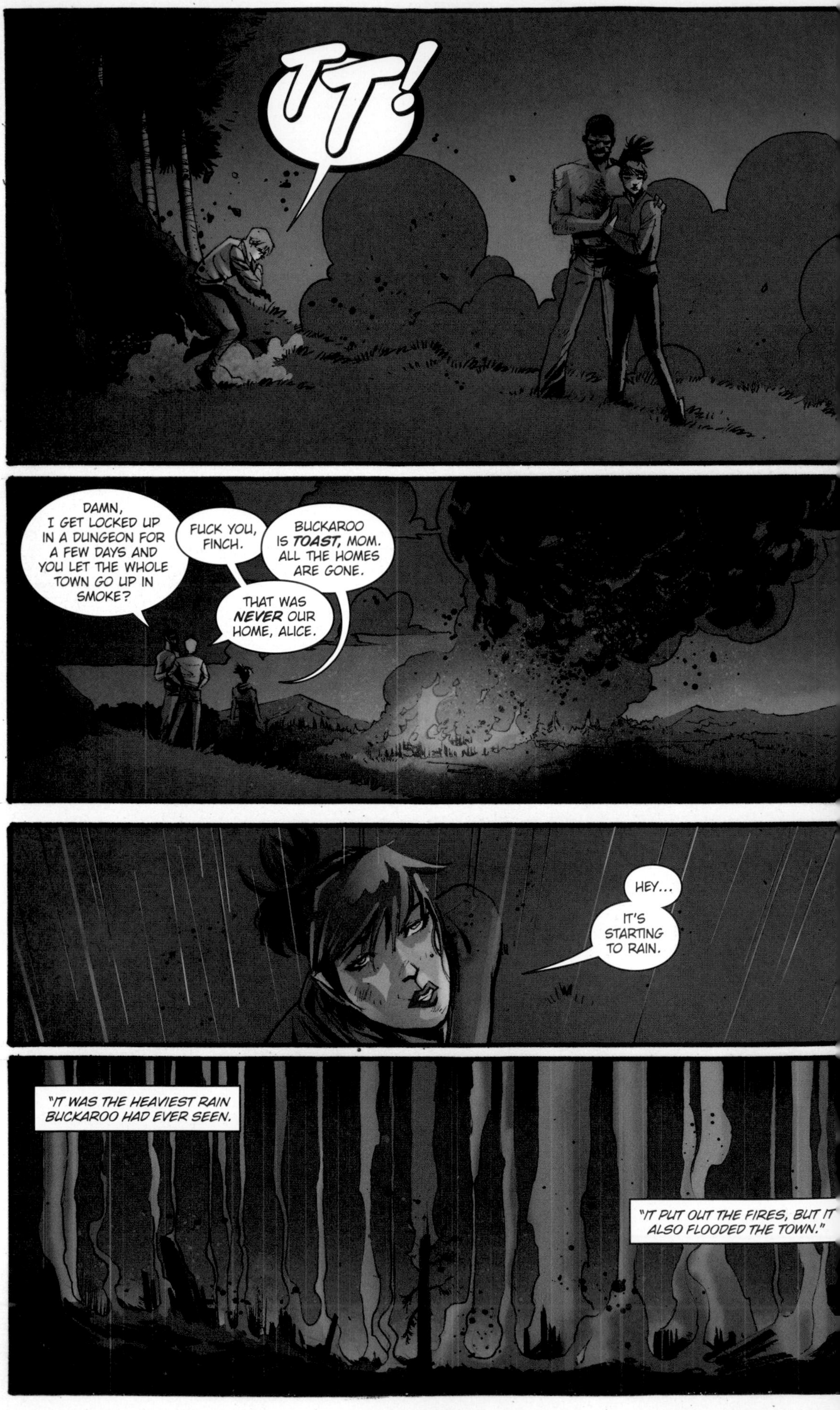
TT!
DAMN, I GET LOCKED UP IN A DUNGEON FOR A FEW DAYS AND YOU LET THE WHOLE TOWN GO UP IN SMOKE?
FUCK YOU, FINCH.
BUCKAROO IS TOAST, MOM. ALL THE HOMES ARE GONE.
THAT WAS NEVER OUR HOME, ALICE.
HEY...
IT'S STARTING TO RAIN.
"IT WAS THE HEAVIEST RAIN BUCKAROO HAD EVER SEEN.
"IT PUT OUT THE FIRES, BUT IT ALSO FLOODED THE TOWN."

"THE FEDS SHOWED UP AND OFFICIALLY LISTED BUCKAROO AS A DISASTER AREA... THEY SEARCHED FOR WARREN, MORTY AND BARKER IN THE TUNNELS...

"AND THEY FOUND A *LOT* OF BODIES.

"NOT JUST PEOPLE WHO DIED IN THE FIRES. THEY FOUND A LOT OF VICTIMS INSIDE THE TUNNELS AS WELL. NO IDEA HOW OLD. IT'S GOING TO TAKE YEARS TO PROCESS IT ALL.

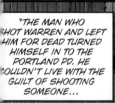

"THE MAN WHO SHOT WARREN AND LEFT HIM FOR DEAD TURNED HIMSELF IN TO THE PORTLAND PD. HE COULDN'T LIVE WITH THE GUILT OF SHOOTING SOMEONE...

"HE GOT A SLAP ON THE WRIST... BECAUSE, Y'KNOW... IT WAS WARREN.

"MY MOM, FINCH AND I MADE A PACT TO TELL PEOPLE ABOUT THE GAUNTLET THAT DROVE THE BUTCHERS MAD... BUT NEVER ABOUT THE TEST..."

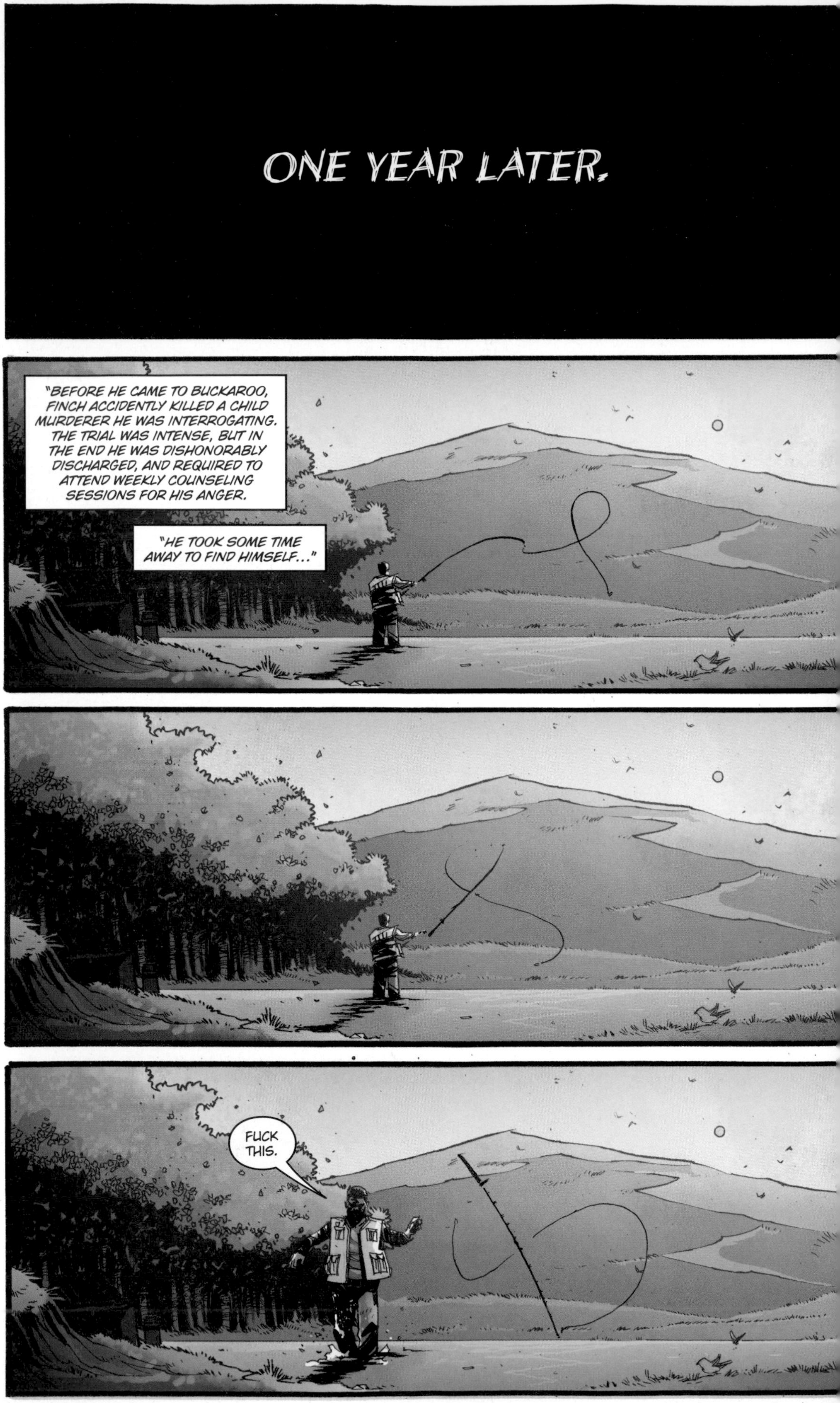
ONE YEAR LATER.
"BEFORE HE CAME TO BUCKAROO, FINCH ACCIDENTLY KILLED A CHILD MURDERER HE WAS INTERROGATING. THE TRIAL WAS INTENSE, BUT IN THE END HE WAS DISHONORABLY DISCHARGED, AND REQUIRED TO ATTEND WEEKLY COUNSELING SESSIONS FOR HIS ANGER.
"HE TOOK SOME TIME AWAY TO FIND HIMSELF..."
FUCK THIS.

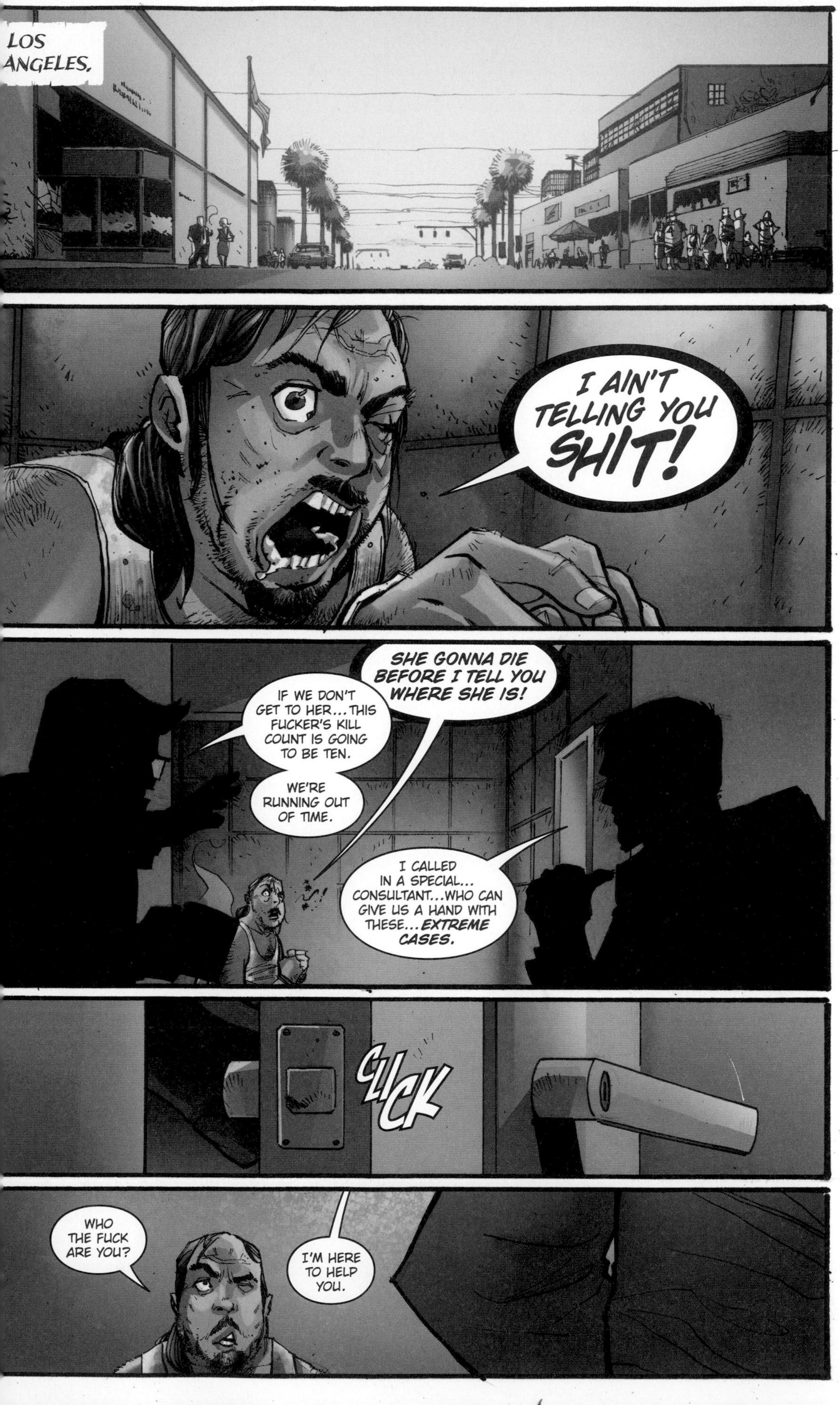
LOS ANGELES.
I AIN'T TELLING YOU SHIT!
IF WE DON'T GET TO HER... THIS FUCKER'S KILL COUNT IS GOING TO BE TEN.
SHE GONNA DIE BEFORE I TELL YOU WHERE SHE IS!
WE'RE RUNNING OUT OF TIME.
I CALLED IN A SPECIAL... CONSULTANT... WHO CAN GIVE US A HAND WITH THESE... *EXTREME* *CASES.*
CLICK
WHO THE FUCK ARE YOU?
I'M HERE TO HELP YOU.

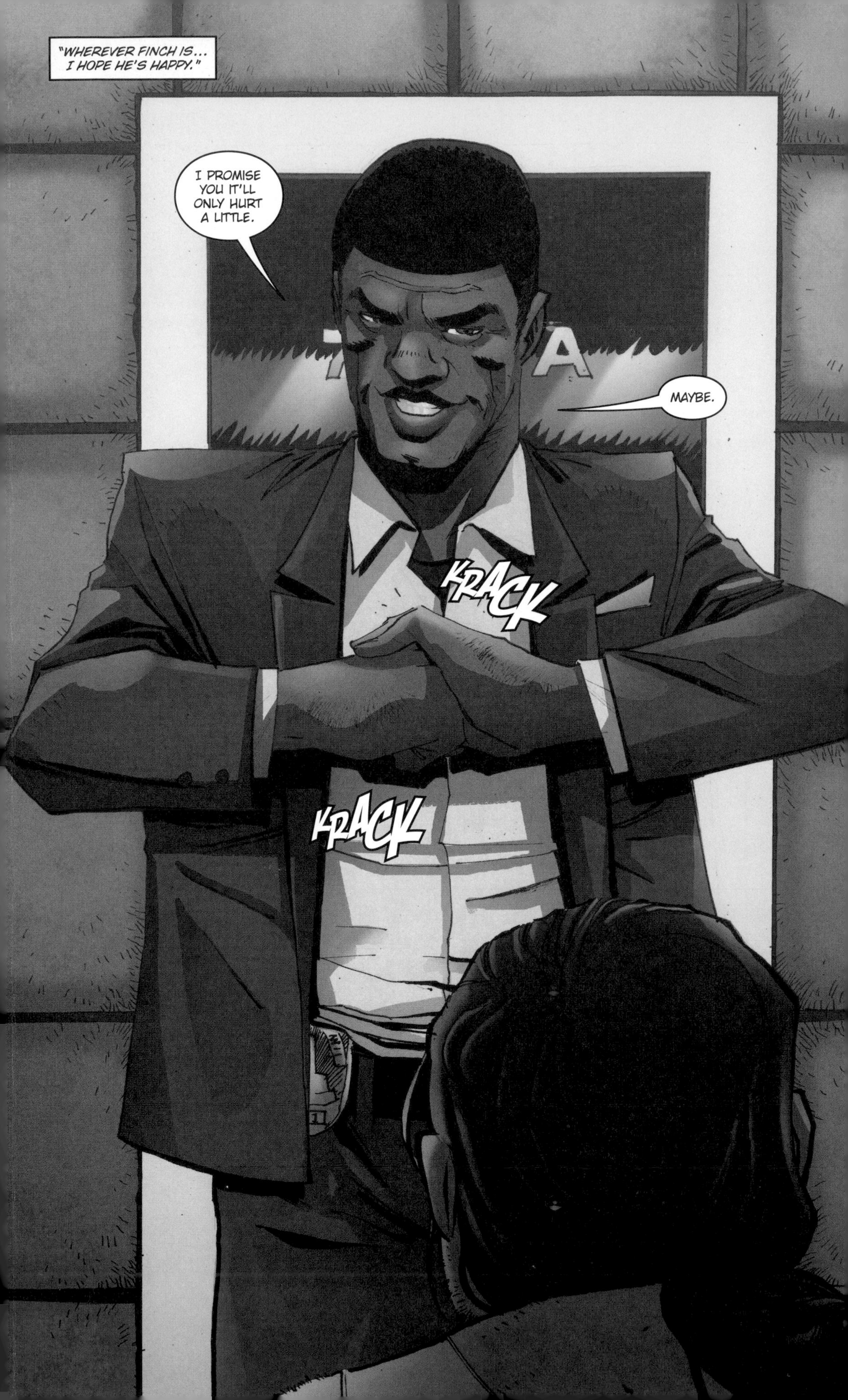
"WHEREVER FINCH IS...
I HOPE HE'S HAPPY."
I PROMISE YOU IT'LL ONLY HURT A LITTLE.
MAYBE.
KRACK
KRACK

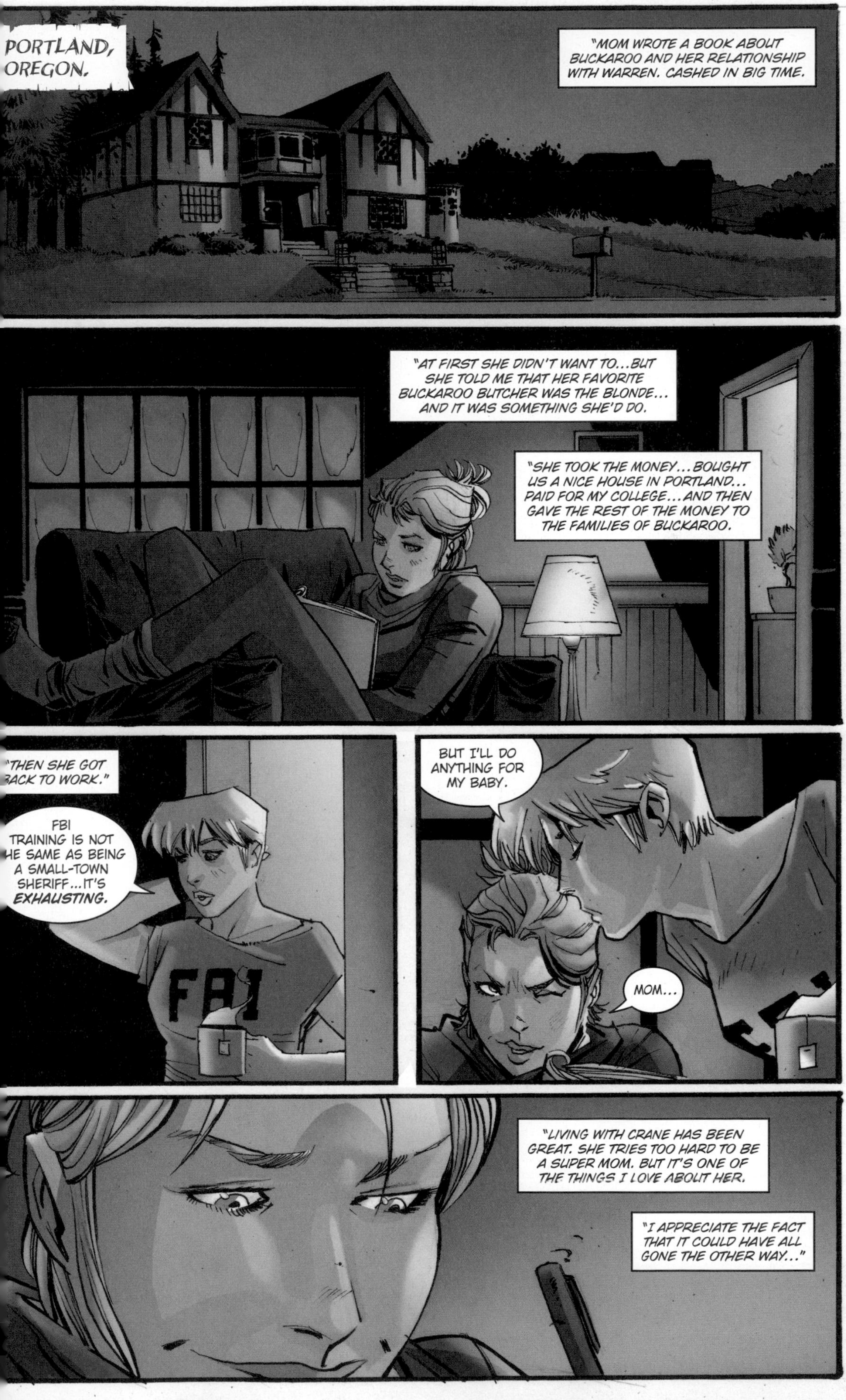
PORTLAND, OREGON.
"MOM WROTE A BOOK ABOUT BUCKAROO AND HER RELATIONSHIP WITH WARREN. CASHED IN BIG TIME.
"AT FIRST SHE DIDN'T WANT TO... BUT SHE TOLD ME THAT HER FAVORITE BUCKAROO BUTCHER WAS THE BLONDE... AND IT WAS SOMETHING SHE'D DO.
"SHE TOOK THE MONEY... BOUGHT US A NICE HOUSE IN PORTLAND... PAID FOR MY COLLEGE... AND THEN GAVE THE REST OF THE MONEY TO THE FAMILIES OF BUCKAROO.
"THEN SHE GOT BACK TO WORK."
FBI TRAINING IS NOT THE SAME AS BEING A SMALL-TOWN SHERIFF... IT'S EXHAUSTING.
FBI
BUT I'LL DO ANYTHING FOR MY BABY.
MOM...
"LIVING WITH CRANE HAS BEEN GREAT. SHE TRIES TOO HARD TO BE A SUPER MOM. BUT IT'S ONE OF THE THINGS I LOVE ABOUT HER.
"I APPRECIATE THE FACT THAT IT COULD HAVE ALL GONE THE OTHER WAY..."

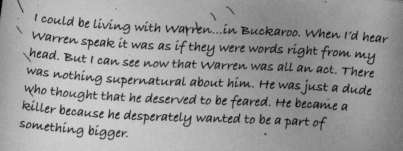

I could be living with Warren...in Buckaroo. When I'd hear Warren speak it was as if they were words right from my head. But I can see now that Warren was all an act. There was nothing supernatural about him. He was just a dude who thought that he deserved to be feared. He became a killer because he desperately wanted to be a part of something bigger.

He pretended he had all the answers but he didn't. No one did.

And that's okay. Some of life's mysteries are better left buried. But after everything that happened to us, the mystery of the Buckaroo Butchers did teach me one thing...

That we should stop being so focused on what makes us kill...and instead look at what makes us live.

OKAY, I'M OFF.

WHERE'RE YOU GOING?

DARIO ARGENTO MARATHON AT THE HOLLYWOOD!

I'LL BE BACK BEFORE THE SUN COMES UP!

BE SAFE!

LOVE YOU, MOM!

LOVE YOU, TOO!

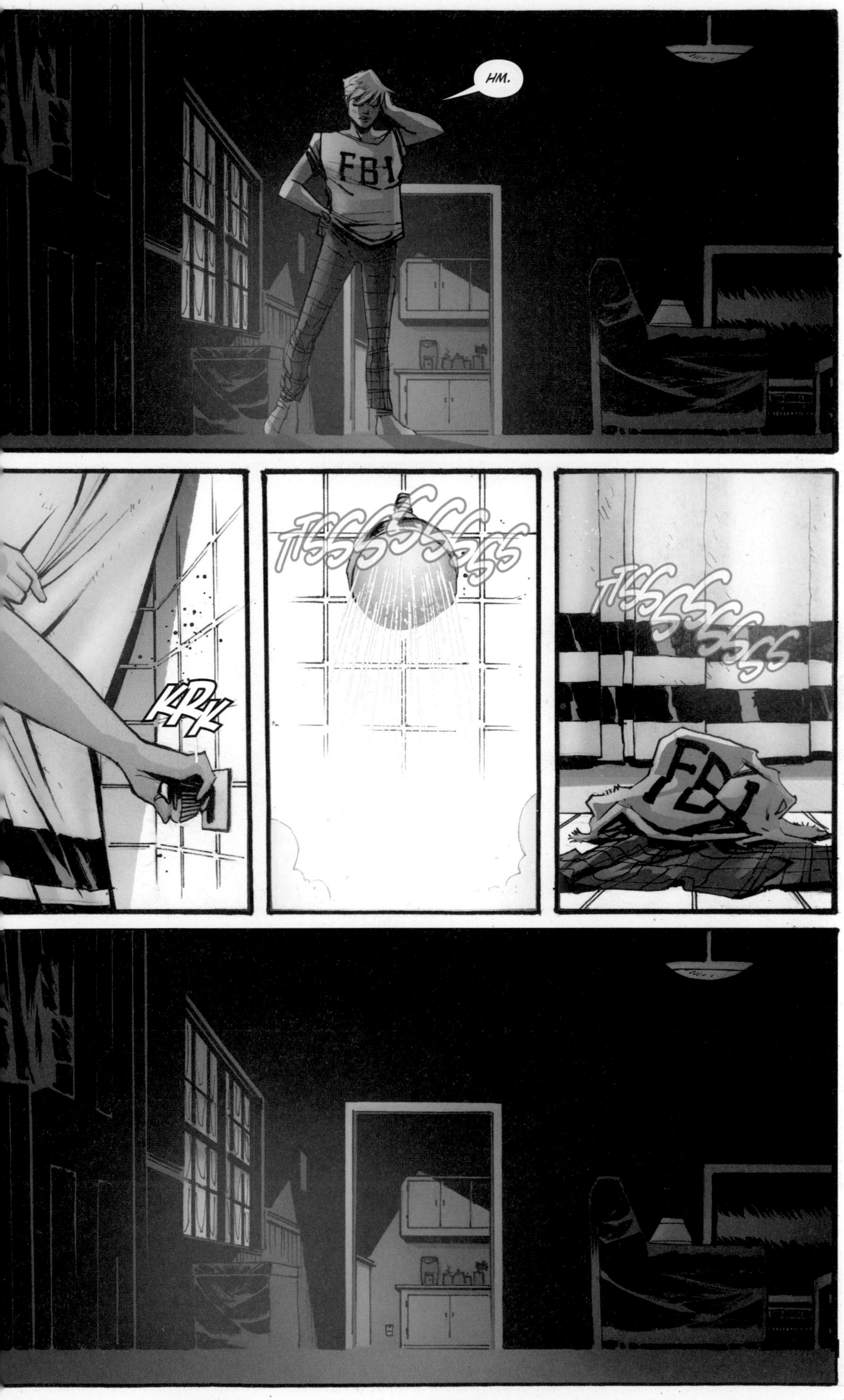
HM.
KRRK
FFSSSSSSSSS
FFSSSSSSSSS
FBI

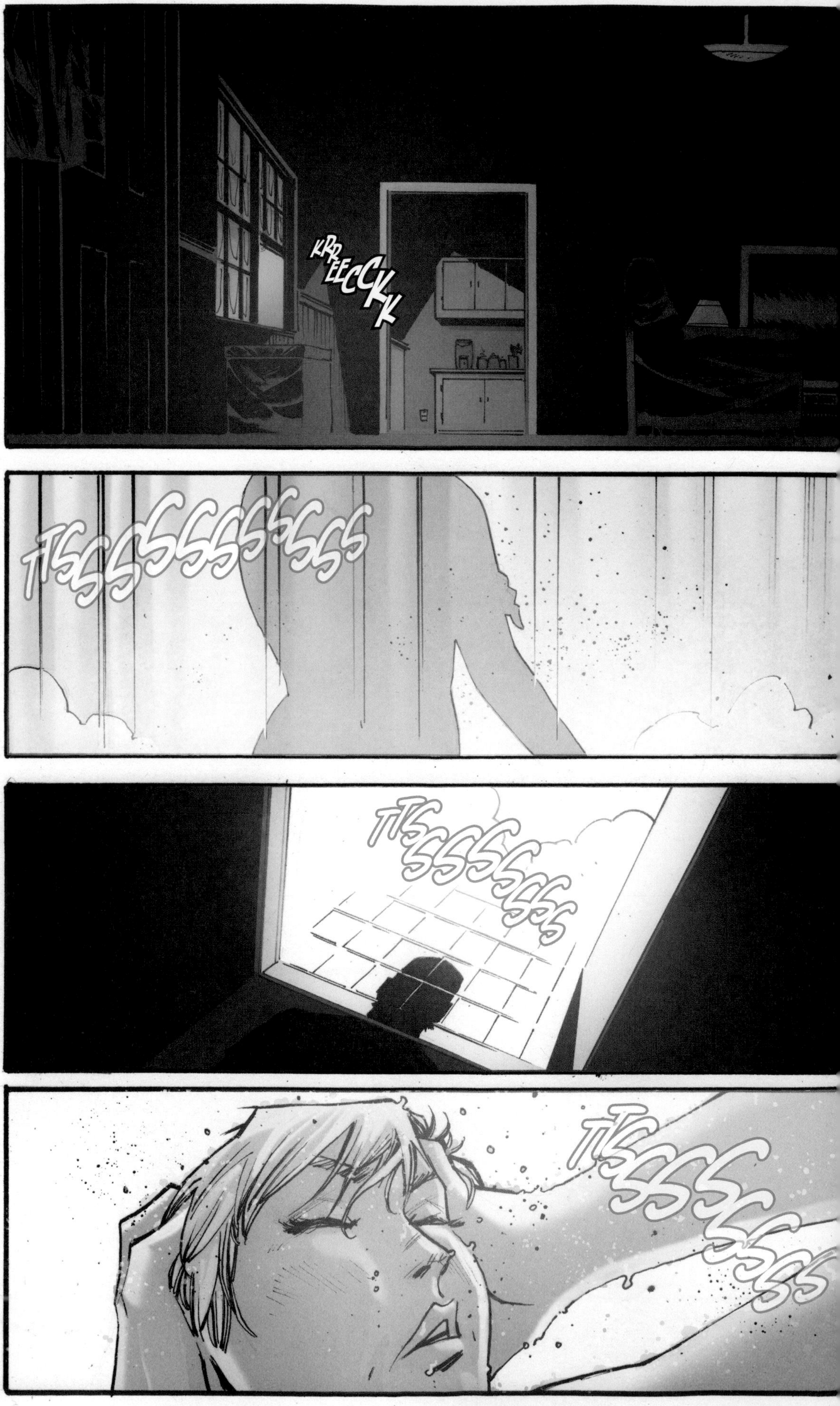
KRREECCKK
TTSSSSSSSSSSS
TTSSSSSSSSS
TTSSSSSSSSS

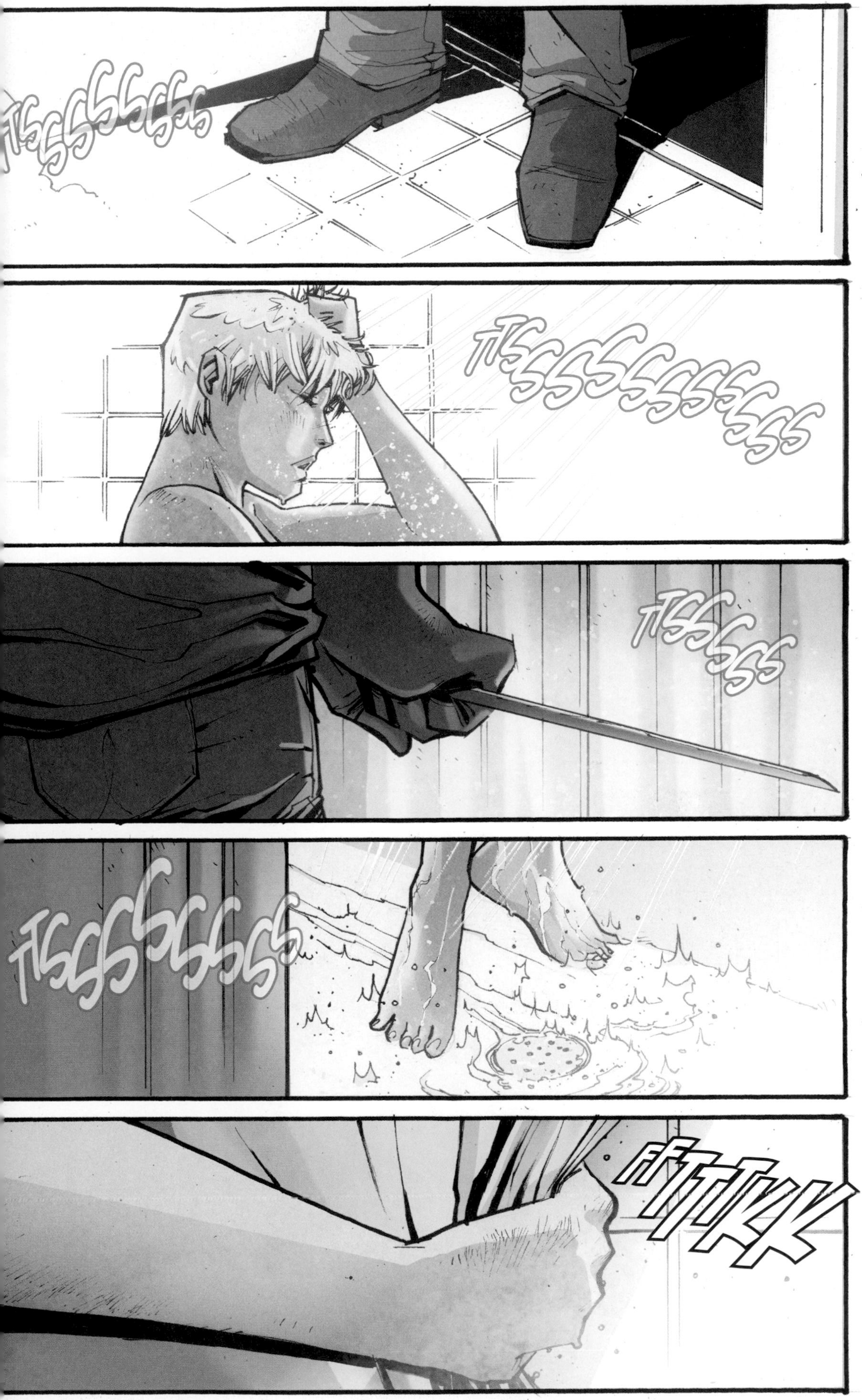
TSSSSSSSS
TSSSSSSSSSSSSS
TSSSSSS
TSSSSSSSSS
FFTTTKK

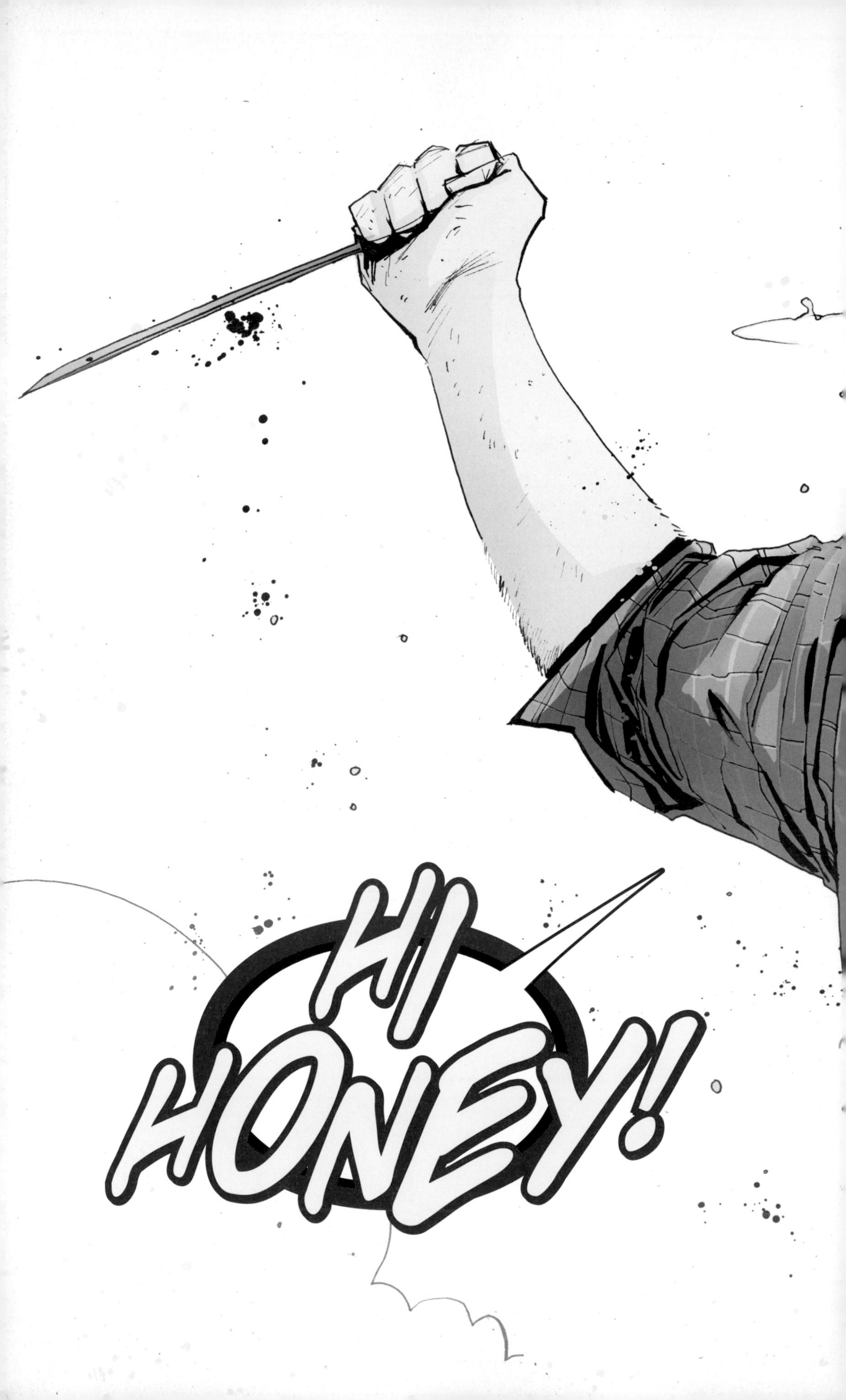
HI HONEY!

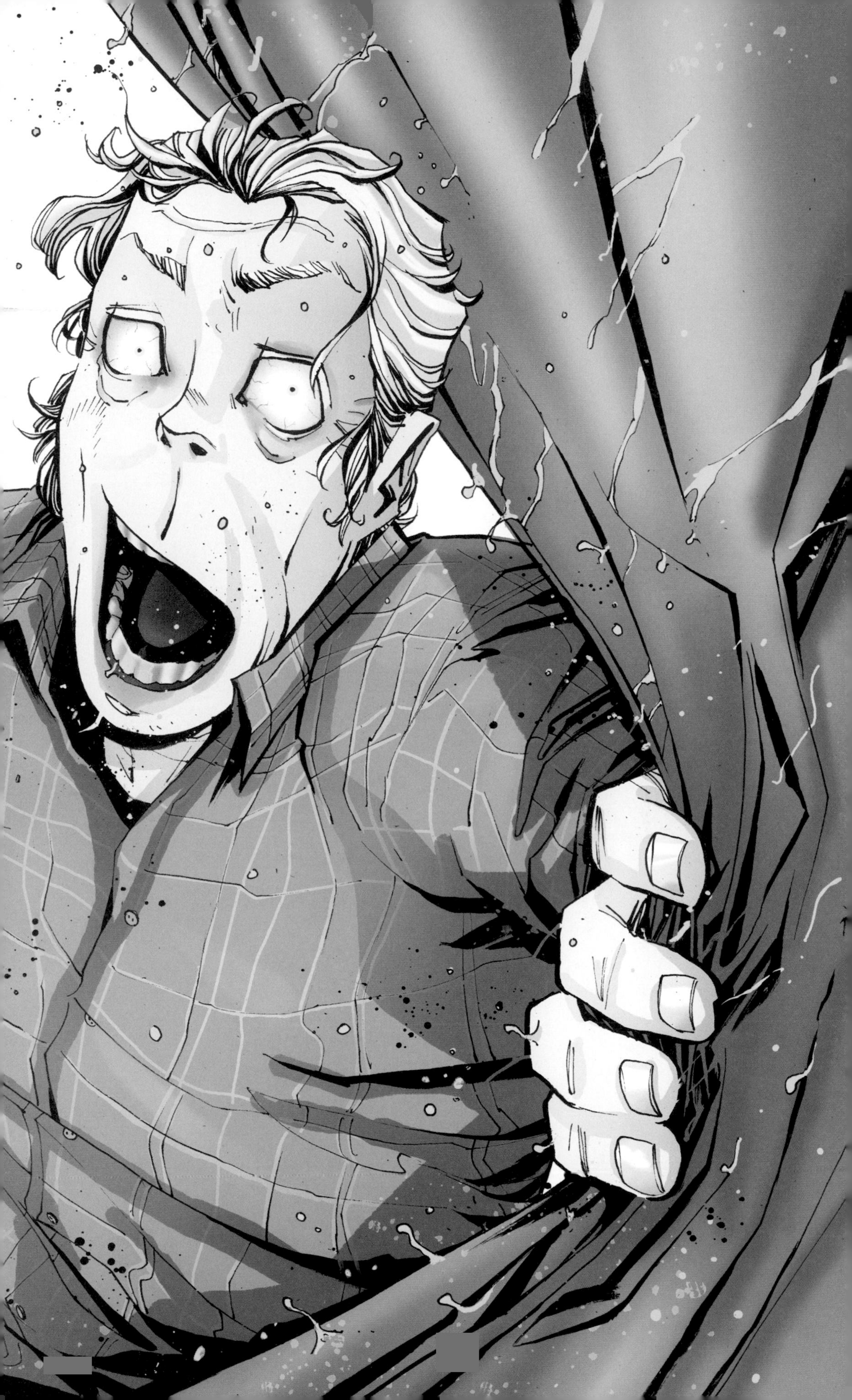

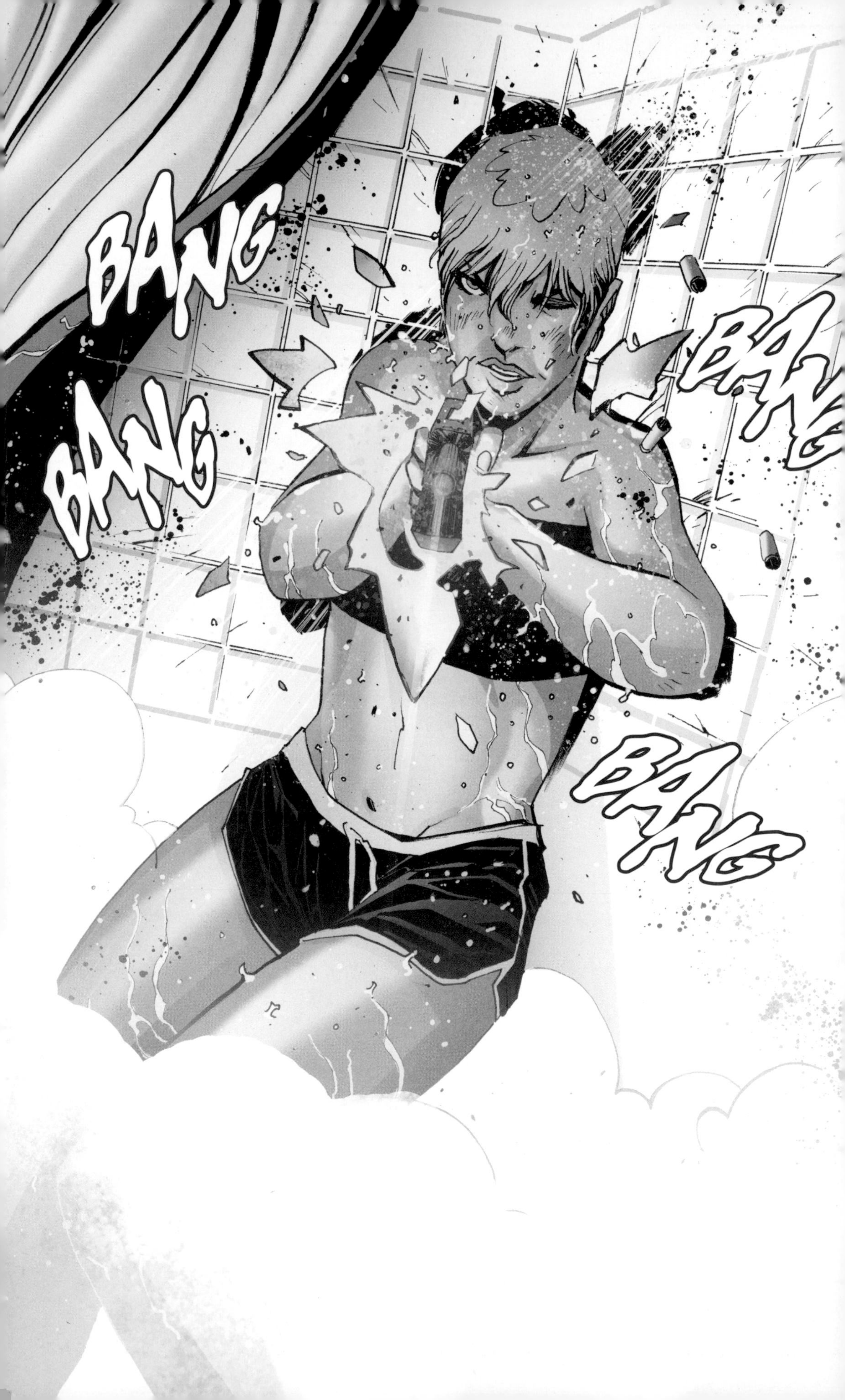
BANG
BANG
BANG
BANG

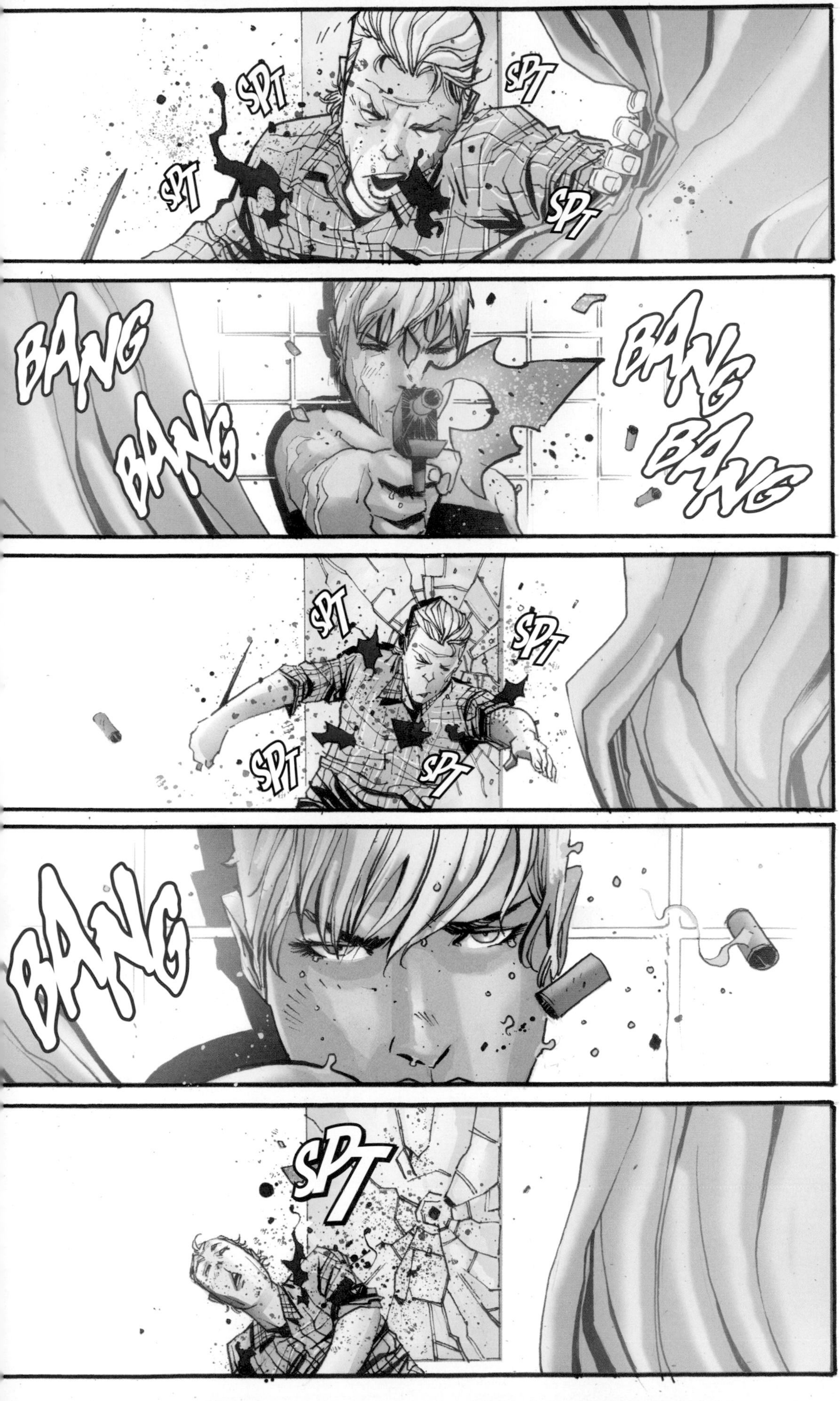
SPT
SPT
SPT
SPT
BANG
BANG
BANG
BANG
SPT
SPT
SPT
SPT
BANG
SPT

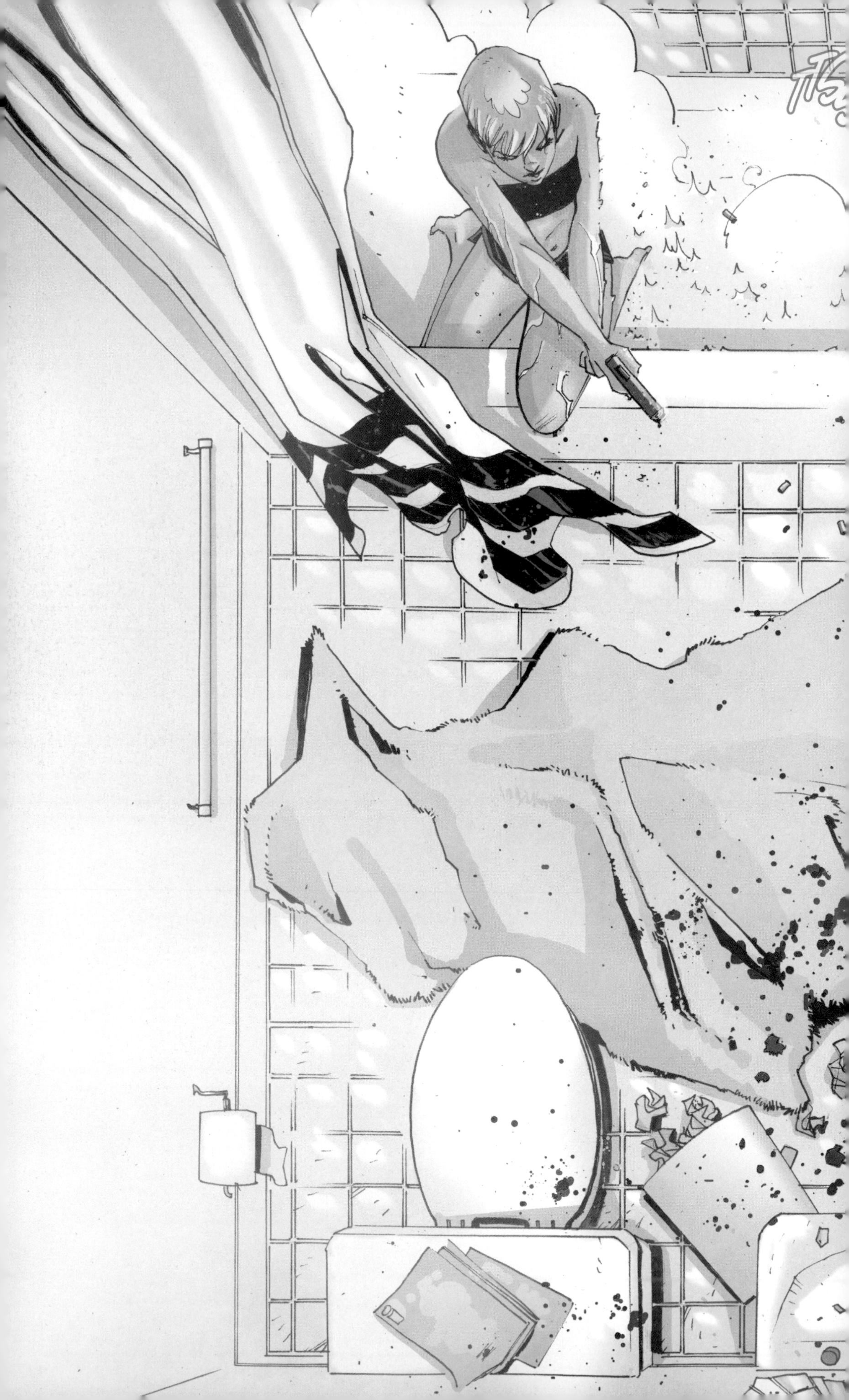

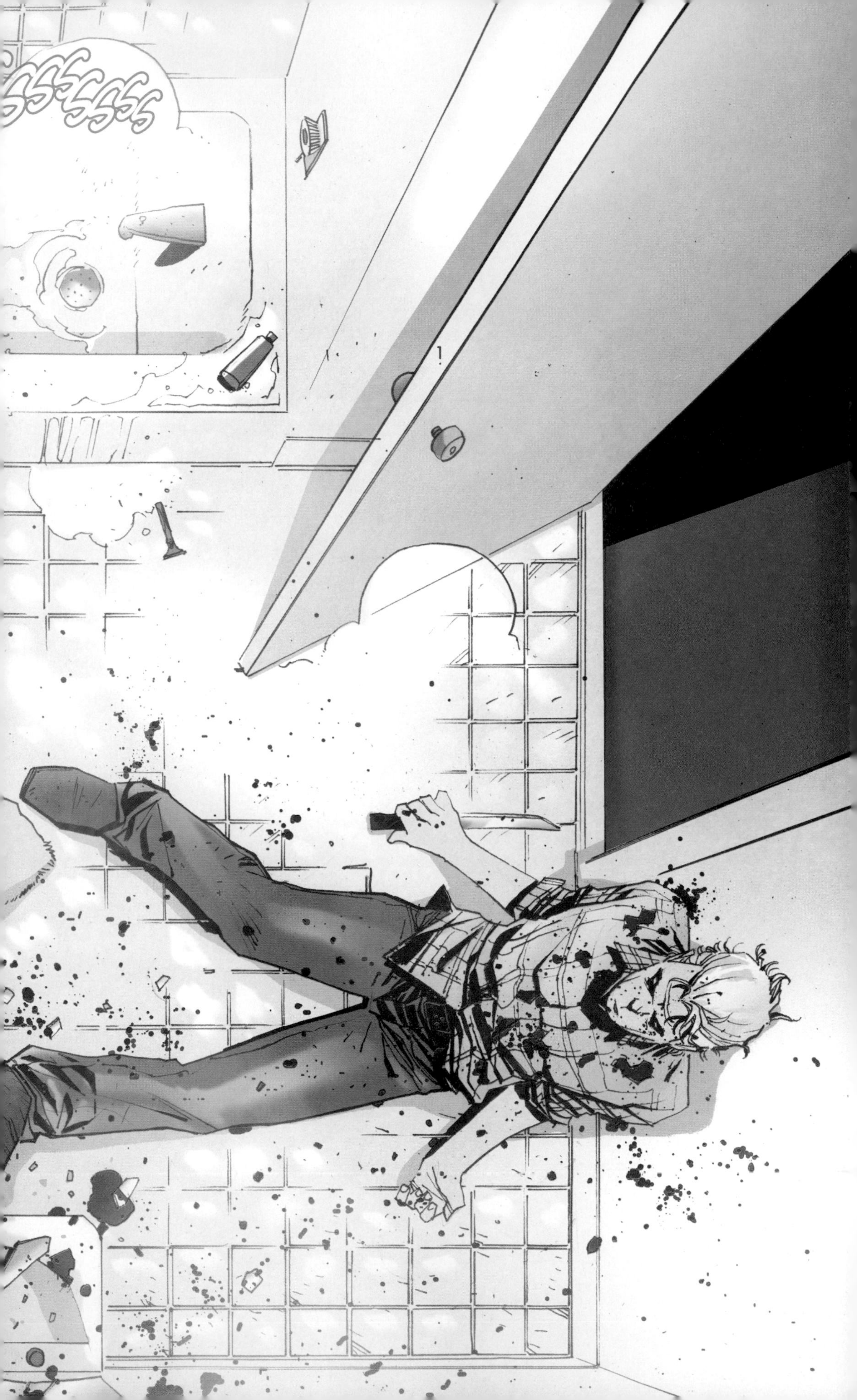
SSSSSSS

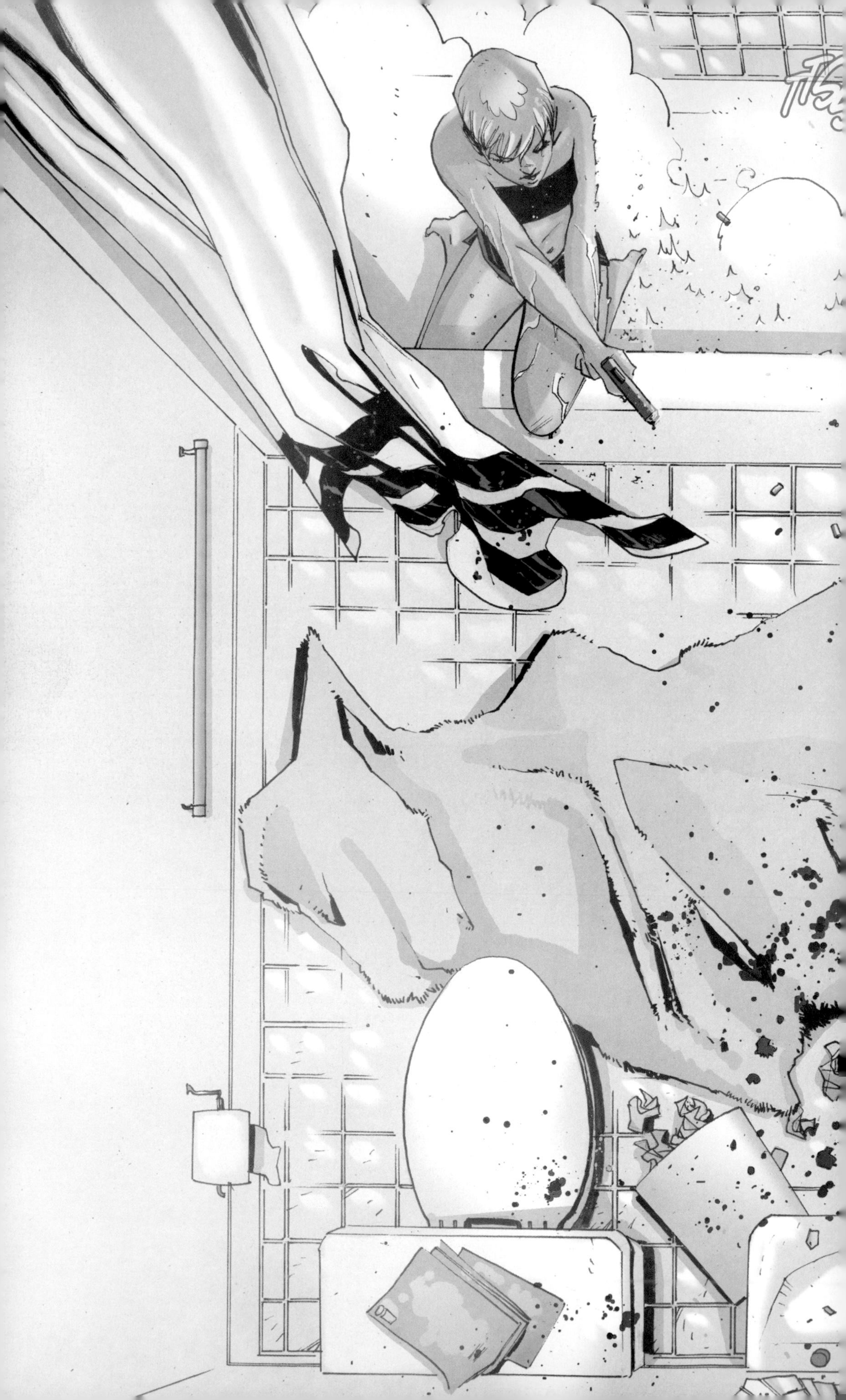

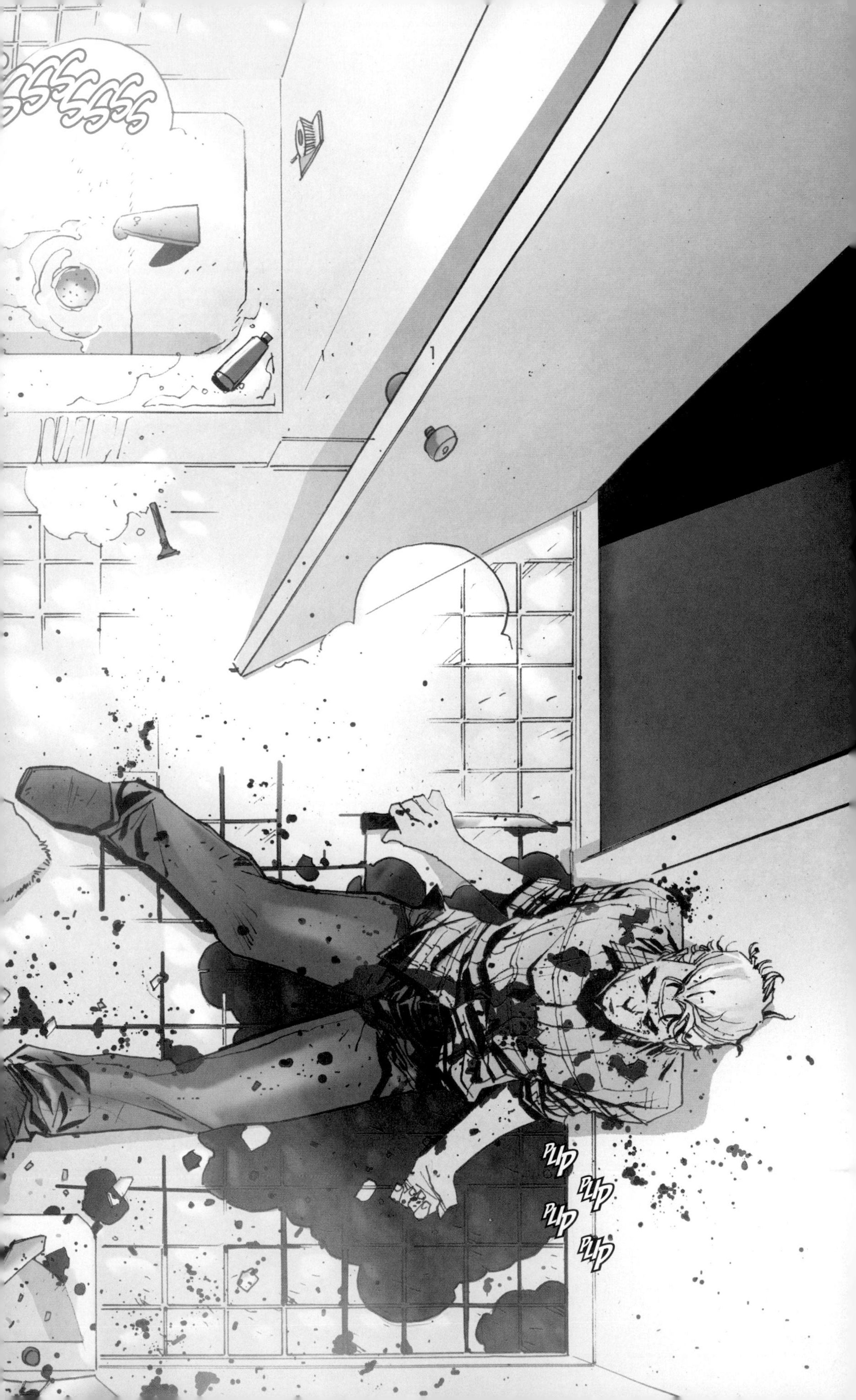
SSSSSSS
PLIP
PLIP
PLIP
PLIP

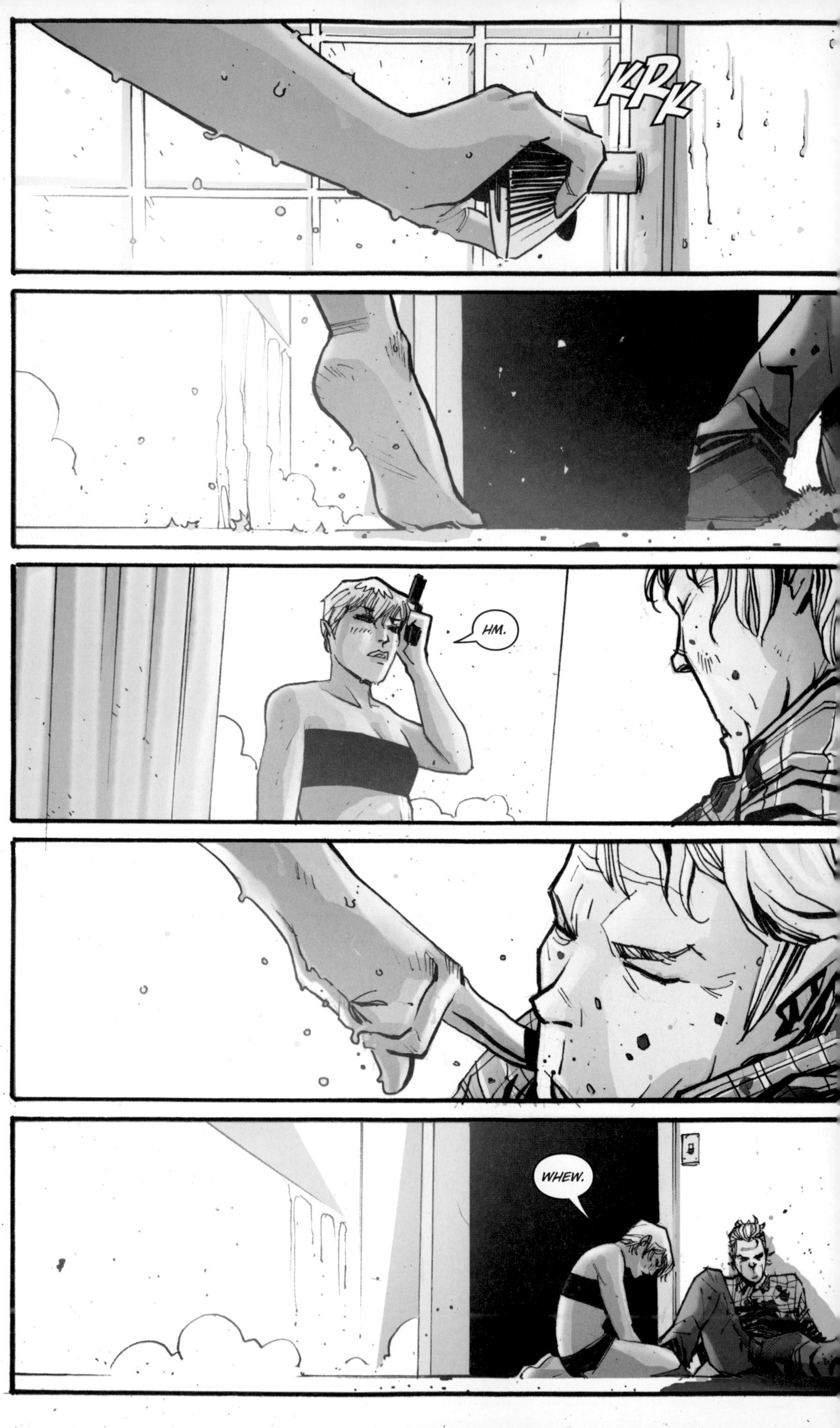
KRK
HM.
WHEW.

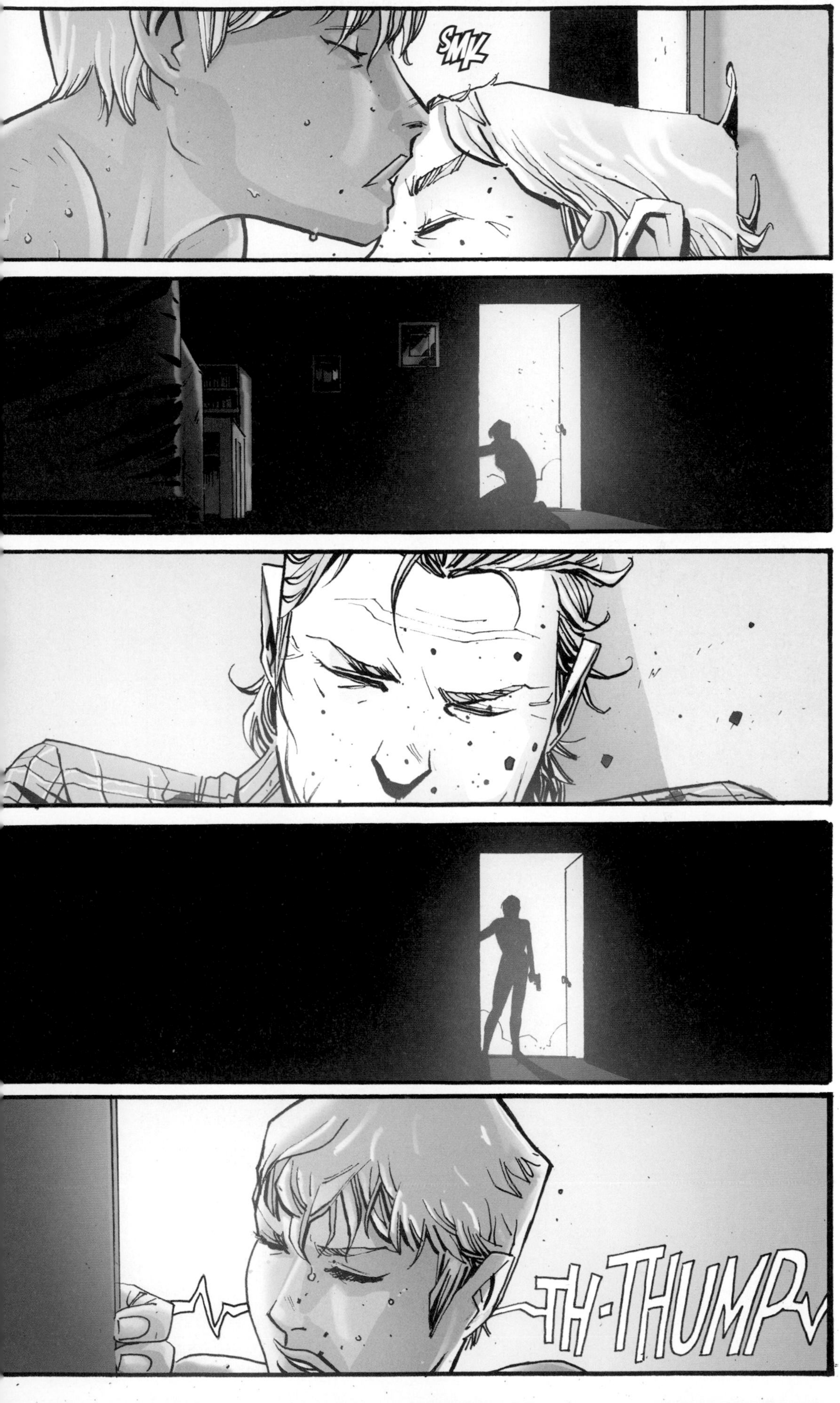
SMK
TH-THUMP

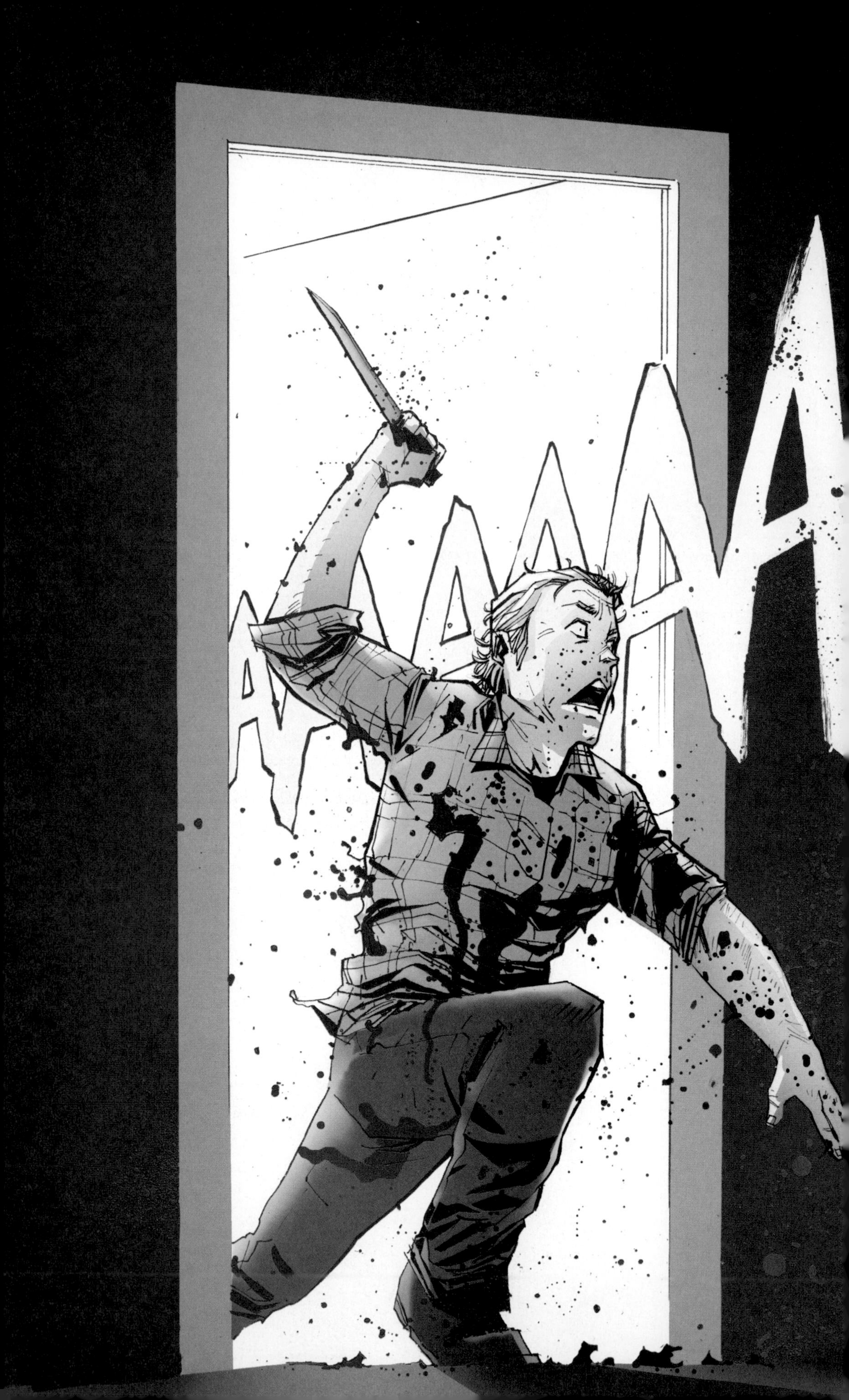
AAAAAA

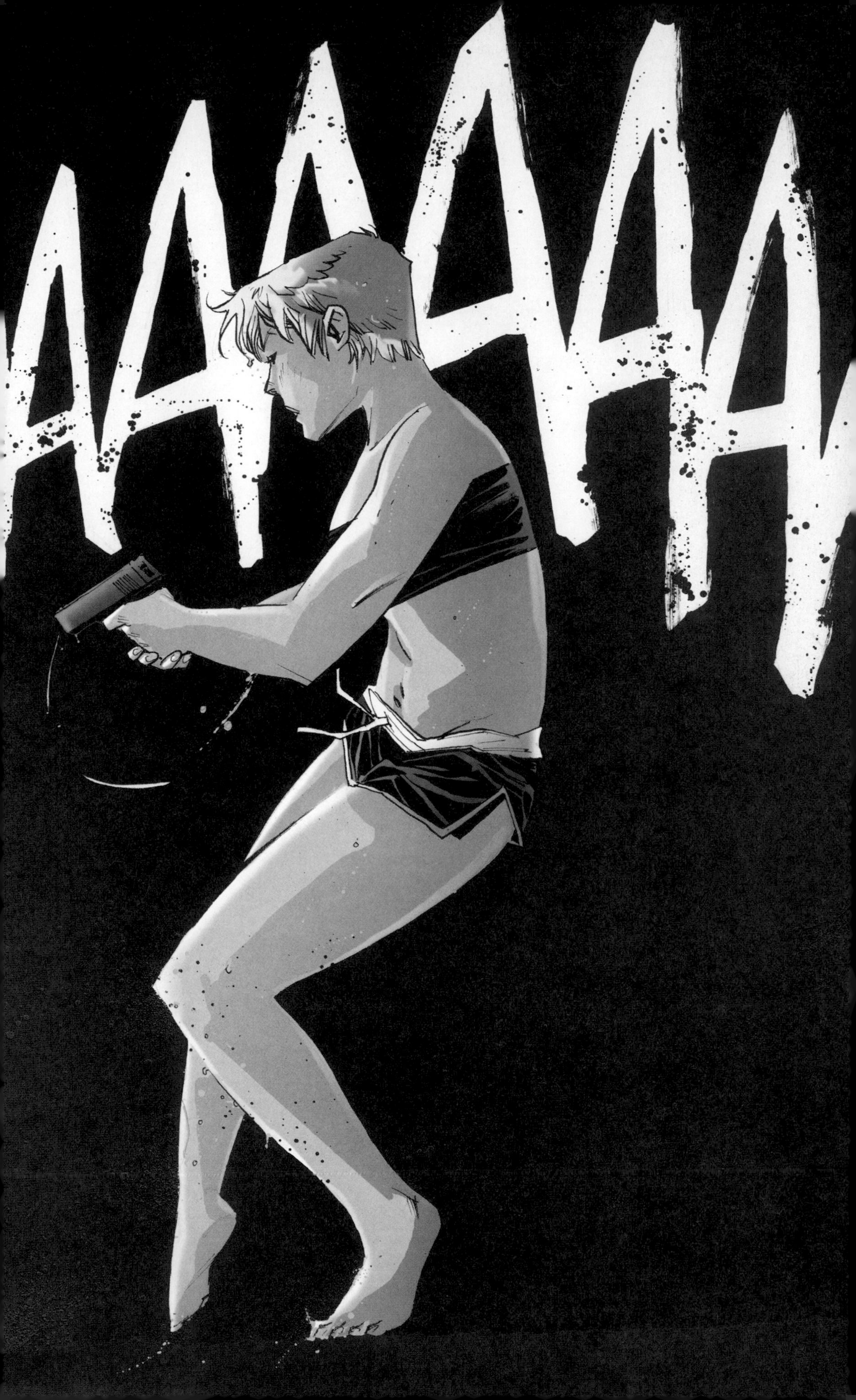
AAAAAA

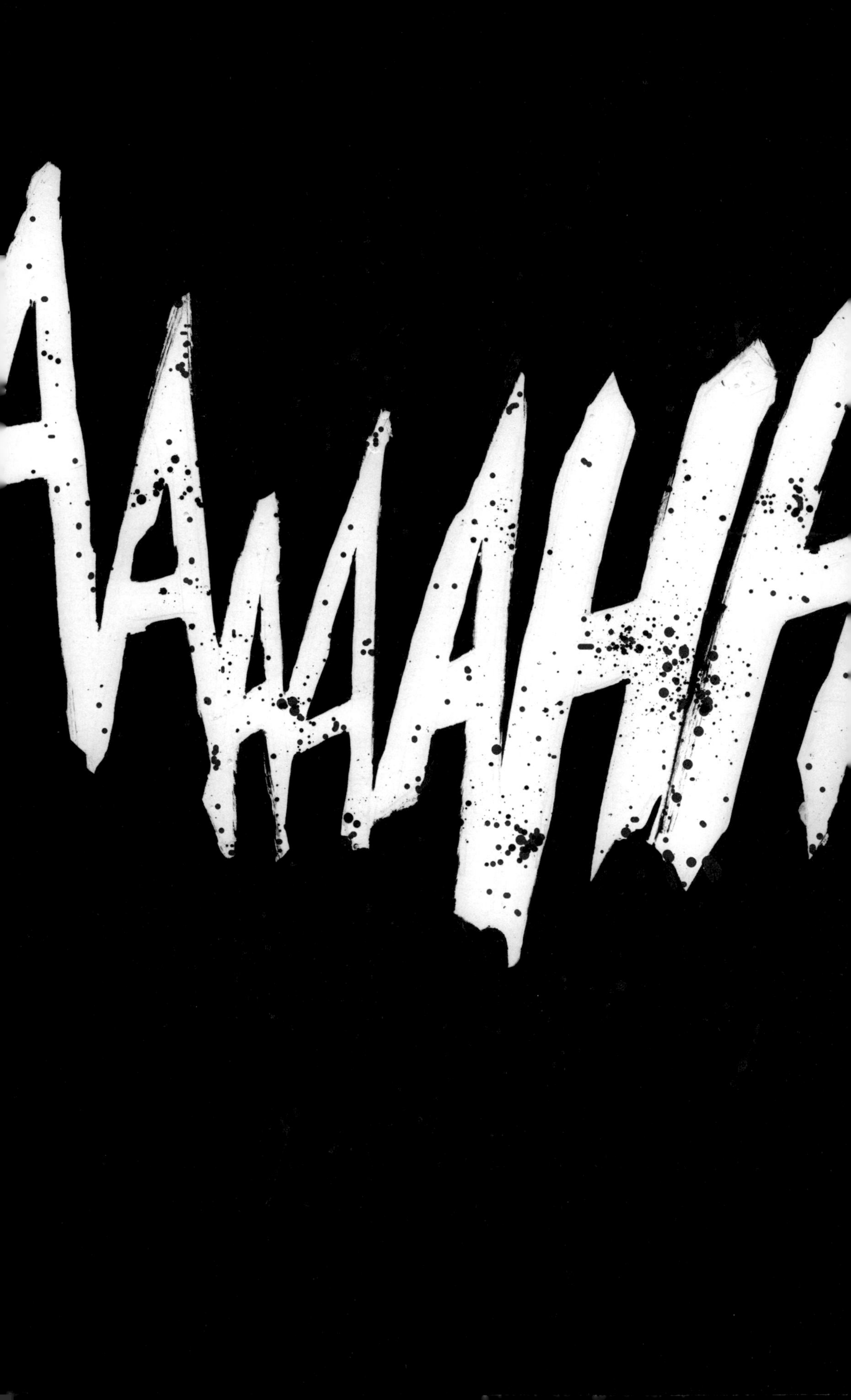
AAAAHH

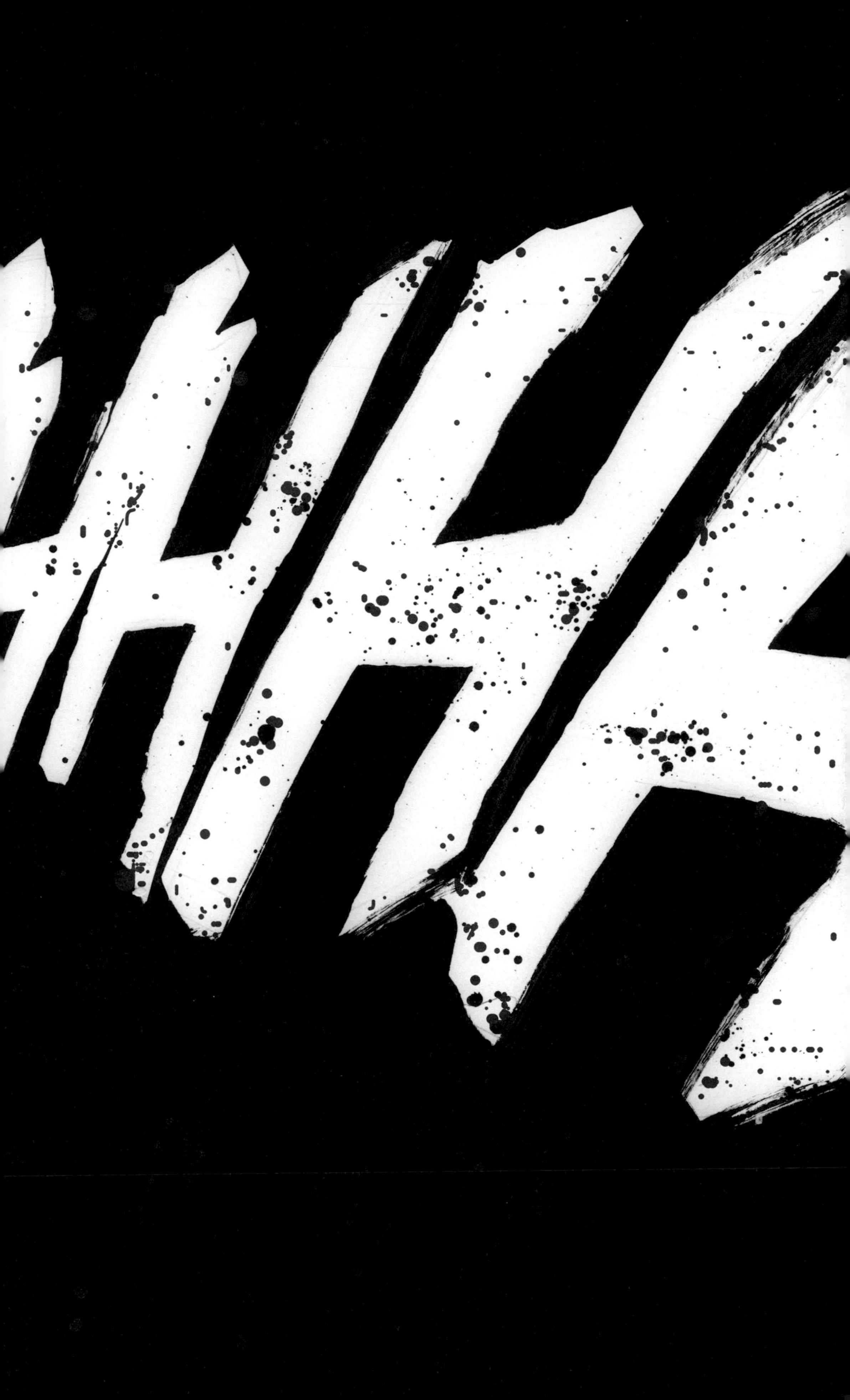

THE
END?

Thank you to Image Comics; the production, sales and marketing staff at Image; Robert Kirkman; Eric Stephenson for saying yes; all the websites that covered this series and the retailers who ordered it. But especially to you the reader... For the last three years, you let us tell a horror story we were dying to tell. We all go a little mad sometimes... thank you for going mad with us.

JOSHUA WILLIAMSON
story

MIKE HENDERSON
art

ADAM GUZOWSKI
colors

JOHN J. HILL
letters / book design

ROB LEVIN - editing   **TIM DANIEL** - logo
MIKE HENDERSON & ADAM GUZOWSKI - cover

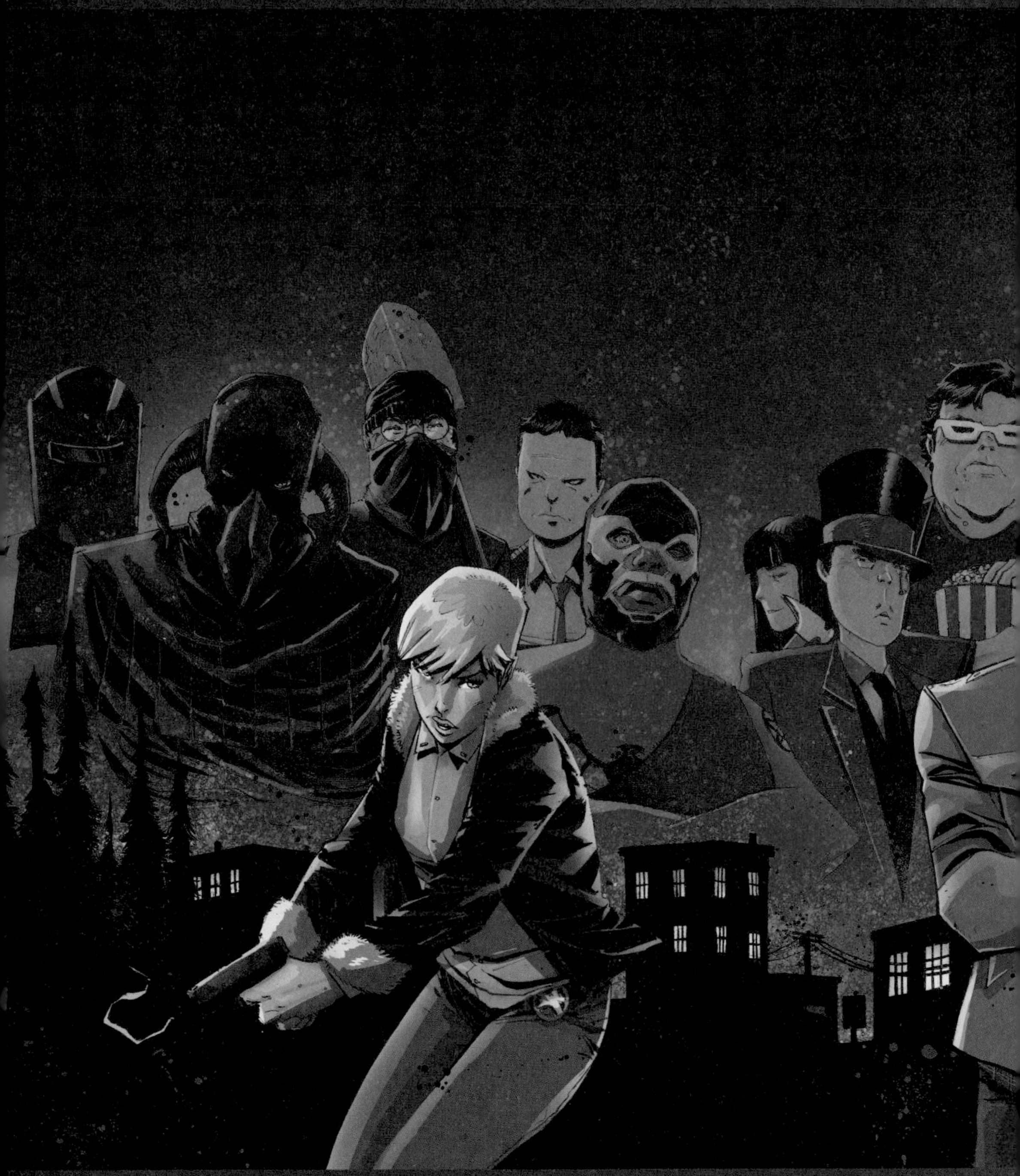

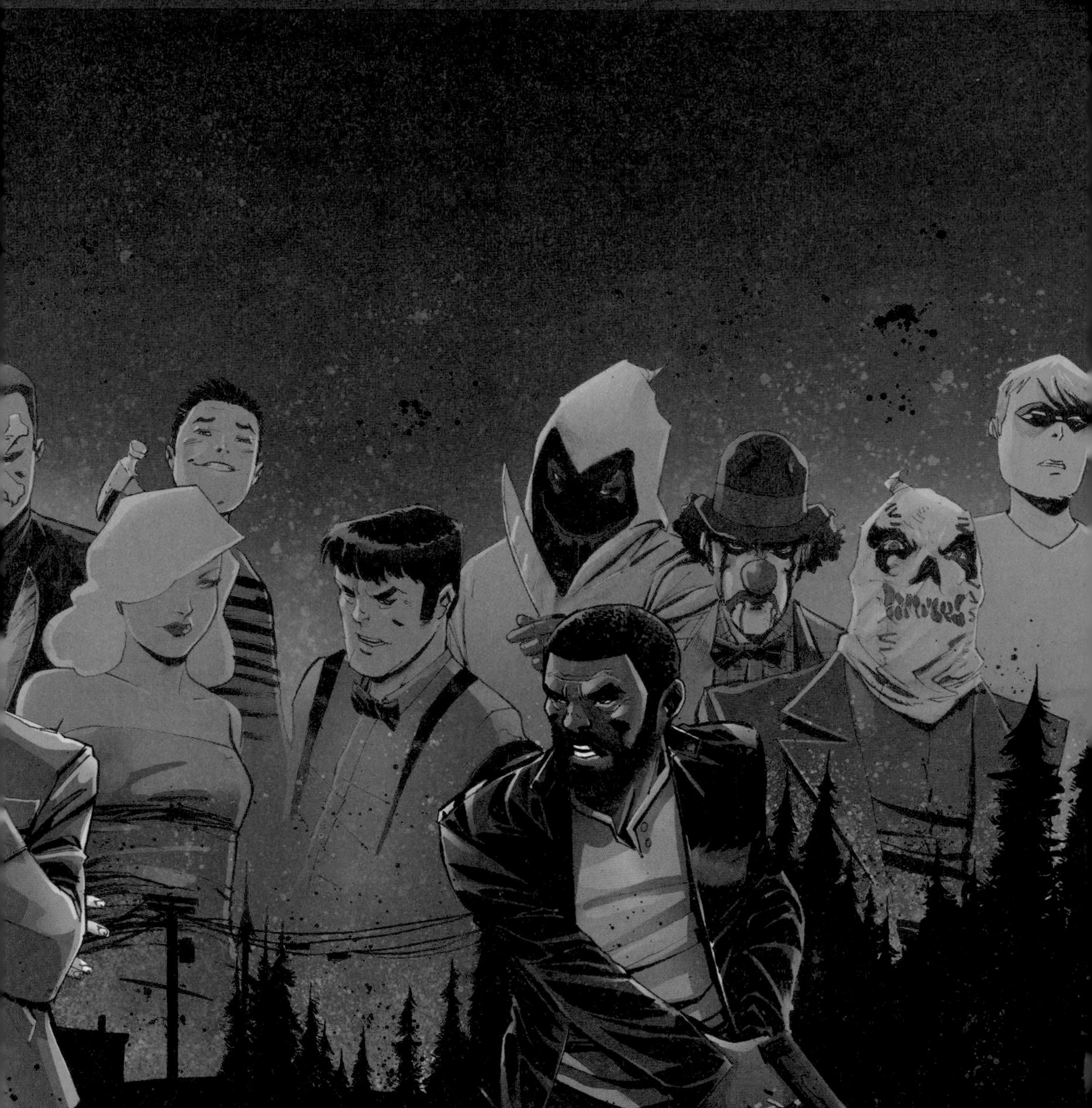

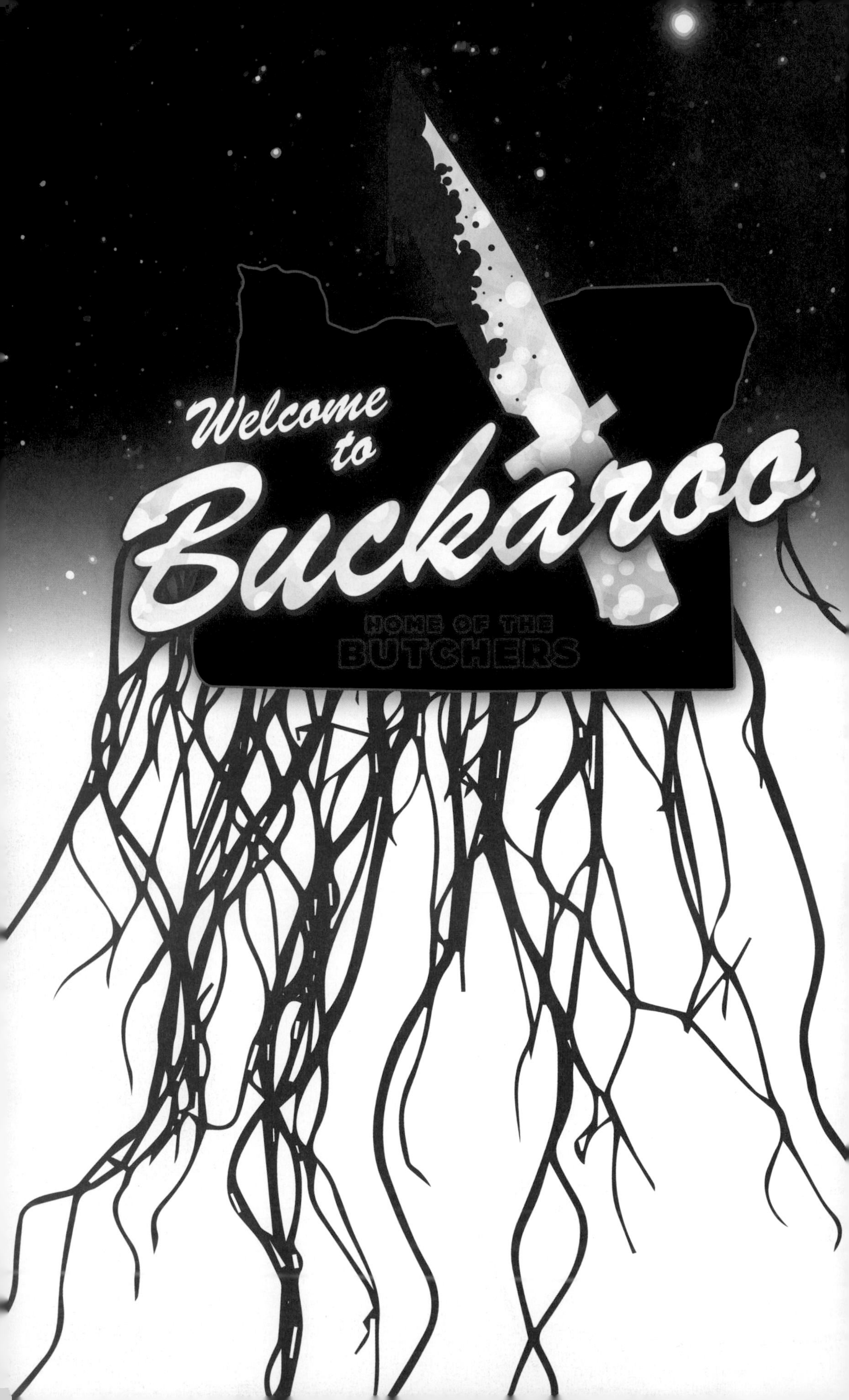
Welcome
to
Buckaroo
HOME OF THE
BUTCHERS

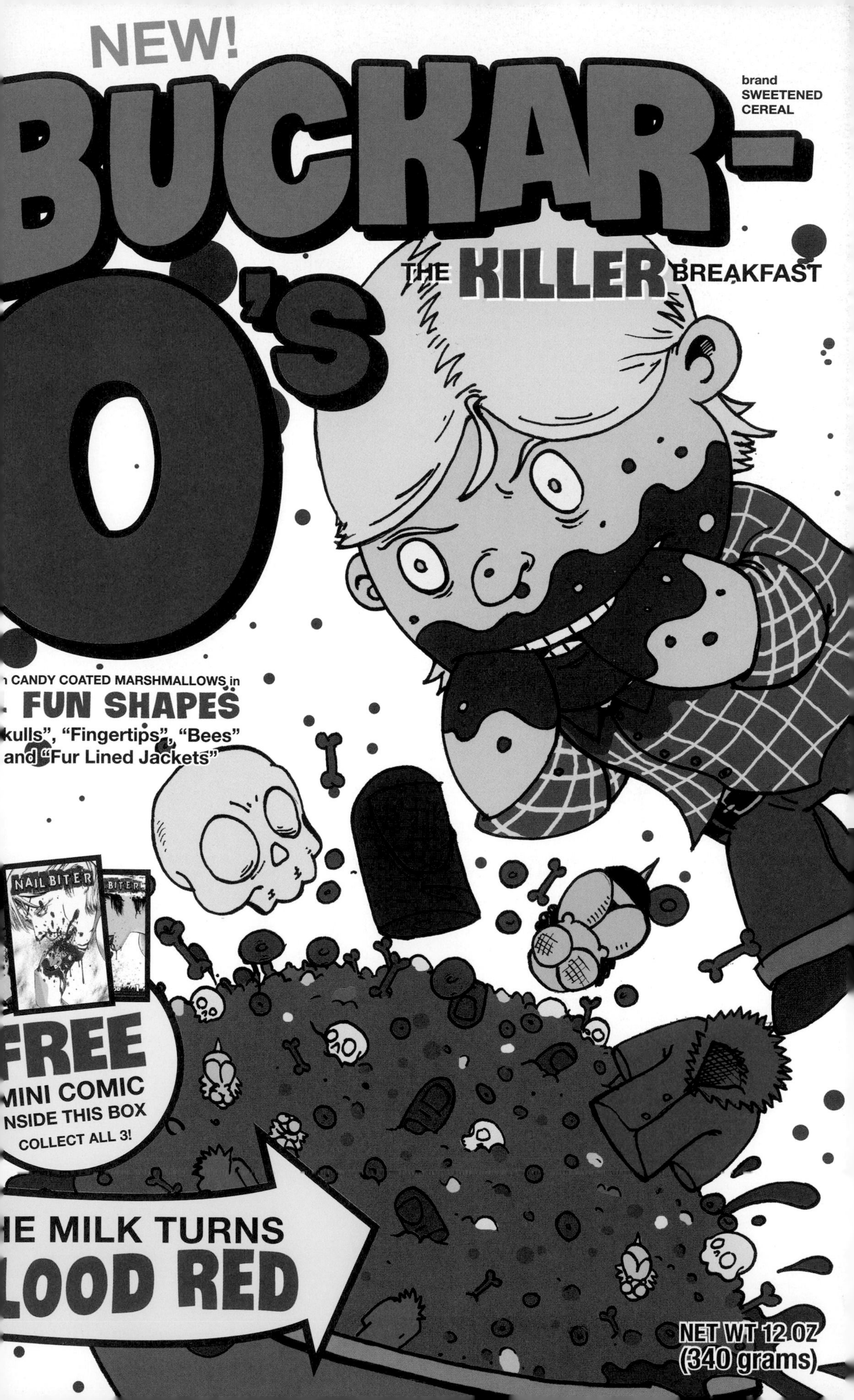
NEW!
BUCKAR-O's
brand SWEETENED CEREAL
THE KILLER BREAKFAST
n CANDY COATED MARSHMALLOWS in
FUN SHAPES
kulls", "Fingertips", "Bees"
and "Fur Lined Jackets"
NAIL BITER
FREE
MINI COMIC
NSIDE THIS BOX
COLLECT ALL 3!
IE MILK TURNS
LOOD RED
NET WT 12 OZ
(340 grams)

IF YOU LIKED

NAILBITER

TRY THESE OTHER COLLECTIONS:

GHOSTED
VOLUME ONE • HAUNTED HEIST

GHOSTED VOL. 1

Joshua Williamson,
Goran Sudzuka & Miroslav Mrva

144 PAGES SOFTCOVER
ISBN: 978-1-60706-836-5

GHOSTED VOL. 2

Joshua Williamson,
Davide Gianfelice & Miroslav Mrva

120 PAGES SOFTCOVER
ISBN: 978-1-63215-046-2

GHOSTED
VOLUME TWO • BOOKS OF THE DEAD

GHOSTED
VOLUME THREE • DEATH WISH

GHOSTED VOL. 3

Joshua Williamson, Goran Sudzuka,
Davide Gianfelice & Miroslav Mrva

120 PAGES SOFTCOVER
ISBN: 978-1-63215-051-6

GHOSTED VOL. 4

Joshua Williamson, Goran Sudzuka,
Vladmir Krstic, Juan Jose Ryp &
Miroslav Mrva

112 PAGES SOFTCOVER
ISBN: 978-1-63215-317-3

WILLIAMSON LACI RYP MRVA
GHOSTED
VOLUME FOUR • GHOST TOWN

BIRTHRIGHT
VOLUME ONE
HOMECOMING

BIRTHRIGHT VOL. 1

Joshua Williamson,
Andrei Bressan & Adriano Lucas

128 PAGES SOFTCOVER
ISBN: 978-1-63215-231-2

BIRTHRIGHT VOL. 2

Joshua Williamson,
Andrei Bressan & Adriano Lucas

128 PAGES SOFTCOVER
ISBN: 978-1-63215-446-0

BIRTHRIGHT
WILLIAMSON BRESSAN LUCAS

image

PLEASE VISIT: **IMAGECOMICS.COM** for more information.
To find your local comic shop call **1-888-comicbook** or visit **www.comicshop.u**

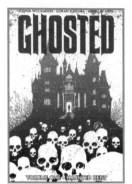

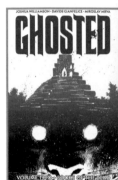